Blood Oath

a novel by:

Jimmy Cherokee Waters

Wolf Klan,
Western Band of
The Cherokee Nation

Follow Jimmy Cherokee Waters on FaceBook

Currahee
Books™

Dedication

This novel is dedicated to the Cherokee, and all of the mountain peoples living on the eighteenth century frontier of America. These Native American, white, and black peoples created the American nation. These people faced the demands of their world, as we do today, based on their perceptions of their world, and while some aspects of their beliefs are hard to understand, or even imagine today, the struggles of these peoples ultimately generated a nation that nurtures and values human life, and at least attempts to foster independent freedoms for all citizens. To these peoples, we owe a debt of gratitude that can never be repaid, and to the degree that our nation does not live up to its ideals, the failures are ours, and not theirs.

This is a work of historic fiction. While most characters are based on historic figures, other characters have been created by the author to enhance this story. I have modified certain religious beliefs of the Cherokee in order to keep this story straight forward and direct. However, this work is intended to represent the types of occurrences that are historically accurate for this period. Historical notes on certain aspects of this novel are available on the Currahee Books website.

Copyright 2009 Currahee Books

ISBN 978-0-615-24394-8

Third Printing: July, 2011

This and other works are available from the Publisher:

Currahee Books

766 Collins Road, Toccoa, Georgia 30577
www.curraheebooks.com

www.Freelancedesign.com • Print & Web Design • Asheville, NC

Prologue: The Hill & The River

This hill is rather nondescript, rising only some 1000 feet on the southern flank of the Blue Ridge along the Tugaloo River. It is not much of a hill really, and admittedly remains unnoticed by almost everyone today. Climbing up the old unmarked logging road, with its shifting ruts created by the rain drenched currents of the October showers, one would never think that anything of importance could have happened here. This hill is just like the others in the shadow of the Blue Ridge Mountains; it is covered with hardwoods and pine, and is quiet now in the afternoon sun. Certainly one would never imagine that so much history had been played out on this slope. In fact, few come to this hill today, and fewer still realize its significance.

The Cherokee know. Yes, we, the Real People, know. Here, our world changed; here my ancestors' concepts of spirit, truth, honor, and courage were formed; here they faced the impossible, and here they died by the thousands. Yet the Real People survive. For the Cherokee, this hill clearly has a story to tell.

Just down this slope along the joining of the creek and the river, a boy who was to become a broad-chested, Cherokee Chief, killed a massive bear from Owl Swamp; legend suggests that the beast was well over 900 pounds! The bear fully intended on dining well that evening on the young Indian boy who was hunting alone and trapped in what would one day be known as Toccoa Creek. His Indian village cluster, centered around Tugaloo Town, was the southern most corner of the lower Cherokee Villages on the slopes of the great Blue Mountains. With 600 souls residing there, it was quite a town. Still it was some distance to the east and the young boy could expect no help with this bear from the town folk. His battle, like every man's, was to be his alone.

Initially, my ancestors died by plague, gunfire, scalping, being sold into slavery, and in many other horrible ways; ultimately for the few that were left, the whites finally decided to kick them out of their own land, and that alone killed many more. My great, great, great grandmother made that shameful walk through history, known in my tongue as the "Trail Where They Cried." After the Cherokee were safely booted off the land, stage coaches ran past this hill for something like two hundred years. The Great Philadelphia Wagon Road came down the eastern spine of the Blue Ridge all the way from the colonial capital at Philadelphia, and brought many settlers to the newly liberated valleys of the Blue Ridge. Of course no one informed the Cherokee that the land was liberated, and my people will tell you quite a different story of those times. Our demise in the East began not with the tragic Trail of Tears, but rather among the first of the Cherokee villages to fall to the whites in the 1760s. It all began here, just on the distant slope of this little, unimportant hill. For the whites, this land was free for the taking in the 1780s.

When the Scots-Irish soldiers of the recent Revolutionary War were awarded land for their services, many a man, tested by the steel of battle, made his fortune and his home on what was then the frontier; it all happened right here, within sight of this hill. Hundreds of soldiers came with their new families, but today we know only a few. Certainly Old Ben Cleveland came to settle across the river in what would become South Carolina. James Wyly, Robert Jarrett, Jessie Walton, all these were heroes of the Revolution, and they tamed a bloody frontier to become the landed aristocracy of the early antebellum South. These were the men who forged a nation, veterans of the Battle of King's Mountain, of Dragging Canoe's War, and of numerous smaller, bloodier campaigns with the Creek and Cherokee. These men created the freedoms that we know today, and they did it, in some small part, along this river—the Tugaloo, and on the lower slopes of this very hill.

James Wyly lived in Jonesborough, Tennessee, but not satisfied that he could make his riches there, he moved his family to the small stream at the base of this hill. Here he made his fortune as the commissioner on the soon-to-be developed mountain road, the Unicoi Turnpike—the rough wagon road that opened up the whole southern crest of the Blue Ridge; it all began right here beside this hill. Wyly's home on the flanks of this hill, just to the southeast, became the stage coach stop known as Traveler's Rest; it still stands today in mute testimony to those frontier days.

We can only marvel at the intricate web of life that played out on the slopes of this hill. Why this particular hill in this particular corner of a rugged frontier; why this parcel of nowhere? Why did the cross-currents of history for so many generations come to be focused on this patch of ground? Part of the answer is geographic; the small river at the bottom of this hill, the Tugaloo, is a critical character in the early story of this bloody frontier. This river is the headwaters of a mighty river system that in time with the distant miles winding toward the coast, becomes the Savannah River; thus this was the highway of early trade. The Indians found tillable bottomland, and their southern-most towns were located here over 1000 years ago. They harvested deer skins from these hills, and traded them for gunpowder, salt, and other necessities; this river was the transportation system into the Indian country of the 1750s.

Later the Great Philadelphia Wagon Road, and finally, the Unicoi Turnpike, came through, right by this hill. Those early wagon trails opened the Georgia mountains, and the lower Carolina and Tennessee mountains to gold hungry, white settlers, and it all began right here. Thus, the conflux of roads, waterways, and the later railroads formed a hub of activity for over three hundred years. The gateway to the entire lower Blue Ridge Mountains, and the plains beyond, was here right at the bottom of this little, unnamed hill.

It is rarely recognized that the story of mountain settlement does not begin on the highest peaks. Rather, mountain history begins in the approaching valleys and dells. Indians and white settlers alike needed to eat, and the peaks were conducive neither to hunting nor the plough. Thus, to understand the mountains, we need to understand the river valley, the stream, the swamp, and the varmints, critters, and land therein. These food sources provided the riches of the mountains, and these were all found well below the highest peaks. The Blue Ridge is understandable, and mountain life can be known, but one must approach the task slowly, creeping silently up the dells, the hollows, into the thorny cane-breaks from the river bottom. The Cherokee knew these lowlands well, and sought them out for their homes and villages. When white settlers followed later, they did the same. Thus, this river and this nondescript hill form the basis for our story—the story of the settlement of a large part of our nation, as told in the experiences of the souls long dead, many resting here, forever on this quiet hill.

The white cemetery on the hill was in use by the 1850's. Devereaux Jarrett IV, an early white settler, along with his two wives was buried here in the 1850's. Though it would have been a surprise to Devereaux, his grave was not the first on this nondescript hill. No, the hill had been a graveyard, though unmarked, for almost a century. Runs-To-Water, the small Indian chased by a large bear, met his first test in life here. He later chose to be buried on the lower crest of this hill; his grave was the first.

Runs-To-Water would fight many battles in life, and lead his people as Peace Chief of the Cherokee. The legends tell us that one day Kanati, the Great Spirit of the Cherokee, spoke to him on the slope of this hill. Just down the slope to the north, he slew his first bear, while he was yet a boy. Here he was tested, here he became a man; here he would rest for eternity, until the Great Spirit Kanati took him up.

Unlike the later white settlers of this area, Runs-To-Water—indeed most Cherokee—felt a humbleness when confronted with nature—her cruelty, her unfairness, her terror, and in contrast, her inspiring beauty. The river below and the distant rising of the Blue Ridge formed the grounding, the very foundation, for his life and his death. The life of my people, the Cherokee, was first and foremost a spiritual life, and that resulted in a certain humbleness in the tribe. No Cherokee, least of all Runs-To-Water, would have ever chosen to be buried at the crest of the hill; that would be much too flamboyant for the conservative, reserved, and mystical nature of the Cherokee. Rather, reserving the crest of the small hill for his ancestral spirits and for the Great Spirit, Runs-To-Water, as he approached his death, chose a grave-site on the lower slope, just down the northern face of this hill. There lies an unmarked Cherokee grave, only a sunken depression in the ground really, and a few remaining stones. There rests the earliest grave in the cemetery, and for generations no white man knew it was there.

The wind freshens a bit, and my thoughts return to the pleasantness and the sadness of this day. Earlier, a couple of hours ago, I buried my friend, Devy Jarrett, on this little hill. He saved my life, as I saved his years ago on the battlefields of Vietnam; only 3 years ago in a battle with a bottle—a battle too many of my people have fought and lost, Devy saved my life again. I could not save him only last week.

Neither Devy's nor my life ever really worked after Vietnam, but when we re-discovered each other so many years after those Vietnam days, we began to search history for our common background. I knew of the family tales that placed my Cherokee ancestors in North Georgia along the Tugaloo River, and Devy's family still lived along that beautiful mountain river. In the desperation of old men whose lives had little meaning, we renewed our friendship and began our search—a search for ourselves really. We understood that we found our strength in the strength of others who have lived and died on this small hill. For Devy and I, that brought some measure of peace to our lives which, by and large, were failures—both his and mine.

Still, when he received word that his only son had died in the 9/11 terror attack in New York, his search for peace at the end of his life was ultimately lost. His son, Thomas Prather Jarrett, like many of the Jarrett men in recent generations, was a firefighter. While his family still resided in Georgia, he was receiving training in New York that September, working with the New York Fire Department. Thus, on that fateful day, when everyone else was running out of the World Trade Center, Ladder Company 18 of the NYFD was running in. Thomas Jarrett died when the building came down; a part of my friend Devy died along with his son.

I know Devy was a brave man, but he did not deal well with that news. Over the next 12 months or so, he missed his only son terribly, and in that time, he just seemed to waste away. Only this project—the research into our people, the study of this land—kept him going. We sought every expert we could find, from archeologists to historians, to local leaders who remembered the stories of their grandparents and great-grandparents—the people of these mountains; we had all of them contribute what they could to this story. We learned everything we could in our search, and from that we gained strength.

That is why we dedicated ourselves to understanding our ancestors on this hill. We wanted to know them; but more, we wanted to know, to experience, and to really understand how they dealt with their world. Surely they knew fear in their time, terror from within their world as we know terror in ours, and while we learned much about who we are from this project, it didn't seem to be enough for Devy, after the loss of his son.

The doctors say Devy died of cardiac palpitations related to a series of strokes; I think he simply died of a broken heart.

A couple of deer feed pleasantly now, on the lower slope of the hill as I sit here, alone. They are unaware of me watching, and I sense the incredible beauty of this scene. At last, something stirs inside my soul—maybe God, or the Great

Kanati—Spirit of the first man of the Cherokee. This unnamed God speaks to my heart, and in a profound sense I realize something; I realize that one phase of my work is finished, and another must now begin. My research is now over, even as Devy's life has ended. At long last, I am compelled to write; I must begin while still sitting here on this peaceful hill by the grave of my friend, a man I love as only comrades in war and life can love. Here, at this moment, I commit within myself to tell the story of this river and this hill, of my friend Devy, of my people and his people, and of the greater, taller Blue Mountains beyond.

As I look down the Tugaloo River Valley, I can see six or eight miles into the Blue Ridge—into the ancient heart of my people, the Cherokee Nation, into the very soul of the mountain peoples. Here, I confront my final great test in life; now I must tell their story; for I have learned it is my story and my friend's story as well. Moreover, I sense that this is the story of every man's struggle writ large on the backdrop of these beautiful rolling hills. That story, the story of this bloody frontier is often a story of cruelty, of justice denied, of slavery, of pettiness, or of raw hatred. There is great pain here, and generations of prejudice that the modern mind cannot wholly grasp. Still, there is great fortitude, great courage here. Moreover, there is an intimate appreciation—often unspoken—of the depth of beauty, the richness of life, the spiritual nature of man's relationship to each other and to the very earth that can today be found only in places like these beautiful Blue Mountains. These people of yesterday held a richness of understanding and security of self that is rarely found in the modern world. They knew their own spirit, while many today, living in a more modern world, seem to have lost theirs—I certainly had. In contrast, the mountains gave these ancestors of mine a personal identity; a self-definition; they knew exactly who they were, and that profound self-assurance is clearly admirable. That spirit still pervades many who are fortunate enough to be born of these mountains. These persons, Indian, white, and black hold freedom to be their birthright; courage to be their duty. Even today, many of these mountaineers are as boisterous, as loud, as rough, as uncouth, and as unmannered as anyone in modern society, but they are also surprisingly, as self-assured as any people on earth. It is almost as if surviving in these hills and rugged mountains, generation after generation, somehow toughened them; gave them an endurance and a rugged independence that the rest of us can only admire. This growing awareness of their struggles has, quite literally, sobered me, and compelled me to tell their story.

Perhaps that rough courage, that self assurance, is their gift to the rest of us. I pray to God that I can capture a sense of that assurance in these pages, when our country, indeed the whole world, needs such assurance so desperately. The people of this hill—without exception—had the certainty that they could survive anything, and these people, my people, did.

I wonder for just a moment, when and where I lost that deep sense of self;

how did I fail to be who I could have been? I guess that is the question that every man eventually asks of himself, but ultimately that is of no consequence. My past is irrelevant, as I am irrelevant to this story. I play an unimportant role here; for in the light of the raw courage of the many souls captured forever on this hill, I see clearly my own failure; my struggles pale in comparison to those who lived and died here.

I now see clearly the task before me. I must write. I must speak of the many others throughout the centuries that Devy and I have come to love and respect. Thus, I humbly try to tell a story so much larger than myself; I try to capture and communicate that spirit, that strength that must ultimately belong to every man. This is my dedication; this will be my life's most important work; this will restore my balance, as a Cherokee. I know I am unworthy of this responsibility, but I pray to God I am up to the task.

Jimmy Cherokee Waters
October 14, 2002

Chapter 1: Runs-To-Water

One Mile West of Tugaloo Town, On the North Slope of the Hill
1729 – by the European Calendar

The bear stood to his great height of almost eight feet, bared his teeth and roared, frightening birds from the trees overhead as he swiped his massive forepaw towards the boy's face. The three inch claws came within inches of the boy's cheek, as he, crouching behind and below the trunk of a fallen pine, began to realize that he was fighting for his very life. He met that sudden knowledge sharply, understanding completely that he was likely to die this day. Nevertheless, he cried out desperately, in his terror; he could smell from three feet away, that sick-sour smell that bears have in the late autumn. The bear's teeth, seen from below the pine log, flashed yellow, long, and showed blood and fur from the bear's earlier feast on a rabbit or squirrel. The bear's growls were horrifying.

Only a few moments before, the boy had heard a low growl, and then seen the bear down near the creek—a narrow mountain stream that would, in time, be called Toccoa Creek. At first the boy had thrown his deerskin water bag towards the bear, certain that he could frighten the creature away. The bear merely looked bewildered at the soft leather, as it hit his flank, then he looked directly at the boy. A shiver went down the boy's spine as he looked into those seemingly lifeless feral eyes. The bear began his long lumbering approach. The boy moved down the creek a bit, to the flanks of the hill, as the bear came nearer. He then used his only weapon, a blowgun, normally used to hunt only rabbits and other small game. The impact of the eight inch dart on the bear's lower shoulder drew a small amount of blood; that only seemed to enrage the animal. Then the bear broke into a lumbering run, which was faster by far than the boy could ever run. As the bear drew near, the boy ran into a blind gully coming down the side of the hill, and crawled into the only cover he found, under a fallen pine, into a small nest of branches. The bear approached from the other side of the nest.

Now, the bear breathed toward him only three feet away, seemingly inspecting the branches that kept him from his prey. The bear growled that low menacing growl again, as the boy slipped further behind and under the log. The bear had come upon the log from the back side, and luckily, a conflux of other branches kept him from the boy. His giant forearms could easily reach two and a half feet into the impromptu enclosure.

The boy had a brief thought about singing his death song, but he had not yet studied to become a warrior, and had no death song to sing. He'd had as yet, no preparation for death in battle. He was ashamed that he didn't understand; didn't know what to do to prepare for his battle and his death.

The seven year old boy, called Toonali, had visited the creek below the hill only two days ago from his village, Estatoe, just up the valley. Here, he discovered that the chestnuts for his mother's grinding stone were easy to pick up, so he'd returned, and with his long blowgun he thought he might be able to knock a squirrel or two down from the higher limbs. Of course, the easy food was the reason the monstrous bear had come up from Owl Swamp to the lower slopes of the hill too—but now the bear planned on a different meal.

At first, under the log, the boy merely cried, shouting for help that would never come. His village was several miles away, and the town that would soon be known as Tugaloo Town was on the other side of the hill. Next, the boy shouted directly at the roaring bear, *"Why have you come out of the swamp? Why have you come to this pleasant hill? Can you not go back to your dark world and leave me here? Can you not let me live, until I am a man and can meet you as a warrior?"*

The noise from the boy seemed to enrage the beast even more. The bear, frustrated when he couldn't reach the boy, now began to strike at the branches and the log itself. The boy was fairly certain the large pine log would hold, but the other, smaller limbs would surely break under the bear's onslaught. One strike by the bear's mighty claw, and the first of the branches cracked and flew away from the log. Another strike and one of the smaller branches got caught in between the claws of the bear's forepaw. The bear took a moment away from his struggle with the branches, backed up two paces, and then placed one paw on top of the other to remove the branch. The boy was sure he would return. Now the whole side of the enclosure was almost free of the smaller branches. The large log rested only two feet off the ground, and the bear could easily make it under the log once he cleared the small branches. Again, the boy felt his own death approach; at that moment, he was sure he would die.

Then, as if by mystical powers, the boy's sensations, his fears, and even his thoughts were changed; he was transported somehow. Suddenly he was far away, sitting by a fire and listening, as he did each evening, to the wisdom of the old men of his tribe. He was a member of the Bird Clan, as was everyone in his village, and the old men of his village had much wisdom to share. His people were a mystical people with fluid understandings of the purpose of all things and all events in the universe. All things—earth, wind, fire—and all the animals of the forest were in balance. Kanati, the great spirit of the first man, had made the world that way, and when a horrid event such as this took place, it was because in some way the actions of his tribe had forced nature out of balance for a brief time; thus Kanati made the world seek to re-establish balance through the death of this young boy.

The boy, in preparing for his imminent death, wondered briefly which member of his tribe had so disturbed the spirit world—who had created the imbalance for which his death would atone? The boy knew that if he listened closely to the stories told by the old men, he would gain great wisdom that would guide him throughout his life.

Then, even with the beast approaching again, he heard quite distinctly, the soft, musically lyrical voice of one of the old men, a man known as Swimmer, sitting there beside him, speaking softly... *"This is what the old men told me when I was just a boy. The universal circle protects us and keeps all things in balance. The cycles of the sun and moon guide our spirits and guide our people, but within your circle, you choose your own balance. When you are troubled, just sit quietly for a moment and realize that you are in your circle; then from within your circle, you may seek guidance of the Great Spirit, and you will get the help you need."*

The boy, not realizing he was speaking out loud, stated in quick breaths; *"I am about to be attacked by a bear and I have only a blowgun. I will surely die this day."*

As the bear turned back to attack the enclosure one last time, the boy heard the wisdom of the old men again; *"The bears are an ancient clan, and were once people like us. They did not like life in our tribe, and as they grew long hair, they became wild. Now they live in the woods and hunt all the time. But why should a mighty bear attack a toonali?"*

Toonali answered the question of the old men. *"I do not know, grandfather. Perhaps something is not in balance."*

The voice, again lyrical, whispered to him quietly; *"Of course you are right young Toonali. Something is not in balance in your world and you will spend your lifetime trying to balance the old with the new. For now, do not worry about this bear. If you die or do not die today, is of no consequence. Just be sure to fight well as long as you can; for you are Ani-Yun Wiya; you are of the Real People of this Earth, and our people must fight as long as they can; for that is all any man can do."*

Toonali answered again, still not realizing he was speaking out loud. *"But Grandfather, I have no real weapon that will kill this beast."*

Again the lyrical voice answered. *"Yes Toonali, I see that. But does not our world provide? Can you not find something to help you? Perhaps you should run to the river, and find a stone. It will not be a good weapon, but it will be a weapon, and that is all a warrior of the Real People really needs."*

In a flash, the boy slipped out the back of his enclosure, exposing himself for a brief moment—a moment in which the bear could easily have killed him. The bear, caught by surprise, did nothing while the boy ran to the small river only ten yards away. Then, the boy heard the lumbering bear pursuing him, only a few feet behind as he stopped in the middle of the knee-deep water. He grabbed a stone from the river bottom and without even looking back to take aim, he shouted as loudly as he could and turned and threw the stone at the bear with all his might. He then ducked immediately and picked up another, larger stone in each hand, noting that he didn't hear the bear approaching. Then, still terrified, he heard a long low growl, and he looked up.

The Village Estatoe

Back in his village of Estatoe, his mother, Nalyeena, was just finishing tending her small patch of selu. Selu was, by legend, the name of the first woman in the mountains, and thus the mother of all of the Real People. Because of the importance of this single crop, Indian corn, these people had used the name of their legendary spirit mother as their word for corn; for corn was the mother of all life for the Real People.

Nalyeena stood for a moment in her selu patch and realized that she had weeded the last row. She took a moment to thank Kanati, the Great Spirit, for her patch of selu, and proudly surveyed her handiwork, as do all gardeners the world over. She was proud of her corn, ready for harvest in just a few weeks. Like all women in this tribe, she spent most of her day tending the communal fields that belonged to the entire town. Still, each woman had a small, private garden patch in which she grew many vegetables—peas, beans, squash, melons, and of course selu.

Standing there in her garden patch, she was the essence of the Native American woman–she was, in a word, beautiful. She was tall for a woman of her people, just over 5 feet and 3 inches, and as did all of her tribe, she had learned to walk gently, with an easy swaying dignity. She wore a simple light tan smock of deerskin that hung across one shoulder and down below her knees. Over this, if the weather was cooler, she would wear a waistcoat made of light cloth, or lighter skins. On her feet she had short leather boots that reached to the middle of her lower leg. She wore the harvest of the mountains in which she lived.

As she looked toward the setting sun, her facial features were somewhat flattened, compared to the Caucasians that would soon come to this village in the lower Blue Mountains, but she and her people were not as dark skinned as the Creek to the west or the Catawba to the north and east. The skin of her tribe had an olive color, as reported by many European traders at the time. Also, her shoulder and upper back were decorated with tattoos made from implantation of gun powder under her skin, in a variety of patterns. She had several flowers on her arms, and several circular designs on her lower legs. She wore her dark hair long, past her shoulders. She did not adorn it or cut it as did the men of the Real People. Rather, she merely ran a comb through it each day. In the dying sun, she looked exquisite, with the easy confidence of a successful woman of her people who had already given her husband a fine son and daughter.

Just as she finished weeding her selu patch she realized that the light was fading. At twenty-four, she was middle aged for her people at that time. She had managed to cultivate more selu and more beans than any other wife in the village, but it took her much longer to keep weeds from around her young stalks. During the Green Corn Festival, which came in the heart of the growing season, in the month Europeans called June, she would repay Kanati and the earth for the bounty of the selu and beans. Because of her good fortune, she took many more gifts to the earth during the harvest month than other families had to make.

She knew her young daughter—three years old—was safe in the lodge, but she wondered where her only son—Toonali—was in the fading light of the late autumn sun. He wandered a bit too much for her taste, but that was the way of boys the world over—as it was the way of their mothers to worry. Still, her thoughts did not linger long on him, but on her work ahead. Soon the harvest would come, and she would have even more work to do.

This industrious group of woodland Indians lived in a village of 35 family lodges, circled around a gaming area with the council house at one end of the playing fields. They called themselves Ani-Yun-Wiya, which means the Real People, or the Principal People, but by way of an early Spanish mispronunciation of their name the tribe came to be known as Che-la'que. When the English traders from Charles Town in the British colony of South Carolina first came into the foothills and mountains only three decades before, the name changed again. The Real People then became known as the Cherokee.

Nalyeena's lodge was to the west of the council house and the playing fields, so her selu patch was slightly west, outside of the village. A triangular rack made of birch logs, stood just outside of her lodge where she dried skins that her husband or son brought in, and her large grinding stone was resting near the lodge opening. A fire pit outside of the lodge to the left completed the domestic scene.

While each woman had a lodge in the village, the most important building, by far, was the council house. It was in the center of the village—an open walled, seven sided building with a thatched roof. The seven sides represented the seven clans of the Cherokee, and each Cherokee was a member of one of these clans; the Wolf Clan, Deer Clan, Bird Clan, Paint Clan, Blue Clan, Beloved Town Clan, and the Long Hair People Clan. The building was large enough to seat everyone in the village, men, women, and children—all were allowed to speak in council. All decisions were made here in the council house by consensus. The seats around the walls of the council house were raised so that all could see who was speaking. Most important, there was a sacred altar fire in a cleared area in the center. The Peace Chief occupied a seat placed in the central area behind the sacred fire. Here offerings were burned for the Great Spirit at the beginning of each council.

The Cherokee called Nalyeena's male child, Toonali, which in their language means boy-child, or child-of-the-Real-People. Of course, Toonali was only seven and thus had not been considered in council for his adult name. At his age, he was still believed to be too young for consideration by the tribal council. In time, the council would sit around the sacred fire in the council house to consider his characteristics, his achievements, his skill with weapons, and his skill in the hunt, as well as his family, and then the council would determine his adult name. Based on his spirit, his actions, his talents, and his gifts to the tribe, they would then give him a name by which he would be known for life, and he would then become a warrior for the tribe. But today, as far as anyone knew, all of that was in the distant future.

At the River

Just as Toonali looked up, holding his next fighting stone, he prepared for the worst—to be disemboweled and eaten alive by a savage hungry beast with no possibility of help. Still as he moved at that very instant, he moved toward the beast; for Toonali had determined in his own mind to fight to the death. He had heard the voices of the old men sharing their wisdom with him when he needed them—just as tribal legends always said he would, and he had obeyed their legendary wisdom. In that fraction of a second before his death, he felt that he was completed, somehow, by the ancient voices, the very wisdom of his people. He had become one with his people, and all was in balance. If his death was required, then he would surely die, but he would die bravely. If death now came to him below this nondescript hillside, so be it. He had a weapon, standing in the river with a stone in each hand, and he would fight until his death. He would meet death savagely and fight as long as there was fight left in him. This single instantaneous thought gave him clarity of purpose, and he knew that somehow he had crossed a threshold—that he understood something about himself that he'd not known with any clarity before. He knew that he could meet the worst that the harsh world had to offer, and if not beat it, at least fight it. If he could not control his own death, he could control how he met his death, and that gave him, simultaneously, great strength and a determined peace. Thus was balance achieved again in the world, and whatever the outcome, Toonali had met this challenge. With these thoughts, Toonali said a silent, quick thank you to the old men for their wisdom. Then he looked toward the beast, ready to fight to the end.

At first, he thought he was dreaming. Two warriors stood over the now lifeless black bear; its massive right forepaw now dipped into the edge of the river only 10 feet away. Toonali didn't understand; had these warriors killed the bear, and thus saved him? He recognized these warriors as men of Tugaloo Town, the neighboring village. These were men of the Wolf Clan; each was an accomplished warrior with many successes in hunting and in war with the Creeks. One had his bow ready, his mighty forearm bristled with muscles as hard as steel, challenged by the pull of the bowstring, and the arrow notched in the gut, drawn tight and ready to fly. The other poked and probed the prone beast with the tip of his Kentucky long-rifle. The bear did not move.

After a few seconds, the younger warrior now questioned Toonali directly; *"Did you kill this bear that we tracked from the swamp this day?"*

Toonali did not respond; he had never before been addressed by a warrior during a hunt; children his age spoke only to their mothers, to the old men, or to other children. Warriors seemed to speak only to other warriors, except, of course in council. The other warrior now poked the bear with his foot; still the beast did not move.

Toonali was confused. He was sure that a simple stone could not kill so great a beast. He was certain that these warriors had killed the bear and were merely jesting with him, yet they asked him again, *"Did you kill the bear?"*

Toonali, still flushed from his terror and his determination, realized suddenly that the warriors were serious. He realized that he and not they had killed the beast, with an un-aimed, incredibly lucky blow on the cranial bone and eye socket that had somehow crushed the bone into the beast's head. Further, Toonali had now breached tribal Cherokee Protocol. Ignoring questions from a warrior was not done!

In his haste to answer, he said simply, *"The bear followed me, and I asked the old men for help. They spoke to me and told me to run to the river for a weapon, so I did. I killed this bear with a stone."*

The warriors appeared skeptical as they looked at each other. There were obviously no old men around. Also, the boy's tone was surprisingly calm for so unusual a feat; still the evidence lay dead at the edge of the river at their feet. Finally, the older warrior, a man of many years, many battles, and great wisdom, mumbled the Cherokee equivalent of *"Well, I'll be damned!"*

After a few moments, he looked at the toonali and delivered his judgment. *"We will talk to the spirit of the bear, and then offer sacrifice."*

Mysticism ran deep in the Real People. They bathed ritually each day with a series of prayers, and danced a variety of ceremonial dances on various occasions throughout the year, each associated with prayers and rituals. The most frequent was the "Eagle Dance" used for celebrations during the Green Corn Festival (held each June, by the European calendar). These dances of public celebration were most often reserved for the ceremonial grounds near the council house. For a successful hunt, tribal spiritualism merely demanded that the warriors involved talk both to the spirit of the animal who was slain, and to Kanati, the Great Spirit of the first Cherokee man who set the animals free.

Kanati had always been the keeper of the animals. Legend said that Kanati had once kept all the animals in a cave in the Blue Mountains, but that through an accident the animals had all been released. Now the Cherokee could hunt them in the woods in order to eat. After each hunt, the spirit of the beast was asked for forgiveness for the killing; also the spirit had to be appeased by the promise that his death would further the life of the tribe. Finally, a sacrifice was offered for the slain beast, and prayers offered to Kanati.

So the two warriors reverently placed their weapons on the ground and sank to their knees by the bear. They waited for a moment until Toonali could come up from the river and join them. Of course, Toonali had never participated in such a prayer before; only warriors ever killed great beasts. Still, the old men of his tribe had told him of this necessity and he knew in a general way the words he was expected to say. He knew it was his role to address the spirit of the bear, and the great spirit, and then offer a sacrifice appropriate for a bear—perhaps by burying a small amount of tobacco, a treasured commodity at that time.

Toonali left the river, and knelt beside the warriors. He looked at the eldest of the warriors to seek his attention, but when the warrior looked at him, Toonali diverted his eyes—this is how a toonali was taught to show proper respect to a warrior. Toonali said, *"I will offer prayer, uncle, but I have no appropriate sacrifice for this great beast. I did not expect to kill so large an animal."*

The warrior with the rifle said, *"What would you have sacrificed for a squirrel or a rabbit?"* Toonali merely held out a small beet from his mother's garden. The warrior looked at the tiny beet and said, *"That will not do for a bear."* He thought for a moment, as he looked this highly unusual toonali over. Then he delivered his verdict; *"You may destroy your blowgun."*

Toonali's heart sank. The blowgun was the most precious thing Toonali owned. The Cherokee blowgun was made of dried river reed, and was slightly over five feet long. The preparation of a good blowgun was no small matter, requiring knowledge on which reed to select, understanding of the drying process, and an extensive "hollowing" or cleaning process. It took several days of work for a warrior to prepare a blowgun, and several weeks to dry it. His blowgun was very dear to him, having been given to him by his uncle some years ago, and it was the most valuable thing that he possessed. Still, Toonali realized the justice—the "balance" of this decision. The bear's spirit, being such a great animal, would demand a sacrifice that was dear, as was proper.

Toonali realized, suddenly, that the warriors had been watching him think about the sacrifice—he knew in an instant they were evaluating him. *"I will break the blowgun."* The warriors diverted their eyes from him, and each acknowledged with a brief nod their respect for his decision. Toonali had acquitted himself well in that moment, if a bit reluctantly. Toonali raised his face to the clouds over the hill and began his prayer. *"Great bear spirit. I came today to the forest of acorn trees for a rabbit or a squirrel, but I took your life instead. I thank you and my tribe thanks you—you will bring us much meat for the winter."*

The warriors understood that the prayer had ended without mention of an appropriate sacrifice. They each looked discretely at Toonali—for it was their responsibility to offer appropriate instruction to this boy. They then noted that Toonali's face was still raised in prayer; for Toonali had another idea. His voiced was raised again, more firmly this time. *"Kanati, Great Spirit of these Blue Mountains. I am also sorry that I took this bear when these mighty warriors had used all of their skill, and much time, and had tracked the beast from the swamp of the Owl. I have offended two great hunters, and I ask their forgiveness as well as yours. We shall share this meat that we may all grow strong, and, in return, I will give to you my blowgun."*

The warriors nodded and this time also grunted loudly, again expressing approval at the justness of this decision, as well as pleasure at this unexpected graciousness from this small boy. Toonali stood solemnly and broke his blowgun in two. He tossed each piece of now useless wood in a different direction, carefully ignoring where they landed. These were now of no consequence.

As they stood after the prayer, the senior warrior with the rifle now stated, *"You are not of Tugaloo Town."*

Toonali replied, *"I am of the Bird Clan, and live in Estatoe by the great Tugaloo River just over those two hills."*

"Then we will take this bear to Estatoe to be cleaned by the women."

With that said, the younger of the warriors sprang to life and began his run to Tugaloo to get others to help carry the bear. This particular young warrior was a *swift runner* of the tribe. Swift runners practiced the art of distance running and were used to carry messages swiftly from one village to the next. These runners could run uninterrupted, and with only a little water for upwards of 30 miles a day through the twisting paths and deer trails in the Blue Mountains. In a day when letters on the frontier were unheard of, and news in the colonies often traveled at the speed of a walking horse, the Indians had in their swift runners a message and communication system that would only be improved upon with the passing of another century, with the early telegraph. Even after the acquisition of horses, the swift runners were still more adept in the low, covered trails of these Blue Mountains. The two miles to Tugaloo Town would take this runner less than 10 minutes. Thus, in a flash many young warriors who wanted to see this mighty beast were soon coming up the trail to help. This began another ritual of Cherokee life.

The Hunt Parade

The hunting procession entering the village of Estatoe that day was grand. While Toonali did not realize it until after the march started, the order of the procession clearly proclaimed his victory over the bear. The two warriors lead the march, as was their right, being senior warriors. They headed past the first of the lodges, and headed straight for the council house where, at the edge of the playing fields, the bear would be butchered. Next, six young men from Tugaloo carried the weight of the dead beast on their shoulders, his body suspended on a pole hastily made from a small, but sturdy oak tree. The bear's head hung to one side, and his huge tongue hung out of his mouth, the blood and hair still visible in his teeth. Even in death, this 800 or 900 pound beast looked fearsome. Immediately behind the kill came Toonali holding one end of his blowgun that the younger of the warriors had retrieved from the woods. In his other hand he carried the stone that he had flung at the bear. This location in the solemn procession proclaimed him alone as the hunter who killed the beast, and while the now useless blowgun was his sacrifice to the spirit of the bear, the successful hunter must carry his weapons with him in his return to the village. Thus, a piece of it was retrieved. Next followed several more warriors, along with others who came to see this parade.

When the little children, playing at the edge of the village, spotted the procession, they ran past the warriors ignoring them. They looked at the beast only briefly, then they ran up to Toonali, and shouted at him to get out of the way. They feared he did not realize he was in the middle of the hunt parade. Still the others in the village—the mothers in their selu patches, the old men, and the younger men, soon to be warriors, saw his proud walk, his eyes never straying from the beast and the warriors in front. They didn't believe this toonali had killed this beast, but they understood something unusual had taken place, and quietly, they began to move toward the council house to learn of this remarkable hunt. Of course, Toonali never spoke to his young friends, and soon they realized the quiet dignity of the occasion, and fell silent. Toonali's mother saw the procession and ran to stand in the line of villagers now forming along the route to the council house. As was expected, she said nothing, but in her heart, she knew fear. Had her son done something terrible to offend these warriors that would require some retribution?

The Cherokee, in order to achieve and maintain balance in all things, had developed a governing principle for dispute settlements; it was an oath which governed their lives—the Blood Oath. To explain it simply, the Blood Oath was an idea common in primitive cultures—blood for blood. As stated in another tradition, it was "an eye for an eye and a tooth for a tooth." Should any offense be noted, the balance desired by all Cherokee would be disturbed and a similar and equal restitution would be called for. Should a Cherokee be killed from one clan, other members of that clan considered it their duty to kill the one committing the offense. However, if that murderer could not be found, the clan merely found and killed any member of the killer's clan in order to restore balance in the universe. The Blood Oath was a guideline for dispute settlement that could, and often did, cost lives, but this principle had ruled all Cherokee tribal interactions from time before memory. While the Blood Oath resulted in much savagery, it also, perversely prevented conflicts. In some cases, as told in the legends of the Cherokee, the Blood Oath had resulted in one death, and thereby prevented all out war between neighboring clans. Further, the avoidance of bloodshed that often resulted directly from the Blood Oath, was one reason for the development of the intricate manners of Cherokee tribal governance—what would become known by white traders as "Cherokee Protocol." This mannerly communication system, like the Blood Oath, governed all Cherokee Councils and other important social interactions.

Nalyeena feared that her son had offended these warriors in some way, and the thought of invoking the Blood Oath terrified her. Thus she hastily prayed, *"Kanati, Great Spirit of the Real People, I pray my son has not found disfavor with these two mighty warriors, and that he acts as the old men of our council house have taught him."*

As the warriors drew near the council house, the old men of Estatoe moved to the front to greet them. Owanaka, the Peace Chief of the village, stepped out in front and greeted the procession with courtly reserve. Each village, by consensus, selected a Peace Chief and a War Chief for leadership, but all of the older men were considered elders, and all citizens—male and female—by speaking in tribal councils, made all the important decisions.

Owanaka did not know how to interpret this hunt parade, for it made no sense that this toonali could slay the giant bear, but his place in the parade proclaimed him as the victorious hunter. His position as Peace Chief required great tact and delicacy at times like this, but he did have the traditions of Cherokee Protocol to depend on. It was his duty to sort out any disagreement with these warriors from the neighboring village.

Had the boy stumbled into danger and then made a kill that belonged rightly to these warriors? Was there even any disagreement here to untangle? He now must engage in the seemingly endless requirements of Cherokee Protocol, and he knew he would be engaged in the delicate balance of spoken words between men of substance. He knew the measure of the senior warrior before him from the neighboring village—this warrior was known for his great feats in battle, as well as for his hot temper. He was a Peace Chief in his village, and thus was a man to contend with.

Owanaka spoke loudly so all present could here. *"We welcome our cousins from the Wolf Clan of Tugaloo to our humble village, and we see your hunt was successful. May the spirit of the bear bless you for all your days. I'm sure it will make a fine blanket for one of your wives."*

With these carefully considered words, Owanaka had complimented the senior warrior in several ways, as was required by Cherokee Protocol. That warrior, Utani, the Longknife, was known for his many successful hunts. Moreover, even beyond the village of Tugaloo, he was known to support two wives, as did many successful Cherokee in his day; that is no simple feat for any man, and thus having it noted was a true compliment.

The senior warrior, Utani, rested the end of his long rifle on the ground. He nodded briefly to Owanaka to indicate his hearing of Owanaka's words, and then diverted his eyes as he considered his reply for a full minute. For the Cherokee never spoke in haste; they realized that words hold great power, and like their weapons, their words were to be used sparingly.

Utani knew that the Peace Chief, Owanaka, was wise, and would, of course, be interested in any possible conflict that might have arisen, so that issue had to be addressed. Also, while the rightful ownership of the bear meat had been decided, those decisions had not yet been announced, and ownership of the bear skin blanket, and ornamental bones and claws had not been discussed. Finally, the warrior determined what must be said. *"The blanket will be a fine one, but it must rest here in Estatoe. While my nephew and I had hunted this bear for two days, he was killed by your young warrior, who graciously agreed to share the meat with us. My nephew will take one of his forepaws, and the claws for a necklace; for like your young warrior, my nephew tracked and hunted this beast well."*

At this, the younger of the warriors from Tugaloo beamed with pride, raised his head and nodded to the assembled crowd in acknowledgment of the compliment he had received.

Of course, Utani knew that Toonali was but a boy—his name proclaimed as much. Still he had acquitted himself surprisingly well, and had not run from certain death. Instead, he had killed this mighty bear. Clearly, this toonali would make a fine warrior one day, and he deserved the subtle respect of being "mistaken" for a warrior, even though clearly he was not.

As this brief exchange demonstrated, Cherokee ritual and custom could become amazingly complex, but it was founded on the mandate that every human being must show respect for every other person, and for all of nature that the great spirit Kanati provided as gifts to his human children. This respect must be reflected in each action and in each word of the Cherokee. To not do so was to become less of a man, and to be out of balance with the world and with the Great Spirit. With this extreme ritual of nearly oppressive sensitivity to others, Cherokee relationships established a level of politeness that modern man would do well to emulate. Still, the intricacies of Cherokee Protocol could be tedious, and many a white man, in later decades, found these customs to be almost unbearable.

The Peace Chief of Estatoe now understood that no conflict existed, and he was thus free to lavishly compliment all concerned *"Then this toonali will take a new warm blanket to his mother's lodge this winter. That gift from Kanati will be most welcome this year, for I fear a cold winter in our Blue Mountains. Further, our village must meet in council to consider this toonali's future this day; our old men must hear from these great warriors of the actions of this toonali. Clearly we have been mistaken in not considering his contribution to our village sooner, as his hunt has shown how valuable he can be to our tribe."*

At this increased recognition, Toonali lifted his head to look directly at the Peace Chief. He had never looked the Chief in the eye before, as that—from a mere child—would show disrespect. Today he faced the Chief directly, then he nodded his thanks, and quickly looked away. At the edge of the crowd, Nalyeena beamed with pride; today her work in raising this child was complete. She wished her husband was here to see this recognition of his son, but he hunted in the distant mountains, and would probably not return for another month. She would be proud to share this moment with him upon his return, so she reminded herself to listen to each word carefully.

The Peace Chief Owanaka continued, as Cherokee Protocol demanded. *"I am sure that having the opportunity to hunt with you and your fine nephew taught our toonali many things. For I have heard of your nephew, Changee, who with great bravery, once chased the mighty panther from the rushes along the northern river. I also hear that he is a swift runner for your village."*

The younger of the warriors from Tugaloo, had indeed had a successful hunt for a large panther beside a creek to the North three winters past. He'd killed the panther with two arrows, and he still wore the panther's claws around his neck, with another tied in the topknot of his hair. It is from that panther hunt, which was transformed into a local legend by the Cherokee, and later by the whites over the next two hundred years, that Panther Creek would get its name. Changee now beamed with pride to hear that his prowess was known in this neighboring village. He lifted his face to the Peace Chief and nodded his appreciation, then quickly diverted his eyes.

Cherokee names were intricate, and seemingly baffling to white men. Some names told of an actual event, as was the case for Changee, which literally meant—chaser of panthers. Names for other warriors spoke of character or perceived strengths of the men in question, and still others' names spoke of gifts brought by the warrior, or given to the warriors by the Great Spirit at critical points in their lives. In knowing a warrior's name, Chiefs from other villages thus knew something about their character or background and could, when Cherokee Protocol required, offer a compliment without knowing a great deal more about the man.

Women, in contrast, took names that were given to them by their fathers, and were not considered in council. While Cherokee women did play an impressive political role in the tribe, much more so than in other tribes in what was to become the continental United States, they nevertheless belonged to their family until they married, and were therefore not routinely considered worthy of a "naming council" meeting.

Owanaka continued; *"I also thank the strong young men who bring the bear to our women for cleaning. They will take a portion of meat to their many wives for their service. Now, I will send swift runners to the other villages to invite our cousins to our council for this toonali."* At that Owanaka looked again at Utani. *"Can I offer refreshments to Utani, to Changee, and to these other fine warriors, who are our guests this day?"*

Thus the matter was settled; everyone had been thanked and complimented, the portions divided; balance was restored and respected. The men moved into the council house to sit around the sacred fire, while the daughters of Owanaka brought in nuts, several types of wild berries, and cool water to refresh them. Most of the women began to move toward their lodges, each to get her knife. Each would work in skinning and butchering the bear, and each would receive a small portion for her services. The work would begin immediately, and the bearskin blanket would go to the toonali to bring to his mother's lodge, as decided.

Nalyeena, quietly turned to her cousin, a woman of similar age who lived at the other end of the village and said, *"Make certain the skin is removed without damage; this blanket will be my toonali's pride as he shows it to his father this winter. Also, get for my hearth a large portion of the brain, the heart, and the loins. Then assure me that the remainder of the meat is apportioned as decided, but be sure that the two warriors of Tugaloo get their choice of the loins, and a large share of the other meat. I must go to council and hear this tale of my toonali's bravery."* With that she hurriedly ran into the council house, carefully moving to the side of the house reserved for the Bird Clan.

In The Council House

By the time Owanaka had taken his seat inside, one of his younger wives had placed additional dried wood and tobacco near the sacred fire for him to use in sacrifice. He placed the tobacco on the fire, the aroma was quite pleasing as the smoke drifted up into the rafters and out the smoke hole at the top of the council house. Owanaka invited both Utani and Changee to sit beside him in the places of honor, but they refused, as was custom, and chose instead to sit on the side of the house reserved for the Wolf Clan—their clan within the larger tribe. The old men of Estatoe sat in the section of the Bird Clan, and since no other clans were represented, the other five sides of the council house remained empty. The council waited for a time for any elders from other villages to come should they wish to.

As they waited, several women from Estatoe chose to enter into this council. Nalyeena attended to hear the story of her son's victory over the bear for she knew that this would become a most important day in his young life, and her husband would want to hear about everything that was said.

Toomi, the beloved woman of Estatoe, also attended. Perhaps once in a generation a woman would become so important to the tribe that she gained the status of Beloved Woman. Her council was then sought as if she were a Peace Chief, since she had distinguished herself in courage or leadership in some way. Beloved

Women of the Cherokee could determine how certain disputes would be settled, and could choose the fate of prisoners of war—anything from total freedom to death. In a day when European countries pretended that women had no abilities, save the occasional rare example such as Queen Elizabeth, the Cherokee routinely committed a most unthinkable breach in judgment by the European standards of the day—they took their women seriously. Moreover, they gave their women respect. Toomi took a seat of honor beside Owanaka by the sacred fire as was her right.

After refreshments were served, Owanaka prayed briefly, thanking the Great Spirit for this fortunate hunt, and for the visit of these great warriors. Next, Utani stood to speak.

"We saw the mark of a bear on a tree on a hill near our village. He bit a tree and the bite was higher than a man's head." All Cherokee knew that male bear marked territory by several means. Urination was certainly used most frequently, but the great black bear would also stand on hind legs and bite a tree as high up as possible to give any male competitors a sense of its strength and size. Other male bears that could not reach that mark were thus warned to find another territory. After Utani spoke, he raised his hand eight inches above his own head to give a sense of the bear mark he'd seen. He turned in a full circle so that warriors sitting in the marked spot for all seven clans of the Cherokee could see his face. Thus he showed respect for all seven clans, even though they were, for the most part, not there. He continued: *"We decided this bear was large, and was too close to our village and our playing fields, so we tracked it into the great swamp where the owl lives, below the little creek that runs between our villages. For two days, we saw increasing signs, and we slept on the trail of this bear. We noted that it headed back for our village along the creek, and then we heard it tearing bushes. We stood on the slope of a hill, and saw your young warrior run to the river. We thought he was running, but we knew he could not escape the bear; we thought that he would surely die this day. Then we saw a most remarkable thing. He didn't run from the bear—he ran to the river! There, he swiped up a river stone, turned, and flung it at the bear, as he screamed his mighty war cry. His medicine is strong, and the river stone helped him; we saw the bear fall dead in the river. I do not know how a stone crushed this bear's head, but I know what I saw. This I say to the Cherokee here assembled in council; Today this young man fought a mighty beast, and he killed this beast with a stone. "*

Utani sat down and the council was silent for a full minute as everyone considered his words. He knew he'd told only half of the story, but speaking too much, even in council, was unseemly.

Owanaka then spoke again, this time to Changee. *"Our village has heard of a brave warrior who chases panthers at the northern river, and we would now like to hear his words."*

Changee nodded to Owanaka, indicating he would speak. He then waited a full two minutes considering his words carefully, as thus he showed respect for the elders present. Then he stood and slowly turned in a circle to face directly all of the Clans of the Cherokee. *"My uncle is a great warrior, and is used to bears; he would not be frightened by one bear, or perhaps by many. We know that any Cherokee warrior can dispatch a bear with an arrow or a rifle. But perhaps my uncle's courage is too great; I ask him in respect, can he see much smaller courage that is still quite large? What toonali is this who faces a bear alone in a river and flings a stone? I have no great victories like my uncle, but I have fought in battle with the Creeks, and I have hunted bear and buffalo in our Blue Mountains during many winters. This young toonali showed more courage than I have ever seen in a toonali, and I think that Kanati, the Great Spirit, spoke to him this day."*

Utani, the uncle, beamed with pride at both the compliment, and at the wisdom of his nephew in posing the question of a toonali's courage. The old men nodded their understanding and contemplated a young boy's communion with Kanati. Does the Great Spirit speak directly to this boy?

After a pause, refreshments were again offered. Several of the old men began to whisper among themselves trying to figure out what these events may mean. Then Owanaka spoke again, this time to Toonali. *"Boy, we have heard the words of two great warriors, and each speaks of your courage. We are convinced of your courage in the river, but tell us, did you speak with the Great Spirit this day?"* For if such communion had taken place, it would signal great things in this toonali's life.

Toonali stood. He had never addressed a council before, but today he stood, and turned slowly in a circle; thus, he too faced all the clans of the Cherokee, and then looked at the Peace Chief. He spoke with a strong, determined voice. *"I killed the bear,"* he said, then he continued, *"But I think that I spoke with the old men. I was told to run to the river and get a weapon. Sometimes we do not have a weapon, and must fight anyway, so I fought. I found balance when the old men spoke to me, and I was ready to die in that river, if Kanati had called to me to die, but he did not call. I threw the stone and killed the bear."*

Toonali paused for a moment, but he did not sit down. He was not yet finished. After a few seconds, he shared—as he knew he must before this impressive Cherokee Council—his full thoughts, embarrassing though these were. He continued. *"Grandfather, I am also ashamed, for I was frightened of this beast."* He then looked away from the Peace Chief, as was proper, and sat down.

Silence permeated the council house for about two minutes, as again, the council considered these words. Each Cherokee present was certain that the boy had spoken to the Great Spirit since the old men were not near the creek. Still, was the boy frightened, and what did that mean for a prospective Cherokee warrior? The silence in the council house stretched to two minutes, then three.

Finally, the voice of an old woman, the Beloved Woman, was heard as she cleared her throat, indicating a desire to speak. Toomi then rose, and slowly turned to face each clan of her tribe, seemingly pausing in each of seven directions. As she again faced the Peace Chief, she spoke. *"As women, we know of great fear, perhaps even more fear than our brave warriors; for which one of our warriors can stand the screams of his wives giving birth?"*

At this, there was subtle laughter in the council house. All believed that even the bravest of warriors would have great fear enduring that agony! Toomi then continued, *"As a woman, I know that fear can paralyze us, even so with great warriors proven in battle. Fear can certainly paralyze any toonali. Fear can make anyone freeze in danger. This is not good for the tribe, and such fear will destroy us."*

She sat, and all considered her words, for her meaning was clear. This toonali may have been terrified, but on this day he had been ready to fight to the death like every other battle-tested Cherokee warrior—such is the mark of a warrior and a man. This beloved woman was wise indeed, having made her point without speaking it. Thus, through her words and her subtlety did Toonali finally learn of the difference between fear and panic. He also learned, while it hadn't been stated overtly, that even great warriors felt fear.

After a moment's pause, Changee rose to speak again. *"Toomi's words are wise; a warrior knows fear often, as I have known fear when faced with a panther. But a warrior knows how to move in fear. Fear becomes a warrior's weapon, like his many other weapons. Today this toonali moved well."* He sat down.

Owanaka sensed that a decision was almost reached, but he needed to hear more. He was about to ask some of the old men of Estatoe what they thought, when Utani stood once again. *"Sometimes we old warriors do forget our first battles— for our old men remember that we have been attacked by the Creeks every year it seems; who can remember?"*

At this point, he looked around, turning full circle again to face each clan section of the council house. Like Owanaka, he sensed that a decision was almost reached—a decision he desired. Still he had let his nephew take the lead in speaking to this council. Even before reaching the village while they were still on the trail, as the toonali quietly considered his kill, Utani and Changee had discussed this very strategy for getting the toonali an early naming ritual. Now Utani wished to express his support. He continued. *"I believe that this toonali spoke to Kanati whom he heard as the old men. He prayed well to the bear's spirit, and offered a valuable sacrifice. This I say to the Cherokee people, this day he became a man."*

Utani had thus let his desires be known; he nodded again to Owanaka, and sat down.

After a few moments, Owanaka again rose. *"Then it is decided, this toonali has earned his right to a name today. He will begin training with the warriors next year at the Green Corn Festival. Can one of our old men suggest a name?"*

One suggestion—quickly made—was bear-killer, but that was discarded since the toonali did not kill the bear alone—for the bear had been stalked for two days by Utani and Changee, and was thus tired by his ordeal. Thrower and stone-thrower were also considered, but were discarded because the stone throw had been essentially un-aimed. The toonali had shown strength but no great skill in that toss—it was merely Kanati's will that he killed the bear at all. Finally, after several other suggestions, Owanaka showed his wisdom in looking at the toonali and asking, *"Toonali, what was the most important thing that happened to you today?"*

The boy stood and without hesitation, he faced Owanaka directly replying *"The old men spoke to me of balance. Then they said to run to the water and seek a weapon. The old men…"* then he corrected himself, yielding to the council's decision, *"No Grandfather, Kanati spoke to me and told me to run to the river and find a weapon."*

Even now, Toonali was just realizing that he had been touched by the Great Spirit in those words. He knew that those words would impact his life again and again. As he reflected on his own answer, he forgot for a moment that he stood before the council.

As soon as Toonali spoke, Owanaka smiled; for he had heard the toonali say his own name without even realizing it. When the toonali finished, Owanaka stood, slowly turning to face all seven of the Clans of the Cherokee; in a great voice, worthy of a Peace Chief of the Cherokee, he spoke. *"Your name shall be Runs-To-Water; for that is what the Great Spirit told you to do. Your spirit will forevermore be led by this. When you seek help or are in danger, you will run to water and listen there for Kanati, the Great Spirit. You will have many battles in life, but use this wisdom always—run to the water, and there will you fight your battles. One day, in one such fight, you will die, but that is of no matter, since all of the Cherokee people die. Still, in these words, Runs-To-Water is great wisdom and guidance; it will be your name and your destiny. This I say to the Real People; this day you became a man, and this is who you are; You are Runs-To-Water. Your body will be marked by a bear and by a swift river. On this day, the Great Spirit Kanati visited you and told you who you are."*

And so it was done. All the old men nodded and grunted their approval, and within twenty-four hours, the young man's body was tattooed with the mark of a bear and a great river across his chest. Swift runners were again dispatched to the neighboring villages to announce the new warrior's naming ceremony, as well as his new name. While this naming tattoo would be renewed many times in his life as he grew, it would always signify his bravery in the river as he faced certain death, at the claws of a great bear. It would also speak of his destiny and the fact that Kanati had spoken to him.

At the conclusion of the naming ceremony, everyone in the council house had a different reaction. Utani and Changee were pleased that this toonali was given a name, for they knew they had witnessed great bravery, and such bravery could only strengthen the Cherokee. Each contemplated one day standing beside Runs-To-Water in battle against the Creeks or the Catawba. Toomi smiled to herself and wondered what she could do to make this boy strong. She knew that the boy would have a hard training—he would begin at eight what most young boys began at 11 or 12. Still, the Great Spirit had touched this boy, and great things were expected from him. Nalyeena, while quite proud, was also worried about his training. Certainly his uncles and the old men would have to begin his training now, so that he could keep up with the other boys at the Green Corn Festival next year.

Perhaps Runs-To-Water had the most unusual reaction. While he knew he was much too young for warrior training, he also knew he had been spoken to by Kanati, and had faced the great bear. Moreover, he understood that he had faced death in the eyes of that bear, and that he could do so again if necessary. He understood that this meant he would have precious little time for play with his friends—for he needed to begin immediately training and acting like a warrior. He understood that his life was changed this day, and while he could never have dreamed of the challenges through which he would one day lead his tribe, he knew he would lead bravely, and one day die as a revered Cherokee warrior. Thus, it began…

Growing Up Cherokee
1735, by the European Calendar

Runs-To-Water, somewhat large for his age, had managed to survive the taunts of his older "peers" during his warrior training. He had now lived through thirteen winters in the Blue Mountains, and while others his age were just beginning to train with arrows, to hunt large game alone, or to run long distances for building strength, Runs-To-Water had already mastered these tasks, and was, because of his large size, moving into the most important stage of his manhood preparations. He was beginning to compete with men who ranged in age from 15 to 25 in the great inter-village games of chungke—the ball game.

The Cherokee took their ball games very seriously. Some historic accounts even note that they were known to postpone hunting or even battles when the team from one village challenged another. In the game of chungke, teams from different villages would throw poles through the holes in the middle of a rolling stone. Teams who were victorious were honored among the villages, and every young warrior wanted to show his prowess on the gaming fields.

In 1735, the games promised much in the way of entertainment and gambling to the community as the Green Corn Festival began. The festival would last five days. Many feasts would be held, hosted by various villages in the lower cluster of Cherokee towns in what would become upstate South Carolina and Georgia. There were eleven towns in the Tugaloo Town cluster, which included towns along both sides of the Tugaloo River below the first high ridge of the Blue Mountains. Each of these towns fielded a Chungke team, on which even the senior warriors would gamble their most precious possessions—hunting rifles, knives, or deerskins.

At the festivals, among the feasts, the councils, and the gambling, the games would dominate, though in addition, all types of trade goods were exchanged. Early each day during the festival, the various teams would move to the selected ball field, which this year was the field at Tugaloo Town. In the villages around Tugaloo Town and Estatoe, some 2000 Cherokee lived, and nearly all gathered for the larger of the inter-village games. In a fashion that can only be described as most un-Cherokee, they would harasses each other, taunting the opposing team, as the players took the field. *"I see your toonalies from Keowee Village. Where is your ball team?"*

"Care to wager your horse on this game? Our village can take your team, as well as all of the horses in Estatoe!"

"Your women must be lonesome; if this is your team then they have no real men in Tugaloo Town!"

So the games and the festival progressed. Whiskey, in abundant supply from white traders who traveled through the area, would brighten the mood and suppress the senses for a time, and inevitably some fights would break out amongst the teams. Still the games were so rough that most anger could be alleviated in the contest itself, and thus most of the violence took place on the large, non-refereed playing fields. Among the older men, much gambling took place, and towards the end of the games—games that often lasted all day and sometimes well into the night—many a Cherokee did manage to gamble away his entire stock of horses and furs. Also, with the ebb and flow of the game, as well as the flow of spirited liquors, many young warriors were soothed by maidens from nearby villages, as couples managed to hide themselves among the river-cane along the river's edge for some rather personal attention, and perhaps a brief explosion of lust.

Should an injured player require a few moments rest, or perhaps some help with a bloody nose, some maiden would appear with cool water from the river and a bit of fruit or berries to eat. The Cherokee were never prudish, and many of these happenstance meetings resulted in a hasty sexual coupling in the nearby grass. The Cherokee took the reasonable position that any young man who wished to become a warrior had better have some experience with women. Moreover, while adultery and pregnancies outside of wedlock were frowned upon, any unmarried woman who was old enough to enjoy it could choose to fornicate with any man she wished. This resulted in relatively lax sexual standards, particularly during festival days.

At times, particularly during the festival, the bushes seemed alive with partners enjoying each other, and after each coupling, the young men headed back out to the bloody field to continue to prove his manhood. In fact, many of the early missionaries were appalled at the sexual promiscuity of the Cherokee, and most complained bitterly; one noted that it was hard to find a place in the grass to step when the necessity to relieve one-self arose, since fornicating couples were so plentiful in the nearby bushes. An early trader, perhaps a bit more wise in the ways of the world, put it more succinctly: *"If you see a Cherokee in the bushes, he ain't huntin' —if he was huntin' you wouldn't see a hint of him! Naw, if you see a Cherokee in the brush, he is doing one of three things; playin', screwin', or waiting to kill ya!"*

Another game championed by the Cherokee was a primitive version of lacrosse. At times only the teams were on the game field, but when these games became heated it was perfectly acceptable for other teammates who were resting to join in—even bystanders took the field when the games got exciting, resulting, of course, in total chaos on the field! At times hundreds would be on the massive ball grounds fighting for any sight, much less any possible contact with the ball. Sticks swung abruptly, noses were bloodied, and bones were broken, but the games went on. Tripping, wrestling, high-sticking—all were not only allowed but encouraged, and short of shooting one's opponents, most everything would be considered good fun, which was convenient since, like the chungke game, there were no referees anyway.

In these games, Runs-To-Water continued to make a name for himself—his arms grew strong, and his chest broad—his chest tattoo of the bear, growing larger with each year. Moreover, most years, he managed to avoid getting broken up too badly, though he did take a nasty blow to his face, leaving a permanent scar across his left cheek. While his mother nursed his wound for some two months after that game, Runs-To-Water really didn't mind the wounded look he now sported. He surmised that many Cherokee girls found the scar to be somewhat interesting. Certainly, given his size, and his prowess—for his early victory over the bear was legendary—he suffered no shortage of female company.

Thus did life proceed for the young warrior. It was good to be in Estatoe, his native village; to hunt the Blue Mountains, and to play in the yearly games. It was good, the life he lead, helping his mother provide for his younger siblings; it was good to stalk deer and bear in the lower hills to the north, and to join the senior warriors in the winter hunts—hunts that sometimes lasted for months. At this point, he was old enough to hunt alone for the great beasts, and taking a mule he had traded for, he would be gone for days—perhaps even for a couple of weeks. In the solitude of the mountains, he would find more than his share of deer to kill and skin. All was in balance during this time.

Once, near a large waterfall, above the great valley that later came to be known as Tallulah Gorge, he encountered a great bear. He'd been lying still above a deer path for some hours in the mystic motionless state known to hunters worldwide. He had assured himself in the early morning light that he was downwind of the deer trail, and he was certain that several deer would fall to his bow on this day. Instead, a large bear came up the Gorge, crossing the path below him, only 20 feet away. Now, bear have tough hide, and the Cherokee would usually hunt bear in groups so that many arrows could be used in the kill. Still, Runs-To-Water saw that this bear had come to him from the Gorge where the loud river flowed; he considered this bear to be another gift from Kanati since it had come up from the river. He silently drew his bow, aiming just behind the front leg for a heart or lung shot. He was determined to take this bear, and was just about to release his arrow when he noted another, smaller paw on the trail. In a moment, two cubs entered the trail following their mother, and playfully pawed at each other.

Runs-To-Water was not sure what to do. He knew killing the bear would provide much meat and a warm blanket, and he believed he would kill this bear with one shot—for he was much closer than usual, and could probably hit the beast in the broadside lung. Still, this bear was giving other bears to the forest and to the Blue Mountains. As he sighted down his deadly arrow into the chest of the great bear, he heard the voice of the old men say… *"This is what the old men told me when I was just a boy—that the Great Spirit Kanati, gives all the animals in the forest for us to hunt. From these Blue Mountains, we take all the things we need to live by the Tugaloo River. We may take what we need, and make sacrifice for these things, but we should never take more than we need."*

Runs-To-Water lowered his bow. He made not a noise, and the bear below him never realized he was there. If he could not take the bear, he could at least observe the bear, and learn what lessons it may have to offer him. While he had finished his warrior training, and his life spread out before him like an exciting array of wonderful choices, Runs-To-Water knew that he still had much to learn. In that knowledge, he was wise indeed; for many young men at the crest of the wave of life, fail to realize that they are not omnipotent. In that sense, Runs-To-Water was wiser than most.

Willow
1745, by the European Calendar

Her name, Akala, in the lyrical language of the Cherokee meant Willow or Willow Tree. The willows of the river valley appealed to the mystic sense of the Cherokee like no other tree—the soft hiss of the limbs as a gentle wind passed seemed to tell of the stately reserve of the Cherokee. It seemed to speak of the mystical, of the ways of Kanati, and of the Blue Mountains themselves. Indeed, her name itself was almost musical, much like the sound of wind passing through the willows by the river.

This young Cherokee maiden was well named, for her lithe body and long limbs at 15, reflected the soft beauty of that name. Her newly formed young breasts were small, but firm under her deerskin smock, her hair was long, in the fashion of women of the Cherokee, and her skin a light brown reddish color, almost copper. Moreover, she was known as a serious worker with a good disposition and a playful laugh, if perhaps, a bit irreverent. In short, Akala was exquisite! In fact, the only drawback to this girl, as noted by the old women of the tribe, was a quick mind and a sharp tongue. Still, the Cherokee were much more tolerant of these traits in a woman than almost any culture on earth in those years.

She was daughter to the mighty Changee, chaser of panthers, who had been killed only a year previous, in a raid against the Creek Villages near the lower Chattahoochee River next to the great mountain of stone in the heart of what would one day be called the state of Georgia. Stone Mountain was considered holy by the Cherokee, who were sure that the little people lived there—a race of godlike creatures the Cherokee sought to avoid. Still, in their minds it was Cherokee hunting ground, and thus, the Creeks had to be driven off. Changee died in that effort.

Had Changee lived, Akala's lot in life would have been secured, but with his death, life had become hard for her, her mother, and her younger sisters. Only one son, 9 years of age, was now hunting small game for this family. Their selu patch was not large, and they had come to depend upon Changee's hunting skill. He often left for months at a time with other warriors to hunt in the great mountains to the north. Many times Changee would bring back more deerskin and other furs for trade than any of the other warriors. Skins would be stacked high on their pack mules as they came back to Tugaloo; skins to trade with the white traders who had lately come up the river from Charles Town, and even from the newer town of Savannah further to the South.

But this year there had been no skins to trade for this family, and they had to live on the vegetables they could grow and the small game their brother killed with his blowgun within a couple miles of the village. He often hunted on the small hill just to the north of Tugaloo town, slightly to the west of the river. For his father had told him of a Cherokee toonali from another village who had killed a mighty bear on that hill in Toccoa Creek, just below the patch of acorns. While this boy dreamed of killing a mighty beast to feed his family through the winter, he found only squirrel and rabbits for the family pot. Thus, Akala, her sisters and mother had to work harder to feed themselves than others in their village.

Akala hoped that her mother would catch the eye of one of the other warriors in town. There had been some talk of one of the older warriors, the famed Utani, taking another wife. He had had two wives die in childbirth over the years, and his first wife was now very old. Still, no one knew if the rumors were true, and for now the women and young toonali were left to feed themselves.

Of course, the other villagers would not let them starve, but Akala and her family realized that accepting selu from their relatives meant taking food from the mouths of their cousins, and all Cherokee were far too proud for this. Such charity was only a last resort before starving.

Akala, at the age of 15, had not considered catching the eye of some warrior for herself. However, many of the old women had thought that this might be the saving grace for the family. All knew that Kanati always had a plan for the Cherokee living in safety in the Blue Mountains, and perhaps if Akala married well, the family might be saved.

The Toothless White Man

Runs-To-Water had reason often to visit his neighboring village of Tugaloo during these years. He was now a young man of 23, and was a well respected warrior of the Bird Clan in his village of Estatoe. The story of his killing the bear with a stone was now legend among the lower towns of the Cherokee, and he was known to fire an arrow straight and true. He played in the yearly games with a skill only noted in more senior players, and he now wore five claws from different bear around his neck. Moreover, he had fought the filthy Creek twice in pitched battles, and had acquitted himself well. His face was scarred from the games of his youth, and he bore in his lower shoulder a piece of stone, an arrowhead from the arrow of a Creek warrior. His chest tattoo of the bear was redone every several years as his mark of courage, and he could point to both the tattoo and the wound with it's rough covering skin with pride in his warrior skills; of course, no Cherokee would ever brag in such an overt fashion, but the wounds of honor were there for all to see.

He'd spent many years learning the ways of the wild deer, the beaver, the bear, and the buffalo, and he'd brought many skins to trade in the shop owned by the Toothless White Man across the river. He found that the old men had been correct in his naming ceremony; for he always had his most successful hunts not on the high ridge, but in the lower valleys down where the water ran. It was here he could seemingly melt into mother Earth, always finding bear, deer, or buffalo for his mother's pot. While the buffalo were becoming scarce, he still found bear and deer plentiful. His hunts were successful enough that he now owned several mules and two horses. He usually took two mules with him on the hunts to carry his skins, and he always left a horse for his mother to use. He had even considered making her a log cabin in which to live, like many of the other Cherokee were doing in the mid 1700s. However, he found that he liked the old ways better—the ways of balance—a balance of his needs and the resources that the Blue Mountains offered. Thus, while he now owned a rifle, he still hunted also with the bow and arrow—he was tied to the older way of life, as was his father, who had died several years ago on a hunt, cut down by the claw of a bear.

Runs-To-Water thought briefly of these things as he entered the town of Tugaloo. He passed some 85 lodges in this flat hollow next to the river. Many fields of selu were planted and seemed to be growing well with the rains from the past spring. Soon the Green Corn Festival would be upon them, and that time of celebration was always one highpoint of the year for the Cherokee. Runs-To-

Water noted the many skin frames next to the lodges, many holding more than one skin: buffalo, deer, rabbit, otter, beaver—all were to be seen here. Many were only partially cured, and several smokehouses were in use, curing the meat and turning the various animals into dried meat for use on the hunt during the fall, or for winter food next year. In the center of the town next to the river were the large playing fields where the men played chunkge—the stone rolling game.

Next to the playing fields was the council house. Tugaloo was the senior village among the lower towns, and thus its council house was more elaborate. It was built on an earthen mound some twenty-five feet higher than the surrounding fields, next to the Tugaloo River. Also the council house itself was larger than those in nearby villages, though constructed in the same seven-sided fashion. All of this Runs-To-Water took in without a second glance. He noted only a few young toonalis on the playing fields, and no one at all around the council house, except for the usual collection of old men. He took his animals forward through the village to approach the trading post across the shallow ford in the river.

The Toothless White Man—that is how the Cherokee referred to him—was named John Sharp. He sat alone in front of his trading cabin. An Englishman by birth, he had deserted his trading partners in Charles Town far to the south in 1736, and established a permanent trading post on the upper Savannah River–just adjacent to Tugaloo Town. Many decades earlier, in the 1690s, a French renegade and rogue trader named Jean Couture had traveled through the Cherokee Country on the southern rim of the Blue Ridge, noting the rich villages along the Tugaloo River as he passed. When he arrived in Charles Town on the coast of South Carolina, he was welcomed as an "Indian expert," and led an expedition in 1700 to establish trade with the Cherokee. Thus, traders had traveled the Cherokee trails many times, but only in the early 1700s were permanent trading stations established. Most of the trade still involved Charles Town in the South Carolina colony, though the Cherokee were now aware of a more recent white settlement to the south on their river. The British had settled Savannah and the Georgia colony in 1733, and had settled Augusta upriver from Savannah, only 3 years later.

Sharp had come to trade with the Cherokee one day and, for reasons of his own, had chosen not to return. The Cherokee often laughingly noted that wherever he had come from, he had surely left his teeth there, as there was no hint of teeth among his head now—hence his name among the Cherokee. Sharpe was not unlike many of European heritage in those decades in that hygiene was unknown or little practiced. Most whites bathed at least once or twice a year, but brushing teeth was unknown. In contrast, the Cherokee bathed in the river daily, usually in the morning, and their selu, fish, and hardtack diet, along with chewing other grains kept their teeth in their head most of their lives. They thought the Toothless White Man to be quite the joke.

However, everyone realized that the frontier of the Blue Mountains during the 1600s and 1700s offered refuge for many whites who had good, though private, reasons to leave their own backgrounds in the newly settled towns along the coast. Sharp had found a Cherokee wife—an old woman whose husband had been killed by the Creeks in a spring raid—and took her into a small log cabin he'd built near the Tugaloo River. Thus, in 1736 was a permanent trading post established near Tugaloo Town, the first "white" dwelling anywhere in the upstate area of the Georgia colony. Sharp was also one of the first white men to experience the pleasures of taking a "squaw wife," but many other white men did so in the years to come.

In his small cabin on the east side of the Tugaloo River, he collected skins and paid the Cherokee in lead for their muskets, gunpowder, cloth for women to make fancy dresses, or with whiskey. He usually sat in front of his cabin, chewing his tobacco leaves and spitting. Sometimes an old warrior would come and sit with him, talking of the weather, the crops, the hunt, or the hated Creeks who perpetually raided the Tugaloo. Sometimes they would drink together; sometimes Sharpe would drink alone. His Cherokee wife was tending a patch of selu out back to help feed him, and all seemed right with the world; just as long as nobody asked too many questions about the background of this Toothless White Man.

Runs-To-Water had just returned from a two month hunt deep into the mountains, near the higher peak with the granite dome, where the cold air lived—this would, in time, be named Clingman's Dome. In the valleys below these peaks, he found running creeks with many signs of deer and bear. He had his two mules loaded with skins, and he carried his rifle across his shoulder, as he led his pack animals through Tugaloo to the Toothless White Man's lodge to trade.

As Runs-To-Water passed the far end of the village, he noticed a young woman in her selu patch, bending down to clear weeds from the corn. He liked the shape of her legs, and as she stood again she flicked her hair to get it out of her face, and Runs-To-Water noticed her young breasts under her deerskin. The tattoo of a river willow on her bare left shoulder seemed to whisper an invitation to touch and caress the young girl's skin. The smock was much too tight; she'd had no replacement for over a year, and her breasts pressed against it. Perhaps that is what caught his eye, as was the way of men the world over.

As Akala stood, for some reason she thought to look around behind her toward the village, and her eyes met those of the warrior—she knew him to be from Estatoe and knew the story of him killing a bear below the western hill next to their village. The warrior had two mules loaded with skins and he was obviously here to trade with the Toothless White Man. This warrior would be wealthy by the end of the day. The look they shared in that moment, and their private, though shared thoughts—unvoiced by each—was all it took.

No one knows why any sane man who is just beginning his successful adult life would decide to take a wife. Indeed, Runs-To-Water would have been hard pressed to state his feelings on the matter at that moment. The Cherokee were anything but prudish in matters of sex; sexual pleasures enjoyed by both men and women, married and unmarried were, as we have seen, quite common. Still seeking release at the end of a long hunt was one thing, and taking a wife quite another entirely. Perhaps it was the deerskin that was just too damn tight. At any rate, Runs-To-Water determined to speak to his confidant—Swimmer—the conjuror from Estatoe, about this. He also decided to talk with his mother, Nalyeena. His mother had grown in wisdom as he himself had matured. She would understand his desires in this matter.

Thus, in 1745 did Runs-To-Water decide to take a wife. He was established as a warrior, and if anything, he had waited a bit longer than most of the other warriors. He stood a full six feet three inches in height, in this, his twenty-third winter. In the manner of all of the warriors of his tribe, he shaved his head, except for a topknot of hair from the rear right of his scalp, which he let grow long—hanging well below his right shoulder. This length of hair he decorated with the claws of his first bear, and a feather for each battle he'd fought with the Creeks. Unlike the Native American tribes on the great northern plains, the Cherokee let their feathers dangle downward toward their necks, and Runs-To-Water's head sported several feathers that year. The great bear, standing on hind legs with paws outstretched, was tattooed on his mighty chest and spoke of his bravery. A great sun disc, tattooed in the skin on his back spoke of the time when the Great Spirit visited him and told him how to kill a bear with a stone. His forearms were powerful; he could draw a bow that would humble almost any white man of his generation, and he could trot, non-stop, for 30 miles in a day up and down a mountain trail or along some riverbank. When he wasn't leading his mules, running was his preferred way to travel the mountains, since most of the mountain trails were not wide and smooth enough for horses, as were trails in the flatlands. He carried what he needed in a small skin pouch—his bow and arrows, his flint for fire, his powder pouch and lead, his rifle, and a bear skin blanket for sleeping in the cool evenings.

Runs-To-Water did not realize it at the time, but his was the last generation of Cherokee of Estatoe and Tugaloo Town to live as his ancestors had lived. In his lifetime, the world would change dramatically, and not for the better—at least in the eyes of the Real People. Still that was not known on this day in 1745, and as he looked at the young girl, he thought only of taking her into a warm lodge for an evening, or for a lifetime.

The marital procedure was fairly simple. That same afternoon, Runs-To-Water expressed his interest in the girl living in the third lodge to the west of the council house in Tugaloo Town, and before the sun set, his mother Nalyeena visited Tugaloo Town to check on the girl's status and availability. Sure enough, the girl was not married, and given the recent death of her father, she was sure to want to escape her own mother's lodge. Of course, among the Cherokee, a warrior did not marry one of his own clan, but Akala was of the Wolf Clan so that was not a concern.

Nalyeena approached the lodge where Runs-To-Water had seen the girl, and learned from her mother the girl's name. She also made more discrete inquiries from the other women in the village and found that Akala was not only a hard worker, but was respectful to all the elders of the tribe. Also, she was known to be of good disposition, though a bit sharp of tongue. Upon finding such pleasing reports, Nalyeena decided that the match was the right one. She returned again to the girl's mother, and advised her that her son would have to pass through the village again the next day to go to the Toothless White Man's cabin. Nalyeena suggested that the girl look over her would-be suitor then.

In Cherokee culture, women were not "purchased" as in some tribes. Rather, Cherokee Protocol dictated a slightly more civilized procedure. First, the suitor's mother would discretely check on the availability of the girl. Then, she would arrange for the young warrior to be "seen" by the maiden. If the young woman was not then interested, nothing further would be said, and it would be as if nothing had transpired—thus no one would be embarrassed or rejected. However, if the young girl expressed further interest, things could proceed.

Courting was almost unknown among the Cherokee. If the mothers consented, and the young couple wanted each other, why prolong the matter? Neither women nor men were assumed to be virgins, rather—they were assumed to be somewhat experienced in the art of love. If all seemed acceptable to everyone it was merely a matter of where the couple would live, and this matter would be settled directly. The groom would find a suitable spot in the girl's village, and build her a lodge; all grooms moved into their wife's village, and became members of the wife's clan. Finally, when the lodge was completed, the warrior presented himself to his soon to be bride's father or uncle and offered a gift—not a purchase price. For a young, attractive woman like Akala, perhaps twenty deer skins would be appropriate. Of course, other things—a rifle or shot, a horse, a mule, ducks, or a set of horses, or other desirable adornments may also be offered. Once the gift was accepted, the matter was done.

The Doubts of a Bridegroom

However, before Runs-To-Water constructed a lodge in Tugaloo, he wanted to consult the conjuror of his village—the same elder, Swimmer, who had shared wisdom with him around the sacred fire when he was just a toonali. Thus, after his mother's discrete discussions with the mother of the young woman in Tugaloo Town, Runs-To-Water sought out Swimmer in the council house of his village of Estatoe.

Upon finding Swimmer sitting on an upturned log, in the shade just outside the council house, Runs-To-Water spoke. *"Great Swimmer, I seek your council and sage advise in a determination I need to make. I have brought tobacco."* At this, Runs-To-Water laid the small pouch of tobacco down before Swimmer, who looked at it with relish. Tobacco was hard to grow at this elevation, and often had to be traded for from the lower villages, or from the Toothless White Man.

Swimmer was worldly wise, like many older Cherokee, and had a notable sense of humor. As Runs-To-Water sat cross-legged in the dirt before Swimmer, the old man spoke. *"And why should an upstart toonali such as you disturb an elder? Do you really need the thoughts of a useless old man on such a fine day as this? Is you pene' (penis) so useless that you can find no sport with the young women, or have our mountains run out of deer and bear to hunt? Has Kanati grown so stingy with his animals that there are none to fall before your arrows?"*

Swimmer had known Runs-To-Water as a toonali, so Cherokee Protocol did not apply here; thus he was free to joke with the young man in any fashion he wished. He grunted and rumbled his laughter to show his joking mood and his pleasure at his own humor.

Runs-To-Water, however, was in no mood for jokes. At first he thought that Swimmer somehow knew of his purpose in requesting the meeting—the comment about "sport" and so forth, but then he realized the old man merely had made a joke. He smiled at the old beloved elder, then looked quickly away as required to show respect. Only then did he speak to his elder. *"A toonali I am in this matter. For I have seen a young girl of the Wolf Clan in Tugaloo, and I know less than a warrior on his first hunt of such things."*

Swimmer immediately realized that this was a serious discussion, so he stopped his joking play, looked at the ground before him, and thought on the matter for a few moments. *"Is this young woman available to you, and is she agreeable? Do you know if she understands the ways of selu, or how to skin the beasts you bring from the forest?"* Swimmer had asked all the obvious questions, knowing that these had been taken care of previously, but this provided an opportunity for Runs-To-Water to state his real concern.

Runs-To-Water spoke again: *"Grandfather,"* an honorific term used with elders, *"I have seen that this girl is available and a worthy wife. My heart is glad; for she is the daughter of Changee, one of the warriors who helped make me a man many years ago. Still, I have doubts."*

Swimmer looked again at the dirt before him, thus showing respect and concern for Runs-To-Water's words. His brief nod told the younger Cherokee to continue.

"I know that warriors should marry one or two wives, and bring children into the tribe of the Real People, but I have doubts about our life on the river. Life does not seem to be in balance. For I have seen the growing farms of the whites just downriver from

*our village, and each hunt, I must go further into the Blue Mountains to find the bear.
The buffalo are almost gone. I have seen our own people build cabins instead of lodges,
and we all hunt now with rifles, as soon as we can buy one from the Toothless White
Man. Are the ways of our people gone? Do I need a wife and family, or should I go to
one of the villages higher in the mountains, and there take a wife?"*

Swimmer thought on these words, for the same concerns had been expressed
by many over the recent decades with the ever encroaching whites. This was the
worry of every Cherokee Chief in the 1700s—how to hold onto their territory.
While the troublesome Creeks were always raiding the settlements and contesting
their territory from the west, the real worry was the whites from the South and
East, whose lust for farmland was never satisfied. Thirty years ago the Cherokee
had to take skins to Charles Town or Augusta to trade; today a trading station was
just across the ford in the river. Of more concern, a large white town—Augusta—
had been established only four days travel down the river. White farms scattered
across the lower valley like a plague, coming ever closer to Tugaloo. In fact, many
minor conflicts had arisen between the Cherokee and whites.

Swimmer thought for several minutes and considered the history of conflict
with the whites. As early as 1715, Colonel Maurice Moore and Captain George
Chicken lead 300 white soldiers into Tugaloo Town for council with the Peace
Chiefs of the lower towns of the Cherokee. This small army met and negotiated
with a man whom they referred to as the "Conjuror," as noted in the history books
today. This Conjuror was Swimmer's father. In what the Cherokee refer to as "the
cooling moon" (October in the world of the whites) the council met with Captain
Chicken, and settled a peace that would last for many years. That council thus
managed to temporarily avert a war between the Cherokee and the white settlers.
However, within the last 15 years, the whites had moved even closer to Tugaloo
Town, and conflicts had increased.

Some Cherokee leaders, such as the shaman Skagunota, warned of depending
on the whites for gunpowder, rifles, and knives, and advocated a return to the old
ways. By 1745, young Cherokee warriors rarely studied the blowgun or the bow
and arrow, but preferred to wait until they could steal a rifle from some unsuspecting
Creek. Runs-To-Water himself now used a rifle for almost all of his hunting.
Clearly, the Cherokee way of life was changing, and many were concerned that
the lower villages would have to be left to the ever encroaching whites. In contrast,
other Cherokee advocated learning the ways of the whites, and becoming more
like them; farming more in larger fields and depending on hunting much less.
These Cherokee argued for a path of assimilation into the white culture, without
foregoing the traditional tribal identity of the Cherokee. By asking this question
of Swimmer, Runs-To-Water had essentially asked Swimmer to solve the most
perplexing dilemma of the eighteenth century Cherokee.

Swimmer gathered his thoughts for several minutes, and at last, was ready to render his words. Knowing his words were very important to this young warrior, he planned his statements carefully. *"When we have been threatened before, we have always found that Kanati, our Great Spirit, comes to us to protect us. You learned that yourself, as I recall, when you faced the beast in the bed of Toccoa Creek. You were but a young toonali then, but still Kanati came to you. Why should we not rely on his council now?"*

With that, the great shaman stood, and moved into the council house, with his tobacco, and Runs-To-Water followed. Swimmer noted that the sacred fire was banked low, but still burned, and he needed only a small fire. This was to be a council of private prayer with only he and Runs-To-Water present. Swimmer took tobacco from the pouch given him by Runs-To-Water, and spread some on the sacred fire as sacrifice to the Great Spirit. His voice raised; *"Great Kanati, Great Spirit of the Cherokee. Come into our hearts that we may understand the happenings in our world. Our lower towns and fields are in the way of the white man, and our young warriors wonder if they should marry. They know that children are needed to keep our tribe strong, and that our fields have been given to us by you. Speak to this mighty warrior and settle his doubts about choosing a wife. You have shown him a woman whom many consider worthy, so let him be at peace with whatever decision he makes. Restore his balance in your world and when he takes a wife, give him many toonalies that our tribe may have a future here in our cherished Blue Mountains."*

As the tobacco burned aromatically, and the whisper of Swimmer's prayer faded away, Runs-To-Water heard quite distinctly the response of the Great Spirit. For at that moment, the sound of children's laughter engulfed him; the sound of several toonali's playing on the playing fields just outside now drifted into the council house. It was as if the Great Spirit had sent the sound of children to answer the prayer. Runs-To-Water understood what he must do. He was to marry the maiden and make his life here, and his children would be raised here, near the hill where he killed his first bear; near the river that had given his people life from the beginning of time. For as long as the Great Spirit Kanati allowed, Runs-To-Water would be a man of Tugaloo Town in the Blue Mountains.

After a few more minutes, minutes of bliss for both men, Runs-To-Water spoke. *"Thank you Grandfather. I have heard your words and the words of the Great Spirit, Kanati. I will marry this young girl of Tugaloo and live on this river until I die."*

Thus, with the instructions of the Great Spirit, Runs-To-Water was ready to commit himself to Akala in marriage; he now needed merely to build a lodge. He would build in the traditional fashion—not a cabin as were many Cherokee of his day, but a traditional Cherokee lodge.

The family lodges of the Cherokee were considered the property of the woman, and stated very pointedly and practically a warrior's intention to wed one young woman or another. They consisted of a main summer house of wattle and daub, that frequently had a smaller winter lodge attached to it. Runs-To-Water began the building process by gathering saplings from the river, 3 or 4 inches in diameter. These he planted in the ground in the shape of his lodge, rectangular, with one of the doors facing the village council house. Twigs and branches, one to two inches thick, the "wattle," was gathered and woven together through the posts in the ground, and tied off on the four corner posts. Daub was then applied to the exterior of the branches. Daub was a sticky substance made from clay or mud and animal grease which, when dried, took on a hardness that resisted rain. The daub was used to seal the cracks in the wattle which made the houses weatherproof. At last, Runs-To-Water had only to whitewash the lodge walls inside and out, and cover the roof with thatch.

The resulting lodge was 10 to 12 feet across and some 15 to 18 feet in length. The earthen floor he packed hard by walking on it, and the roof he latticed with small saplings from one wall to the other and covered with bark or grasses. The lodge would have no windows, but Runs-To-Water left an open door on each long side, and built a stone fireplace at one end of the house that would be used for cooking and heating. Bedsteads made of canes were on each side of the fireplace. The bedsteads were raised from the ground about two feet and covered with skins. It took Runs-To-Water three weeks to build Akala's lodge, but he selected his location well. He found a spot about 500 feet from the council house, but in an open area where Akala would have plenty of room to plant her selu patch.

One afternoon towards the harvest month, Runs-To-Water looked at the lodge and realized with a start that it was all but finished. He had only to bring over his sleeping couch from his mother's lodge up the valley in Estatoe and it would be ready. As he hunted over the next years, he would make other sleeping couches and skin lined furniture. On this day, however, he would bring his couch, and then his bride to her new lodge.

He first went up the river, perhaps a mile, to the curve with the swamp to the west, to bathe alone out of earshot of the village of Tugaloo. He stripped off his skins and leggings and slipped into the cool water. It felt bracing, as only mountain rivers can, and even in the early autumn, it was cold. Still, Runs-To-Water was used to crossing cold creeks, and he was joyously happy. He reflected that his first impulse was to come to the river for a ritual bath and prayers before he claimed his bride, just as his name suggested he would. For in his life, he had many times found comforting wisdom here near this river. On this day, he sought the securities that every man seeks as he begins a new life with his wife.

Runs-To-Water, while bathing alone in the Tugaloo, raised his face to the sky towards the east from where the sun comes; thus he spoke to his god. His manly voice, loud, and pure with emotion, rang into the lower Blue Mountains. *"Kanati, Great Spirit. Thank you for my life. Thank you for the many gifts you give to me. Thank you for the Blue Mountains that sustain us, and bring bear and deer to our lodges. I thank you also for my many successful hunts. I thank you for the times that I did not kill, but missed with my arrows and my rifle. In those hunts, I learned more of the ways of the animals. Great Kanati, today I, have built a lodge fit for a strong young woman. She is a good woman who will bear many children. I ask that you bring joy to this lodge for this woman and I that we may be worthy of the many gifts you bring to us from the forest, the river, and the selu fields. Make my actions in balance with the world, that my hunting will be successful. Make my pene strong, that many children will feed in this lodge in each new winter. Make me a worthy husband and father, so that I might give many souls to the tribe, and be blessed with many sons in my old age."*

Here his prayer could have ended. The fact that he continued spoke volumes about his constant worry, that even his discussion with Swimmer did not totally abate. *"Great Kanati, keep us strong that we may keep these mountains which you gave to us. May I and my sons fight well against the Creeks and the whites to save our fields and our sacred hunting grounds, and our sacred fire in the council house. Make my arm strong to protect my children and my wife in our village."*

Here, Runs-To-Water finished his prayer, and dipped his head seven times in the river, one to represent his remembrance of each clan of his people. Then he stood and left the river. He was almost ready to claim his bride.

When he left the riverbank, he ran one last time to his mother's lodge in Estatoe two miles from his new village. As he entered the lodge, he saw that she had packed many skins together in a bundle—some 30 deerskins from his last hunting season; other skins were there as well. She also had packed the skins that covered his sleeping couch, and untied the frame branches from that and from another couch. Nalyeena looked at her fine son, the son who killed the bear so many years ago, the son who had grown into a fine warrior. Then she spoke. *"These couches will make a nice addition to your new lodge, for I am sure that you will need a child's couch before the next Green Corn Festival."* At this, Nalyeena deferred her eyes, wanting to joke but not embarrass her son.

Runs-To-Water did not know what to say, so he nodded to her, and picked up the skins and the frames for the couches. *"There will be times when we have more meat than we will need, and I will bring it to you."*

Nalyeena smiled at his concern for her. *"Keep your meat, but bring me many grandchildren that I may teach them of our Blue Mountains and of the ways of the Cherokee."*

At this word from Nalyeena, Runs-To-Water merely nodded and left. He was never one to express such intense emotions well, but he knew he owed this woman his very life.

Taking His Bride

As Runs-To-Water entered his new village of Tugaloo, many noticed the large bundle of skins, and knew this to be his gift for the family of his new bride. The whole village had noted that he was nearly finished with the new lodge, and many had noted the painstaking way he finished the walls. Some of the old women had even joked that he was taking extra time—that while he feared no bear, no panther, nor any Creek warrior, the great Runs-To-Water was terrified of taking a young wife!

To these accusations, Runs-To-Water had only laughed in recent weeks, but today as the many wives and old women of the village taunted him again, he merely walked on to the new lodge where he deposited the frames for the sleeping couches and the skins that covered them. He thought for a moment that he might tie them back together, but he was sure that the taunting would only grow worse until the important deeds of this day were done. Thus, he again picked up the other bundle of the newly tanned deerskins, and began the long walk to the lodge of Akala. He had to pass almost the entire village—for he had chosen for his lodge, a new site at the other end of the village away from his in-laws. Thus, the village elders and old women noted what was happening with excitement; like lightening, the news spread throughout Tugaloo Town! Runs-To-Water was taking his bride!

While the Cherokee were shy, extremely respectful, and often demonstrated a quiet dignity, matters of great joy for the village brought out another side of their collective character—an ever present willingness to celebrate, to joke with each other, and to laugh at the joys in their collective life. Soon every soul in the village seemed to be lining his path, and many shouted encouragement. *"Your back is strong, and your children will be also!"* Shouted one young warrior, as the crowd murmured an agreement.

"Please do not keep us awake with your noise tonight! Go someplace upriver!" An old woman shouted, and the crowd laughed outright!

"Don't hurt the young girl, or you will taste her wrath forever!" One of the elders warned, in jest, to which his wife replied, *"Never mind, she is a strong girl, and he will taste her wrath soon enough anyway!"* At this the entire village laughed and many friends patted the strong shoulders of Runs-To-Water.

Akala, of course, had heard the commotion and was waiting with excitement in her mother's lodge. Her mother and her uncle, who would serve this role in the absence of the deceased father, waited inside with her. Her mother pretended to be busy at the hearth, but it was soon obvious that little work was being done. Her sisters and younger brother were supposed to be in the selu patch, but were, rather, in the midst of the growing crowd. Soon Runs-To-Water came to the door of the lodge, and the brief ritual began. The crowd became quiet, as the entire village huddled behind him. *"I have come to take your daughter to her lodge, and I have brought you a gift worthy of her."* Runs-To-Water began the ritual scene.

The uncle, the same Utani who had witnessed Runs-To-Water slay his first bear, stood and came outside. *"I see a mighty warrior has come to take my daughter to a new lodge. I see a couple of furs offered as a gift."*

Runs-To-Water was surprised and greatly pleased to find Utani here. This was a great honor for Akala and for himself. For Utani, the Longknife was widely known, and he was a great leader, now serving as War Chief of the tribe. While any of a dozen "uncles" could have performed this role, Utani had made certain that he was not hunting when the lodge was nearing completion. Today, he proudly stood in for his brother's deceased son.

Runs-To-Water continued the prescribed Cherokee Protocol. *"I fear the great warrior, Utani, has lost eyesight in so many hunts."* Next came the announcement of the bride-gift, and the voice of Runs-To-Water arose more strongly. *"For I have brought 35 new deerskins, and two bear blankets, and a buffalo robe for this young woman, Akala."*

The crowd murmured loudly now, grunting and nodding in pleasure and celebration, for no one had ever heard of such a bride gift before. Still, Akala was a true beauty, the finest Cherokee maiden to have been claimed in Tugaloo in quite some time. The gift also demonstrated the resolve of Runs-To-Water. Again, they all grunted and nodded their satisfaction with the arrangement.

Utani smiled openly at the gift, thinking all the while that he had done a great service by getting this warrior an early naming ceremony many years ago. He then shifted his gaze downward. *"I will ask what my daughter thinks."* While this was a foregone conclusion, Cherokee Protocol demanded that the tribe witness this preference of the bride, so that should serious disagreements arise and a couple wish to divorce, the tribe could attest to the fact that both parties entered the bargain of their own free will.

Akala waited inside for her cue, and just as she expected, she heard her uncle call to her. *"Akala, come out and see the gift this warrior brings to us today."*

And out she came, looking splendid in her tight smock, bare over one shoulder with the willowy tattoo on her back. With her hair long and flowing, and her slender form, she was beautiful; perhaps even as beautiful as the Blue Mountains visible behind her. Not waiting to be asked the all important question concerning her desires, Akala spoke before she should have and thus, playfully, breached Cherokee Protocol. *"I see a large pile of very fine skins. To what do we owe the honor of this warrior's gift?"* She beamed her radiant smile looking directly at her Uncle with complete, though artificial, innocence, and then directly at Runs-To-Water, both of whom were completely stupefied.

Not knowing what to do, they turned to look at each other, then, comically, turned in unison back toward the young girl. The crowd was hushed, since with this breach of Cherokee Protocol, no one knew what to say.

At just that moment, an old woman's voice—that of Toomi—was heard from the rear of the crowd. *"He can wrestle bears in his sleep, but can he tame this young beauty's tongue?"*

And that was all it took. The crowd laughed loud and long, bending over in mirth. Utani beamed and clasped the forearm of Runs-To-Water, and then gave him a manly hug. *"You now have a wife, with a sharp tongue, I fear. Watch out for the tongue, even as you watch for giant bears or arrows from the Creeks."* The crowd heard this and laughed even more.

Runs-To-Water, never the great orator, merely responded, *"I will."* Then he smiled at his new bride.

Utani spoke again, more loudly. *"Send swift runners to all the villages—a feast is to be held tomorrow for this new lodge in our village. Invite all of the seven clans!"*

At that Akala took the hand of Runs-To-Water, and in an easy canter suggestive of such pleasure that it left the other men in the crowd hungry for their wives, she lead him out of the village towards the river for prayers and a ritual bath. This was her proudest moment, and she looked radiant. She and Runs-To-Water would stop and speak with many in the crowd during the next minutes. Still, she constantly lead him out of the town as the crowd dispersed, and they headed down towards the river ford a mile to the north. They would complete the ritual baths together, and pray in the ancient stream, feeling the coolness of the water from the Blue Mountains surrounding them.

Thus, it is written by the sages of old; *"For a man shall leave his father and mother, and a woman shall leave her home, and they shall cleave together as one."*

And cleave they did. Later that night, as is often the way of things in this world, a new life and a new family was begun in Tugaloo Town.

Chapter 2: The Cherokee Wars
1749 – by the European Calendar

Within only a few years, it had become a running joke among the Cherokee in Tugaloo Town that Runs-To-Water was always wrestling with a bear, a Creek invader, or his sharp tongued wife; for Akala was always remembered as the young woman who broke Cherokee Protocol with her joking, sharp tongued taunting of her husband as he delivered the bride gift. Still, the old men noted that they must "cleave" often; for children seemed to come with astonishing regularity. Obviously, both Runs-To-Water and Akala very much liked to cleave, as the evidence seemed to appear with each passing year.

Akala, pregnant again, had blossomed into a beautiful woman of 19, and had learned the wisdom of reflection. By that age she had already mothered two children, a boy and a girl. Perhaps the duties of motherhood had led her to prize silence more than in her intemperate earlier years. Now, she was known to hold her tongue respectfully in council meetings, at least on most occasions. However, when she did choose to speak, it was with great passion and cunning forethought. Some in Tugaloo Town were already talking of her as the next "Beloved Woman" of the tribe, though that honor would come, if at all, much later in her life.

Akala's little toonali showed every indication of being his father's child. He was born only nine months after Akala and Runs-To-Water first entered their marriage lodge, and he was quite large and grew fast. Further, he seemed quite determined in his own mind—stubborn, in a word. He gave Akala fits when he was only two or so, but the Cherokee were quite indulgent when it came to their children. Their next child had been a daughter. Runs-To-Water was there for her birth, and it frightened him more than anything in his life—even the bear he killed when he was seven. As he watched his huge, pregnant wife in their lodge in seemingly great pain, he saw her cry and scream so much that he was certain something was amiss. At long last, the midwives realized his uselessness and ran him from Akala's lodge. He sat with the other men outside listening to women's chatter in the lodge. He decided then and there that hunting bear, or even fighting the filthy Creeks was child's play compared to what his young beautiful wife was going through.

The Great Spirit Kanati makes all men suffer in order to harden them, but he never makes them suffer too long, and as surely as the sun would rise over the Blue Mountains in the morning, the long screamed-filled night ended at daybreak, with the cries of a new young bundle—a smelly, bloody daughter. The midwives let Runs-To-Water hold her only briefly before taking the child to the Tugaloo River to clean the birth filth away. The mountain stream water was considered good for Cherokee children, and if the cold water of the mountain river led them to cry—as it always did—that was believed to be good for their young bodies, too; for all the midwives knew that the Cherokee of Tugaloo Town took their very life from this river.

Thus did life for the Cherokee and for the young family go on. Of course, there were many worries for the Cherokee of the 1700s. At least three times in that century, the dreaded small pox swept into the tribe and killed thousands. Only a few winters before (in 1738 and 1739) this dreaded disease swept through the tribe killing over half of the entire Cherokee population. As if that weren't enough, the whites around the new settlement of Augusta seemed to be moving ever closer. They had now moved into the traditional Cherokee hunting territory, and they were killing whole forests as they came. Cherokee raids against the outlying farms were frequent, and many horses were taken. Finally, the horrid Creeks were always raiding the villages along the Tugaloo, stealing horses, and those raids would occasionally lead to a warrior's death. There seemed to be no peace for the tribe, and the lower Cherokee towns of Seneca, Tugaloo, Estatoe, and Keowee seemed to bear the brunt of these threats. These towns were the closest to both the white settlers and the Creek. Still, as if by a minor miracle, life did go on and the young family of Runs-To-Water was generally happy during those years.

Of course, Runs-To-Water would lead his hunts a couple of times each year. He always returned with many furs for trading with the Toothless White Man, and the younger warriors were eager to hunt with his party. They felt their own hunting would result in increased success if they could only hunt with a legend such as Runs-To-Water, who had killed a bear when he was only seven. The hunt parties were often made up of between four to fifteen warriors, and would travel quite extensively to reach good hunting grounds. They would trek up the ancient Unicoi Trail for a brisk five hour trot toward the Dividings—a cluster of trails that converged where a city to be named Clayton, would one day spring up. From there the hunt team would select a course into the steeper mountains to the north, sometimes ranging as far as the famed domed rock high in the distant mountains. This rock would later become famous as Clingman's Dome in the higher reaches of the Great Smoky Mountains, but in this age, the Cherokee had no special name for the mountain other than the "high rock where the wind blows."

More frequently, however, the hunt team would select a streambed at a much lower elevation that had not been hunted during the previous season. They would then camp for a time, and say prayers for a successful hunt. Next, they would plan a series of brief hunts involving small groups of three or four warriors. These were exploratory expeditions to locate signs of deer, bear, and buffalo. Each group would take a pre-selected section of the streambed, further dividing themselves into working groups of two or three warriors. These smaller groups would approach the streambed from both the stream itself and from the sharp hillsides. When hunting for bear or deer, the scent of a man was critical, as was the direction of the wind; for if the game caught the scent of men approaching, the game would quickly depart the area, and the hunt would be fruitless. Thus, not only did the hunters in the smaller groups need to be ever cognizant of the wind directions, but also of where the other warriors were in relation to the wind and the streambed. Still, the experienced warriors had hunted for years, so such things were second nature to these men. More often than not, the hunts were successful, and meat for the town was acquired in abundance in these years. In this time, life seemed to move along at a reasonable pace, and everyone ate well. This time of balance in Cherokee life was not to last for long.

Death In Tugaloo Town

It is too easy, in the modern mind, to consider these Cherokee as noble savages; in some sense, as pristine creatures of a longed-for yesteryear. We can envision nobility in their lives, which, in the case of the Cherokee, is certainly justified to a large degree. However, lest we forget, the world of those distant days was one of struggle, pain, and heartache, as these people scratched their meager existence from the river and from the hunt. Sometimes nature seemed to conspire against them. Perhaps a fire would sweep through the selu fields near the town and many would go hungry through the next winter. At times, Kanati refused to send rain and no corn or beans or squash would grow. No fish would set in the Cherokee fish traps along the Tugaloo, or accidents that barely broke the skin would fester and become deadly in these distant decades. Men and women alike died from foolish handling of knives while skinning a deer, or of games played with the newly acquired rifles. Death could come a thousand ways to anyone in Tugaloo Town, and on this night, it came from the hated Creek—the dreaded, long-standing enemy of the Cherokee.

Runs-To-Water was on an autumn hunt in the early fall of 1754 when the Creeks struck Tugaloo Town again. Of late the attacks—brief raids to steal horses, rifles, or furs, rather than major military engagements—seemed to be coming more frequently, and Runs-To-Water had been somewhat reluctant to leave his young wife and growing family for the fall hunt. However, Akala, in her taunting and playful way, had poked fun at his concern and let him know that she wished for him to lead the hunt, as he had been doing for the last several years; for Utani, the Long-knife, had become too old to lead the young men in their quest for furs. In recent years, he stayed in the village where his knowledge and skill were invaluable for instruction of the many young toonalis. It was during this fall hunt, exactly when many of the young warriors of Tugaloo Town were many days-run away, that the Creek struck.

They came just before dawn one morning in the early fall. Had they been a few weeks later, the fall hunts would have been over, and they would have found all of the warriors of Tugaloo ready to meet their assault. Of course, they knew that fact, and chose to strike like cowards, when women, children, and old men were alone in a defenseless town. To begin, several Creeks set fire to a fur drying rack outside of a lodge on the east end of the village. They then melted back into the night, while the villagers ran to assess the damage and assist in putting out the flames before the whole lodge was gone.

However, Utani and the other old men knew that drying racks and fresh skins didn't burn by themselves, and they sent word to every lodge to wake any older toonalis that were available and hastily they began to give orders for defense of the town. The growing noise awoke the entire town, and all headed for the fire. Across the Tugaloo River, the Toothless White Man was even seen in the doorway to his cabin. First, he watched the drying rack burn as he calmly loaded his Kentucky rifle on the dirt porch of his cabin. Next, he took a pull of cheap whiskey to "clear his head" and then poured powder down the barrel of two flintlock pistols. He knew from long years living in the shadow of the Blue Mountains, that you can't have too many loaded guns when the Creek are about.

Even before Utani could get his instructions across to the group of young warriors—in reality there were only 15 young toonalis, too young for a naming ceremony, each looking both solemnly determined and totally frightened—the other Creek struck at the west end of the village, far away from the distracting fire but near the horse corral. To continue the confusion, four young Creek warriors ran into the village toward the horses, letting fly six to ten arrows each minute; their fire was deadly.

Historians have never truly understood this aspect of the woodlands Indian wars of the sixteenth and seventeenth centuries. This amazing rate of arrow fire was one reason that an Indian attack using the venerated bow and arrow was much more deadly overall than an attack by Indians with Kentucky long rifles. Of course, the famed Kentucky rifles could fire much further, and were, on a shot by shot basis much more deadly than arrows, but the faster rate of fire for arrows relative to the slower muzzle loading long-guns of this age meant that in any close-encounter engagement between white men with rifles and Indian warriors with bows, many more arrows filled the air than rifle balls. If the range was close, there was usually no contest. It is for this reason that Native Americans—Cherokee among them—fought from behind trees, and cane-breaks rather than in the open; that tactic allowed the Cherokee to get into better killing range for their more primitive weapons.

For a few minutes during the initial part of the attack, the air seemed to be filled with arrows, and the Creeks shot at anything that moved in the dim, predawn light. While running at full speed, they fired at drying racks, shadows that seemed to move, butter churns, and even lodge doorways, on the chance that someone may come out. Two members of the family of Runs-To-Water were hit—the young daughter, and the lovely Akala, the sharp tongued wife. Akala had run from the door to her lodge only a few feet towards the fire at the other end of the village, when she heard the fearful words of her uncle Utani. *"The Creeks have come to kill us! Prepare to fight them!"*

The words stopped Akala in her tracks only twenty feet from her lodge, but as she turned to return to her children and the safety of the building doorway she faced the specter of four Creek warriors not thirty feet away running in a dead heat into the camp directly at her, shouting war cries as they ran. She heard them shouting horrid insults at the Cherokee, and saw them firing arrows by the scores. Next, her sight fell to the door of her lodge, where she saw her daughter, too young to know any better, leave the relative safety of the lodge, and doing what all children do when frightened—run to her mother. In an instant, Akala saw what mothers fear most; her flesh seemed to melt into terror, and her dreams died as two Creek fired their deadly arrows point blank into her daughter's three-year-old body. They shouted their war cries as they killed her child; they didn't even turn to watch the child die. The young girl obviously posed no threat, and she died simply because she was there and made the mistake of moving into the sight of the rabid Creek warriors.

To Akala, it seemed to happen so slowly, watching through the fire-shadowed night, as her daughter fell half in and half out of the lodge, with two arrows sticking in her chest. The child breathed only once after being hit, and looked up, making eye contact with her mother, only a few steps distant. Those eyes pierced Akala, so much so that she didn't even realize the danger she faced, as the Creeks turned their next arrows on her. She then felt the arrows enter her belly, and knew she would die also, but her most horrid pain in her last moments of life, was for the daughter, who already lie dead in her lodge, and for the unborn child in her belly who would never see a dawn in the Blue Mountains along the Tugaloo River. Before she died, she did manage to crawl the last few steps to her lodge, and, after the Creek left with their newly acquired horses, the Tugaloo villagers found Akala's body, hand outstretched. Her final act in this life had been touching the face of her dead daughter, to close her daughter's eyes.

The villagers found that five of their clan members had been cut down in this raid on Tugaloo. They began to wail their death songs, and to put out the several additional fires the Creek had set. Several of the toonalis collected the stray horses that the Creek had not managed to steal, and the old men began to collect the five bodies for the death rites.

Unknown to the Cherokee that day, two white men, young hunters from the eastern Blue Ridge in North Carolina were watching this deadly raid. They had been tracking a band of Indians for two days. While their original idea had been to hunt in the lower regions of the Blue Mountains, they'd come across sign of some dozen Indians crossing the trail and heading to Tugaloo Town. They knew that John Sharp operated a trading station there across the river, and they planned to follow these Indians into town and resupply their kit for the last months of the fur hunt. However, when they came across the Indian camp, they realized it was Creek and not a Cherokee party they were tracking, and they then knew they were following a raiding party.

The white men knew the woods almost as well as the Indians, and even at 16 and 17, they were veteran hunters, accustomed to long stretches of time away from their distant homes. Jessie Walton expressed himself, eloquently, as usual by spitting his chew of tobacee on the ground, barely missing the boot of Ben Cleveland, who for no good reason everyone called "Early." These white men, along with John Sharpe, were the only Caucasians in history to ever witness first hand, a Creek raid on a Cherokee village.

"Hit that boot with your damn spit, and them savages won't be the only thing you got to worry about. Recon' I'll go cross your scalp myself with my huntin' knife if you spit on me again," said Early, who didn't take his eyes from the battle before him as he spoke.

Jessie, never one to miss an argument, responded, *"Shut up, you whinin' old buzzard! I didn't hit your damn boot, did I?"*

Early didn't raise to the bait of name calling—he knew it to be friendly banter—not uncommon among the white men of this period who often hunted together for months at a time. He looked back toward the town. *"What you reckon those Creeks was up too? Did they come all this way for a few horses, and why couldn't they have got them from some other town further down the valley?"*

"Reckon we'll never understand these damn Injuns at all. They got damn near the prettiest land on God's Earth, and they don't do nothin' but fight each other over horses." In that statement by Jessie Walton, laid a simple man's summary of the eventual demise of the Cherokee.

While one of the noblest tribes on the U. S. mainland—a spiritual tribe that in time would largely accept Christianity, a tribe that deeply respected all life, the only tribe to develop a written language or create an independent representative government modeled on the growing democracy in Washington. The plain fact is that few whites ever did understand the Cherokee or any other Indians during this or the next century.

History tells us with repetitive clarity, that when cultures clash, one will invariably dominate the other. Only rarely does one find historic examples where one culture, in such a clash, doesn't disappear entirely. In this exact moment, when white men first witnessed the historic conflict between Indian tribes, lay the demise of all of the woodlands Indians east of the Mississippi River—for white men would exploit these historic tribal hatreds again and again during the next decades. In the French/Indian War, the later American Revolution, and in the focused conflicts on the great American plains many decades later, white men on all sides would pit one tribe against another, and the Indians of the continent would be decimated. Most of the Woodlands tribes east of the Mississippi, from Florida to Canada would not survive at all, thus leaving the land to the white man.

These thoughts would have been much too advanced for Cleveland and Walton that day on the little hill by Tugaloo Town. Neither were highly educated men, and neither would ever study history in any formal school. Though only teenagers, each were already a seasoned frontiersman, and in an age in which Daniel Boone would become famous, many young men were venturing into the distant Blue Mountains and growing in their understanding of the frontiersman's life. With little schooling, each of these men had learned to read, each would fight Indians his entire life, and each would play a part in the later history of the hill and the Tugaloo River Valley.

While the exploits of Walton and Cleveland in later years are well known and documented, it is only by happenstance that we know of their observation of this Creek raid on Tugaloo Town from the undistinguished hill that is the focus of our story. Only through the dim memories of one of Cleveland's great, great, great granddaughters, do we know that these men watched this Indian-versus-Indian fight in the Tugaloo Valley of the lower Blue Ridge. Ms. Elizabeth Hagen, descent of Cleveland still lives in the Tugaloo Valley. She remembers writing a school paper on her ancestor's view of the Indian battle, based on a 200 year old family legend, a legend handed down through the white families who later settled here. The family legends tell of this battle, and it is interesting to reflect that within only 25 years of this raid, the Cherokee would cease to exist in the Tugaloo River Valley of the lower Blue Ridge.

Suffice it to say that Walton was right. The whites never did understand the Cherokee.

The Revenge of Runs-To-Water

Revenge, like hatred, is one of the great motivators of human history. Anger, rage, greed, and love are others, but it has long been recognized by civilized man that among the great motivators in human nature, the negatives outnumber the positives by a considerable margin. While men and women of all cultures make pretenses toward a more subtle nobility in order to excuse their actions, these base motivators—hatred, anger, revenge—often do more to truly shape our history and our actions than we would ever acknowledge. Revenge certainly shaped the actions of Runs-To-Water after his wife's death at the hands of the Creek raiding party. Of course, like many military or political leaders, Runs-To-Water cloaked his need for revenge in loftier terms, but all knew upon looking on his mighty countenance and his stony, long-scared face, that revenge was driving him. Many of the women, even in their grief over losing kinsmen in the recent raid, began to feel pity for the first Creek caught in the clutches of those powerful arms. It seemed that even the great bear tattoo on his powerful chest would squeeze the life out of someone on that very day when he returned to find his wife and daughter dead. The infamous Blood Oath of the Cherokee culture demanded retribution so that balance might be restored. Runs-To-Water was to be merely the instrument of that terrible retribution.

Upon his return to Tugaloo, his bundle of furs bulging the backs of his several horses, Runs-To-Water found not the loving family he'd left only six weeks previously, but funeral fires still smoldering. His son was living in Utani's lodge, and his possessions were stacked in a corner of the Council House for him to claim; his home was no more, for in keeping with Cherokee custom, Akala's lodge had been burned after her death.

After the raid, Utani, who was now the Peace Chief of Tugaloo, had sent a swift runner to find the hunting party of Runs-To-Water and the several other parties of warriors to tell them the news. It was only a matter of two days before a saddened Runs-To-Water emerged from the trail with anger in his eyes, to find the fires lower now, and the body of his wife and daughter gone. The tribe was in council in the council house at Tugaloo Town. The Cherokee had gathered from all of the lower settlements, including the Keowee settlements to the east.

Debate on what recourse the Cherokee may take had continued for a full day, as the various hunting parties gathered. Some wanted a massive raid to steal horses on the nearest Creek settlements toward the Oconee River to the Southwest. Others wanted a blood fight with the upper settlements of the Creek near what was to become, in the next century, the Dahlonega Gold Fields. Various voices were heard, but all knew that the younger warrior leaders who were still returning from the various hunting groups would make the final decision—for they were the ones who would carry the battle to the Creek.

Tsu-la Kingfisher of the Deer Clan, a mighty warrior from the Keowee settlement of the Cherokee, was speaking as Runs-To-Water entered the council house. *"I have seen many winters in these Blue Mountains. I have fished many streams, and killed many deer. The Creeks have always been found in our hunting grounds, and sometimes come to our village as they have to Tugaloo Town. But this time, they come to kill, and we must now go to meet them and kill. We must kill them as our Blood Oath demands."* With that sentiment, Kingfisher made the sign of death, a knife-blade against the throat, and many warriors grunted in agreement. Kingfisher sat down.

All were silent for a few moments as Runs-To-Water entered and took his place with his clan. He noticed, as he sat, a surprising number of warriors from settlements in the Keowee Village cluster some twenty miles to the east. Normally, these would not be here, after just one small raid, so he assumed, correctly, that their villages had been raided also.

After a couple of minutes, Utani spoke. *"Our brother, Runs-To-Water, lost a wife and a daughter in the raid on Tugaloo Town. I would hear his words."*

Runs-To-Water, of course, knew the retribution options available, as these had been discussed before after many raids. While he did not know who had already spoken in council, he could easily guess. He knew these other warriors completely, as only men who have fought together and faced death together can know each other. He had stood shoulder to shoulder with these warriors many times, in battles large and small. He looked around before he stood to speak.

Utani, the Peace Chief, could be counted on for reasoned thought and wise council. The Cherokee, unlike the western Native American tribes, elected two chiefs—a Peace Chief to rule the council house, and a War Chief for battle. Utani had served many winters as Peace Chief. He would suggest a raid likely to result in the same rough level of damage—some twenty horses stolen, many fur racks burned, and five or ten women and children killed among the villages. Many here would agree with him.

In the section of the council house reserved for the clan of the deer, there sat many warriors. Kingfisher, who had just finished speaking, was a War Chief of the Keowee village to the east. He had lost a young child in the attack on Keowee, and he was obviously ready to kill. Doublehead, a War Chief from a village far to the west, was known for his pointed anger and quick knife. He sat in the section reserved for the Paint Clan. He was mighty of chest, with many tattoos on his torso—the most obvious being a half-man/half-panther that represented Kanati. He was a deadly warrior; his slashing knife had left many Creek warriors without hair, many others without their life. It was said he liked to scalp his enemies before he killed them—and at that precise moment, they often had two heads of hair! From one such early attack he'd earned his name—he had left his enemies alive with double heads! On this day, he would call all warriors together and urge everyone to join in a series of raids lasting for the whole next year. He wanted to attack all the Creek villages along the disputed tribal boundaries.

Runs-To-Water knew that in spite of the presence of such luminary warriors as Utani and Doublehead, his own words would carry weight. He was a young warrior and would probably lead one of the raiding parties; moreover, he had lost as much as any of them. Still he did not stand immediately because he needed time to gather his thoughts. After a minute or so of silence in the council house, he was ready to stand.

Before he could speak, however, the voice of old Toomi—Beloved Woman of the tribe was heard. She rose with her great bulk and faced the seven sides of the council house. *"Horses we can steal from the Creek anytime. For our warriors are brave and can creep into the villages to the South, and take what is ours, and whatever else we need."* She took a breath, looked down in consideration of her thoughts, and then continued. *"We can kill more animals for furs, and even take women from the Creek or the whites to replace the lives of our sisters."* In all five young, child bearing age wives had been killed in the raid. *"Our Blue Mountains give us many gifts of animal furs, and horses we grow, but I do not think we can forgive death of our children, as they play in our own village. These filthy Creek did not attack a mighty party of warriors. No! They attacked our town when our warriors were gone. Our Blood Oath now demands their blood; we must attack them, as they have done."*

As she sat down, many warriors grumbled, and Kingfisher in particular grunted, and coughed out loud to show his approval—he had been arguing exactly that point for a number of hours. Utani and Doublehead also nodded to Toomi in agreement. After a moment, Runs-To-Water also nodded and grunted vigorously; for a brief second he reflected that this woman seemed to voice his exact thoughts even when he couldn't. Indeed on the very day he had taken Akala as his wife, it had been Toomi's voice that was heard when Akala had breached Cherokee Protocol. Now, because of Toomi's words, he understood his own mind, and as the final few warriors from the last hunting party entered the council house, he stood to speak. Slowly he turned to face the clans of his people, often meeting the eyes of men he knew well. Then he spoke. *"I would rather kill bear, panther or deer than a warrior; even a Creek warrior. I do not think that killing a warrior is wise, because the bear, or panther or deer give us meat for our fires and furs for our lodges. A dead Creek warrior gives us nothing to use."*

At this, Doublehead began to look directly at Runs-To-Water in challenge. He didn't like the way these words were heading, but he held his tongue out of respect for the man's loss. All in the council house were quiet as stones as they noted that Runs-To-Water had not taken his seat; for he was not yet finished speaking.

After a respectful pause, Runs-To-Water continued. Now, however, his tone was much harsher. *"But when our lodges and our villages are attacked, it is time to kill. My woman and my daughter are dead today. Kingfisher has lost his child. Now I think it is time to kill. It is time to attack villages, and to kill them all. This I say to the Real People–Kanati does not wish us to be killed by the Creek without fighting them. We will fight them in their villages, and we will kill them all in our Blue Mountains."*

At this, almost all of the warriors nodded and many grumbled in agreement. Each man there reflected that this warrior, Runs-To-Water, had talked directly to Kanati when he killed his first bear. Therefore, his words were to be considered carefully, for he had been spoken to by God.

Again, many expected Runs-To-Water to take his seat at that moment, but still he stood. He silently faced each of the Clan sections of the council house for a full thirty seconds; this let everyone present know that he considered his next words critically important. He continued, *"Now I will go to the river and pray. I will take sweat in the sweat house, and then wash off the smell of my recent hunt, and then pray again to Kanati for victory over the Creek. On the dawn tomorrow, I will go the Creek country to the Southwest, and I will kill Creeks. Their blood will color my knife, and my arms, and the ground under their villages. The Blue Mountains will be red with their death. Their horses will become mine, and I will not stop until the valley beyond the low mountains to the west is clear of the filthy Creek. The Chattahoochee River will run red with their blood. When the sun comes tomorrow, I will fight Creek and drive them all away, or I will die."*

With this statement his purpose became crystal clear—he would rid the Blue Mountains of Creek, or die in the attempt. Should the tribe determine not to go, he was now committed to go alone, and fight alone even until he was killed. Runs-To-Water, like leaders of men in all ages, had without realizing it, voiced the essence of the thoughts of his followers. While he was not the senior warrior present, and was certainly not then a chief, he was a leader to whom others deferred. The Cherokee would do more than mount a revenge raid. This day, the Cherokee would go to war, and hell itself hath no fury like these vengeful warriors on that fateful day.

After he spoke, Runs-To-Water bowed a final time to each of the clans in the council house, noting that each of the clan sections had some warriors present. This was rarely seen in any of the Cherokee councils. Then he picked up his bow and left the council. He would let the War Chiefs determine the final outcome—his fate was decided, and if he needed to, he would fight the Creek alone, for he was committed. Now, he simply wished to be alone for a time with his thoughts, to pray, and to say good bye to the spirit of his wife and child.

He walked into the bright sun of the afternoon and was somewhat surprised that there was still daylight left. Without another word to anyone, he walked to the river above Tugaloo Town, and as he walked he began his ritual chants to Kanati, in order to prepare himself for prayer and purification. After a ten minute walk up the river, he dropped his weapons and all of his garments beside the flowing mountain stream and stood naked beside the waters. Here he paused for a moment and reflected that only a few years earlier, he had come to this same spot with his new bride for prayer and purification after his marriage. Still, those thoughts he put away, for he had more serious business with his god on this day.

He picked up from his trousers a pack of tobacco, and took some of the loose weed to sprinkle on the ground as a small sacrifice to Kanati. On this day, above all others, he wanted his prayer to be heard. As his feet and then his hips entered the water, he felt the cold sensation of the river on his skin, but this he ignored. He always felt better praying from the river. As the water reached his chest, he heard Kingfisher, and his woman Nan-ye'hi begin their prayers just down the stream; he was far enough away that he would not bother their meditations. As he walked further into the cold stream, he began his prayer. *"Kanati; Spirit who gave us the Blue Mountains, and all the deer, and bear, and rabbit to hunt. Kanati, you gave us the selu from our fields, and this water for our cooking pots. You gave me a bear when I was only a toonali, and you have since given me many animals with each hunt. You gave me a wife and children so that my lodge is warm even in the cold, short days after the fall hunts."*

Runs-To-Water did not realize it, and would have been surprised to notice, but tears streamed down each side of his face at this point. Cherokee men, like all men, cry, but heaving sobs among warriors were unknown. Such sobbing would have been unseemly. Rather, when tears came, they simply came, streaming down his face, as if from some unstoppable source, with no sobbing and no sound. To an observer, had there been one that day, the tears would thus have been more poignant.

The warrior continued his prayer. *"On this day I have no lodge, and my wife is now gone. Her selu patch has been burned and I have no warm sleeping couch for this night. Still, I slept with the stars in the Blue Mountains last night, and will do so again tonight. Tomorrow, when the sun comes, I will go to fight the Creek. Let me have strength in my arms that I may be mighty in battle. Give me swift arrows that I may kill my enemies, and let us drive the Creek from our mountains. For this I say, I will drive the Creek away or I will die."*

At this, he paused in his prayer, wondering if more needed to be said. When he could not think of anything to add, he left the stream, and forgoing his time in the sweat-lodge, he found a suitable place to lay his fur robe, making himself a bed for the night. He lay down, just as the sun began to set, and he slept the sleep of a man who is committed to his purpose and comfortable with his future, whatever that future might be. He had thanked his god for his life and the many blessings in that life, and then he told God explicitly what he felt he had to do. Runs-To-Water was, as always, a man of his word. Tomorrow he would go to war.

War at Taliwa

How mighty Runs-To-Water looked that fateful morning, walking into Tugaloo Town just before Kanati brought the large fire into the morning sky. His stately, dignified walk was itself a thing of fearsome beauty, and this day he was going to battle. Runs-To-Water stood taller than most Cherokee, his topknot of hair decorated with many bear claws, including one from the first bear he killed— it was powerful medicine to bring one's former enemies to one's next battle. How mighty his forearms and chest looked proclaiming his strength; he was naked to the crisp morning from the waist up, but his torso was covered with his tattoos of his personal victories over the bear, and his personal medicine that required him to seek Kanati in the rivers and streams. The scar on his left cheek, from a Chungee game in his youth only made his countenance more fearsome. Any who fell under his war hatchet on this day would surely think they'd been massacred by the devil himself.

On his face, the women of the tribe could—at a glance—read the pain of his loss, as well as his fearsome determination. One was heard to remark, *"I would rather be a bear in the sight of his rifle than a Creek in his path. For a bear would die swiftly, but a Creek warrior will endure many small deaths."*

Even the Toothless White Man, watching from his porch across the river, noted the fearsome countenance as Runs-To-Water walked toward the council house; he spit his chew from behind one of his few remaining teeth (contrary to Cherokee rumor he still had several) and spoke out loud to himself, *"That is one damn mad Injun."*

Runs-To-Water did indeed look fearsome and determined. He wore his bow shouldered over a powerful left arm; his deerskin quiver worn over his back held many arrows. These were tipped with large points for big game or humans. The arrows he used for killing bear and deer, he would now use for killing Creek. He had two knives, one in a sling around his neck hanging down between the powerful muscles of his chest, and another in his legging on his right calf—each had been used to kill before, and each would kill Creek in this battle. He wore his fighting hatchet in his deerskin belt, and he held a rifle; his powder horn and deerskin pouch of lead balls were attached to his belt.

He was fearsome indeed that morning. Already a veteran of many battles, he was as fine a fighting man as any army anywhere in the world could place on the battlefield in that year of 1755. At twenty yards, his powerful, swift, and silent arrows could penetrate a tough dear, bear, or panther hide. The thin human skin of a Creek guard on the perimeter of their town would offer no match for those arrows, and the silence of that attack assured that no one in the town would be the wiser. No civilized nation in that century had a silent weapon that could even compare.

At a hundred yards with his Kentucky rifle, this man's aim was deadly. In hand to hand fighting he was awesome; in close combat his hatchet in one powerful hand and his knife flashing in the other, he could fight as well as any Roman Centurion who had taken the battle to his enemy two thousand years earlier; in his determination he was as fearsome as any Mongol invader of the middle ages. On this morning, Runs-To-Water was death itself.

He spoke not a word to others in Tugaloo Town, merely walked to the council house and stood for a few moments. At first, he stood alone; he was determined to go to war this day, alone if need be. He would rid the land of the Creek or die in the attempt. He vaguely remembered this same determination many years before in the small stream where he killed his first bear, and that thought brought a peace, a balance into his soul. At that moment, he understood what soldiers throughout the ages have understood—that to accept one's own death before the battle even begins is to become immortal.

Then, as if by some strange magic of these mountains, warriors appeared—warriors coming from the morning mist, streaming in on a lightly chilly wind, spat out from the river and the nearby woods—bred from the heart of the Blue Mountains themselves. They came ready to do battle, and like Runs-To-Water, they were all ready to die.

Then came the fearsome Doublehead, his tattoos proclaiming his strength; his walk was slow, stately, and majestic; his war hatchet in his belt, and his rifle in hand. He would kill many on this day. Then came the Kingfisher, smaller than Runs-To-Water, but many years more seasoned in battle, still leading warriors from his village on epic hunts each year. Then came old Utani, the Longknife, a veteran of many years and many battles—his pride in his Kentucky rifle still obvious as he brings his weapon to war. When Runs-To-Water saw Utani step forth, he nodded and grunted loudly, overcome by the thought that this same Utani had first proclaimed him a man after the killing of his first bear so many years ago. Today they would fight shoulder-to-shoulder, side-by-side.

How proud these four looked, how magnificent, standing together before their council house that distant morning in Tugaloo Town, and how fearsome. Their top knots and tattoos proudly proclaiming them as Cherokee. In that day, September 4, 1755 by the European calendar, no finer fighting men existed anywhere in the world and none could be found more determined.

Over a hundred other warriors stood together in just over a minute with no greeting, other than simple nods to each other as their eyes met. All of these men had been waiting just inside their lodges for Doublehead, Kingfisher, Utani, and Runs-To-Water to appear. Runs-To-Water watched as they gathered, meeting many eye-to-eye. These men were going to war this day.

In a few moments, after a brief nod from Utani, the senior most Chief from this village, the voice of Runs-To-Water was raised in prayer, as the final warriors gathered. *"Mighty Kanati. Bring the large fire soon to begin this day. Our arrows cry for blood, and our warriors are ready to make war. If we die today, it is of no concern. We know that you will make our spirits happy in these, our villages, that we may hear the flowing rivers in these Blue Mountains forever, and be in balance with your spirit. And today, let us kill all the filthy Creeks."*

After a few more moments, in which each warrior contemplated the prayer, and the possibility of his own death, Kingfisher and Doublehead came to the front of the group. Doublehead said, *"Kanati brings the great fire into the sky, and our warriors wish to find Creek warriors in their rifle sights. Perhaps it is time to walk."*

Without a word, these four led the warriors out of the village. Runs-To-Water began his walk with a powerful stride, walking quickly for the western path at the other end of the village. When they reached that path, they began a gentle trot that they would continue until dusk. They would repeat the same run again the next day, and just over a hundred Cherokee warriors followed. Within only ten minutes the path took Runs-To-Water by Estatoe, the village of his birth, and there an old woman named Nalyeena watched the running procession.

The recent years had not treated the mother of Runs-To-Water kindly. Women in every culture find the frontier life brutal, hard, and short, particularly after the death of a husband. Still, Runs-To-Water found some extra deer meat every few weeks. Stopping often before returning to his own lodge, he frequently managed to give her something to eat. She tended her vegetables and selu as she had done as a young Cherokee maiden, and she helped tend the children of the other families of the Bird Clan in Estatoe.

He did not look directly at his mother when he ran past the village; a warrior going to war had other things to concentrate on than his frail mother. Still, he knew she noticed him, and he saw the pride in her eyes as he ran past with this mighty Cherokee army. Runs-To-Water did nod at the additional thirty five warriors from Estatoe standing patiently by the path—these he knew would join the end of the war party. For swift runners had been sent to every Cherokee village that could be reached along the route, telling them to gather their warriors for this battle, and each village that was passed offered more warriors.

These warriors in each village marveled at the procession passing by at a trot. First, they saw Doublehead, the legendary firebrand from the west and Kingfisher, the War Chief and great hunter from Keowee Village. Next, came the mightiest of all War Chiefs, Oconostota, a leader of some of the middle mountain villages of the Cherokee, who had arrived in Tugaloo Town late in the night after Runs-To-Water had begun his prayers. Next, was Runs-To-Water, whose chest told his story of killing his bear. Only rarely in history had the Cherokee assembled so many war chiefs and mighty warriors. The trail they took followed the ancient Unicoi Path up into the mountains before turning southwest. At each village, each creek and crossroads, more Cherokee braves were waiting to join the war party. By the end of the run after two days, some 500 Cherokee warriors approached one of the larger Creek villages in the lower mountains forty miles to the west of Tugaloo Town. This Creek village ruled many smaller villages, and if this stronghold could be destroyed, the hated Creek would withdraw to the southwest, leaving the disputed lands to the Cherokee.

While whites in Europe had developed ritualistic rules for organized fighting by the sixteenth century, no such rules guided battles when Indians faced Indians. These battles among woodland Indians tended to be mismanaged affairs, and while elaborate battle plans were often formulated, after the action began, each warrior tended to go his own way. Thus, these battles were often uncontrolled, bloody, and short, with one tribe or another driving the other off the field temporarily, but with little permanent damage done, other than a few deaths of warriors on either side.

However, the battle of Taliwa was to prove to be an exception to this general rule, because Runs-To-Water wanted to exact such a terrible revenge. He wanted not only the blood of warriors on his mighty arms, but literally to rid the Blue Mountains and lower valleys of the hated Creek forever. Many Cherokee leaders were present; Doublehead was lusting for battle; Kingfisher, the War Chief, sought vengeance for his personal loss; Swimmer, the conjuror, had come along to pray to Kanati for victory for these warriors; and Oconostota, the mighty War Chief had lead some 60 warriors from the Cherokee settlements further into the Blue Mountains. Even old Utani had managed to stay with the younger men on the two day run. These leaders would lead various war parties in the attack under the overall command of Oconostota, the senior War Chief present.

By consensus, they chose the largest of the Creek towns to attack in the lower Blue Mountains, a town called Taliwa, literally meaning ball ground. This large town of 200 lodges boasted the largest ball ground in the lower mountains.

At this moment just before noon on the third day after leaving Tugaloo Town, these Cherokee leaders crouched low in a stream bank together just 200 yards short of the unsuspecting Creek village. This was a mighty town with a surrounding fence of brush encompassing the gaming fields, the main gate, a pen for cattle, and a few selu patches—though most of the fields were outside the fence to the South. The gate lay slightly to the west of what would one day become Dahlonega, Georgia.

As these chiefs and war leaders gathered, they sorted themselves by clan; for even without a Cherokee council house nearby, the chiefs sat according the positions of their respective clans in the council house. Runs-To-Water sat in the position of his Bird Clan, his original clan, while Utani sat, as was proper, in the position of the Wolf Clan. Doublehead and Kingfisher sat where the Deer Clan was to be. Runs-To-Water was surprised to see Nan-ye'hi, wife of Kingfisher, drop into the council circle beside her husband—he didn't realize she had come along on the long run.

After a moment, Oconostota, as the most senior War Chief present, dropped some tobacco on the ground in the middle of the assembled group of leaders as a final offering to Kanati. Then he spoke, referring to himself. *"Oconostota is growing old; for these bones do not feel well after a two-day travel."* The levity helped relieve some of the stress, for men of all ages are nervous before going into battle. Oconostota continued, *"Since we have come this far, we should perhaps take a few horses and furs from these filthy Creek, if they have anything worth taking."*

All grunted in agreement. In a moment, Doublehead continued the thought. *"The sun is still high, and we may as well attack now. We can run through these Creek as if they were old women, and be gone by tonight's darkness."*

Again, many nodded and grunted in agreement since immediate attack was often the way of Indian wars throughout history. With virtually no plan, many horses and furs could be claimed in short battles; that type of attack didn't result in too many deaths on either side.

However, the hatred of Runs-To-Water was much deeper. He wanted more from this battle than merely a bombastic bloodletting raid and a few horses. He considered his words and his place in this assembly, as merely a young warrior. Still a slave to Cherokee Protocol, he waited an extra moment to consider carefully the last words of Doublehead. Then he began to speak just as the last of the leaders, old Swimmer, seated himself in the circle.

"Doublehead is wise, and we all know of his fighting skill. Even now his war hatchet cries for more Creek blood, and I wonder if he will find enough to quench that thirst." With that statement the mandatory compliment for Doublehead had been stated, and all grunted agreement. Runs-To-Water continued. *"Still, can we make sure all the Creek are here, and that none run away if we attack only from this small stream and only from one side?"*

With that question, Runs-To-Water had made his point—he wanted everyone in the village dead. In fact he wanted nothing less than the extermination of the Creek. While no one immediately grunted agreement, they each considered these words and reflected that such was their intention when they mounted this war party. In only a moment the others became just as determined as Runs-To-Water. After a moment of silence, he spoke again, at length. *"Kanati once told me to go to the river to find a weapon. In my life I have, many times, hunted in rivers, and sometimes fought Creek in rivers. I have come to see that a river is a weapon."*

Then he gestured to the stream bank itself, descending into the village, and then continued, *"See how this small river leads into the village, and see how just there it enters the village of my enemy. I can use it to enter the village also. If the warriors are drawn to the horse corral at the other end, I can enter here in the river and kill everyone. I will take no rifles—I will kill with my knife and arrows."*

Thus, did a battle plan emerge for the upcoming battle to the death. Oconostota would begin the battle with his war cry, as was proper for the senior War Chief. Next, while a force under Oconostota and Doublehead would attack the large town from the southwest, making noise, using their rifles, and shouting their courageous war cries, Utani would select a point on the opposite side of the village to the northwest, and fire burning arrows into the center of the village. This would set the village afire and result in confusion. Kingfisher was to lead his men into the village from the west end, just after the attack by Doublehead. By then, he would probably be facing all of the Creek warriors, who would certainly charge to meet what they assumed was a two pronged attack on the west end of their town near the horse corral. These advances would serve as the initial Cherokee attack, and the Creeks would assume that the entire attack came from that quarter.

However, after the warriors were well engaged at the other end of town, Runs-To-Water would lead his group of some 50 warriors quietly into the creek bed at the east end of town. Entering silently from the rear, he would move through the town, killing silently as he went—for knives and arrows make no noise. All agreed that they would kill everyone in sight.

The three distracting forces, each numbering over 100 warriors, were given "the walk time from Tugaloo to Estatoe" some twenty minutes to surround the village. No signal was given—the noise of the preliminary attack itself would be the battle signal. Runs-To-Water and fifty warriors from Tugaloo and Estatoe—only veteran warriors, each of whom had fought Creeks before—would quietly slither down the stream bank to the eastern end of the village, and slip under the brush that masked the joining of the defensive fence and the stream.

The stream bank was depressed by four or five feet, so these warriors could not be seen from the lodges unless some woman came for water. Just as the last of his warriors entered under the brush fence, Runs-To-Water heard the battle begin at the other end of the village. Suddenly there was shouting and running, as Creek warriors sounded their war cries to bring out all of the Creek warriors. All ran towards the noise of battle at the west end of the town.

Oconostota had begun the battle from the Southwest as planned, and had fired into the village, dropping many warriors from the outset. Next, the fire arrows of Utani's band created havoc in the town. Kingfisher's force, mostly armed with rifles, were attacking from the Northwest, and the shouting of war cries was lost amid the firing of guns. Kingfisher crouched behind a log, firing his rifle as quickly as he could load it. His wife, Nan-ye'hi, hid behind him and chewed each of the lead balls for Kingfisher's rifle before he loaded it—this made the ball more deadly in battle. It was well known that a piece of lead, well chewed, would gouge out bigger hunks of flesh.

At the east end of the village, in the streambed, Chucha, the Cherokee warrior beside Runs-To-Water, heard the battle begin and, true to form, immediately stood up to begin his climb out of the stream bank to advance into the village. A mighty arm grabbed his shoulder in a crushing vice, and with the strength of ten men, pulled him back down. Runs-To-Water wanted the diversion attack to proceed until all of the Creek warriors were engaged at the other end of the village. He knew he could forestall the advance of his own force for only a few seconds since all of those warriors were itching to get into the fight. So without thinking he started talking. He whispered to Chucha and those nearest. *"We will attack the village lodges. Steal what furs and weapons you can, but do not be drawn into the fight at the other end of the village. We do not want the Creek warriors to know we are here until the village is destroyed. Kill everyone."*

With those terribly cruel words, Runs-To-Water saved the battle plan and changed the history of the Blue Ridge Mountains forever. That few additional seconds at the beginning of the battle assured that the Creek warriors were all running the other way, and this fact assured a major Cherokee victory. The Creeks

The Battle Of Taliwa

Dahlonega, Georgia
1855 by the European Calendar

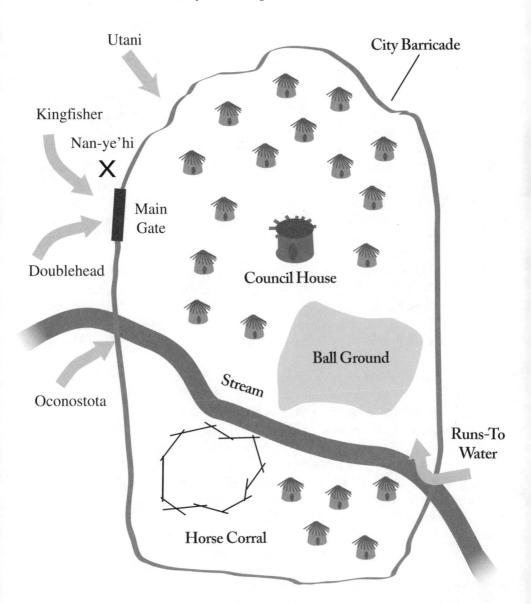

only mustered around 350 warriors for this fateful battle, but of the 600 old men, women, and children who would be attacked by the warriors with Runs-To-Water, not a single soul survived.

After a few more seconds, Runs-To-Water looked into the eyes of Chucha and nodded. He then raised up, drew his knife from his neck case and placed it between his teeth. This was another smart move that Runs-To-Water had planned in advance. The other warriors greatly admired Runs-To-Water, and thus did likewise. With knives in their teeth, all were prevented from giving a war cry and silence was maintained for a few seconds longer. Runs-To-Water then began his climb and a swift run to the nearest of the lodges. He entered the lodge with an arrow notched into his bow, and within one step had fired it into the face of an old man in the lodge. The arrow entered the man's right eye, and before the old man hit the floor, Runs-To-Water had another arrow flying 12 feet into the belly of a woman who had begun to stand up, rising from the couch at the other end of the lodge. As she died, Runs-To-Water with merciless eyes, took the knife from his teeth and slit the throat of the two young toonalies who stood on the couch behind their fallen mother. In just under ten seconds he had killed four Creek.

It must have been fearsome for those young toonalis to have looked into the eyes of Runs-To-Water at that moment before their certain death. While Runs-To-Water knew that this mother had died trying to protect her young, as had his lovely Akala, his eyes did not register this. His eyes showed no emotion at all on this day of killing; he had no thoughts of whose family he had slain. His dark eyes were like a panther's or a shark's eyes—hauntingly blank, cold, and fearsome. Runs-To-Water was merely moving through his enemies cutting them down as his wife once cut corn stalks in her patch of selu—no emotion, no thought, no remorse.

As Runs-To-Water emerged from the lodge, he saw many of his warriors in front of other nearby lodges examining furs, knives they had captured, or pots and pans from various lodges. One was taking a bear skin from a fur rack by a nearby lodge, and another held up an old rifle as his victor's prize. One Cherokee was scalping an old man near the door of one of the smaller lodges. The old man, still alive, was screaming terribly. Another Cherokee made sport of a captured young woman, slowly and systematically cutting off her fingers with his knife. Her screams were dreadful, but were buried under the overall sound of the battle. Runs-To-Water knew that he needed to get his attack back on track, but he also knew that the old adage, "To the victors, go the spoils" was nowhere more appropriate than in wars between the Cherokee and the Creek. In a fraction of a second, he'd formulated exactly what to shout. *"There are many more rifles in these other lodges. We will attack and find them."*

With that, a mighty war-cry erupted from the warriors still fighting with his group as they ran toward the next set of lodges to seek opportunities for killing and for additional spoils.

Two hundred yards to the west, just outside of the village, the Cherokee were still outside the wood barricades and still attacking vigorously. Kingfisher, Utani, Doublehead, and all of the warriors, armed with either rifles or arrows, were happily firing at any target that presented itself. By now, the Creek warriors had decided to open their gates and press their battle into the woods. They hoped to save their village by taking the Cherokee out of range of the burning arrows. Thus, they sealed the fate of that village, without ever realizing that another Cherokee force was in their rear.

Kingfisher fired his rifle methodically, carefully selecting his targets and hitting most of them, while his wife calmly continued chewing his rifle balls, passing them to him as he reloaded. Suddenly, she felt his leg jerk and looked to see that his face had exploded—he had caught a rifle shot just behind his eye; it killed him instantly. The back of his head disappeared in a massive spray of blood, as he fell across the log in front of him.

Nan-ye'hi simply moved forward, lying down beside her dead husband, and picked up his rifle. She noted that it was already loaded—Kingfisher had been seeking another target when he died, and as that thought floated through her mind, she was pleased. A warrior should die in battle seeking the death of his enemy. She smiled to herself at the thought, just as the unlucky Creek threw open the gates to their village and charged toward the trees. Nan-ye'hi's smile was deadly, nearly satanic, as she thought, "How lucky I am to have a loaded rifle at just this moment." She aimed and fired as did 200 other Cherokee—the charging wave of over a hundred Creek warriors were slain before they could advance twenty yards. The momentum of the charge died as quickly as the first rifle fire, and then the younger Cherokee warriors with arrows fired as those with rifles reloaded. Within a minute the Creek retreated, and the Cherokee ran out of the trees and toward the open gates.

Many of those Cherokee died of arrows or rifle balls from the Creek still left in the town, but others did make it inside the gates, and brought the battle into the heart of the village of Taliwa. Amazingly, at this late point in the battle, not a single Creek warrior yet realized that they were caught between two forces. Nan-ye'hi charged with the other Cherokee warriors into the gates, loading and firing her rifle as she went. She still chewed a rifle ball, but forgot to load it. She would end the battle with the same hunk of lead, well chewed, between her teeth.

Runs-To-Water entered a second lodge with Chucha right behind him. Each fired an arrow into the chest of the woman they found there. Each noted she was expecting a child soon, and neither bothered to care. After a quick look around, they moved on. As Runs-To-Water entered the third lodge, he noted the smell of burning. Fire at the other end of the village had overtaken a lodge and a fur drying rack, casting a dark gray smoke over the battle. He was distracted for just a moment as his mind registered this smell, and that was long enough for a young toonali—no more than seven or eight—to have thrust a knife into his left shoulder from the rear. The boy had been hiding behind the hanging skin entry way of the lodge. With a sure swing of his left arm, Runs-To-Water backhanded the boy, and sent him flying into the wall of the lodge. He was unconscious when he hit the floor; in less that five seconds Runs-To-Water's arrow found his chest and pierced his beating heart. This was important only in that this was one of the several battle scars that Runs-To-Water would take with him to his death.

Thus the attack progressed; lodge after lodge was ransacked, as Runs-To-Water and the Cherokee exacted a terrible retribution for the small raid at Tugaloo Town. Within twenty minutes, the forces of Oconostota, Doublehead, and Kingfisher had merged inside the gate at the other end of the village, and only minutes later the last of the Creek warriors abandoned the town by whatever route they could find and ran into the woods. By that time, under the terrible, calculating rage of Runs-To-Water, the Creek village had lost its heart—its mothers, sons, and daughters; it's grandfathers, it's medicine men, it's midwives, and it's old women—all were slain.

The Cherokee found and tortured only two captives. They systematically cut off fingers, toes, arms, and legs, leaving them to die, which they did in fairly short order. After that entertainment, the warriors gathered their spoils, and burned the remaining lodges. In just over three hours, this mighty Creek town had ceased to exist.

One black slave was found under some furs in one of the lodges. While it is not widely known today, many Indians of that frontier period owned black slaves, having either captured them or purchased them from whites. By consensus, the slave was given to Nan-ye'hi, for her bravery in battle.

This battle was not viewed by any white man—for the only white trader who happened to be in this Creek town huddled in one of the Creek lodges, and was slain as quickly as the Creek women and children. This battle is known today among white men only from the tales of the Cherokee because of its ultimate outcome. This battle determined the fate of the Creek in the Blue Ridge Mountains. Never again would the Creek raiders attack the lower Cherokee villages themselves. Ultimately, the smaller Creek settlements in the lower ridges of the Blue Mountains were moved further to the southwest, thus yielding this land in the Blue Mountains to the Real People. The Creek became Indians of the flatlands towards the coast. Further, this battle settled the conflicting claims of the Cherokee and Creek on the rich hunting grounds in the sacred Blue Mountains. After this battle of Taliwa, they were to be the hunting grounds of the Cherokee forever.

One unhappy result of the battle was the untimely death of Utani. He had moved a bit to slowly in loading his rifle during the beginning of the fight with the warriors, and unlike the women, old men, and young children slain on the knife of Runs-To-Water, the Creek braves at the west end of the village shot back. As Utani ran his powder and ball down the barrel of the rifle, he stood to extract the ramrod, and two Creek musket balls found his chest.

He was breathing heavily after the battle, and some blood came in his breath. He lay just outside the walls, and Runs-To-Water sat by his side. Utani talked in a labored fashion to his friend. *"I think I will find the Great Spirit Kanati this day. My chest is heavy and I cannot get enough air to breath."*

Runs-To-Water diverted his eyes, and thought fleetingly, will the killing never stop? Must I lose everyone I love? He did not realize then that, such is the cry of everyone who grows old, and outlives his companions in this life.

Utani continued, *"I will die tonight, but I want to rest near the Tugaloo. Many of my hunts were there. Would you take me to the creek of the Panther, and there say prayers to Kanati for my spirit?"*

Runs-To-Water looked down at his friend. For the second time in three days, tears streamed down his face as he considered the words of his beloved uncle. Since Utani knew him so well, the potential embarrassment of the tears made no difference. For Utani had given Runs-To-Water one of his first lessons as a warrior, years ago, in telling him to break his blowgun as a proper sacrifice. Even now Utani offered a good lesson for any man—a lesson on how to die well.

Runs-To-Water spoke. *"I will take you to Tugaloo, to the creek of the Panther. There you will rest with our brother, Changee. But you will not only rest in the Blue Mountains—for you are the Blue Mountains, and I will tell toonalis for many generations of your battles and your victories. Your story will be told by the old men in the evenings in the council house, and thus your spirit will be as vast and beautiful as the earth and sky."*

At this Runs-To-Water looked down at his uncle and his lifelong friend; only then did he realize Utani was gone. Thus did evening set on that fateful day over the burning of Taliwa. Various ritual chants began for the dead and dying Cherokee with no chants or weeping at all for the many dead Creek. The strong voice of old Oconostota was heard—he had lost many warriors from the middle villages of the Cherokee. Just inside the woods, Nan-ye'hi wailed and chanted for her slain husband where he died, even as her newly acquired black slave stood frightened and bewildered with his arms tied around a nearby tree. Other warriors were tying bundles of furs together or gathering horses, rifles, and anything else of value. Runs-To-Water added to the growing noise his chant for Utani, his lifelong friend, even as the sun set over the Blue Mountains.

Tugaloo Mourns A Fallen Leader

Runs-To-Water did manage to procure two Creek horses and thus did he bring Utani back to Tugaloo Town. He'd wrapped the body of Utani in several deer furs, but that had not helped the decomposing corpse much. Only the early freeze and ensuing snow the night after the battle had allowed Runs-To-Water to respect the wishes of Utani. While the Cherokee had many dead—from Estatoe and Tugaloo Town alone some twenty-five warriors were now immortal—Utani was the senior among them and thus was accorded the honors of the town. As he laid his burden before the sacred fire in the council house two days after the battle, Runs-To-Water bowed to each of the seven clans. As usual many sides of the council house were empty, but the Wolf Clan, the Bird Clan, and the Deer Clan were well represented.

Runs-To-Water sat in the first row of the space for the Wolf Clan, his clan since his marriage to Akala. There he waited for the senior chief of the town to stand and speak. By Cherokee Protocol, whenever a notable warrior fell in battle, the leaders of the tribe provided a great oration on the life and contributions of the man. Only after two full minutes had gone by did Runs-To-Water carefully look up and see that many eyes were discretely falling upon him. With a shock, he realized that the entire town expected him to speak; thus was he elected Peace Chief of Tugaloo by acclamation.

The thought frightened him, as nothing he could have foreseen. He quickly looked away from the faces around him, seeking to avoid their eyes. He did not wish to be Chief, for since finding his wife dead and his remaining child homeless, he'd thought of little else but killing Creek warriors and killing is clearly not the business of a Peace Chief. In fact—and this thought struck him like a lightening bolt—he realized for the first time that he'd not even expected to survive the battle at Taliwa!

As these thoughts came rushing in a jumble to him, he began to think of who should become Peace Chief for Tugaloo. Who was sitting here in the council house to carry the tribe forward? He'd seen old Nalyeena come into the council house, along with Chucha, the younger warrior who had fought so bravely beside him at Taliwa. A good warrior, Chucha, but much too young and inexperienced to become Chief of so important a town as Tugaloo. He noted that Swimmer had come, and sat in the space for the Clan of the Bird, beside Toomi. As he thought of the many other warriors sitting in the council house, his mind of its own accord began to reject many as potential chiefs—this one was too young—that one too rigid minded. This one was a loudmouth braggart whom no one would follow. That one visited the Toothless White Man too frequently and drank too much. As his fear began to mount, he thought of others, and as quickly as a man came to mind, he found a reason that the tribe would not support him.

At that moment, if Runs-To-Water had been able to find another to whom should fall the mantel of Chief, he would have gladly looked directly at the man, and nodded his support; however, much to his consternation, he could find no one better qualified or more senior than himself. This conclusion had nothing to do with bragging, or self-promotion. Runs-To-Water had hunted successfully for years, stolen horses from white men's farms, and killed his share of Creek. All here knew that he'd saved the battle plan at Taliwa—he'd heard Chucha telling Oconostota of how he'd stalled just long enough to let the battle plan develop, and of his later bravery.

Runs-To-Water began to see a certain inevitability to his unanticipated succession. Had he not killed many bear, and demonstrated his courage time and time again? Was he not the oldest warrior present from Tugaloo that survived? In fact, had he not been spoken to directly by God when only seven? Had he not followed throughout his life those words, "Go to the river?" At each major crisis, had those words not guided him? Without realizing it, he thus managed to consider himself as a possible Peace Chief, and ultimately he'd found no one more qualified.

Just as he reached that conclusion, his eyes rested on old Toomi, sitting with the Bird Clan—his original clan. She was looking straight at him, and her eyes seemed to bore into his soul; just then she grinned a mighty toothless grin—for she was now well past 70 years old—and Runs-To-Water saw her nod in his direction. She had read his mind again, and proclaimed his thoughts correct; her grin let him know; he was now Peace Chief of the Cherokee. Thus it was done.

At times in the lives of certain men, fate seems to reach for them, to single them out in some fashion. Historiographers often reflect on this question: Does man make history or does history make the man? Would Abe Lincoln have been a great President had not the Civil War ennobled him? Would Franklin Roosevelt have become the nation's father for some fourteen years, without the threat of aggression from Germany and Japan? Would Washington have been the Father of a nation, had Britain not taxed her colonies so terribly? Would anyone remember Jefferson, had he written only poetry, while farming his Virginia plantation?

Perhaps we can never know the answer to that broader question, but we can say that on this day, a man stood up in this Council House of the Cherokee at Tugaloo Town to meet history face to face. Thus, did the town of Tugaloo get a new Peace Chief. Where only minutes before a mighty warrior had taken a seat among the Wolf Clan—now a new Peace Chief stood, arisen from the acclimation of this council—the very heart of his people. He cleared his throat loudly as he stood—thus acknowledging the inevitable wishes of his tribe.

With a slow dignity, indeed a majesty rivaled only in the great ancient courts of Egypt, perhaps of China, or Rome, this new Peace Chief walked slowly toward the vacant seat beside the sacred fire. While he yet stood, he reached for tobacco, which he then sprinkled on the fire, as sacrifice. Then his voice arose—the very voice of his ancient people, heard loud and strong throughout the council house. All present knew that they were witnessing history that would be told for generations among the Cherokee.

"This day, I say to the Cherokee, a great one among us is fallen! Spread tobacco on the sacred fire, and place mourners in the heart of our village. We will wail, and cry out in our grief. For this day we have lost Utani, the Longknife. He was born of the Blue Mountains and of the river Tugaloo, and he hunted these many years the deer and the bear. He taught the great Changee to hunt panther, he lead me to find the Great Spirit Kanati, when I was but a toonali. Who among us has not heard his voice when we faced danger or looked up to see him teaching our toonali the ways of the bow and the knife?"

The oration of Runs-To-Water lasted over an hour that day, emphasizing and describing the many battles and deeds of Utani throughout his long lifetime. Each small skirmish was remembered for the people in astonishing detail—each of Utani's many wives were likewise honored, and their contributions to the tribe described. Few would have thought—least of all Runs-To-Water himself—that he was to become a "Long Talker" one of the great orators of the Cherokee, but on this day, his heart moved him, and the mystic balance of the Blue Mountains mandated that he speak long and lovingly of his mentor and his friend.

Runs-To-Water did not realize it, but he ended his mighty oration as he had ended his words to Utani on the battlefield. *"Again, I say to the Cherokee, we have lost the great Utani, the Longknife. I take him now to the Tugaloo, to the creek of the Panther in the Blue Mountains. There Utani will rest with our brother, Changee. But you, Utani, will not sleep in the Blue Mountains—for you are the Blue Mountains, and your spirit will soar to the heights of these Blue Mountains, and fly as free and beautiful as the earth and the sky."*

Chief Runs-To-Water, or Wauhatchie in the Cherokee tongue, was indeed a long talker of the Cherokee. None knew this at the time, but that name would be written in a history of blood for all generations of the Cherokee. The name would be preserved in the oral histories of the tribe, as well as the written histories of the whites who would later settle along the Tugaloo River in the Blue Mountains. Moreover, the oration of Runs-To-Water was to be the last of its kind—the final great oration for a chief ever heard in the council house at Tugaloo. Within only a few years, that council house and village would be forever destroyed.

The Burial of Utani

As the body of Utani was taken up on a horse for his final ride in this world, the professional mourners of the Cherokee cried and wailed loudly their grief for Utani. All of the people of Tugaloo did likewise. The Cherokee lined the sides of the playing fields in Tugaloo Town that day, as Runs-To-Water and all of the others followed the funeral procession.

At times, the Cherokee were buried under the ground of their own lodges. At other times, mighty leaders—both male and female—were honored by burial under the ground of the council house itself; indeed centuries later, several such graves were found in the council house mound at Tugaloo Town by archeologists. However, Utani had spoken his wishes, and the tribe would honor them, in order that the spirit of Utani the Longknife might be in balance with the Great Spirit, Kanati. The funeral procession left the playing fields of Tugaloo Town and turned northwest, to pass Estatoe—another village mourning her dead—and then continued on to the banks of Panther Creek, where the great Changee was already entombed.

There the body of Utani was laid on a prepared piece of ground, a six inch depression in the rocky soil, on a high bluff overlooking the creek. As he was laid, the mourners and family members (for Utani still had one old wife who was destined to outlive him by some 15 years) continued their loud mourning. Two young warriors laid many of Utani's personal possessions in the grave beside him; Runs-To-Water saw the bow Utani used when teaching the young toonalis to shoot. Also, all of Utani's personal robes and skins would be buried with him. All present noted that the Kentucky rifle and the powder horn were not being buried here. During the grave side ritual, these were waved over the prostrate body of Utani, symbolically thanking him, and then the rifle and horn were handed to the oldest of Utani's many grandsons—for the Cherokee were much to sensible a people to bury all of one's valuable possessions as grave goods. However, Runs-To-Water again felt his grief most sharply, when he saw the large knife laid on the corpse; that knife had cost Utani 100 deer skins many years ago in a trade with the Toothless White Man, and was worth much more than the other grave goods. However, upon reflection Runs-To-Water grunted loudly, signifying his approval—it is right that Utani, the Longknife, was to take his long-knife with him as his spirit hunted the Blue Mountains forever.

The younger warriors, having finished the grave goods portion of the ceremony, then began to pile large rocks on top of the body. They continued alone for a while, but in time the family members and other participants began to help, finding stones of all sizes to build a cairn of considerable size. Many such Cherokee burial cairns were six feet high or more. This work continued for many hours, and the grave constructed would last for many decades. For all knew that the smell of the body would draw many scavengers, some who were strong enough to remove all but the largest stones, thus a great number of stones were placed on the cairn.

That evening, the funeral procession returned to Tugaloo with one more duty to perform. One Cherokee, designated for this purpose by the tribe, entered the lodge of Utani, and dismantled his sleeping couch. He took this, and one small stool used by Utani out into the nearby woods and broke them in order to prevent future use. He also removed all the ashes from the fireplace and swept it clean. Next, he made a new fire for the use of the one remaining wife of Utani. With Utani's many sons married into other villages, only the wife remained.

After the cleaning of the hearth, she went alone to plunge into the river seven times, alternating facing east and then west. She would retire for four days, into the woods, and only then return to the council house to accept the final condolences of the tribe. For many months this old woman would let her hair grow loose, without dressing it in any way—thus showing her continued mourning. For years afterward, many in Tugaloo would reflect that this woman, the last of Utani's many wives, did her husband proud—for she mourned longer than was required,—thus showing her great love and respect for the great Utani the Long-Knife, Peace Chief of the Cherokee.

Runs-To-Water and the Whites

Runs-To-Water always sought balance in life, but the years of his reign as Peace Chief were spent in constant bickering. While it soon became apparent that the battle of Taliwa had settled the problem with the Creek, Runs-To-Water had assumed leadership in his tribe at a critical juncture in history. Not only did he have to deal with the usual bickering between tribal members, he became increasingly concerned with the relationships with the whites.

During the years from 1755 and 1759, those racial relationships became increasingly complex. As whites moved ever closer to the foothills of the Blue Mountains, they cleared farmland, developed primitive roads, established communities, built churches, and perhaps worst of all, sold their way of life to the Indian. Whiskey, ever the bane of tribal existence, became the number one preoccupation for some of the young warriors, and they refused to hunt. Thus their pretty young Cherokee wives and countless children starved, or froze under bear blankets that had seen too many winters. The Toothless White Man seemed to show no realistic sign of dying any time soon–Runs-To-Water thought that he must be nearly 70 winters old, and he sold rum to anyone with a penny, or a chicken, or a deer skin to trade.

However, a more subtle grievance was noted by many of the older tribal members. The elders were just beginning to realize that their relationship with the whites had changed; the racial relationship had moved from the earlier tolerance of white faces, to a sort of symbiotic relationship of mutual service between the races. Whites seemed to need furs—deer or beaver—and the Cherokee certainly needed rifles, lead, cloth, and gunpowder. By this period, the elders loudly and vocally stated that the tribe had become totally dependent on the whites.

Skiagunota, one of the elders in Tugaloo, summarized this quite succinctly, in words that the son of the Toothless White Man recorded in a letter to a trading partner in Charles Town—thus these worries come down to us from history. *"My people cannot live independent of the English. The clothes we wear we cannot make ourselves. They are made for us. We use their ammunition with which to kill deer. We cannot make our guns. Every necessity of life we must have from the white people."*

His assessment was completely accurate. By the 1750s, the Cherokee were the most "civilized" of all the tribes. The young warriors now wanted a long rifle rather than a bow, and few could shoot an arrow straight anymore. Almost all of the young men rode horses, and finding a swift runner was becoming a problem. Most of the lodges had been replaced by more sturdy log cabins such as those build by the whites; so much so that a white stranger arriving in Tugaloo Town on the frontier might well mistake it for a white village. Some of the Cherokee had even abandoned Kanati and the ancient animistic wisdoms of the elders for the new white religion. They apparently worshiped two crossed sticks, and some weak, dead member of a foreign tribe named Jesus.

How this had happened Runs-To-Water could not understand. How could any Cherokee be displeased with Kanati, with selu, and with all the gifts from the Blue Mountains—particularly now that the filthy Creek had been sent away forever?

Meanwhile, life went on in Tugaloo Town. Runs-To-Water found another woman, whose husband had fallen dead at Taliwa, and promptly built her a lodge. He reclaimed his son from the village, and immediately began to produce several more children. At each birth, he wondered if these toonalis would know the wonder of the lone hunt in the Blue Mountains where the air grows cold. Would they see the rock where the wind blows, or know the falling waters of Panther Creek? How could he be sure they learned the stories of Changee, the Chaser of Panthers, or Utani, the Longknife, or Kingfisher? Would his new wife, know a long life along this beautiful river—a life that had been denied his beloved Akala? These questions haunted Runs-To-Water more with each passing year.

Once in 1757, Runs-To-Water determined to take his prayers and reflections on this matter directly to Kanati. He had often watched a promising young warrior of his tribe choose to drink his life away, or seen a young Cherokee Maiden chose to neglect work in the selu every seventh day and go to the new cabin across the river down by Ward's Creek—they called it a church. His heart was increasingly troubled, and he was no longer in balance with the world.

Thus, on one morning several weeks after the Green Corn Festival, Runs-To-Water left Tugaloo Town and began to trot to the west for four hours until he came to the mountain called Currahee, which in the Cherokee tongue means "He walks alone." For on this mountain, Kanati, the Great Spirit, was said to live; here he looked down over all of his people in the lower towns of the Cherokee.

The Cherokee people believed that communal prayers were essential components in various ceremonies and in town governance and many corporate prayers were sent forth to Kanati from among the Cherokee people gathered in the council house. Still at times every man must approach his God alone, and Mount Currahee, with its breath-taking 360 degree views, was designated as the place to approach Kanati; for that is where Kanati lived. Thus the name of the mountain, "He walks alone", meant that a man had come to a time when he must speak privately with his God. Runs-To-Water would climb this mountain alone to bring peace to his troubled mind.

In this way, did Runs-To-Water seek wisdom to lead his people through the troubled times ahead. After a sharp trot to the top of the mountain, the vista opened before Runs-To-Water; he could see off the top of the rocky face northward for over thirty miles, well into the heart of the Cherokee Nation. Many men of various backgrounds have had the same inspiration from that lofty height, and, on that day, Runs-To-Water was sure that he had approached the very council house of his God. After a few minutes of respectful silence, Runs-To-Water offered tobacco, by sprinkling some on the ground; He then spoke. *"Kanati, Great Spirit of the Cherokee. I have come to your mountain today to ask why you have sent the whites into these Blue Mountains. These whites seem to have no understanding of balance; they kill the forest and everything in it, without any sacrifice to you. They take all, and they give nothing back. I can look from the top of your home on this mountain and see your Blue Mountains and my home in the river valley. I can see that you have given these Blue Mountains to the Cherokee forever; that is why you gave us victory over the filthy Creek two winters ago. Great Kanati. I can hunt bear and deer that you provide, and I can help my people in their petty disagreements, but I cannot see how to help rid them of the whites, or of the whiskey at the table of the Toothless White Man. Please help me to see how to lead my people. Make me more worthy to be your Peace Chief that I might lead your people as you would have them go."*

With that, Runs-To-Water could think of nothing else to say, so he sat on the rock over-ledge, looking back to the Northeast towards Tugaloo Town. Like all men, Runs-To-Water was a man locked into his own time, and like almost all men, he could not envision another way of life, other than the simple village life of farming and hunting—the life of the Cherokee. He wanted nothing more than to live that life for fifty years, to tell the stories of great Cherokee warriors to his children, and then to die peacefully in this village, beside the river he loved. He sat for many minutes on Mount Currahee, perhaps an hour or more, looking down at the world of men, as Kanati must look down. He did not sense that he had received an answer to his question, but he had faith that he would, someday. He firmly believed that in silence and in simple faith, Kanati, the Great Spirit, does speak to mankind.

The view he saw that day can still be enjoyed by anyone seeking a God's view of the trials and tribulations of this world—a view that does help one to put problems into perspective. In fact, some 190 years later, many a white man would run to the top of Curahee Mountain and behold the same breathtaking view, while training for yet another war. Many of those men would say prayers here—just as Runs-To-Water did on that day long ago, before they themselves left for another desperate battle. For this was the mountain used by the Camp Toccoa Paratroopers Training Facility during World War II. The now famous "Band of Brothers" trained here on Currhaee, having run "three miles up, three miles down," on the flanks of this mountain many times. Thus the Cherokee name "Currahee" would, in the 1940s, become a battle cry and source of inspiration for a whole army of white men. It would become a term signifying rigorous training to be spoken with great pride, and some reverence, in distant battlefields in Normandy, Holland, and Germany. Still, all of that was in the dim, distant future. It was a future that Runs-To-Water could not have imagined, but to be fair to this great Cherokee Chief, can any one among us truly imagine our own destiny or our own future? Perhaps it is sufficient, that on that distant day those many years ago, Runs-To-Water sought his god on Currahee, and found, if not clear answers, some measure of balance.

British Forts and The Great Philadelphia Wagon Road

As the years passed, Runs-To-Water continued to be concerned with the whites. He tried desperately to foresee how the red man and the white could share these Blue Mountains, but he feared for his small band of Cherokee. He knew that the whites had established forts at various locations throughout Cherokee country. One, Fort Loudoun, was built near the middle Cherokee towns, some sixty miles to the north, but the one that most troubled Runs-To-Water was called Fort Prince George and was only a morning's run away. That fort of the whites stood only a few minutes run from the Cherokee village of Keowee, in what would one day become the upstate area of South Carolina. This fort directly overlooked Keowee, the same village from which the great warrior Kingfisher had come, and could fire its mighty cannon directly into that Cherokee village!

Runs-To-Water was pleased when the wife of Kingfisher had married a white trader named Bryan Ward. Thus, a Beloved Woman of the Cherokee became a woman with a white name—Nancy Ward. Her husband had set up a grist mill on the lower creek only three miles below Tugaloo town, and the Cherokee in the valley now had much of their selu ground at this mill rather than grinding it by hand as had the Cherokee women for so many generations. Many began to refer to that running stream as Ward's Creek, and so it is known to this day.

As he reflected on the battle at Taliwa, and the ever encroaching whites, Runs-To-Water wondered if he'd fought the right enemy. At least the filthy Creeks had not destroyed traditional ways of life among the Cherokee.

But perhaps he was just getting old. He reflected—as all older men do—on where the time had gone; where his life had gone. He was, in this his 38th year, a substantive warrior and the Peace Chief of his village. Still in his century, among the Cherokee, that was not young. Had it really been four years since the battle of Taliwa? It seemed long ago, and yet it also seemed like only yesterday. As the

Peace Chief, everyone considered him the most important elder in Tugaloo Town. His peers were now the elders of the other Cherokee villages, and they all talked of their trouble with the whites. The whites never seemed to stop coming!

In 1755, Governor Glen of Charles Town in the British colony of South Carolina became concerned about relationships with the Cherokee. Another war between Britain and France loomed on the horizon, and French influence had always been strong among the "over-the-hill" towns of the Cherokee—the towns that were across the Blue Mountains. These "over the hill" towns were much closer to the French influence which emanated from the Mississippi River, than was Tugaloo Town. Thus, the over the hill towns were under French influence whereas Tugaloo and the other lower towns were more influenced by the British. Governor Glen knew that in a war with the French, the Cherokee would be critical allies. The war, which in the colonies was referred to as the French and Indian War, promised to be brutal and cruel.

Governor Glen knew that some distant Indian settlements were falling under the influence of the French, and that the French and their Indian allies had attacked British colonists all along the frontier. He sent a party into Cherokee country to treat with the lower towns of the Cherokee and thus, to keep this closest cluster of towns under British influence.

This treaty meeting took place on the Saluda River just 35 miles east of Tugaloo Town. The Cherokee were represented by a Peace Chief from one of the Middle Cherokee towns, a man known as Little Carpenter. He was known to be friendly towards the whites, and, with Runs-To-Water looking on, a tentative peace was established between the lower Cherokee settlements and their British neighbors. The Cherokee gave some land to the British—an inconsequential amount really—and in turn the British stated that they would not settle west of the Blue Mountains. The Cherokee, including Runs-To-Water, were very pleased with this treaty, but like so many such treaties, this agreement was useless the day it was signed. Nothing in that paper or in any other treaty could ultimately protect the Cherokee lands in the beautiful Blue Mountains from whites who craved the land.

In fact, that otherwise insignificant treaty sounded the death song for the Cherokee in the lower towns in the Carolina colonies. The French and their allies among northern Indian tribes were attacking British colonies from the Virginia settlement all the way up into what would become Canada. Thus white settlers who wanted to move to the frontier and homestead their own land found the western frontier of all the northern British colonies closed to settlement, or at the very least, inhospitable. These settlers, thousands of them from the great northern cities, then looked south where they found that a treaty offered land in the mountains to whites.

As a result, scores of thousands of white settlers streamed southward down a series of rugged trails and roads along the eastern edge of the Blue Mountains. This route came to be known as the Great Philadelphia Wagon Road, though that name suggested that there actually was a road—a very liberal interpretation for this trail in the mid-1750s certainly. Still they came, some ten thousand a year, for the entire decade. Historians have described this road as the busiest road in all the colonies during the 1750s and 1760s. Many of these whites settled in Cherokee country in the shadow of the Blue Ridge. Thus, the treaty made by Little Carpenter and Governor Glen, which was intended to protect Cherokee land, essentially made that land irresistible to thousands of new settlers with white faces.

Runs-To-Water, never an avid student of geopolitical population influences or emigration trends, simply found it hard to believe how many whites there were! Still, the evidence of the new settlement was all around him. Apparently the British colonies of the north were even more crowded than the Charles Town colony or the newer towns such as Augusta or Savannah. These northern colonies were spewing their overpopulation into southern foothills of the Blue Mountains, more quickly even than settlers coming upriver from the British coastal cities!

At just that inopportune moment, the Cherokee experienced hunger for the first time in decades. For several years during the mid-1750s the selu crop was terrible—not enough rain, and the deer were scarce because of all the new settlers. Thus, in 1759 Runs-To-Water did what no leader should ever be required to do— he watched as an increasing number of his people starved. With this conflux of events, there is little wonder that hostilities soon broke out. The war between the French and British, while many think of this as primarily a European affair, was to result in the decimation of one population, who would become the biggest losers of all—the Cherokee.

The Cherokee War

Historians today say the war was inevitable; some say it was a logical result of the Cherokee Treaty of 1755, which held out the hope of peace on the southern frontier. Others talk of a clash of cultures—Cherokee and white—each of whom held different perspectives on the land. Some consider the Cherokee War merely a minor extension of the troubles in Europe. The war was not a minor affair to Runs-To-Water who, when the time came, characterized the war much more simply, yet eloquently. *"The whites wish to take my home in the Blue Mountains. I will not let them. My Clan and my people were given this land by the Great Spirit Kanati, and I will not give it to the whites. My lodge is here; my Council House is here, and the Sacred Fire of the Cherokee is here. This I say to the Cherokee, I will fight for my home on this river in the Blue Mountains, and drive the whites away, or I will die."*

The precipitating cause of the war was an unimportant matter, as it so often is in the broad history of great conflict. When the British Governor of the Virginia colony had called on the Cherokee as allies against the French in the north, many Cherokee warriors left their villages and fought with the British. The French and Indian War was in full swing, and the Cherokee sided, naturally enough, with their British trading partners. These Cherokee rode to Virginia, and were then told to leave their horses and continue to the battle on foot as did the British troops. However, when they returned from helping the British win the battle, the guards at the fort refused to return the horses! Instead they fired on these Cherokee, killing nineteen warriors—since they believed they were at war with all Indians! In disgust, these warriors returned home, steeling horses from white farms along the way.

Moreover, the blood oath of the Cherokee required a life for a life, and these warriors were duty bound to take nineteen lives from the clans among the whites, the same number as their brother warriors who had been slain. Now various Christian missionaries in the mountains had already informed the Cherokee that all whites belonged to one clan, so these warriors were free to exact retribution and thereby re-establish balance by killing any whites they happened to find. In their return home, they killed exactly nineteen white settlers, all of whom were innocent in the earlier murder of the Cherokee. Most of these unfortunate settlers were merely farming along the Yadkin River in the North Carolina colony. In the Cherokee mind, this settled the matter, but the British saw this as the killing of innocent civilians. There was anger and resentment on both sides, such as always seems to result when people do not seek to truly understand each other.

In view of these recent killings in the North Carolina colony, the Royal Governor of the South Carolina colony did not see it as his place to be understanding as to why the horses had been stolen and white settlers had been killed. Thus, in 1759, in yet another effort to keep the peace a delegation of Cherokee leaders, including the venerable old War Chief Oconostota, and Saloue, the Peace Chief of Estatoe along the Tugaloo, traveled south towards Charles Town to treat again with the Whites. Instead of meeting these Cherokee openly and hearing their complaints, the Governor of the South Carolina colony amassed his army and rode to meet them. Once met, the Governor showed no desire at all to be diplomatic with the Cherokee leaders, or even to let them speak. He was fed up with the raids on outlying farms and wanted an end to the problem. Thus, before the war even began, a number of chiefs who thought they were traveling south to keep the peace were instead captured, returned north to Cherokee country, and placed under guard as hostages in Fort Prince George along the Keowee River.

In order to defuse the situation without a pitched battle, the governor did allow some of the chiefs including Oconostota, the War Chief who had lead the Cherokee at the Battle of Taliwa, to leave, to argue for peace among the Cherokee. However, when these Chiefs departed, they were in no mood for peace. They talked with the Cherokee, explaining what had happened, and enraged Cherokee warriors surrounded both Fort Prince George and Fort Loudoun, in the Tennessee country. They then began killing white soldiers whenever a white face showed above the parapets.

In a matter of days, the commander of Fort Prince George, Colonel Coytmore, was killed as were many others, and command of the Garrison fell to Alexander Miln. The British soldiers inside, angered at the death of their commander, swore to kill every hostage inside their walls. Miln tried, ineffectively, to prevent the slaughter. Still, in one fit of anger, these ill-disciplined soldiers killed the entire group of remaining hostages—thus did 22 Cherokee leaders die while held hostage by the whites inside of Fort Prince George. This sealed the fate of the entire frontier; no more peace was possible and The Cherokee War had begun.

The Cherokee went into council and many argued for joining the French. Lantagnac, a Long Talker from the middle Cherokee towns, gave an impassioned plea for war against the British colonies. Seizing a war hatchet he shouted, *"Who is there that will take this hatchet for the King of France? Let him come forth!"*

Many Cherokee shouted their support. Saloue, the War Chief of Estatoe along the Tugaloo River, shouted the loudest, *"I will take it! The spirits of our dead warriors call! He is less than an old woman who will not answer them."*

His friend and comrade in arms, Runs-To-Water stood, and took the hatchet and shouted his solemn vow. *"This I say to the Cherokee, I will fight for my home on this river in the Blue Mountains, and drive the whites away, or I will die."*

War erupted all along the frontier, with the warriors of the lower towns of the Cherokee leading the carnage. The guns of Fort Prince George fired directly into the Cherokee village of Keowee, destroying forever, the town. The Cherokee kept up their siege of the fort, and killed many white settlers—as far south as Augusta—who were caught alone in their cabins and their fields. Others fled to the safety of Charles Town or Savannah. Within two months blood flowed in a swath from the settlements at Keowee through Georgia and into what would later become Tennessee. The new Governor of the South Carolina colony summed up the carnage as he understood it, in an impassioned speech before the provincial council in Charles Town. *"Twenty-two killed, two scalped but yet alive, and the entire frontier terrorized!"*

The Cherokee siege of Fort Loudoun in February of 1760 trapped the entire British garrison inside. Thousands of Cherokee warriors took shots at the fort from the surrounding woods, and it was clear that the garrison would starve, in time. Thus, in the late Spring of 1760, a large British force, 1500 men under Col. Montgomery, arrived in Cherokee Country intending to relieve the siege of each fort. The Cherokee surrounding Fort Prince George near Keowee melted into the mountains, and thus, Montgomery found himself with nothing to do there. He moved forward towards Fort Loudoun, and destroyed many of the Cherokee towns along his path. Remaining Cherokee cabins at Keowee were reduced to nothing, thus did the Cherokee loose the home of the famed Kingfisher.

Much to the surprise of Runs-To-Water, the village of Tugaloo was ignored by Montgomery in this raid; it was considered too far south of the advancing column. However, the village of Estatoe—Runs-To-Water's home town only four miles up the Tugaloo river, was laid waste by Montgomery's men. Amid this carnage, the mother of Runs-To-Water–the old woman Nalyeena, was killed by a British musket. She was dead before the British scalped her. Her thinning hair was later turned in at Fort Prince George in exchange for two British sovereigns—the standard fee for killing an Indian.

Next, the British moved toward the more numerous Cherokee towns to the north as that was a more direct route to Fort Loudoun. This mass of men destroyed villages and patches of selu as they went. The butchery shown by this force is unsurpassed in eighteenth century history. Captured Cherokee, if not slaughtered on the battlefield or in the Cherokee towns, were often tortured. Cherokee women and children, if they did not flee into the Blue Mountains, were gunned down in their cabins. No one was spared, and scalping was rampant on both sides.

However, before Montgomery could reach Fort Loudoun, old Oconostota, the experienced War Chief, laid a clever trap along a narrow portion of the trail. With Runs-To-Water and many other warriors from the lower Cherokee towns in his force, the Cherokee hid in ambush on the steep hillsides along a creek. The narrow creek-side path which the British force followed curved back on itself below the Indian warriors' position, and on that battlefield, carefully chosen by the wise War Chief, Montgomery could not bring his entire force to bear. In contrast the Cherokee simply had to shoot into the British forces down-hill. It was a massacre. In less than three minutes, the Cherokee had used their Kentucky rifles with deadly resolve; they had killed a hundred men from the front ranks of the British column and wounded many more. Fortunately for the British, the limited powder and shot of the Cherokee forced them to retire, and most of Montgomery's column was spared. Most of those men never even saw a Cherokee warrior during this fight.

By then Montgomery and his British forces had had enough; he turned back toward Fort Prince George, where he immediately proclaimed a great victory for the British. He pointed out that his orders were to invade Cherokee country. Thus, rather than admit he had suffered a defeat at the hands of the Cherokee and failed to relieve Fort Loudoun, he argued that, in fact he had accomplished his mission. Fort Prince George was now safe, and his force had entered Cherokee country and destroyed several villages along the little Tennessee River, just as his orders specified. After a brief stay at Fort Prince George, he retired to Charles Town, and disembarked with his force to the New England colonies.

Meanwhile, with no relief in sight, and abandoned by the British column under Montgomery, the commander of Fort Loudoun determined that his men could no longer hold out without food. Thus, in August of 1760, he asked for terms from the Cherokee leaders. Much to his surprise, the Cherokee, lead yet again by Oconostota, demanded only that the garrison leave the fort, and abandon to the Cherokee any powder, guns, and ammunition that still lay in the storehouses. The Cherokee even let the British infantry keep their own rifles. The British commander, in a move too crafty for his own good, considered burning in secret some of the garrison's powder and spiking the cannon on the evening before retiring from the fort. However his officers dissuaded him. Thus, when they took the fort, the Cherokee came into possession of 12 cannon, a thousand pounds of powder and shot, and eighty rifles.

The next day, proudly flying the British flag, the British regiment marched in good order out of Fort Loudoun towards Fort Prince George, some 60 miles distant. However, within a few moments, the Cherokee fell savagely upon the retreating column, in spite of the assurances of safe conduct. Their Blood Oath and their sense of the necessity of balance demanded it. The Cherokee killed 22 men in the fight—exactly the same number as the number of Cherokee hostages killed earlier that year at Fort Prince George. They took the remaining members of the column prisoner.

Of course, Runs-To-Water and his many warriors from Tugaloo Town had fought in these struggles, and had been in on the carnage when the British column had been attacked. However, the Cherokee had restored balance, and thus, after the defeat and capture of the garrison from Fort Loudoun, the Cherokee calmly returned to their farms and villages, where they encamped for the winter of 1760. Many began the hunting that would sustain them through the next year. In their view, the war was over, and that conclusion seemed even more reasonable when they learned that the overall struggle between the British and French had come to a conclusion as well. A British force had ended French domination of Canada, and thus, at long last peace seemed to be coming to the Tugaloo River Valley.

Destruction Comes To Tugaloo Town

Perhaps history at that moment could have taken a different turn—a turn which would have allowed the Cherokee to survive for another generation or two in their peaceful towns in the lower Blue Ridge Mountains along the Tugaloo River. Perhaps Runs-To-Water and his children could have lived out their entire lives peacefully along the stream where he had killed his first bear. However, history was not destined to be so kind. The British general in charge of the all British forces in the colonies, General Ambrose Jenkins, didn't need his massive army anymore, since the French were already defeated. Still, he hated not to put such a resource to use for his own personal glorification.

When he learned the outcome of the action at Fort Loudoun, he expressed outrage that a group of "savages" had managed to dislodge a British outpost. This represented a black mark on his record, which he could not tolerate. He stated, *"I must own I am ashamed, for I believe it is the first instance of His Majesty's troops having yielded to the Indians."* Therefore, on the whim of a British officer's inflated pride, the Cherokee War was to continue for another year, and neither Tugaloo Town nor Runs-To-Water would survive.

Colonel Andrew Williamson, a former subordinate of Colonel Montgomery, was ordered to take another army of 2000 men and invade Cherokee Country once again, in 1761. This was, by British thinking, necessary in order to wipe out the disgrace of the Cherokee victory the previous year.

Strangely enough, the Toothless White Man—the same James Sharpe that had always run the trading post for Tugaloo Town, was the first to know that the British were coming. By 1761, he'd taken a second Cherokee woman as his wife, his first wife having died some 10 years previously. By marrying into the tribe, he'd managed to stay in his trading post for the entire duration of the Cherokee War. While other traders who were less well liked by the Cherokee had been killed, scalped, or both, the Toothless White Man had merely loaded his numerous guns and stayed out of sight inside his cabin when the warriors were up in arms. After they marched out to this or that battle, he continued to trade in cloth and deerskins with the locals. He made a point during the war of having no gunpowder or shot to trade to the Cherokee.

Sharpe was an interesting character, surprising in many ways. While dental hygiene was not his strong suite, he had acquired along the way the rudiments of education. He knew his sums, and he'd written letters for traders who came by from time to time. Much of what we now know of the local history of the Tugaloo Valley during those years comes from his grammatically incorrect scribblings, or those of his son. More importantly, he received a newspaper periodically from Savannah by way of the flatboats that routinely made their way upriver from Augusta with cloth for his shop. They then returned with various letters, and loaded to the gunnels with deerskins. He thus, knew of Williamson's march and mission into Cherokee country shortly after it began—literally having read about it in the Savannah paper.

They came in the Green Corn Month, just as the Cherokee were preparing for the Green Corn Festival. Young warriors had been sent to the lower Cherokee towns to establish which Chunkee teams would play in which towns, and almost all of the warriors from the lower towns were at home in their own villages—thus the mighty army of the Cherokee was dispersed throughout the lower Blue Ridge. When several of the younger warriors returned from the recently burned Keowee Village with tales of yet another army of whites coming, Runs-To-Water did not believe it. He thought that the war was long over, since the affair at Fort Loudoun had been finished. Further, neither he nor his warriors from Tugaloo had raided any white settlements in well over a year, nor had they given trouble to Sharpe, or Bryan Ward or other whites who had wandered into the area and settled near their town. Still, during the following two days, the reports continued to come in of a "long march" of soldiers coming their way. He determined that when the soldiers arrived, he would greet them as guests, offer them tobacco, and treat with them by the sacred fire in the council house. His greatest hope was for peace in the Tugaloo River Valley. He did not understand that the mission of the British was not peace, but rather punishment.

The attack came at dawn, from a brace of light cannon that Colonel Williamson had mounted on the hills to the east above the Tugaloo Council House. The British column had moved into position much faster than anyone had anticipated, and even with the rumors of a British army on the move, the Cherokee of the lower towns were still dispersed and totally unprepared. The first cannon salvo rudely awoke the 400 Cherokee in Tugaloo Town on the morning of June 12, 1761, and those first several shots destroyed for all time the Tugaloo Council House, and the sacred fire within. That building was the largest in the town and was thus the logical aim-point for Williamson's artillery officer. Further, with so many Cherokee living in outlying cabins at this point rather than in the traditional Cherokee lodges, the town had no protective wall. Moreover, the cabins were scattered rather haphazardly for over a mile along the river. Each one, in turn, received attention from Williamson's brace of cannon.

While Runs-To-Water and the other warriors gathered and returned fire toward the enemy in the hills to the east, the Cherokee woman and children attempted escape across the Tugaloo River to the west, following Toccoa Creek into the heart of Owl Swamp. Here they would wait for the conclusion of the battle. The wife of Runs-To-Water, thus escaped with three toonalis fathered by Runs-To-Water in recent years, along with 248 other Cherokee.

Runs-To-Water and his warriors initially took whatever cover they could find and began to return fire upon the 2000 infantry on the slope above. Thus did 187 brave Cherokee warriors, who were totally unprepared for battle, turn to meet a much larger force of veteran British troops. Still these warriors were defending their town, and each had been tested in battle. Further, they had the hope that warriors from the nearby towns would come quickly to the sound of the guns, and join in the unexpected fight.

Only seconds after the first cannon fire, many warriors had grabbed their rifles and powder horns, and were returning concentrated rifle fire in defense of the town. Their Kentucky rifles were much more accurate than the smooth bore muskets of the British troops in the hills to the East; the range of the Kentucky rifle was also much superior. It is interesting to note that in this battle, as in much of the Cherokee War, the supposedly modern British army took to the field with

The Battle Of Tugaloo Town

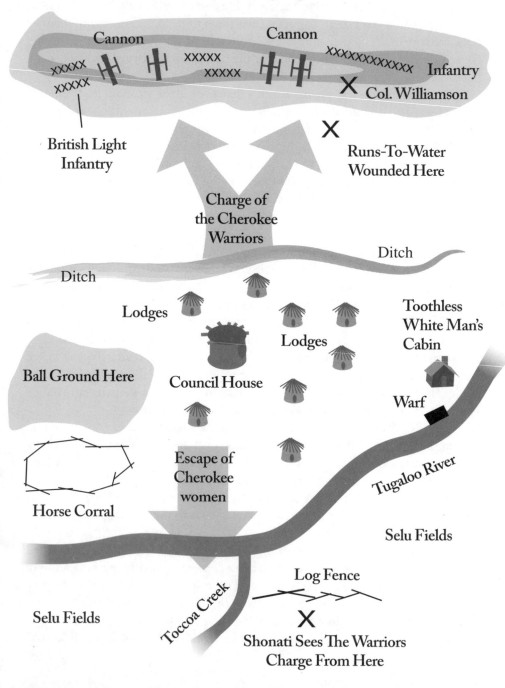

Eastern Hills Overlooking Tugaloo Town

Cannon

Cannon

xxxxx

xxxxx

xxxxx

xxxxxxxxxxxxx
Infantry

xxxxx

xxxxx

X
Col. Williamson

British Light
Infantry

X
Runs-To-Water
Wounded Here

Charge of
the Cherokee
Warriors

Ditch

Ditch

Lodges

Lodges

Toothless
White Man's
Cabin

Ball Ground Here

Council House

Warf

Horse Corral

Escape of
Cherokee
women

Tugaloo River

Selu Fields

Selu Fields

Log Fence

Toccoa Creek

X
Shonati Sees The Warriors
Charge From Here

inferior muskets while their supposedly savage enemy employed one of the finest firearms of the period. The Cherokee, skilled in hunting with their highly accurate rifles, could pick off British soldiers at 100 or even 200 yards, whereas the British had to depend on concentrated musket fire at much closer ranges.

However, the disproportionate numbers on each side precluded any possibility of Cherokee victory, and Runs-To-Water realized that as soon as he saw 2000 muskets in enfilade fire on the hills above the town. The British had the high ground overlooking the town, and, with the rate of fire from so many more soldiers, the battle was so lopsided that the Cherokee never stood a chance.

Runs-To-Water, never having been elected a War Chief, nevertheless fell into the role of command of the Cherokee—the War Chief had been killed only minutes after the battle was joined when several musket balls penetrated his chest and stomach. The remaining Cherokee warriors lay in a ditch, really only a small depression in the ground to the East of the River. This ditch nevertheless afforded them some cover from the deadly, massed musket fire from the hills above. As Runs-To-Water considered the options, it quickly became apparent that he could no longer control the anger of his warriors; many wanted to take the battle to the enemy on the hill, and fight it out hand to hand. Many had no rifles at all, but wanted to charge forward with only their war hatchets and knives.

The young warrior Chucha, who had fought beside him at Taliwa, was by his side again, quickly loading his rifle and firing. Like many he was hungry for white blood and argued that they should charge the enemy and drive him away from the cannon on the hilltop. Runs-To-Water considered that plan foolish, and stated so plainly to all those warriors who would listen. Few did. Chucha argued the opposite, that such a charge would allow many more warriors to fight in the battle, since many only had weapons for hand-to-hand fighting. Such a charge would also shame the British and possibly even force a withdrawal. While Runs-To-Water was known as a great Chief, he was still the Peace Chief, and thus could not order these warriors to do anything, in particular he could not order a retreat from this battle.

A decision was quickly reached among the younger warriors. While the older warriors would return covering fire, the younger warriors would load their rifles or take up their war hatchets, arrows, and knives. At the signal of Chucha's war cry, they would charge up the hill and drive the British away from the deadly cannon. As the warriors built up their courage by sounding their war cries and loading their weapons, Runs-To-Water remained silent. He was sure that this plan was suicide, but at least it had the effect of buying time for the escape of the women and children across the river. Perhaps it was the will of Kanati.

The charge of these Cherokee into the face of the British guns on that day made the now famed charge of the Light Brigade of Great Britain pale in comparison. These Cherokee knew what scattered shot from cannon and concentrated musket fire could do, but they valiantly charged into the teeth of the British cannon. They had already seen their townspeople die on this morning, and the blood oath demanded killing as many of the enemy on the hill above the town as possible. They thus charged into the guns, with two thoughts—to save their families and kill their enemy.

At the cry of Chucha, a mighty war cry erupted from over 100 Cherokee warriors all along the ditch. They arose in mass, and charged up the hill to the East of Tugaloo Town. Swift and mighty they ran, shoulder to shoulder, thus drawing strength from each other. Chucha was surprised on this run; for after he fired his rifle, he paused briefly to reload and then he saw the mighty Runs-To-Water—a Peace Chief who was supposed to stay in the ditch and provide covering fire, sweep past him charging bravely up the hill. The powerful bear tattoo on his chest seemed to come alive and breathe fire, and a mighty war cry tore from the warrior's throat. As the morning sun rising over the Eastern hills framed his powerful scarred body in the morning light—he looked like a terrible God bent on retribution as he ran up that hill to save his home and his family.

At just that moment, across the river, crouched behind a log fence with her three toonalis in tow, Shonati looked back at the battle scene. She saw the morning sun glisten off the forest of musket barrels on the eastern hill, and she saw 100 brave warriors charging forward to challenge over 2000 of the enemy. Right in the middle she saw the massive shoulders of her husband, his rifle before him, his topknot of hair flying behind. Before she even realized it, she stood up, exposing herself and pointed to the battle. She shouted to her children, *"Look there on the mountain. See how mighty are the warriors of the Cherokee! Look now and see your father die; for he is a great Cherokee warrior!"*

These words would enter the folklore of the Cherokee for all time. This bravery would be spoken of by the old men at sacred council fires that eventually stretched half way across the continent, along with many other stories of Runs-To-Water. These words would be spoken reverently for generations, for such stories of greatness define the Cherokee People.

The British were even more shocked by this unexpected charge, and for a few seconds the musket fire totally stopped. Colonel Williamson heard the guns go silent as he heard the terrible war cry. He looked up from his maps and spotted a massive Cherokee warrior with a bear tattoo on his chest running directly towards him, along with scores of others just a few paces behind. From his perspective, he could also see many of the Cherokee escape across the river. One woman even stood up, and seemed to point directly at him. Meanwhile these brave Cherokee charged directly into his guns, thus buying time for the women and children to flee. Even before he realized he was speaking, he was heard to remark *"My God! I have never before seen such bravery, especially in the savage!"*

After a few seconds, several British commanders ordered their companies to fix bayonets; these inexperienced commanders expected a hand to hand fight within the minute, and this order took 250 British soldiers out of the action for a critical ten to fifteen seconds, as their men played with their clumsy bayonets. However, the veteran commanders knew there was no need for this maneuver; for over 1500 men were still massed on the eastern hills, their muskets loaded. The final battle orders came from Colonel Williamson when the Cherokee were a mere 40 yards distant. At that moment in the relative silence, all the British on the hill heard his shout: *"Pick your target! Aim at the savage directly before you! FIRE!"*

The carnage was just as one would expect. No Cherokee warrior made it any further up the hill, and nearly 40 died in one fearsome second. Four of the British regulars from the Scottish Highlanders Brigade of Scotland had aimed at the filthy looking savage directly in front of them—the big one with a nasty scar on his left cheek and a massive bear painted on his chest. Three musket balls found the tattoo, and one dropped lower into the abdomen of the savage—each individual wound was mortal. One of the Highlanders named Archibald Carmichel was heard to shout—*"I got the biggest of 'um all. And a mean son-of-a-bitch he was too!"*

As Chucha stood again to fire, he caught a musket ball in the side of his head, which removed a part of his lower jaw and eliminated several teeth, surprisingly leaving him both breathing and conscious. He saw the mighty Runs-To-Water fall just up the hill, so after the terrible musket fire, in the reloading pause, he stood again, grabbed Runs-To-Water by the arm and began to drag him back down to the relative safety of the ditch.

The few Cherokee remaining there determined that there was no further point in fighting. Only twenty warriors remained unimpaired, and mostly they were the older ones who had remained in the ditch to cover the charge. Only 35 or so warriors had been able to come back down the mountain after the deadly fire. With their youthful bile spent in this foolish carnage, even the most rabid of the angry young warriors were willing now to listen to the wisdom of their Peace Chief.

As he breathed his own blood, with more blood seeping from four wounds as well as his mouth and nose, Runs-To-Water gave his last instruction to his people. *"Take your weapons, and run to the river. The river is a weapon, and it will help you escape."* He then lost consciousness.

The British did not fire on the retreating warriors. Instead they turned their cannon on the various cabins in the Tugaloo Valley, where they destroyed everything. Brigades were sent down the hill to burn the patches of corn, and the horses that were still in the various corrals were confiscated. After 30 minutes, an old white man with shoulder length hair, smelly and toothless, came up the hill asking to speak to the commander. John Sharpe explained that he was a trader, and asked that the cabin where he lived with his Cherokee woman be spared. Colonel Williamson readily agreed, and then had this man Sharpe identify some of the bodies of the Cherokee that still lay about the battlefield. Sharpe knew almost all of these warriors—for the battle had not lasted long enough for warriors from other towns to arrive, and Sharpe had traded with many of these men for over 20 years.

The Colonel was destined to leave this battlefield disappointed however; when he asked to see the body of the great Chief Wauhatchie, Old Man Sharpe said simply, *"You mean Runs-To-Water? He ain't here."*

Still many others were there, and, in this destruction of Tugaloo Town, over 140 Cherokee lost their lives. The old conjuror, Swimmer, was among the dead— he should have left with the women, but that was not to be. His, and all of the other bodies of the Cherokee were burned in a communal pile just to the east of the remains of the council house, leaving only their ashes behind, to eventually wash into the beloved Tugaloo River.

After the destruction of Tugaloo Town, Williamson's army continued into the middle towns of the Cherokee, killing and burning for a number of months. Over fifteen Cherokee villages were destroyed, and some 1500 acres of corn were simply burned. Five thousand Cherokee took to the hills as a result of this onslaught, most were women and children who were ill prepared to meet the demands of the frontier life during the next winter without a home. Many would starve when the cold weather set in.

While Williamson relished his "victory," others wondered about the wisdom of the whole campaign. Did the British really need to "teach these savages a lesson?" One British irregular who participated in the destruction of Tugaloo Town was Lieutenant Francis Marion. This man was destined for fame in his own right, for in only a few years, he would become the bane of the British forces in the Americas. As the legendary "Swamp Fox," he would destroy many British units in militia actions during the coming Revolutionary War. At Tugaloo, he reflected on the devastation of the lower towns, and he wondered how history would see this series of battles. His thoughts have been preserved for history, in his personal papers.

"We proceeded to burn the Indian cabins. Some of the men seemed to enjoy this cruel work, laughing heartily at the flames, but to me it appeared a shocking sight. When it came to cutting down the fields of corn, I could scarcely refrain from tears. Why did we need to do this? I saw everywhere the footsteps of the little Indian children where they had lately played under the shade of their rustling corn. When we are gone, thought I, they will return and peeping through the weeds with tearful eyes, will mark the ghastly ruin where they had so often played. "Who did this?" they will ask their mothers, and the reply will be, "The white people did it—The Christians did it!"

Thus was Tugaloo Town destroyed forever. The council house was never to be rebuilt. Though some Cherokee families would try to return to this valley to farm during the next decade, the soul of the town was gone. The council house destroyed and the sacred fire—the heart of this proud Cherokee town—was put out forever.

The Burial of Runs-To-Water

Runs-To-Water was carried from the field on the shoulders of his friend and protégée, Chucha. Only once did the mighty warrior regain consciousness. Later that night, approximately a mile west of the battlefield, he stirred, and asked where he was. Chucha, though severely wounded himself, was able to mumble through his shattered jaw that he'd headed up the Toccoa Creek towards Owl Swamp. That is where the other members of the tribe were believed to be. Chucha had lain down to rest on the rump of a small hill by the creek, and because of his loss of blood he had fallen asleep. When he looked at Runs-To-Water again, he thought the old warrior had lost his mind—while severely wounded, with his very blood still seeping from his body, gurgling with every breath, the old man seemed to smile as tears streamed silently down his face. *"I know this hill,"* the old chief said. *"This brings balance to me."* He then asked, *"Did Shonati and the others escape?"*

Chucha replied. *"She escaped across the river with the women."* He noted the growing smile on the face of Runs-To-Water. Then he heard his Peace Chief speak once again.

"I wish I could have found peace for my people. Still it is good that some escaped. Yes, that is good. My toonalis will live to fight the whites on another day." Then the old warrior seemed to turn reflective. His breath was ragged now, and much blood came from his mouth. He was clearly dying, still he continued. *"I killed a bear once beside this creek, when I was but a toonali. I used a stone from the river."*

Chucha had heard this legend from the old men many times, but he'd never heard Runs-To-Water speak of it. Such bragging ways were not Cherokee, but now the old warrior was dying; it was only right that he speak of his victories in this life. It would put things in balance for the old man.

"The great Utani, the Longknife, helped to make me a warrior on that day, by this little stream. He made me break my blowgun for the spirit of the bear, and now the spirit of that bear lives on my chest." Runs-To-Water paused for a ragged breath, and then continued. *"Utani wanted to be buried by the creek to the north, he is covered with stones near Changee, by the creek where the Panther runs, but I shall be buried here. I fought many times here and this is where the Great Spirit Kanati spoke to me of my destiny. This water will hold my spirit until the Great Kanati takes me up. You will bury me on this hill, above this creek, and I will rest in these Blue Mountains forever."*

Within a minute of his final words, Runs-To-Water had breathed his last. As Chucha watched, the blood ceased to flow from his body, and his ragged breath stopped, while the tears for his people were still fresh on his scarred face. So it was done.

Chucha, though severely wounded, carried out what he thought would be his last duty as a Cherokee—he buried his Peace Chief on a small hill to the south of Toccoa Creek. As the only one present, and with his lower jaw shattered, he could not chant the death rituals, but he did bury the war hatchet of Runs-To-Water beside the warrior, along with one of his knives. He made certain that the nine bear claws, each representing a separate kill of this mighty chief, were removed from his topknot and placed on his breast. Then he gathered many stones from the creek to cover the body of the mighty Runs-To-Water, least the animals disturb the body. Many trips did he make to the creek, coming back with ever larger stones, building a burial mound four feet high that would last on the side of this hill for over 200 years. By the following morning the deed was done. He whispered a brief prayer for his fallen Peace Chief, as best he could with his shattered jaw, a prayer that has been lost to history, and then he fled toward the setting sun.

That is how we leave the Cherokee fields in Tugaloo Town, on the upper reaches of the Tugaloo River in the winter of 1761. While a few Cherokee remained in the area for another 50 years or so, the town itself was never rebuilt, nor would the ancient Council House ever see the sacred fire of the Cherokee again. Every cabin and Cherokee lodge within three miles of the council house was burned or destroyed by Williamson's cannon, their residents fled into the Blue Mountains. Only Sharpe's trading post was spared. The rich bottom lands along the river, once home to the selu fields of the village, were reclaimed by nature for over 15 years, and the next plough to part this fertile land was guided by white hands, or by black hands.

The remains of the ancient council house mound can be seen to this day. In fact, these ancient remains have been excavated several times over the years, most recently in 1957 just prior to the building of Lake Hartwell in Georgia, on the Tugaloo River. The council house mound is now an island in the middle of the lake that can easily be seen from Highway 123, east of Toccoa. Of course, at the death of Runs-To-Water both the highway and the lake were hundreds of years in the future.

Several days after the battle, much to the surprise of the retreating Cherokee, a severely wounded Chucha caught up with the band from Tugaloo Town, as they made their way toward the Cherokee villages of the west. Chucha would survive his wounds and live two more decades, with the new name of Anu-we-ai, which translated as "Half-Face." His wound thus became both his new name and his badge of honor among the Cherokee.

He eventually learned to mutter a guttural form of his language through his half-jaw, and he became a revered elder in the tribe. Over the decades living in the Blue Mountains far to the west, he told many tales of the mighty Chief Runs-To-

Water. He told of the many battles and of the death and burial of Runs-To-Water, a great Peace Chief who died with both tears for his people and joy for their escape in his heart. Half-Face attested that Runs-To-Water had finally found his balance in his death on the hill near Tugaloo Town. As Half-Face told these stories, several of the young toonalis who listened most attentively were the sons of the mighty chief. With other stories from Shonati, the legend of Runs-To-Water grew among the Cherokee.

Wauhatchie—Chief Runs-To-Water—lives today in the hearts of his people, and is remembered in history as a man who fought many battles and led his people bravely. Moreover, he is revered as a man who sought and found his balance within the joys and the terrors of his turbulent world. He lived a full life, a spiritual life, which is ultimately the only type of life worth living. He is known for his bravery and his leadership in his village beside his beloved Tugaloo River. He lived well until the Great Spirit Kanati called him up.

Would that we all could emulate the balance seen in the life of that great man. Ultimately, his life has provided a lesson to us all, and in thankful reverence we may wish him well. May his spirit rest peacefully on an unnamed hill beside the Tugaloo River that he so loved.

Chapter 3: The King's Mountain Men
1780 – Four Patriots Going To War

For one brief moment, just before the crack of the muskets and the deadly uphill charge, four men, each uniquely gifted, stood together; James Wyly, Ben (Early) Cleveland, Jessie Walton, and Robert Jarrett. None realized the significance of this meeting at the time; none realized they would each play a role in opening the frontier of the lower Blue Ridge and the Tugaloo River Valley. Moreover, none realized that each—in his own way, would lead his generation into the next level of civilization in the wild deserted frontier mountains.

In fact only rarely in the broad conflux of history do such men meet. While all were natural leaders, these men were not kings or presidents, not dictators, diplomats, or aristocrats in any sense of the term. All had arisen from less exalted stock. Most had backgrounds in European peasantry, all were frontiersmen, and while most of them could at least read, extensive education was not prevalent in this group. All of these men eventually acquired some wealth later in life, but none ever had a portrait made, as did other, more educated aristocrats of the day. Today, we do not even know what they looked like, except by descriptions in rare family correspondence.

They didn't know their position in history; they would have been surprised that history remembered them at all, but, to be honest, few of us would think ourselves important enough for historical notice. However, these men made history; each of these men would help settle the frontier of the lower Blue Ridge, and carve an existence out of the unforgiving mountains. During their youth, the Tugaloo River Valley was Cherokee Country, totally unsettled by whites, but by their death this frontier would be tamed, explored, and liberated from the Cherokee, and these men would lead the way in settlement. In fact, the entire track of the lower Blue Ridge, and thus much of the lower and mid-south of the North American continent would be open to white settlers by these men. They would tame a frontier, and ultimately create a nation in this American wilderness but they did not realize that at the time. They would not have believed that hundreds of years after the fact, their names would be remembered.

Among these men, James Wyly was, by far, the most capable. He was both accomplished leader and visionary. Moreover, he was the only one to keep a diary, and with his insightful concern for history, not to mention his irreverent wit, we are indebted to this man for much of our understanding of this bloody frontier in the late eighteenth and early nineteenth centuries. He was a man who, when called upon, could speak the language of common, uneducated men of this frontier (note his irreverent dialogues with his contemporary, Early Cleveland). In contrast, his education allowed him not only breath of understanding, but intellectual sophistication which is reflected in his written thoughts. His writings make clear that he never anticipated that these thoughts would be dissected by history. Rather, his diary revealed his inner reflections—his musings, his plans and his fears. While these are clearly reflective of the prejudices and bigotry of his day, these thoughts still provide a rich source for us today and, thankfully, his diary and some of his other papers survived. Thus, we do have some personal insight into who these men were and how they, unknowingly, shaped history.

They came together by happenstance at the foot of King's Mountain, these four men who would mean so much to the Tugaloo River Valley and the lower Blue Ridge. They met briefly on the early afternoon on the day of the desperate, now-famous battle that changed the course of the American Revolution. The battle occurred at a mountain just 75 miles east of the Tugaloo River, and the men who would shape the future of the Tugaloo—Cleveland, Wyly, Jarrett, and Walton—were all there. Wyly's diary, written only a few years after the battle, sums up the result of that conflict, as well and any subsequent history that has yet been printed (Note his reflective style, his obvious good manners and breeding, his wit, and his amazing economy with words).

"Though it is most ungentlemanly to say, we clearly whipped their arse! Our forces, this ragtag collection of near-do-wells, drunks, mountain settlers and poor white crackers fought the King's men to a standstill, and then eliminated them as a fighting force. Who would have thought, on the morn of that rainy October day (October 7, 1780) *that this collection of mountain hunters and trappers would send the British forces in the Southern colonies reeling. Some say old Cornwallis actually shat his breeches, visibly shaken by news that his entire left flank had been wiped out at the King's Mountain.*

As a result of our victory at King's Mountain, Cornwallis abandoned his plans to move up through the Carolinas. His left flank for that move northward was gone, and the sheer viciousness of our Patriots in the battle certainly caused him pause. He changed his plans for an early confrontation with the other Patriot army led by our greatest General, the Honorable George Washington. Moreover, after our Patriot victory, any support for dammed Tories in the colonies dried up completely. The Brits found that without this support, they could not do battle at such a distance from their base at Charles Town. We subsequently discovered that this Patriot victory caused such an upheaval in popular opinion in Great Britain that some have, of late, suggested that this battle ultimately set up Washington's victory at Yorktown only 12 months later. Yes, we certainly made our mark at the King's Mountain. May God bless those cussing, cursed, unwashed men—the stink, waste and refuse of the distant mountain frontier; for these fought so valiantly that on that day they changed the history of our nation—a history that few of them could foretell, and fewer still could read. Our freedom was both forged and glorified in their sacrifice, sanctified in the blood of these brave men of the Blue Ridge. I am, and will always be, proud to count myself among them!"

Reflections on the Late Revolution
James Wyly's diary, 1782

Today at the crest of King's Mountain, a monument stands. In tribute to these men, it reads simply: *"On this spot, in October of 1780, the American Revolution was won."*

Of course that realization was in the distant future in October of 1780. On the eve of the battle, both Jessie Walton and Ben (Early) Cleveland were mature, seasoned militia leaders of some years. Much blood was on their hands, most of it Cherokee blood. These were the two who had, inadvertently, witnessed a Creek raid on Tugaloo Town some years before, during an extended hunt for deer skins. Each had fought the Cherokee and the Creek many times. Each knew and understood war.

In contrast, Robert Jarrett was much younger; merely a boy of 16. He was serving as the orderly for one of the commanders, as well as a "runner" for the rough, ill-defined Patriot leadership in the anticipated battle. He had been chosen for that role by Early Cleveland only several days prior to the battle. Early thought the boy too puny for a real fight, and he knew that Jarrett had never faced battle with Indians, as had almost all of his other men. Still, the boy could run like the wind, so "runner" was a natural assignment for him.

The job of "runner" involved running orders to commanders at different locations on the field. In other, more seasoned armies of the day, flag corps could be counted on for that duty, but the veteran Indian fighters who made up the Patriot force at King's Mountain—while experienced fighters—had little need for such communications; for most conflicts with the Indians were brief affairs, rarely involving large forces, or extended time-frames. In conflicts involving 25, 50, or 100 fighters on a side, and generally lasting less than 15 minutes, no battlefield communications were needed beyond a shouted order, and so the men comprising this Patriot force had never trained a flag corps. However, this battle promised to be much larger, so with no trained flag corps, this Patriot force would need runners. Early figured that the boy Jarrett, this puny upstart from Pendleton Court

House in South Carolina, could at least manage that.

Wyly, our chronicler, was still in his teens like Jarrett, though Wyly did have some formal education. Further, James Wyly was a brilliant man, a reflective man, who was possessed of a vision for the Blue Mountains; he often considered what *could* happen—rather than merely what had happened—in the development of the American frontier, and his papers demonstrate such reflection.

"I have often considered the future of these desolate hills, where the land is so rich and begging for the plough of civilized man. When one considers the continuing arrival of new foreigners in our coastal cities, and every man among them hungry for land, one can only conclude that these men, with families in tow, will soon come to this wild frontier. Should a man of means provide the toll roads, bridges, taverns, and farm implements needed here, if one had such capital, he would do quite well for himself."
James Wyly's diary; 1785

Wyly was that rarest of men—both a dreamer and a doer; a visionary and a practical, hard-nosed leader. The demands of every frontier—the Appalachian frontier in the late 1700s, the South African frontier a century later, or the frontier in outer-space in the 1960s—calls forth to both visionaries and accomplished practical men. While these four leaders on King's Mountain on that fateful day were to become influential leaders because of their good judgment and practical common sense, James Wyly was so much more. He was a man who could see not only the harsh demands of a hard land, but could also envision things as they *might one day be*. He would be the first white man in history to see that the location of Tugaloo Town would be the critical juncture for both transportation and settlement of the lower Blue Ridge—with both roads and rivers converging there—and he would profit well from that insight. He would live through much of the first century of American history, passing away well into his nineties, remaining an influential leader for most of those years. More so than the other Kings Mountain Men, this man would define development along the Blue Ridge frontier. Moreover, his diary catalogues his thoughts and plans such that we can see his very visions. There is no richer document of these times than the diary and papers left by Wyly to posterity, and I shall use them liberally here for obvious reasons, not the least of which is, these papers are a joy to read!

The Tugaloo River Valley

The Battle of Kings Mountain did not directly impact the Tugaloo River Valley as it was known by Runs-To-Water. In fact, little had transpired there in the 20 years since the death of Runs-To-Water, and the destruction of Tugaloo Town in 1761. Most of the Cherokee had left the area, and only a few white frontiersmen continued to visit the Tugaloo River Valley in the years after the Cherokee War ended. Moreover, only sporadic settlement took place. Most of the settlers in the recent waves of new immigrants from the northern coastal cities of New York or Philadelphia could now find free land all along the eastern slope of the Blue Ridge in states to the North, and many settled on that eastern slope in North Carolina or Virginia. In fact, several men—including Thomas Cash and Early Cleveland—who would play a major role in Tugaloo River history in the near future, resided at that time in Surrey County, North Carolina, having come down the Great Philadelphia Wagon Road only far enough to cash in on the free land in upstate Carolina during the 1760s.

Meanwhile, the settlements in the lower reaches of the Georgia Colony continued to grow, and white settlers from Savannah and Augusta continued to probe the Tugaloo area in hunting parties. At the frightening news that the Revolutionary War had begun in the north in the autumn of 1776, several new leaders grew from among the hearty frontiersman in these former colonies. Colonel Elijah Clarke, though bombastic and illiterate, was soon to become the leader of the Patriot forces in the upper reaches of the Georgia Colony. He never missed an opportunity to promote himself or to lose a battle, but he still managed to do some good towards both settling the high country of Georgia on the lower southern slopes of the Blue Ridge, as well as leading Patriots forces in the Revolution. As a military leader, he left much to be desired; like most of the other Patriot leaders in that war, George Washington among them, Clarke managed to loose more battles than he won. Still, his contributions are notable, including developing a Georgia Company of militia which proved to be an effective fighting force in the Revolutionary War. He thus provided another Patriot force with which the leaders of the British forces had to contend, and this kept the British wary of their distant mountain settlements. Some British commanders referred to the frontier along the Blue Ridge as their "Mountain flank" since, in moves northward from the ports at Savannah and Charleston, the various British armies always confronted the formidable Blue Ridge and the rag-tag settlers of those hills on their left flank.

In contrast to Clarke, the Tennessean John Sevier was an experienced Indian fighter and a natural leader. As both a frontiersman and a gentlemen with considerable education, he was known to detest "savages." While the lower crest of the Blue Ridge was not yet opened, whites had forced their way through the Cumberland Gap in the north, and many were settling in Cherokee hunting grounds to the north of the Great Smokies and the Blue Ridge Mountains, along the Nolichucky, the Holston, and the French Broad Rivers, in areas that would become Tennessee and Kentucky. Sevier lead these settlements, and was named head of the Tennessee Militia in 1779, because of this unusual combination of credentials, both education and frontier skills. In the late 1700s education and frontier skills were not typically compatible. Thus he led many of the Patriots from the Tennessee settlements in various militia campaigns during the war, including the Battle of King's Mountain. Sevier, called "Nolichucky Jack" by his militiamen— he had settled on that river—would lead these forces in battles against both the British and their allies, the Cherokee. This seasoned militiaman and Indian fighter was eventually to become the first Governor of the state of Tennessee.

By the late 1770s, both Elijah Clarke and Nolichucky Jack Sevier had a history of fighting the Cherokee, the Creek, the Catawba, or any other Indians who got in their way. Each had carved a living out of the frontier, each was to become a leader in the American Revolution, and each would lead brigades up the slopes of King's Mountain in October of 1780.

Meanwhile at the Tugaloo River, some few Cherokee families had moved back into cabins along the river to farm a few of the old Indian fields. Wyly's diary portrays a desolate land populated by only a few savages and somewhat fewer whites, during those years from 1760 until the 1780s.

"The area in which so many veterans of the late Revolution were to take interest seems to have been a rough, unsettled river basin, in which only a few savages, most well into their drink, abided. One toothless reprobate—Sharpe is his name—peddles a homebrew whiskey to these Cherokee. That keeps many quite passive and thus, in line, I should think. However, the rich land once farmed by the Cherokee is there aplenty for the taking, should one wish to move so far from one's peers. The Creek occasionally attack, considering these parts one of their distant hunting grounds, and the rambunctious nature of the few white men—most like the Cherokee well into their cups—lent a certain desperation to this bloody and distant frontier. I had previously considered this area as one option for me after the Revolution, but I could not then have decided to dare to undertake such a settlement alone."

James R. Wyly's Diary (1788).

One man living in the Tugaloo Valley during these years is critical to our story. Chucha, the Cherokee who buried Runs-To-Water, had a son named Ekaia. Ekaia had missed the battle for Tugaloo Town entirely during the struggle of 1761; he was literally away from home on a hunting trip.

The Cherokee term "Ekaia" is essentially untranslatable, and strictly speaking was not a name, even in the Cherokee tongue. Its various meanings include "Ghostlike," or "Spirit," "Disappearing" and "Reclusive in nature," and all of these meanings are appropriate for this unique Cherokee warrior. For this Cherokee hunter and scout had an amazing ability to "disappear" when hunting or scouting out the Patriots for his British paymasters. Thus did he earn his Cherokee name. At times he covered himself entirely with the loamy insect filled earth and merely lay down amid a carpet of earth and leaves. Amazingly, he could do so for uncounted hours, all the while feeling the insect rich earth of the lower mountains seemingly crawling all over his skin. In that living humus, he could lie still, never moving, until a deer or bear walked into his gun sights. Anyone who knows the living richness of the earth of the Blue Ridge, understands that to be a minor miracle. Ekaia, however, was spiritually connected to the rich earth during those times, just another living being, both in and of the Blue Mountains.

At other times Ekaia cut branches and climbed trees where he could make himself disappear entirely in the upper canopy of the thick forest of the Blue Mountains. In later wars, men would train incessantly to camouflage themselves in such positions, in order to prepare for battle. Ekaia seemed to be able to do this naturally; for this Ghost of the Cherokee, hiding was as easy as breathing. Thus did Ekaia become, in some sense, the world's first sniper.

Ekaia had been out hunting deerskins during the unexpected battle that destroyed Tugaloo Town in 1761. When he returned several weeks later, rather than heading west to catch up with the fleeing Cherokee, he merely traded his skins with the Toothless White Man—Sharpe—as he always did, while he listened to Sharpe tell about the battle. Then he calmly began to rebuild his family's lodge, assuming that his family would soon return to their village and their fields. In that assumption he was entirely wrong.

However, after only a couple of months, he saw the future much clearer than had his Half-Faced father. Ekaia believed that the whites would soon dominate the Cherokee, and he saw no reason to fight against the inevitable. Thus, he decided early that he would learn the ways of the whites. Sometime around 1765, he even adopted a white man's name—Thomas Prather—the later name being a bastardized version of "panther" and representing the rocky creek near his lodge. He then built, a somewhat larger log cabin a few miles closer to old Tugaloo Town rather than continue to live in his more traditional Cherokee lodge. Next, he replanted the family fields in the river basin. He would soon marry a half-breed daughter of John Sharpe—the Toothless White Man—and from that hybrid blood would come the beginnings of the large "Prather" family, a family of ill defined origin that soon "passed" for white in the Tugaloo River Valley.

Billy Sharpe, another half-breed result of the Toothless White Man's drunken entertainment with his second Cherokee wife, now ran the trading post, and struggled to turn it into a more respectable frontier store. John himself, totally toothless after living for some 69 years, finally expired one day in 1763, while sitting in his chair on the porch of the cabin. Nobody really missed him much, and few came to his funeral. After one evening of mourning, Billy buried him behind the cabin in an unmarked grave that, like the cabin itself, has long since been overgrown and lost to history.

With his only sister married off to Thomas Prather, Billy determined it was time to find a wife, and this promised to be a problem; for he was himself a half-breed, and while that mattered not a hoot on the rough frontier, it did matter in the coastal cities. In those days a half-Cherokee would find no willing women in the distant white cities of Savannah or Augusta. Billy had decided that he did not want a traditional Cherokee woman. First of all, none were available in the valley. More importantly, he had never lived as a traditional Cherokee himself. Thus, he was not sure that he would get along, had he found a Cherokee woman. The more he considered his unusual situation, the more he became interested in a white wife. After many weeks of consideration, he solved his problem in a straightforward and relatively unique way.

Trading on the fact that he looked more like his father than his Cherokee mother, he paddled down river the next Spring all the way to Savannah, where for a few deerskins he acquired the services of a very willing, and quite robust whore. She was a truly big woman, ungainly, and loud, who having not bathed in some time, cast a certain unpleasant aroma into any room she entered. Still, she had a pleasant face, and her smile was quite inspiring—particularly when she eyed the obviously valuable collection of deerskins brought to the market by the ignorant dark-skinned mountain man from up-river.

She was Scottish, with bright red hair, and greenish blue eyes, and had she had the opportunity she would have tipped the scale at slightly less than 200 pounds. She was also certain, one evening in April of 1764, that she'd made a smooth trade, giving her services for an evening to this ignorant backwoods trader in exchange for 200 deerskins. Deerskins, delivered to the docks of Savannah for shipment to London were worth a small fortune, and she was sure that this drunken mountain hick didn't realize what he had! The idiot obviously didn't know he could get other gals for less than one tenth that rate! So she silently counted her blessings, and told the smelly olive skinned man—Billy was the only name she'd heard him use—to order some grog, and prepare for the night of his life.

However, after ingesting an obscene amount of homemade liquor this rotund Scottish girl awoke the next morning and found herself hogtied and covered over, in the bottom of a flatboat along with the 200 skins, heading back upriver to Tugaloo Town. Billy sold the skins four days later when he passed through Augusta on the way back home. He didn't untie her until they were well past the last cabin owned by whites north of Augusta; what's more, he didn't even offer to give her any of the money he got for the skins!

Of course, by then, there was absolutely nothing she could do, other than acknowledge that this ignorant hunter had outsmarted her! The woman would be "convinced" to marry Billy after only several weeks hogtied to the bed and wallowing in her own feces, in his rough cabin along the banks of the distant Tugaloo River. After all, she could see no easy way to get back downstream. Within a year she had determined that it was indeed preferable to become the wife of a tavern owner on the frontier than to live as a whore on the docks in Savannah. In just a few short years, this woman—Sadie Sharpe—was to become quite a leader in the Tugaloo River Valley community. Within a few more years she would became a cornerstone of the Tugaloo Presbyterian Church, the first church made from sawed wood rather than logs, to go up along the Tugaloo River.

Bryan Ward, along with his Cherokee wife Nancy, remained on Ward's Creek; just off the Tugaloo River, grinding corn for the few white settlers in the area and the few Cherokee that remained. In a few short years, Nancy became tired of her husband's constant drinking, and one evening she slipped away to the Cherokee town in the north called Hiawassee. Bryan never saw his wife again and he subsequently faded from history, but not before leaving a covey of "Wards" in his wake in the Tugaloo River Valley. However, Nancy was to rejoin her family in the Deer Clan of the Cherokee, and would become famous as a "beloved woman" of the Cherokee tribe. She would live a long, influential life. Today, books are written about her, as the preeminent Cherokee Princess of her day, and even in her absence from the Tugaloo Valley itself, she continued to play a critical role in the settlement of the lower Blue Ridge. We shall hear much more of this remarkable woman later in our chronicle.

A couple of white families moved in down river within several miles of the Tugaloo Town site. Wyly details the progeny of one, Archibald Carmichael.

"Carmichael himself asserts that he fought the Cherokee with British forces in 1761 along the Tugaloo. By his claim, he fought with Williamson under Captain Theobold Grant during the battle that destroyed Tugaloo town, and had helped kill the largest Cherokee charging up that hill (if true, that would have been Runs-To-Water). *Within two years of the battle, he returned to this country with a pretty but, by all accounts, stupid German girl from Augusta and settled in by building a small cabin to the South of Ward's Creek; He never married and never paid for the land on which he settled; He merely settled on it and began to both farm and fornicate with great vigor. His progeny, those infernal Carmichael's would breed like the rabbits they killed so often for their stew pots, and within only 20 or 30 years, there were seemingly scores of them, and no one knew who was related to whom or in what way. Such is the trash and refuse of these mountains, and one can only implore true gentlemen to settle here and move civilization forward. For those here now, will take the cause of the white man nowhere!"*
James Wyly's diary, 1788

Thus did the first settlers, most of whom would have been unremembered by history, save for Wyly's diary, come to the Tugaloo. Still, it is quite clear that the upper Tugaloo River Valley was largely unsettled, and little of historical note took place here during those years from 1761 until 1784 or so. In those decades the future of this area and of the lower Blue Ridge, was formulated elsewhere.

A Wanderer Along the Tugaloo

One event should be noted from those years, and Wyly, ever the dutiful historian recorded the events long after they took place.

"One Billy Bartram traveled into the Tugaloo area in an effort to explore the regions to the north. He traveled without a guide, and seemingly did not know his way, or where he was going, other than to "Charge the Blue Mountains." Who would have believed at the time that much of our insight into those dark forbidding mountains would come from one unschooled in the frontier, not to mention one so frail? Having read through many of the papers of Mr. Bartram, I can personally attest that, while inclusive of many important insights, I found no devastatingly sharp mind in these works, no rapier wit here. This, of course, forces the question; Why? Why, indeed would the Almighty have chosen to reveal the secrets of the sacred Blue Mountains to someone whose mental faculty was, quite clearly, such a very blunt tool?"

James Wyly's diary (1798).

History has been kinder to Mr. Bartram than was Wyly. In 1775, Billy Bartram, one of the earliest and most famous of the uplands explorers, entered the valley with the express purpose of looking for plants. Bartram was the reclusive son of a Philadelphia aristocrat, who, for amusement hunted plants for medicinal purposes. He was the last person one would consider as a rugged frontiersman—small of stature, and neither robust or strong; indeed he had always been frail as a child. After having failed in several business ventures as a young man, Billy determined that if he could do nothing else, perhaps he could explore the frontier of the southern colonies for medicinal herbs, and at least add information to the growing science of botany if not adding a few British coins to his pocket. Thus did Billy travel south on a dilapidated coastal freighter, directly to Charles Town. There, he equipped himself for the frontier and departed for the lower Blue Ridge Mountains, determined to study the flora and fauna of the area.

As happenstance would have it, he departed Charles Town on April 22, 1775 moving toward the upcountry and thence into the Tugaloo River Valley. Only four days after his departure, a few rabble-rousers fired a musket shot at a desolate and relatively unimportant river crossing called Concord Bridge in the Massachusetts colony. That single rifle shot changed history; it was forever famed as the "Shot Heard Round the World." That single rifle shot, of course, began the American Revolution. Billy Bartram, however missed hearing about it at all. Further, as he was spending his time in the mountains, he managed to miss hearing news that a war had even begun for the next four years, as he happily roamed the highest peaks in the Great Smokies in blissful ignorance of world events.

In his move northwards, he stopped at various trading posts, including Fort Prince George in the South Carolina foothills, near the ruins of the Cherokee village of Keowee. Billy, as a naturalist, was forever stopping to look at plants and footprints of various animals, thus always seemed to be looking down at the ground rather than outward toward the dangers of the mountain frontier. Perhaps for that reason, he decided to seek a guide to lead him into the mountains. With that in mind, he also wandered into Sharpe's tavern near the Tugaloo River.

Sharpe and an old Cherokee were seated on two stools near the fireplace, and when Billy entered, Sharpe welcomed him warmly—as he did most of his customers. Without looking up, Sharpe shouted, *"Drinks are a ha'penny, and you pour your own. I'm too damn old to get up every time some bastard walks in here."* With that welcoming greeting Sharpe turned back to the fire.

Billy merely said, *"Thanks,"* and walked across the packed dirt floor towards the bar. There he found a clear liquid—obviously a home-made hooch, in a half-full bottle, along with several empty cups turned upside down to keep out the flies. Undeterred, he turned up a cup and discovered to his surprise that it was relatively clean; he then poured himself a drink.

In a moment he said, *"I'm Billy Bartram, and I need to find a guide into the mountains to the North. Do either of you gentlemen have a suggestion as to where I might find one."*

Clearly, neither man seated by the fire was a gentleman, and Sharpe, if not the drunk Cherokee, took some objection to being called one. Still, Sharpe had known of Billy's presence in the area for a couple of days, since Billy had inquired about a guide in the settlements toward the coast as well. However, Billy's reputation as something of a klutzy naturalist preceded him and no one could be found to lead him into those forbidding hills. Further, those mountains were known to be infested still with the more militant of the Cherokee, and most whites were afraid to travel further into the hills.

Sharpe didn't want to offend his customer any further, so he merely replied. *"I'm not sure anyone here' bouts would head into those mountains much further than the gorge a few miles north. The Goddamn Cherokee 'r likely to slit your damn throat."* Sharpe, in his vulgarity and racial bigotry, had conveniently ignored the fact that not only was he sitting by a Cherokee, but he himself was half Cherokee—such was the total lack of political correctness on this rough frontier.

Billy then finished his drink, paid, and left the tavern. However, Sharpe's prediction was accurate; no one could be found to serve as a guide for Billy. Further, while searching for a guide, Billy soon discovered another interesting fact; he quickly determined that while several white traders have moved into the foothills of the Blue Ridge, not a single frontiersman had yet crossed those high mountains; in fact no one had even explored them.

Now, klutzy he was, but in Billy that trait was offset somewhat by a bravery that many of the day thought foolish—others considered it suicidal. When he found no one to lead him into the higher mountains, and then subsequently discovered that no one really knew the way, he quietly repacked his kit, stocked up on salt, bacon, shot and powder, and headed across the low hills and up the Tugaloo River alone. Those that saw him go considered him a damn fool, and none believed they'd see him again.

He soon passed, just across the river on the western bank of the Tugaloo, a beautiful, incredibly peaceful hill, overlooking a stand of young pine trees. Billy never realized he was looking at an area that had been cleared selu fields of a Cherokee village only 15 years before. He ignored the small hill above the stand of pines entirely—for many in that valley are equally as beautiful. However, as he walked beside the river, he did notice a large rise near the river, and wondered what it might be; he did not realize it but he was then looking at the council house mound where once the sacred fire of the Cherokee had burned.

After a few days travel upriver, when Billy was in and among the higher peaks, on hands and knees looking at a particularly interesting plant—one of the delicate flowering plants in the area—he heard a noise and looked up. His blood immediately ran cold; for on the rise above him, he looked into the eyes of his own death.

There stood several Cherokee warriors on the slope; one had a loaded musket, cocked and pointed at his midsection. Another approached Billy, while looking with envy at Billy's pack. Remembering the fear of the settlers at Fort Prince George, Billy was absolutely certain that he'd soon meet his maker. However, he also recalled an earlier experience of the famed frontiersman, Daniel Boone, which he'd read about, and in the desperation which is sometimes born from a total lack of reasonable options, he determined to use the same unreasonable strategy. If it worked, it just might save his life.

He stood up slowly, smiled broadly, and gently extended his arm in greeting and spoke the words that come from the soul of all honest men—*"Hello, Brother."* When spoken in heartfelt honesty, with a smile, those words are understood regardless of language.

To the Cherokee, this white man was obviously crazy; for who would study a single plant so closely and let his guard down on this rough, bloody frontier where bear, wolf, and panther still killed men regularly—not to mention the filthy Creeks, and several interesting varieties of poisonous snakes. They stumbled upon this fool while they stalked a deer, and they quickly determined that—even for a white man—Billy was obviously quite deranged. Still, while Billy was brandishing that stupid grin, the Cherokee determined that he was not threatening. Thus, after relieving him of some of his shot and powder, with Billy smiling at them all the while, they gave him a gift in return—a deerskin they'd previously collected. Then they kindly went out of their way for two days, and lead him back to Sharpe's trading post on the banks of the lower Tugaloo River. Apparently, they thought the whites should care for their own imbeciles, and after the kindness of returning him to his own, they wanted nothing further to do with this madman.

Billy was undeterred; he figured he was one up on life, since he'd survived his first Cherokee encounter. Therefore, as soon as the Cherokee left the trading post, Billy Bartram again replenished his supplies and departed upriver. He was persistent as well as determined. For the next four years did Bartram travel all over the Blue Ridge identifying many plants native only to this region. He filled several notebooks with specimens, and his artwork of the flora was particularly appealing to botanists of Europe. He'd send his notebooks every few months to his father, via the occasional post from some trading station or fort in Georgia, or lower Tennessee; once he made it all the way to a distant trading post that would one day be named "Asheville," in the Carolinas. His father would publish these pictures, with whatever commentary Billy had provided, and the emerging society of botanists worldwide—particularly in Europe, would purchase these small books with amazing regularity. Billy did indeed find a way to make his fortune, as well as his mark in history.

His next encounter with the Cherokee was similar to the first, and Billy used the same strategy to break the ice—thus defusing a tense situation in which he again believed he could easily die. However, this time he'd had the good fortune to run into a Cherokee who truly liked the white man. Little Carpenter was over seventy years old at the time, and as a Cherokee who knew English, he'd often visited Charles Town. When Billy greeted him in English as *"brother,"* he responded in that language. Thus a friendship was formed immediately, and Little Carpenter lead this naturalist throughout the mountains for several months.

Bartram departed the lower mountains after only a few years, and was never to return. However by then he'd identified, catalogued, and drawn over 100 species of plants known no where else on earth. His view of plant life was not unlike that of his Cherokee friends—he believed that all life was intertwined, and that insult to any single plant was an affront against all life. Thus, was he "Cherokee" in spirit, if not in blood, and in that fashion did the mountains and the Cherokee embrace the first naturalist to see the beauty that, heretofore had been known only to the Cherokee and to God.

Bartram's name is remembered largely because of his contributions to botany through his European best sellers; Wyly, in contrast, mentions him only briefly, suggesting his impact was more readily noted in the great European Universities than on the frontier. Still he left a legacy of amazing contributions to botany when that was still a fledgling science, and he was immortalized in the myriad of trails along the Tugaloo River, and the Chatuga River, that bear his name to this day. At the very least, one may note that these Blue Mountains were first explored for the Europeans by a white man who truly appreciated them.

The Family of Runs-To-Water

Some 50 miles to the west of Tugaloo Town, the oldest son of Runs-To-Water, Stands-Tall, was in the process of training his son, Ridge, in the traditional ways of the Cherokee. The Cherokee elder known as Half-Face, the very same Cherokee, who had buried Runs-To-Water in 1761, had taken Stands-Tall under his tutelage some years ago for his manhood training, and in that fashion Stands-Tall had learned the traditional ways of the Cherokee. Now Stands-Tall, was training his son, Ridge, much as Runs-To-Water had been trained many years before.

While in traditional Cherokee villages, it was the elders or "Uncles" who trained the young toonalies, Cherokee village life had been so disrupted by the recent wars, that Stands-Tall could find no warrior worthy to train his son. Of course, there were many brave warriors, but few knew the arts of the blowgun, or the bow and arrow well, having forsaken those tools for the rifle and musket. More importantly, Stands-Tall did not believe that a Cherokee warrior who did not know the traditional ways of the tribe ever totally achieved the "balance" that was the defining characteristic of all great Cherokee warriors. Thus, Stands-Tall undertook the training of his own son, in order to assure he knew all the traditional arts of the Cherokee.

Ridge was to learn the ways of the blowgun, the swift runner, and the bow and arrow. On many days his father would take him to a location many miles away from the village in the distant mountains and instruct him to *"be still."* This meant that the boy was to fast throughout the day, and remain perfectly still for hours on end; he could maintain himself only with small sips of water every few hours. During these day long silent times, Ridge was to observe the trails of the deer, the panther, the beaver and bear, to see how the animals moved, ate, mated, and raised their young. He was taught to merge with the forest, and become one in spirit with the land. On dark nights, Stands-Tall and Ridge would investigate the animal's nocturnal habits; how they slept, when they came to the river to drink, and how they watched for intruders. Ridge was taught to seek the balance of life in the Blue Mountains, since balance is required by all living things. He was also taught a reverence for Kanati, and deep respect for the moving "silence" of the Blue Mountains. For in the silence both the forest and the animals speak and the Cherokee, unlike the whites, could hear them and learn from them. As a reward for all his troubles and his efforts to learn the ways of balance, the Great Spirit Kanati saw fit to whisper some of his powerful secrets to Ridge, after many hours alone in the woods. Ridge became, as was his grandfather and his father, a Cherokee warrior, not only in the physical sense, but in the spiritual sense as well. For all traditional Cherokee warriors, detecting and becoming a part of the spiritual balance of the universe was the most important struggle of all.

Ridge was taught many evenings by the sacred fire, the tales of the Cherokee, of Kanati and his release of the animals, and of how the morning fire is brought into the sky each day. He was raised listening to the tales of his brave Grandfather, and how the whites had stolen the land of the Tugaloo River and destroyed the village, putting out the sacred fire of the Cherokee in that cluster of villages forever. Stands-Tall would tell of the tranquility of the Tugaloo River Valley, of the stark beauty of the Blue Mountains from atop Currahee Mountain, the mountain that stands alone, and of how the sacred fire burned in the council house on top of the hill in the village of Tugaloo Town.

The early education of Ridge involved many such stories, from many tribal leaders. The honorable elder Half-Face, and his son Ekaia, often spoke of life along the Tugaloo River. Ridge was told that Ekaia still lived along the river, pretending to be white, and that he only visited his father occasionally on his many extended hunting trips. During one of these trips, Ekaia himself taught Ridge how to hide in the forest, and how to stalk deer and bear, and all Cherokee of the lower Blue Mountains knew that Ekaia was the best hunter of all; for he was a ghost who could disappear completely in the forest.

Shotani, who was now many years old, likewise told Ridge many tales of the battles of Runs-To-Water; how he killed a mighty bear while but a toonali. She spoke of his vengeful wrath at Taliwa and his heroic charge in defense of Tugaloo Town. She told of the mother of Stands-Tall, the first wife of Runs-To-Water, and of how Stands-Tall and she escaped under the cannon fire of the whites, while Runs-To-Water and the other brave Cherokee charged the guns. If bravery was expected of Ridge, as it was of every Cherokee warrior, then good upright character was demanded; for the Cherokee well knew that, it does indeed take a village to raise a child. Thus, the traditional myths of the Cherokee merged with the oral history of the family in the mind of young Ridge, and the family memories were passed on to the next generation. So these tales would be for many centuries to come.

Other men who would decide the fate of the Tugaloo River Valley were, at that point, living in other areas of the Blue Ridge. Neither Jessie Walton, nor his friend Early Cleveland had returned to the Tugaloo area, after watching the Creek raid on the town many years ago. They lived in the North Carolina colony, but they often hunted across the mountains in Tennessee or Georgia, and often talked about the less settled Tugaloo River Valley around their campfires at night.

Wyly's diary records that, on one such hunting trip in 1774, they had been relieved of their deer skins, their rifles, and their shoes by a roving band of Cherokee. They were then told to march barefoot, to the east heading out of the Blue Mountains and not return. Cleveland, the bigger man with the bigger temper was furious and vowed to take his revenge on the Cherokee who stole his skins. Still, without rifles and shoes, it took an additional year to return from the mountains, and by then the Revolution had begun, serving to prevent him from taking his vengeance on the Cherokee. After some consideration, he figured he'd rid the Americas of the damn British first, and then deal with the Cherokee. Once Early Cleveland decided to do something, it was just a matter of time before it was done!

Thus, in those desperate years of the American Revolution, many men of different backgrounds gathered for a great battle on the slopes of King's Mountain. Some would live and some would die; some would open the Blue Ridge mountains and the bloody frontier beyond, and many of those frontier folk would travel right through the Tugaloo River Valley.

Patrick Ferguson and His Tory Army

It is interesting to note that in the most important Revolutionary War battle in the Southern colonies up to 1780, not a single soul from Great Britain participated. The "British" forces, like the Patriot forces were all from America—they were Tories from various American colonies. Their leader, Major Patrick Ferguson, was Scottish.

Ferguson was leading a group of around nine hundred and fifty men, most of whom hailed from the coastal cities in the Carolina colonies. Others were from New York and New Jersey, but few had been on the frontier before, and none had been in the mountains. Still, his troops were highly motivated to preserve the relationship between the British colonies and her mother country, and like everyone else in that fateful year of 1780, they were sure that a British victory in this petty frontier rebellion was only a matter of time. After all, the Patriot forces under Washington had lost almost every battle that had been fought, save for a few minor skirmishes at Trenton and Princeton. A part of Washington's army had then run to the Southern colonies to "hide" from the powerful British forces in New York and Philadelphia. Washington and the rest of his men seemed to be able to do nothing other than retreat from the overwhelming British forces in the North.

In fact, by 1780 the large British armies all over the continent were seeking out the Patriot army on every front. The British had shipped an entire army by sea, into the Southern ports of Savannah and Charlestown. Since that time, Cornwallis himself had defeated the rebel general Horatio Gates at Camden, South Carolina, sending the Patriot general scurrying from the field. Some said that Gates didn't stop running for three whole days! After that British victory, Cornwallis had decided to advance his army into the North Carolina colony to the city of Charlotte, a newer inland city which had fallen to him in a pitched battle on September 26, 1780. It was clear to everyone that the inevitable British victory was only a matter of time, so the Tory force under Ferguson at King's Mountain in October of 1780 was feeling quite confident.

More importantly, Col. Ferguson was an effective leader. By all accounts he was a very good tactician and he was a specialist in armaments. Earlier in his career, some years before the Revolutionary War, he had invented a breech loading rifle called for no known reason, the "Bulldog." In a day when other weapons were loaded in a rather cumbersome fashion from the front of the barrel, this breech loader was decades ahead of its time. The highly accurate Bulldog increased the rate of fire from four or five shots per minute—the average for a typical British infantryman using the British Brown Bess musket—to eight or nine shots per minute. Thus, in terms of the rate of fire, this rifle turned one soldier into the equivalent of two. Had it been adopted by the British for their infantry during the Revolution, as well as by the various Tory armies in the field, that rifle could have made a difference in the battle on King's Mountain, not to mention several other major battles. Most importantly, the breech loading Bulldog could be loaded from a prone position on the ground or behind a low breastwork; this important fact would have been a critical advantage on King's Mountain, as we shall see.

Still, the British leadership was no more—and no less—foresighted than military procurement officers worldwide, and they declined purchase of this impressive rifle. Only 200 or so Ferguson Rifles were ever made, and today only 12 Bulldogs are still in existence; these are highly prized by collectors as examples of innovative weaponry. Unfortunately, the British soldier entered the Revolutionary War armed with the same "Brown Bess" smooth bore muskets that had been in use for several decades previously.

In contrast, most of the Patriots at the bottom of King's Mountain on that fateful October day in 1780 had Kentucky long rifles—a much better weapon than the Brown Bess. These famed guns had "rifled" barrels—grooves on the inside of the barrel that sent the lead ball spiraling in flight. Unlike the Brown Bess muskets which were smooth on the inside of the barrel, the Kentucky Rifles of the Patriots had much greater range and accuracy; each Patriot on that mountain could easily kill a man with the 50 caliber ball from their Kentucky long rifle at 150 yards. Many said that a good marksman could hit a man's head 200 yards away.

While named the Kentucky Rifle, none of these firearms were ever made in that state. Most "Kentucky Rifles" were actually made in Connecticut or Pennsylvania; moreover they were made in those distant states by German gunsmiths! Still, the rifle had evolved specifically to meet the rugged demands of the frontier, and by this time the frontier was in the mountainous woods of Kentucky, Georgia, the Carolinas, and Tennessee. Virtually every rifle made by the Germans in Pennsylvania found its way into the Kentucky or Tennessee highlands, and thus the name "Kentucky Rifle" evolved, and these weapons were highly prized. In fact, many frontiersmen knew their lives depended on their rifles on the frontier, and they developed a special attachment for these venerable firearms. Many men gave their rifles names such as "Bearkiller,"

"Honeydue," or "Leadfly." One of Sevier's men, a sinewy teenager named Robert Young, even called his rifle, "Sweet Lips." One may make of that name what one will, but it may help to reflect that a mountain man spent all his life with his rifle, and typically only saw his wife or his gal for six or eight months out of the year—he'd be hunting for skins the remainder of the time. In that context, what could a name such as "Sweet Lips" possibly mean?

The naming of weapons of war has long been noted in history. This tradition would find its finest hour in the nose-art of the heavy bombers in the "Mighty" Eighth Airforce of the U.S. Army during World War II, several centuries after the Battle of King's Mountain. Still, the tradition is a long one; for even during the Revolutionary War, men going to battle both loved and named the weapons on which their lives depended.

Thus, as in the previous Cherokee War, the Tory Army at King's Mountain fighting for the British entered the battlefield with an inferior weapon. In contrast, the crude, largely illiterate rebels—today we call them Patriots—were all better armed. Further, these mountain men were much better shots, and had much more experience at wilderness warfare, particularly shooting in these mountains. These differences were to be critical in the hell on top of King's Mountain, on that fateful October day.

However, the Tories at King's Mountain did have one advantage—an advantage in leadership. Ferguson was, indeed a dashing officer. Raised and educated in Scotland, he was a man of breeding and refinement. He was also a crack marksman, which instilled great pride in troops under his command, and he had served in the British infantry long enough to have been under fire several times in various colonies.

It is recorded that on one battlefield in the countryside of the Maryland colony, he had an unsuspecting Patriot officer in the sights of his famed Ferguson Rifle. With that highly accurate breech loading weapon, Ferguson could have easily killed that officer—sitting atop his white horse in full view some 250 yards away. However, Ferguson refused to shoot, telling the man beside him that he considered such a shot to be no more than murder; it was therefore beneath consideration for a true Scottish gentlemen. Thus, did Ferguson miss an opportunity to become the world's first sniper, and the unsuspecting officer—General George Washington— lived to fight another day, having never known how close he came to death at the battle of Brandywine Creek.

The Best Laid Battle Plans...

In mid October of 1780, Ferguson knew that a ragtag militia of vulgar rebels— pompously calling themselves the "over-mountain men"—were marching toward his forces. He'd challenged them previously with a well published taunt, which was widely circulated in the Tennessee country, along the Tugaloo River, and all through the Blue Ridge. Only a few months before, Ferguson had sent a message to John Sevier, the Patriot commander of the Tennessee militia, suggesting the Patriots should *"...desist from their opposition to the British arms, and take protection under my standard, or I will march with my army over the mountains, hang your leader, and lay waist your country with fire and sword."*

Publishing this taunt was incredibly stupid, as Ferguson had badly misjudged his enemy. His challenge had exactly the opposite effect from what he intended. First, on this frontier many men had had their lives *"laid waste with fire and sword"* by the Creek, the Cherokee, or the Catawba, and that taunt hit home. Moreover, no frontiersman would ever give up his rifle under any condition—such an action would be suicide on the frontier. His life—not to mention that of his family—depended on that rifle! Rather than causing the rough, vulgar men of the Blue Ridge to reflect on their position and possibly lay down their arms, it merely angered them; *"Excited them greatly"* was the phrase used by Wyly in his diary.

Sevier, a politically wise man, knew his illiterate constituency well, and thus caused the insulting ultimatum to be read everywhere, particularly in the various drinking taverns dotting the frontier. He then sent out a stirring call to arms.

In the Tennessee country, even men who might have been disposed to the Tory position were ready to fight when one talked of taking away their rifles. Within a fortnight, an entire Patriot militia army—newly formed—was marching south to meet Ferguson's Tory force, and this Patriot force of mountain men grew larger at every crossroads, every tavern, and every town. They would meet Ferguson's Tories a month later at King's Mountain.

Ferguson himself didn't know the size of the Patriot force pursuing him, so he wisely retreated for a time. He hoped to reach the relative safety of Cornwallis' main army which was then encamped in the new settlement of Charlotte, North Carolina. Still, the slow loping gait of his pack train mules, and the muddy red-clay ground in upstate North and South Carolina, heavily soaked after some days of rain, dictated his speed. As he breasted a rise in the land leading his forces through the backwoods of South Carolina, just below the North Carolina line on a rainy Friday afternoon, one of his Cherokee scouts—a man of dubious reputation known only as Prather—rode up to him and gave him the news that the rebels were only one day away. As Ferguson listened to the oral report, he noted a hill nearby rising above the surrounding countryside, and he decided to encamp on its bare crest.

In only an hour, he was more at ease. He was happy with his location, and in fact, his defensive position was quite strong. The hill, which would forever become known as King's Mountain, is a low rise, some 60 feet in height. It stands 600 yards long and 120 yards wide on the east end where Ferguson would make his camp. On the western end, it is only 60 yards wide. The top was very flat and in 1780, almost barren of trees, though there were some stands of oak and poplar on the western end, as well as rocks everywhere across the plateau. All of the sloping sides of this hill in each direction were heavily wooded. The hill was shaped somewhat like a short boat paddle, with the wider end toward the east and the narrow "handle" to the southwest. At certain points, his men built log breastworks at the crest. In a short time Ferguson felt invulnerable on his mountain; he knew he could hold off a force many times the size of his small band. He didn't, however, realize either the importance of the Kentucky rifle, or the innovative fighting nature of his opponent, and he would not live long enough to understand either.

Later, during the battle, he would sit astride his horse, and ride from one end of the crest to the other, signaling with a whistle he'd brought along for that purpose, and thus moving his scant reserves as needed. He deployed his men in equal numbers facing each direction, all around the top of the hill. All his forces had to do was sit and wait, and then kill any rebels foolish enough to climb up the wooded slope.

In contrast to the Tory force, the Patriot forces, totaling 940 men, had no defensive position at all. Had they needed to fall back, they wouldn't have stopped running until they hit Tennessee! Of course, they were still enraged at Ferguson's threat, and didn't even want to consider the possibility of falling back. However, another problem was soon apparent among this Patriot force; they had little clear leadership. To put it simply, they were overstocked with Colonels!

Historians have attributed overall leadership of the Patriot forces to Col. William Campbell, who had been elected from among the group of leaders, but that seems to be mere historical hindsight. It is true that Campbell stood six feet and six inches, and was a natural leader. Still, these frontiersmen from across the Blue Ridge were generally large men, and were particularly notorious for fighting in their own style and ignoring their leadership once a battle commenced. The devil himself could not have forced them to stand shoulder to shoulder abreast and fight in the traditional battle line used by most formal European armies in the late eighteenth century.

Moreover, there were really too many experienced commanders among the Patriots on that fateful day! Campbell having been elected by the Colonels themselves, assumed overall command during the planning, and he then showed great wisdom in recognizing the veteran fighters among his disjointed forces. He used the leadership he found among these men, and it was one of the wisest decisions ever made by any commander on any field of battle.

Jessie Walton, for example while not well schooled—he could barely read— was a natural leader and a man of substance. He was a restless man, a spiritual man, who never seemed to find himself at home. At times, history produces a man whose fate it is to wander, and leave parts of himself wherever he goes. Jessie was such a rolling stone, and history is graciously blessed by his wanderings. Not only was he a leading frontiersman—rivaling the famous Daniel Boone in westward explorations in the 1760s and 1770s. Like Boone, Walton was a man who took his family with him. By 1780, he was a veteran fighter and frontiersman, 41 years old, who knew this country well, and knew how to fight. He could load his Kentucky Rifle in 12 seconds flat, and hit a wild turkey at 200 yards! He didn't say much, but Campbell had noted that when he did talk, his men listened. This Walton fellow would have been an asset to any Patriot commander on the field that day.

Only two years previously, in 1778, Walton had been instrumental in settling the first British outpost in an area of Cherokee country north of the Blue Ridge that was to become Tennessee. He named the settlement Jonesborough, a name typically and incorrectly attributed to Daniel Boone. Walton was also a savvy businessman, and had acquired nine lots in Jonesborough personally, expecting to make his fortune there. Then this damn war had intervened. Like his friend "Early" Cleveland, Walton had served on the early "Committee of Safety" in the Tennessee and Carolina mountains where his company had disarmed Tory sympathizers. His company ranged all the way from the Moraivian settlement at Salem in North Carolina to Jonesborough, Tennessee. Thus, he was a frontiersman of proven dependability who had been leading men in battle for some years. He was a man who could be counted upon in a pinch. In this battle, Walton would lead 150 Patriots ascending the rise on the right end—the southwest end—of the hill, forming the right flank of the Patriot attacking force. Robert Jarrett would act as his runner, and ascend by his side. At the first sign of problems Jarrett would ride back to report to Campbell.

Cleveland, another solid man, if a man of too much girth, and a vulgar mouth, would lead another 150 men and ascend the mountain on the left end of the Patriot line. Campbell didn't really trust the loudmouth Cleveland, considering him an uncouth braggart. After all, how could anyone trust a man so prone to eating and drinking to excess? Ultimately, Campbell placed James Wyly in Cleveland's force as his personal runner, and nominally his second in command, in order to keep an eye on the left flank. Cleveland and Wyly knew each other well, and if Campbell didn't care for Cleveland, he did have confidence in the young man Wyly. For Wyly was shrewd, and could tell the forest from the trees—he was always good at determining the big picture.

Elijah Clarke, the illiterate upstart with the quick temper from Georgia, would lead his force of 400 men right up the northwest face of the mountain to directly into the Tory main line. Campbell didn't like the fact that he had to use Clarke at all, but Col. Clarke had lead more Patriots to this particular battle than anyone else, so Campbell couldn't very well leave Clarke out of the leadership. Still, that type of assignment is what a wise commander like Campbell does with a braggart and loudmouth like Clarke—charge him straight into the teeth of the enemy guns.

John Sevier, and his smaller band of 120 Tennessee men would be held in reserve, to ascend in the wake of Clarke's force. Thus did Campbell plan on an ascent by three separate forces, with some 200 yards of unprotected terrain between each of them. The plan was formulated in camp some 3 miles from King's Mountain on the evening of October 6, 1780. At daybreak, the Patriots would march to the mountain and immediately attack. At that point, they were sure they had the larger force, but in this belief they were wrong—the forces engaged at King's Mountain were roughly of equal size. Still, like all upstart rebel armies from the frontier, these Patriots were confident of victory.

Of course, things went wrong from the start; Campbell's mules were no faster on the muddy-rut trails than were Ferguson's so under a heavy downpour on the morning of October 7, the Patriot advance was delayed. The Patriots wrapped their blankets around their rifles and powder horns to keep their powder dry. With rain pouring down for most of the morning, they didn't even get into position until two in the afternoon. Still, the rain did abate around 2:30, and Campbell was confident he could attack that day; he knew that his men were itching for a fight, and he really didn't believe he could have made them wait another day, had he wanted to.

The savage anger and ferocity that motivated the Patriots that day can only be understood by considering two factors each of which enraged the over-mountain men; Cherokee warriors and Tarleton. Once again, the British were using the Cherokee as a weapon; Cherokee were serving as scouts, and British agents were inciting the Cherokee to fight against the Patriots all along the Blue Ridge. Thus, in many cases the Cherokee were fighting against the same frontiersmen who had been encroaching on their land for decades, and both Cherokee and whites were using the same bloody tactics; cruelty, torture, and terror. Almost every Patriot on the mountain that day had fought Indians all his life, and many had lost loved ones to the savage butchery of the Cherokee Wars of the previous 20 years. Using the Cherokee in another war against these rugged settlers was like waving a red flag before a raging bull. The Patriots didn't really care that only a few Cherokee scouts—Prather among them—were actually serving on the mountain with Ferguson. Most of these over-mountain men hated the Cherokee with a fanatic passion; they were just as happy to kill Indians as they were to kill Tories.

The "Tarleton" factor is a bit more difficult to understand; for this unfortunate man has left his name written in blood for all posterity. Moreover, Colonel Banastre Tarleton of the British Royal Dragoons, impacted the Battle of King's Mountain without even being there!

History records that in the battle of Waxhaws, in South Carolina, Tarleton had chosen to give "no quarters" to defeated rebels. Thus, no prisoners were taken, and any Patriot trying to surrender during or after the battle was simply shot as he stood there with his hands raised. Such a rash policy was sure to result in increased

The Battle Of Kings Mountain

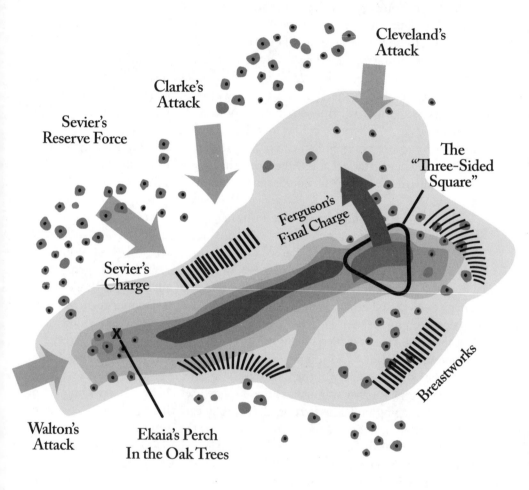

Cleveland's
Attack

Clarke's
Attack

Sevier's
Reserve Force

The
"Three-Sided
Square"

Ferguson's
Final Charge

Sevier's
Charge

Breastworks

Walton's
Attack

Ekaia's Perch
In the Oak Trees

savagery on both sides, not to mention extreme bloodshed. Patriots and innocent bystanders alike hated both the policy and the man behind it. Tarleton's name has thus been cursed throughout history, and even today, *"Tarleton's Quarters"* literally means *"death to all who try to surrender!"*

Now, Tarleton and Ferguson were known to be good friends, having served together for many years. While Ferguson generally disapproved of the policy that came to be known as Tarleton's Quarters, he was, in the minds of the Patriots painted with the same brush, and his earlier threat of *"fire and sword"* did nothing to dissuade the Patriots of these notions. Thus, would Tarleton's barbaric policy lead to much useless bloodshed in a frontier battle on King's Mountain, when he himself was not even present.

Hell on the Mountain

As a natural leader of men, Ferguson knew his men well and understood how to inspire them. Just before the battle, before the musketry began, and just before the Patriots began their ascent, he put on a red checkered shirt and climbed atop his white horse. From that vantage point, he road down his entire defensive line, and to inspire his forces, he stopped in the middle of the hill, and proclaimed the preeminence of the British crown. Loudly he shouted down the north face of the mountain toward the rebels. *"I stand today on the King's Mountain. Today, I am the King of this Mountain, and neither God Almighty nor all of the Rebels in Hell can drive me from it!"*

While his troops cheered, he rode at an easy canter back toward the eastern end of the hill, speaking to many of his men as he passed, assured that his tirade had had the desired effect on his troops.

Of course, the reaction of the Patriots down the hill was quite different. With that statement and his earlier threats, he really managed to piss off the independent minded, rough, and vulgar men just down the slope behind the tree line; thus did the battle begin. With Tarleton's Quarters on their minds and such taunting from the British Commander atop the hill, Ferguson may as well have kicked over a hornet's nest, and as a result of this bravado, he would die within the hour.

Still, as strange as it may seem, from Ferguson's taunting in this deadly, bloody battle, a children's game of strength and agility was derived. What parent has not heard their children rough-housing on some small hill in the backyard, while playing King of the Mountain?

And that is precisely when it happened; the men who would formulate the subsequent history of the Tugaloo Valley and lower Blue Ridge stood shoulder to shoulder. With all of the Tory and Patriot forces arrayed around this otherwise unimportant hill, the four men who would conquer the bloody frontier, build the future of the Tugaloo River Valley, and open the entire lower Blue Ridge for settlement came together for only a couple of minutes.

Campbell had called his commanders in for one final talk before the battle; thus did Wyly, Cleveland, Walton, and Jarrett stand together in the sheltering tent with Campbell, Clarke, Sevier, and several other Colonels. A greater assemblage of rugged frontiersmen had never before been seen, nor would ever be again. In most battles of this century, the frontiersmen, or "Over-mountain Men" were considered irregulars, and were not depended upon for critical phases of the fight. Thus there were very few battles that included more than one or two militia groups, and therefore only a few militia commanders were ever gathered together. Here on this mountain these superb frontiersmen—seven different militia groups from all over the Blue Ridge—were all that the fledgling colonies had to bring to the fight. Together, these men heard the taunting words from Ferguson atop the hill. While standing there shoulder to shoulder, they looked in unison, rather stupidly it would seem, up into the rising mist at the wooded battlefield, and they no doubt wondered if they were destined to die on that mountain.

Then a shrill gruff voice was raised—a vulgar voice that could only spring from these rugged mountains. *"You God Damn, King Lovin,' Son of a Whore! I hope your ass grows together and your eyes turn brown!"* Early Cleveland simply had to respond verbally to the previous British taunt, and he shouted this uncreative repartee at the top of his lungs; for his temper was unbounded, as was both his sense of humor, and his phenomenal ability to string together totally unrelated vulgarities.

However, on this particular day, he thought that he'd made damn good sense with his first effort, so he continued. *"Now shut your shit kissin' mouth before I stick your poxed British face into the ass end of my mule train."*

That was all it took! All along the line Patriots began to cheer. When faced with death at the business end of a Brown Bess musket, one wants at least one fearless leader on one's side, and if Early Cleveland was a bit less than totally cultured, that was just fine with these frontiersmen from the Blue Ridge; for in years of fighting Indians, he was known to be fearless, and he'd never send any man to any place he would not go himself.

Campbell of course, had heard all of this, and he knew his men were ready. He merely smiled to himself, and waited for the cussin' to stop. Then he gave his final instructions to his Patriot commanders. Wyly's diary dutifully reports his few words. *"Men, when I hear firing from both the right and left flank, Col. Clarke and the rest of us will begin the main assault with the ascent up the north face of the mountain. Now ride to your formations, and begin your climb. May God go with you; for I fear we shall see hell on this mountain today!"*

The Patriot commanders then mounted their horses and rode to their respective commands, each quietly reflecting on his own fate in the upcoming battle. Walton and Jarrett headed to the west end, and Cleveland and Wyly headed to the east.

When Cleveland reached his forces east of the mountain, he dismounted briefly and had the men gather around him. Because of Wyly's presence, Early Cleveland's words to his company just before the ascent were recorded for history. Now deadly serious, Early pointed up the mountain and said; *"Patriots. Yonder is your enemy, and the enemy of mankind. I will show you today, by my example, how to fight. I can undertake no more, you will expect nothing less. Now let's go up that mountain and kill 'um all."*

With that brief oration behind him, he mounted his unfortunate horse–for on that day, Cleveland weighed in at 285 pounds—and began his assent up the mountain towards Ferguson's men. It was all the animal could do to stand up and move, but when lead starts flying even horses can become quite motivated, and under considerable duress the animal began to struggle up the slope of the hill.

The Battle Is Joined

Shots were first heard at the right flank of the Patriot army. While about 900 Patriots would climb the hill that day, it seemed to be Walton's bad luck to be the first who actually headed up on the western slope. He was a savvy, experienced fighter, and unlike his friend Early Cleveland, Walton wouldn't be caught dead riding a horse up that hill. He didn't have his friend's need for bombastic self-promotion, and he wasn't about to go up there mounted. He merely wanted to get the damn thing over with, and live through it; also he knew he could shoot best from behind a tree. While he was notorious for spitting his chew wherever and whenever he needed to, he even chose to forgo a mouthful of tobacee when he knew that he was headed into a fight. He looked at the rustic, filthy, smelly men before him, still drying out from the morning rain, and without preamble, he said; *"Alright, you sorry lot. Let's climb this damn hill."* With that inspiring pep talk ringing in their ears, they started up.

They had not advanced 200 yards before they were spotted from the top, and several lower level Tory commanders who had never seen a battle, much less participated in one, gave the order to fire. Of course, in their panic they had given that order much too soon. Ferguson was at the east end of the ridge, some 500 yards away at that moment, but had he been on the west end, he would have immediately countermanded this foolish order. Still, in his absence the Tories, well hidden behind rocks and stacked-log breastworks, fired on the rebels with no effect whatsoever. Their Brown Bess smooth bore muskets didn't have a chance at killing anyone at 100 yards—the maximum effective range was something like 50 to 60 yards for that weapon. Still, this first volley did serve to let the Patriots below them know that a fight had begun, so several returned fire with their Kentucky long rifles and one or two of the Tories on top of the hill fell dead.

Some 200 Tories had fired that first volley on the western summit while they crouched behind their rocks and breastworks. Now these men had to reload, and much to the surprise of every single Patriot on the lower western slope, they stood up to do it!

The first Patriot to see this highly unlikely and incredibly stupid maneuver, scratched his head and said, *"What the hell are they all doin'? Taking a piss together?"*

His friend and cousin, standing beside him in line, said, *"I don't know what they be up to, but keep an eye on um!"*

The fault for this stupidity of standing in battle lay with the Brown Bess musket. The venerable old Brown Bess flintlock muskets served His Majesties forces well for almost 100 years, and many of the Tories on top of the mountain had known no other gun besides the Brown Bess. These muskets were very large, ranging from six feet two inches to six feet eight inches in length. These were thus quite hard to load in an era when the average British and Tory infantryman was only five feet four. Further, these muskets had an extremely long ramrod, which made the loading procedure even more cumbersome. In fact by regulation, it took 12 distinct steps to load the musket from a standing position, and it was all but impossible to do this behind a 3 foot high breastwork. Fixing the standard 21 inch bayonet on these cumbersome things was even more of a problem. Still, no one in the military procurement office in London saw any problem with this procedure at all! In the British military mind of the eighteenth century, no true gentlemen would fight while crouching behind a log or rock, so why should the British equip their army based on such concerns?

The standard "Volley fire" tactics of the British infantry, were also problematic for the Tories at King's Mountain. The Brown Bess could throw lead about as well as any smooth bore, particularly when used by massed infantry at close ranges. In standard volley fire procedures, one line of men would kneel in front of a second rank, with those kneeling firing first and in unison. Then the line in back would advance 3 paces, take aim, and fire in mass, while the kneeling men, thus bypassed, would stand up to reload.

Consequently, with both the practical necessities for loading and the volley fire procedures demanding it, after these Tories fired the first volley they stood up. They then calmly and in a disciplined fashion, began their 12 count process to reload their muskets—some even counted their loading procedure steps out loud!

At various times throughout history, world changing events do seem to hinge on such ill-conceived stupidities, and this battle was to be an example. Of course, such idiocy as standing to reload can only transpire when nobody had challenged the procedures, and the British had never fought a true frontier army before. Exposing oneself to reload was one such lunacy that had never been challenged, and on this day, this obscure procedure changed history.

To the veteran riflemen coming up the slopes below, their Kentucky rifles primed and loaded, this was a dream come true. To a man, these rugged hunters, Indian fighters, and frontiersmen below gawked at this unexpected bounty of targets—truly a "target rich environment" in today's terms.

One shouted, *"By damn! Them fools is dumber than dirt! Why they doin' that, I wonder?"*

His friend, crouched low while loading his rifle behind the next tree, soon shouted back. *"Who the hell cares? I just want 'um to do it again!"*

Sure enough, they did. The Tories fired again in volley fire under orders from their younger commanders, and stood up a second time to reload, thus negating all advantage of both their elevated position and the logs they had placed as breastworks for concealment. Perhaps they thought their disciplined volley fire would impress the rebels.

And it certainly did! When they stood again, another Patriot shouted, *"Damn! It's just like a turkey shoot back home! Time it right, and you win the prize!"*

"Naw." another said. *"Not a turkey shoot. Its more like flushing a gaggle of wild turkey! I can only shoot at one of 'um, when 15 of 'um fly!"*

By the time the Tories stood for the third time, the Patriots had learned the timing. The Tory men on top of the hill stood to reload, and Kentucky rifles flashed all down the Patriot line. Fire flashed seemingly behind every tree, log, and rock on the slope of the mountain, and the Tories on top began to drop with deadly regularity. Hell had come to the mountain, indeed, as rifles named "Honeyhole," "Precious Bottom," "Bluefly" "Mama's Grits" or "Sugarplum," sent their deadly package of lead into the breast, the throat, or the head of young men from New York, Brunswick in the New Jersey colony, or New Berne in the Carolinas.

While that third reloading was in progress, one skinny boy, a veteran fighter at 16 years from the newly established Jonesborough settlement in the Tennessee country, took his shot, and then thought out loud to himself. *"If them damn fools is gonna' do that again, I could sight 'em a damn sight better from a tree!"* This young frontiersman had shot deer from trees when he was only seven; climbing with a Kentucky rifle was as easy as breathing to him. He looked straight up the old oak he hid behind and sure enough he saw a branch just within reach. In 30 seconds he was 24 feet in the air, heading further up with his rifle in hand—he'd named his rifle "Hotlead." He found a comfortable spot 39 feet in the air, and thus was much closer to the top of the mountain. He began to stuff his powder and shot down the barrel of Hotlead, with the assurance of a man who had done so all his life; he needed no 12 step plan to load his weapon. In just under a minute he was situated, primed, cocked, and ready, so he shouted down to his cousin on the slope below, *"When you recon' they gonna stand up again?"*

Within three minutes some 30 Patriots, with no orders what-so-ever, had decided to fight this battle from the treetops. All climbed as high as they could given their particular tree; some reaching a height of 45 feet, which placed them almost level with the Tories on top of the bare hill. Robert Jarrett realized that Walton wasn't likely to need his services as things were going fairly well, so he picked a small poplar and climbed up too. From that treetop spot, this ancestor of that great Jarrett family of the Tugaloo River Valley killed his first and only Tory in the Revolutionary War.

The persistent, withering fire from the trees brought bloody death to the western flank at the top of King's Mountain. Tories died from horrid, ragged wounds in every conceivable location on their bodies; enemy fire seemed to coming from everywhere, and one lower level Tory leader with a heavy Irish brogue, was heard to shout, *"By God, I never saw so much lead coming at me men! It was coming from rocks, and trees, and the sky, just like hell itself!"*

On the other flank, Early Cleveland sat atop his poor horse, as the animal struggled up the hill; his men were behind him, on foot. They had a longer trek than did Walton's men. Of course Early, by riding, offered his ample girth as the most inviting target coming up the steep slope. He was the only man mounted, and the unfortunate horse struggled along uphill at barely a canter. Still the Tories, using their old Brown Bess muskets and firing much too soon on the east end of the mountain as they'd earlier done on the west, managed to kill only the horse. They thereby dumped Early in a large pool of muddy water, and relieved said animal of the necessity to carry the monstrous load all the way to the top.

That poor shot by some unnamed Tory in this first volley also saved Early's life. As wide as he was, he would have been impossible to miss sitting on that slow horse as soon as he got within a reasonable range. As he got up he jumped behind a tree and exhorted his men, with his usual combination of cussin' and vivid humor. *"Well, by damn. I guess I'm walkin' just like the rest of you sons o'bitches, now. Come on, and let's get that shit-faced peacock up there in that damn red-checker shirt."*

Just then the Tories on the eastern end of the plateau stood up to reload after their second volley, as they had at the other end of the line. Early was heard to gasp, *"Well I'll be damned"* as Kentucky rifles all around him fired.

Wyly, just behind and to his right, said. *"That's the second time they've done that. You missed the first one, Col. Cleveland, what with your broad ass in the mud and all!"*

Early didn't mind such ribbin' from his younger friend and second in command—as long as the other men didn't hear. He answered back. *"Well, that was a good horse those bastards kilt. Recon' I'll have to get one of theirs, and I fancy that white one ol' Ferguson's ridin."* He looked back up the mountain, still not believing what he'd seen. *"Did they really stand up to reload twice?"*

Wyly fired his Kentucky, and answered, *"Damn sure did. Wouldn't 'a believed it if I hadn't seen it with my own eyes."*

Early then repeated himself; *"Well, I'll be damned."* He seemed, for just that moment, to be utterly incapable of creative cussing at all—which was, for him unheard of.

With the third volley, several of the Patriots were wounded horribly–the Brown Bess did throw deadly lead when it was within a reasonable range. Early saw several of his men go down, apparently shot in the gut—what in later military jargon would be called "center mass." Such wounds in the Revolutionary War were almost always mortal; between blood loss and infection, these wounds usually overcame any resistance the human body could muster. Early said, *"Guess they got the range now."*

Wyly, loading again from behind the same tree, said, *"Yea. They sure as hell do!"* He finished loading and fired a shot at Ferguson, who for some reason had remained mounted and within sight. He thought he may have hit him, but he couldn't be sure.

Early then had an idea, and shouted to his men. *"Next time they stand up, don't nobody shoot. Nobody at all! Ya hear? Any of you shoot next time, and I'll personally crack his skull!"*

Several of his men didn't get the message, and fired anyway the next time the Tories stood to reload, but most of the Patriots had heard these strange orders, and thus held their fire; in that fashion they conserved their loads of powder and shot in the barrels of their deadly Kentucky rifles. Then, the Tories fired again. As they stood again to reload, Early shouted at the top of his lungs. His booming voice was heard by 178 Patriots on the field who were still in the fight. *"Mountainmen, let's go get 'um! I'll see you at the top!"* With that he stood up and charged, leading his men, just as he'd promised from the front. He'd momentarily forgotten the fact that his rifle still lay below his dead horse, and that he had no weapon at all; he was simply too much into the fight to notice.

By all accounts, he did the unthinkable, running unarmed straight up the slope of King's Mountain, with no variance in his stride to throw off his opponent's aim. Early knew that he'd picked the right time and he ran up in the relative safety of the reloading pause, while all the Tories on top of the hill could do was cuss at him—they were all standing up and smack in the middle of their 12 step reloading procedure. Early quickly, covered over 25 yards, and his line advanced with him, with some men covering 30 yards or more! Then they all took cover, falling behind trees, logs, and anything else they could find, just before the British fired the next volley.

Meanwhile Tory fire discipline on the top of the hill had broken down, and several were now firing individually as quick as they could reload. Many had realized that it was pretty dumb to stand up again, but others still did so, having never practiced loading while crouched behind a log. Thus, while all of the Patriots on the east end of the mountain still held their load, many of the Tories did not, and the Patriots had managed to advance 30 yards without a single casualty! They shot the next time the Tories stood, and then repeated the maneuver—skipping every other "standing reload" of the Tories, and using that time to advance another 15 yards or so. This time there was some limited fire from the hill, but there were still 170 Patriots moving forward. Thus, did the company of Early Cleveland play hopscotch up the left flank of King's Mountain, right under the Tory guns. Predictability on the part of one's enemy is always an advantage, and Early Cleveland intended to use that predictable loading pause to get all the way to the top!

When Early got his force within 35 yards of the summit, he still had 159 effectives—the rest were wounded on the slopes. He then waited for a reloading pause from the top and shouting *"Charge,"* he ran to the top. Unfortunately for Cleveland, while the Tory muskets were largely inferior, they did have one major advantage over the Kentucky rifles; each one could mount a bayonet.

Bayonets, of course, were widely used instruments of war in that century, but the venerable Kentuckys were made for hunting in the mountains and the various dangers therein—not the battlefield. Thus, unfortunately for Cleveland's force, none of his weapons held a mount for the bayonet. In contrast, the Tory forces at the top already had their bayonets mounted and were in a much better position to repel the latest rebel charge. Subsequently, during several such attacks, the Tories responded to a charge with a charge, and each time the Patriots were driven back. Thus, Cleveland's first attacks all ended with a Patriot retreat back to the tree line some 50 yards below the summit.

Ferguson, missed these enemy advances; while still astride his magnificent white horse, he was at that precise moment, galloping down the middle of the mountain plateau to the west end of his line to check on things there, happily blowing his whistle all the while. He was confident that his trained troops could hold back this rough rabble of ill-educated men. He shouted encouragement to his men, calling many by name as he road past, as does almost every effective military commander. He'd originally had his forces disbursed around the entire mountain top, but the Patriots seemed at first to be attacking from only either end. Ferguson was about to order his men on the north face of the mountain to the west end of the mountain, and have his units from the south slope reinforce the east end of his line.

However, just at that moment, Elijah Clarke's large force of Georgia men emerged from the lower pine trees on the north slope of the hill, and the Tories above them became engaged. Ferguson said a hasty *"Thank God!"* that he hadn't had time to issue the movement orders. Quick prayers such as this are the norm for men in combat throughout history. Ferguson reconsidered his options. No doubt these damn rebels—how many of them were there anyway—had a force slithering up the south face too, so he kept some 200 Tories facing down that slope for another 30 minutes into the battle. They were thus wasted for the most part in this endeavor; having no Patriot force advancing on them, they had no targets for their guns at all.

Meanwhile Walton's Patriot force was now advancing steadily up the right flank, and several of the youngsters high up in the trees could see a new target that, wonder of wonders—was even less believable than the Tories standing up to reload. In a flash, here came a disgusted looking British general—to every illiterate Patriot on the mountain that day any enemy officer who was mounted was a general—riding on a white horse with his whole damn body exposed to enemy fire from the treetops! To top it off, he was wearing a red checkered shirt that no Patriot could miss! Ferguson may as well have been shouting, *"HERE I AM! SHOOT ME FIRST!"*

Of course Ferguson didn't know his enemy had climbed trees for better position; he thought he was safe as long as he stayed away from the crest of the hill. He was about to learn of his error, as twenty Kentucky rifles sounded as one, from the trees, the rocks, the logs, the grasses. The whole slope seemed to erupt in fire, and several pieces of hot lead found their mark on Ferguson's body. In that moment, he was hit in the lower calf of his left leg, his left arm just above the elbow, and most seriously, in the right shoulder. He was thrown back in his saddle, but in what amounted to a minor miracle, he managed to stay mounted, on his white horse, and by some quirk of fate, the horse was not wounded at all. He quickly maneuvered his horse to duck out of sight behind a thicket of rocks under several massive oak trees that still stood atop the summit. He'd also been wounded at the other end of the line, though superficially, merely a scratch on his left wrist. His body had now suffered four separate wounds.

Just above Ferguson, approximately 85 feet up, the leaves and branches of a mountain poplar appeared for some strange reason to be growing from a fork in an old oak tree. An interesting biological phenomenon that—a poplar branch growing from an oak—but in the midst of the hell of the battle below of course no one noticed. Meanwhile, the half-breed Cherokee scout Prather–Ekaia to the Cherokee—a longtime resident of the Tugaloo River Valley, calmly ate a piece of dried jerky, and watched the battle progress below him. It had taken him most of the night to put together this perch, virtually invisible from the ground—he was surely very "Ekaia" during this battle.

While Ekaia had frequently scouted for the Tories since they paid him so well, he really wasn't terribly vested in this fight. At this point, he just wanted to live through it. Further, he couldn't help but agree with the Patriots on several points. It was really stupid to stand up to reload in the middle of a battle, but to ride a white horse while wearing a red checkered shirt into a nest of pissed off frontiersmen with Kentucky rifles was plainly insane!

Upon seeing this stupidity, Ekaia immediately understood which side would carry the day in this battle; thus he began to plan his escape from this mountain of hellish death. After dark, he figured, when all of the Patriots had come and gone, he'd sneak away. All he need do was sit tight and be quiet, and he knew he'd be fine; after all, he'd been disappearing like that all his life.

Elijah Clarke's forces—400 strong—were not men of the Blue Ridge, as were most of the other Patriots on the mountain that day. Some of Clarke's men had never seen a mountain before a couple of months earlier, and certainly they had never shot at anything in any type of sloped terrain, and that lack of experience would prove critical. Now, any man of the mountains will tell you mountain hunting is different. When the Earth itself is at an angle to your proposed shot, one tends to overshoot when shooting downhill, and undershoot when shooting uphill. These Georgia boys from the distant flat lands to the south didn't know that, so while they were doing an excellent job of plowing up the earth in front of the Tories on the hilltop, they were consistently missing their shots, and thus were having no real effect on the battle at all. Most of their shots were landing immediately in front of the Tory breastworks on the north slope of the mountain, and for that reason they were not killing many of the enemy. Further, for 20 minutes or so they'd remained in the same positions behind the first logs they found, and remaining stationary in any battle is always a mistake.

Of course, the opposite problem confronted the Tories atop the mountain. These men from the large coastal cities—again, many had never seen mountains, much less hunted in them—tended to overshoot. Once, when Ferguson looked over the battlefield down the north slope, he was surprised that he saw only a few dead Patriots below the crest of the hill. These aiming errors were confirmed after the battle ended, when the Patriots noted fewer casualties overall, but also noted a much larger number of men killed by head shots than one would normally expect—the Tories had been firing high throughout the battle. With both Tory and Patriot units on the north face stymied by the same unrecognized terrain problem—Clarke's Patriot forces had been in a stalemate with the Tories facing them for almost a third of the entire battle.

Old Elijah Clarke, ever the hothead, and always one to come up with a bad idea at just the right time, had almost decided to do exactly the wrong thing. He had determined that the enemy position at the summit was too strong for his assault, and he was about to order his men back. In fact, these brave men would probably have pursued the battle much more vigorously and effectively, if some Tory had had the good grace—and the aim—to put Elijah out of his misery. Such was not to be however, and Col. Clarke was about to issue these wrong-minded orders, when, much to his surprise, the reserve force lead by the lean and mean Tennessean, Nolichucky Jack Sevier, came charging up the hill, and ran right by Clarke's forces. Mountain men to the last, this incredible wave of 120 brave frontiersman carried the battle further up the north slope, firing and loading as they went, and unlike the shooting of the Georgia men, these Tennesseans knew what the hell they were doing. Even when firing uphill, it seemed that they couldn't miss!

History of another kind was made that day on the north slope of King's Mountain, as those brave Tennesseans charged. Here they came, sweeping up the slope, jumping from tree to log charging like banshees from hell, and strangely enough, screaming a high-pitched scream at the top of their lungs. These frontiersmen long ago had picked up the habit of screaming a high pitched, wailing scream as they charged their enemies; for screaming gave one both power and energy in battle. In fact the fathers and older brothers of these men had stolen the same idea from the war cries they'd heard in the Cherokee War only 20 years previously. Clarke was thus, the first man in history to hear a battle sound from the throats of a charging line of white men, a terrifying scream that 81 years later, in yet another war, would become known as the "Rebel Yell." Today, in the clarity of hindsight, we are left to ponder the strange but interesting fact, that the famed "Rebel Yell" was first screeched by Cherokee warriors in the Blue Ridge, almost exactly 100 years before the American Civil War started. King's Mountain was the first battle in which the "Rebel Yell" was used by whites—these uneducated, but ferocious mountain men from Tennessee, Kentucky, and the distant Carolina mountains. Such are the vagrancies of history.

As luck would have it, the timing for Sevier's charge was right—most of the Tories on top were reloading right then. Thus, these men from Tennessee charged not into loaded rifles but into the relative calm of a reloading pause, and because of this dumb luck, this charge managed to reach the top of the plateau. However, they then discovered the same drawback Cleveland's force had noted only minutes before—they had no bayonets, and their enemy did. Like Cleveland's force they too retreated to find positions lower down the slope, some 25 yards from the top of the hill.

Still, the battle on the north face was now edging further up the slope, and Clarke could not, with any honor, withdraw. Even more to the advantage of the Patriots on that day, most of Clarke's men now ignored their hotheaded, ineffective commander, and merely followed along with Sevier's better disciplined and more experienced men. In fact, several of those men actually reached the top of the mountain with their rifles loaded, and thus dispatched some of the Tories prior to their retreat. For that reason, Clarke could not—and did not— do any more harm on the battlefield on that particular day. All that can be said of Clarke's performance at King's Mountain, is that he did manage eventually to get himself wounded slightly in the arm, and thus had a sign for all posterity of his self-proclaimed bravery in this critical battle. He would brag on that singular wound until the day he died. Because of that wound and his ceaseless self-promotion, a county in Georgia would be named in his honor, and therein would be located one of the great Southern universities, the University of Georgia. Thus would Clarke's name live forever.

Walton's forces were heavily engaged but were not advancing, so after a few movements of individual infantrymen, Ferguson, still mounted, began to gallop back to the other end of the mountain top. Ekaia, sitting calmly in the fork of the oak tree above Ferguson, was glad to see the Commander leave, as that took a tempting target further away from his stealthy but not bullet proof perch high above the fray. Ekaia thought to himself, *"Good riddance–that idiot Ferguson is sure to get himself killed this day!"*

Ferguson had instructed his commanders on both the north and south slope to send a support unit of 150 infantrymen from their units, should they hear his whistle call. Sure enough, Ferguson had worn that whistle around his neck during the entire battle. When he got back to the east end of the hill, he could see that the Patriots below him had advanced significantly; by then they'd actually been on the plateau twice, so he began to blow his whistle like crazy. He expected that 300 men would thus leave their posts on the north and south breastworks, and come charging to the east end of the plateau. However, when several units tried to reposition, they found that they were even more vulnerable than when loading their rifles! Many were cut down before they reached the east end of the plateau. Still this did have the effect of involving some men from the south face—the only mountain slope that was unmolested by the Patriots up to this point in the battle.

Thus did the battle progress; Patriots attacking in several positions all around three sides of the mountain and Tories defending. The Patriots frequently charged to the summit, but on each occasion the Tories charged with bayonets and sent the Patriots scampering back down the hill a few yards. Each time the Patriot sharpshooters—that is how the Tories now thought of the men in the treetops on the western slope of the hill—would cut down a few more of Ferguson's men. Then another group of Patriots would advance from another quarter, and Ferguson would have to recall his men on the north slope, to create a defense of the east or west flank.

The battle continued for a time, with Walton's men picking their targets from their tree top perches, and many men in Early's command still playing hopscotch. Sevier, now the de facto commander of some 450 Patriots attacking 300 Tories on the north face, was steadily advancing. Some of his men had sighted Walton's treetop sharpshooters, so they began to climb too. Ferguson—never a man to give up easily—road down the entire line at least one more time, shouting encouragement to his men, and collected another superficial wound in the process. His shoulder—by far his most serious wound—hurt like hell and was bleeding badly. Still he rode on, and from his ever changing vantage point things began to look pretty grim for the Tories all along the line. He wondered to himself, *"Where the hell did this rabble learn to fight like this?"*

He would not have believed the answer had someone been there to give it to him. These frontiersmen had fought just like this since they were old enough to load a weapon for their paw, their maw, their older brother, or sister, and by the age of five, for themselves. The very fact that they were here at all attested to their fighting fortitude on the roughest frontier anywhere in the world in the late eighteenth century. Such men had faced the terror of unexpected Indian attack for every second of their lives, and they had fought all of their lives, unlike the more settled city merchants or farmers from the eastern tidewater regions who comprised the Tory force on the mountain that day. Like the warriors of ancient Sparta, the Zulu nation of southeastern Africa, or the Apache of the western plains in North America, these over-mountain men were born fighters—on that day, they were some of the toughest frontier fighters in the world. Such men make for a bloody frontier indeed, and hell had, in truth, come to the King's Mountain, as Campbell had foreseen.

Ferguson was, by then very concerned about the fight on the north face, and he considered it critical that his command not be divided by Patriots achieving the summit in the middle of the hill. What Ferguson didn't realize was that the real threat was on the western end of the plateau. There Walton's men in the trees had picked off enough of the Tories, that the others were becoming truly scared. From the perspective of these Tories, hot lead seemed to be flying at them from everywhere, even the trees, which of course they knew was impossible! These men were at that stage of fright, when they were beginning to look into their comrades eyes, with the heartfelt, though unspoken question, *"Would this be a good time to get the hell out of here?"*

Only ten minutes after Ferguson rode off for the final time, the west end of the line began to crumble; slowly at first, but then more quickly. First, only one Tory, a 14 year old boy from Summerville, New Jersey, broke from the breastworks and ran back toward the center of the hilltop. Having seen this flagrant cowardice, his lieutenant immediately turned with his pistol and shot that man in the back. Fear was understandable, but running away from enemy fire in the heat of battle was not tolerated by any army in the world, no matter how old, or how young you were. Still, the first Tory runner had been only the tip of the iceberg. Another stood, and instead of loading took a ball right in the middle of his face; his head exploded and his brains and blood shot out to cover the face of the man next to him. That man then threw down his Brown Bess and inadvertently screamed the same high wailing scream used as a weapon by his enemy. Next, he turned and began to run like hell. Several others followed, and several more tossed down their weapons and stood with their hands raised in the worldwide signal for surrender. The hapless lieutenant, watching all of this, hadn't had a chance to reload from killing the first of his cowardly men. Still, one of the other fleeing Tories didn't realize that, so he paused just long enough to ram a bayonet through his commander's stomach; he didn't want to be shot in the back by this lieutenant like his companion had been only moments before.

By then, Walton's men were at the summit, having charged several times, and with Tarleton's quarters on their collective mind and with their blood running high, they shot anything that moved, including the Tories with their arms raised. After all these damn Tories had been stupidly standing up all afternoon, and who could tell if they were surrendering or not? In fact, who could tell what these idiots thought?

While some Patriots turned away from the carnage, others considered this the same type of to-the-death struggle they'd had with the Cherokee all their lives; for them it was kill or be killed, and they didn't even consider the enemy's arms raised as an issue. Still others enjoyed this hell, calmly reloading and shooting at every target they saw. One frontiersman in a rough deerskin coat was making the Tories lay down side by side, as if already in the grave. Then he and his fellow soldiers marched up to their heads and shouted *"Here's your Tarleton's quarters."* They then shot the prone Tories right between the eyes.

Now on the northern flank, the fighting was fierce, bloody, and hand-to-hand. The Tories from the coastal cities of the Carolinas, New York, and New Jersey were mostly shopkeepers or farmers, and none had any real experience in knife-fighting. It is one thing to fire a musket at a man, and many of these Tories had never done that prior to this battle. Still, it is considerably more emotionally engaging to kill a man with a knife, a man who is within arms reach. Some Tories tried to fix their bayonets a bit late in the battle, and standing up yet again for this purpose, many were cut to pieces or shot. These men died with an unloaded Brown Bess in one hand and an unused bayonet in the other.

Sevier's over-mountain men, in contrast, were born with knives in their teeth, and many had experience at slashing Indians, or each other, at close range. Some had fought bears with only a knife on a Saturday night bear-baiting or at the yearly county fairs, then to be paid by a drink of homemade liquor. In this fight, the Tories never stood a chance once the battle became one-on-one.

With the western end and northern slope of the plateau falling to the Patriots, Ferguson ordered a "Three Sided Square" a formation designed to increase the effectiveness of their volley fire. At this range using that formation, the Tories could deliver a massive volley, that cleared the plateau top of the Patriots for a time. At just that moment, Ferguson did the unexpected—he ordered a bayonet charge of his own, and his men charged the Patriots, with Ferguson, still wounded and astride his horse, leading the way. With no bayonets themselves, the Patriots retreated again down the slopes. This pattern repeated itself several more times, in only a matter of minutes on the eastern end of the hill.

Even with the western end of the hill lost, many of his men wounded, and Patriot rifle fire taking a fearsome toll, Ferguson still refused to see the writing on the wall. When his second in command recommended surrender, he shouted, *"Never will I yield to such damned banditti!"* He issued orders to close ranks, and then he led a final charge, with the pitiful few Tories that would still follow him. With sword drawn and still astride his horse, he charged directly towards Sevier's over-mountain men—the very men he'd taunted for over a month with his famed "Fire and sword!" message. He had indeed kicked over a hornet's nest, and these hornets had come to sting!

It is an unfortunate fact that good men die on both sides in almost every battle in history. One could not, at that moment have found better fighting men, or men with more overall potential than Early Cleveland, William Campbell, John Sevier, Jessie Walton, or James Wyly on any continent in the world. These men would tame the first American frontier, and in large measure, create our nation. All were good men; indeed all were great men, and many such men would die that day.

Of course, we must also mention the Cherokee half-blood, Ekaia, who still sat in his God-like treetop perch at the far end of the ridge calmly eating his jerky while these world shaking events unfolded below him. He was a man on whom much would depend. He would eventually create a family dynasty of considerable wealth and influence; he would succeed in a white man's world, simply because he was savvy enough to know when to appear and when not to.

Opposing the march of history that day was Patrick Ferguson—an innovative, charismatic, highly effective leader who, as he saw it, was doing his best in defense of the colonies of his beloved country. Unlike his friend Tarleton, Ferguson had always fought with honor and with great bravery. He'd refused a shot at George Washington, because he considered it immoral, and such heartfelt distinctions mark the character of this incredible man. There was no finer officer in the entire British army anywhere in the world on that day than Patrick Ferguson.

Clearly, great men fought on every side in this conflict, and even when dealing in death, the soldiers on either side of such a bloody conflict can, and often do, recognize this simple fact. It sometimes causes a moment of reflection, a moment of pause, as it did on King's Mountain that day, when a man of such stature is about to die. Almost every man on King's Mountain, Tory and Patriot alike, knew that Col. Ferguson was about to perish in glory; Most who were there believed to their dying day that Ferguson even realized it himself.

The diary entry of James Wyly, written shortly after the battle, reflects his thoughts at that exact moment.

"Ferguson looked magnificent astride his white horse, with his blood running down his shirt and the horse's flank, in that final charge into our rifles. He'd collected many wounds, but he managed to stay in the saddle to the end. I am convinced that God wanted this man to die gloriously. As he drew his sword one final time, and shouted the order to charge. He whirled facing his steed toward his enemy, and the battle seemed to

pause as every man on the hill—Tory and Patriot alike—looked at this magnificent leader." James Wyly's diary, 1780

All present at that moment knew this would be his last desperate action in this life, but Ferguson would not consider defeat even though he was already defeated. As he made his advance, his raw courage inspired a few of his remaining ambulatory men to rise to the occasion and follow him, charging toward the Patriot guns.

At that moment, at least fifty Kentucky rifles were aimed directly at the bloody red-checkered shirt, and many more were aimed at the few men who ran beside him in that climatic final charge. One of Sevier's over-mountain men calmly licked the front sight of his Kentucky rifle; this was the best way to clean off the black powder residue. Just as Ferguson began his charge, that man, Robert Young tossed the rifle to his shoulder in a fluid well-practiced motion, and said, *"Let's see what ol' Sweet Lips can do!"* Over 100 rifles shook the very air on the mountain; "Sweet Lips," "Bearkiller," "Leadfly" and scores of others with and without names, sounded as one.

Every man in that final charge was hit several times. Ferguson went down with fourteen more wounds in his body, and as he finally fell from his horse; his left foot was shot completely off and hung in the stirrup. The horse stampeded off the mountain, right into the ranks of the Patriots. From his position lying on the ground, Furgesen pulled his pistol and killed one more Patriot before being killed himself, while lying on the ground. Furgesen's mighty charge had reached only 15 yards, and Furgesen died without ever talking to a Patriot commander.

Still, more barbarity was to result from this battle. Ferguson's horse, ignored now by the Patriots, galloped right up to the Patriot line, still carrying Ferguson's foot and lower leg. The bridle was finally grabbed by a large filthy man with mud on his breeches, and a slight wound on the left lower rib area of his massive body. Early Cleveland then shouted to his friend Wyly, *"Told you I'd get me this white horse."* He tore the foot and leg from the stirrup and calmly tossed it away in the woods, where raccoons devoured it that night. He then mounted his captured horse, and proudly rode it back toward the dying battle on the top of the mountain.

Hell Hath No Fury

As a general rule of thumb, you don't want to piss off men from the Blue Ridge, particularly if they are armed, and these rugged frontiersmen were always armed. For only a few more minutes after Ferguson's fall, did the battle continue, but as more white flags were raised by the Tories the true hell on the mountain began. Like the attempted surrenders on the west end of the Tory line, the Patriots on the east end of the mountain were in no mood to allow any to surrender. As the Tories raised their arms and pleaded for *"quarters!"*

Many of the Patriots responded with a shout of, *"Tarleton's Quarters,"* as they continued to fire into massed Tory troops, most of whom had their arms clearly raised in the air. In one location on the mountain top, Ferguson's second in command raised a white flag, which was honored by Campbell, and the two walked towards each other and briefly stood together talking. However, in plain sight only 200 yards away, the firing on the now surrendered Tories continued. Campbell was outraged; he grabbed the nearest horse and rode through his Patriot army knocking down rifles before they fired. He shouted, *"For God sakes, don't shoot. It's murder to kill them now, for they have raised the flag!"* Still, the firing continued some time, as the anger over "Tarleton's quarters" played out. In time, the various militia commanders managed to gain control of their men, and the firing stopped briefly; a pause which was not to last.

As fate would have it, that brief respite was not the end of the bloody carnage on King's Mountain. At just that moment, even as things were coming under control on the plateau, a foraging party of some 100 Tories that Ferguson had sent out earlier that morning before the battle, returned leading a group of pigs and some cattle. They emerged from the woods on the southern flank, some were even holding chickens or small goats they'd collected. They saw the Patriots atop the hill and opened fire from down the slope, and that was all it took.

Immediately the fight—more accurately the massacre—on the mountain began again. At that point, many of the Tories had been disarmed and were seated together under guard, and for them this was truly unfortunate. Sure now that the white flag was a betrayal, Campbell ordered his men to shoot any prisoners who tried to escape. In the heat of that moment with lead from Tory muskets flying over the plateau, that order was misinterpreted as *"Shoot the Prisoners!"*

Thus, did a dozen Patriots fire several times directly into the faces of 200 unarmed Tories seated together and under Patriot guard. Three, then four times, they loaded and fired into the group, who could do nothing but huddle together behind their comrades dead bodies, and the few logs and rocks nearby. One Patriot later reflected on that moment; *"We killed near a hundred of them and hardly could be restrained from killing the lot, the bastards!"*

Once again, it took some time to gain control of the various militia units, but the commanders did so, as the Tories in the tree line retreated and ran for Cornwallis' force encamped in Charlotte.

The Patriots losses in the battle were light; 28 killed and 64 wounded. However, because of the bloody after-battle carnage, losses on the Tory side were steep. In this hour-long fight, the Tories lost 157 killed with 163 wounded. Over 698 Tories were taken prisoner.

In a final act of senseless carnage, Ferguson's body was defiled by some of the Patriots as the final prisoners were rounded up. Several men from the Blue Ridge laughed as they urinated on the body of the man who had threatened their homes with the phrase, *"...lay waist your country with fire and sword."* One shouted to the corpse, *"Here's how I'll put out your damn fire"* as he relieved himself on the bloody red-checkered shirt.

However after that spectacle, others who were acting more humanely, stopped the desecration and eventually they buried the body of Ferguson in a shallow grave near the crest of the ridge he defended so valiantly. One or two Patriots, while saying a brief thankful prayer for their own deliverance, remembered to mention the brave Ferguson in their prayers. Ferguson's leadership and courage in his final action was to be recorded for all history—by Wyly and many others—and he is remembered well by posterity. Many years later, on the 150th anniversary of the battle, a simple stone was raised to honor this man on the summit of King's Mountain. It was raised by the descendents of those who defeated him, and dedicated to: **"A soldier of military distinction and of honor."** It stands on Kings' Mountain to this day.

However, other graves dug by the victorious Patriots for the Tories left a lot to be desired. Most graves on the mountain were horribly shallow—only a foot or so below the level of the rocky ground, so by one or two days after the battle, the wolves, raccoons, and bear of the mountain ridge had dug up the corpses of the dead Tories and feasted on the bounty of meat for days. For many decades after the battle, this hill was known as "Wolves Ridge," because of the abundance of wolves in the area. Most locals attributed that population to the rich food sources resulting from feasting on the Tories' bodies during the fall of 1780.

Other than the usual night of drinking and braggin' after a battle, the four white men who would determine the future of the Tugaloo River Valley did not meet again. Walton and Cleveland would fight together again within only a couple of months, and Cleveland kept Ferguson's horse for many years. Robert Jarrett would return home and Wyly would return to his family, and continue to write in his diary. Still, that evening of October 7, 1780, none knew of their future role in settlement of the lower Blue Ridge—each was merely concerned with getting back home and building his own future, making a living for his family. Of such mundane desires are great nations made. The Revolutionary War would come to an end within 12 months at Yorktown, but these men of the Blue Ridge would, by then, be fighting the Cherokee again.

Now, however, it was time to go home, and any soldier cherishes those times; the battle is over, and peace is at hand. Cleveland, Walton, Wyly, and Jarrett were no different; they each looked forward to some time at home, without having to take up arms. After a final night of comradeship and drink, these men, like militia forces in every great conflict, simply hopped on their horses and headed home.

In 1780, Early Cleveland still had a small spread in Surrey County, North Carolina, and all 285 pounds of him—still imposing mightily on Patrick Ferguson's horse—made the trek back up the Great Philadelphia Wagon Road to his wife and his sons Larkin, Thomas, and Paul. Jarrett returned to his home near Pendleton Court House, just below the Blue Ridge in South Carolina. From that spot, he opened a dry goods store and, by all accounts, did very well with his business. Jessie Walton and James Wyly were neighbors in the Jonesborough settlement in Tennessee, so they rode with "Nolichucky Jack" and the other Tennesseans back across the Blue Ridge and eventually ended up at home in Jonesborough, some 30 miles northeast of the Great Blue Mountains. However, the frontier was anything but a settled place, and these men would soon find themselves embroiled in yet another conflict—for in these days, in the Blue Mountains, war seemed to be inevitable.

Chapter 4: Blood on the Frontier
Dragging Canoe's War

History can, and often does, play cruel jokes on men, leading some to attempt the impossible, and others to believe in the importance of efforts that are doomed to be futile. Such men, once deceived by history, struggle on where no hope exists. These leaders may never grasp the role that they may be playing on the world stage, and others fail to understand that they have no notable role on that stage at all. Such was the fate of the Cherokee War Chief, Dragging Canoe. He never realized how very unimportant his war was, but then, from his perspective, his fight was critical. Moreover, how many of us really understand even the most basic view of who we really are, much less how history might perceive us, if it remembers us at all—in a century or two?

It has become popular today to act as if the Revolutionary War stands alone as a seminal historical event. Indeed some see it as a defining event in all history, when the common man for the first time demanded and fought for his freedom and for his say in government. However, a more accurate read of history demonstrates that such was not the case. Indeed men had demanded freedom for centuries prior to that revolution. Further, the American Revolution of 1776-1781 was only a small part of one of the numerous European colonial conflicts of the day. Indeed, at the time the British royalty saw this messy little rebellion in the North American colonies as merely a sideshow to their larger ongoing war with France. In fact, both France and Britain claimed land in the northern hemisphere of the new world, and each played a critical part in this American Revolution. Of course, for the Patriots and Tories who happened to live on the northern American continent, the war with France, while much more global and certainly of longer duration, was nevertheless the sideshow, and Dragging Canoe's War wasn't a war at all! Thus, the "important" conflict in any historical period may, ultimately be a matter of one's perspective.

Still, embedded within these two larger conflicts—nested inside this geopolitical fight for global control and colonial influence, and hidden under the smaller continental struggle that was the American Revolution, buried like the increasingly smelly layers of an decomposing onion—the Cherokee on the frontier of the Blue Ridge managed to stage their own little war in the 1780s–a war lead by Dragging Canoe. While the battles of the Cherokee in the upland country of South Carolina and the lower reaches of the Blue Ridge during this period must be considered as a part of the broader Revolution, the war chief who now led the Cherokee didn't see his war from that perspective at all. To Dragging Canoe, War Chief of the Cherokee, this war was a fight to the death—a fight for the very existence of his people; this was a fight against the private holocaust of the Cherokee.

Dragging Canoe had reached his manhood as white culture and influence had come to dominate his tribe, and like Ridge—the grandson of Runs-To-Water—Dragging Canoe had been raised in the traditional culture of the Cherokee. He hated all white faces with a fierce passion. Still, as an astute leader, he was able to see advantage in using the British against those whites who would claim his land, and while the British faces were also white, at least they claimed they would remove all white settlements from the land to the west of the sacred Blue Mountains. Thus, in Dragging Canoe's mind, this land would be forever Cherokee.

Yes, Dragging Canoe hated white faces deeply, with a burning intensity. Still, he was a cousin of Nancy Ward—the same Nancy Ward that once lived along the Tugaloo with a drunken owner of a stream-fed grist mill. As a Beloved Woman of the Cherokee, she managed to maintain something of a moderating influence over this firebrand Dragging Canoe for a time. Still, in the years from 1776 through 1781, Dragging Canoe and his warriors—numbering perhaps a thousand effectives—forced many whites to flee the frontier in the Blue Ridge by killing, torture, and scalping. In his mind, this Cherokee War was a war for the very life of his people. As always, Wyly chronicled the temperament of Dragging Canoe and the Cherokee during that period, with an understanding of the mind of "the savages" that was uniquely astute for his day.

"No sooner had we returned victors from the fight at King's Mountain, than we received word that Dragging Canoe was kicking up his heels again. He is a bloodthirsty savage, schooled in the arts of torture and warfare against defenseless women and children. Some in the Tennessee settlements attributed this round of threats to the typical warrior bombast coupled with strong drink, but I fear they may be wrong. Those who look more deeply can see that the Cherokee loose their precious hunting grounds to the whites at every turn. When this bloody war against the tyrannical crown of England ends, one can barely conceive of the numbers of whites who will make toward the frontier in the ever growing quest for new land, and the Cherokee, like the Creek before them, are bound to be pushed out. The Cherokee, like all savage civilizations, are

doomed once that great migration commences. I shall have to look into the opportunities that such a migration presents for the astute businessman."

James Wyly's Diary, October 29, 1780

Wyly was right to fear the Cherokee. For Dragging Canoe saw that the whites were once again fighting each other, and therein lay his opportunity. In one council in the final months of 1776 when considering yet another treaty offered by the whites, Dragging Canoe turned to every clan in the Council House, making his greeting silently by bowing in the direction of each clan section. When he finally spoke he made his position clear.

"We speak of another treaty to take our land. I have thought on this matter, and I have listened to my brothers speak for two days, and I now know what I must do. We know that whole Indian nations have melted away like snowballs in the sun before the white man's advance. They have scarcely a name for our people except those wrongly recorded by their destroyers. I ask you, where are the Delawares? They have been reduced to a mere shadow of their former greatness. We had hoped that the white men would not be willing to travel beyond the mountains. Now that hope is gone. They have passed the mountains and have settled upon Cherokee land.

They wish to have that sanctioned by treaty. When that is gained, the same encroaching spirit will lead them upon other land of the Cherokee. New cessions will be asked. Finally the whole country which the Cherokee and their fathers have so long occupied will be demanded and the remnant of the Real People, once so great and formidable will be compelled to seek refuge in some distant wilderness. There they will be permitted to stay only a short while, until they again behold the advancing banners of the same greedy host. Not being able to point out any further retreat for the miserable Cherokee, the extinction of the whole race will be proclaimed. Should we not therefore run all risks and incur all consequences rather than submit to further loss of our country? Such treaties may be all right for men who are too old to hunt or fight. As for me, I have my young warriors about me. We will have our lands, or we will die. I have spoken to the Real People. Kanati will be with me defending my land, or I will die."

Then in 1776, after hostilities between Patriots and Tories began, Dragging Canoe called together as many warriors as would follow him and, using his muskets and powder supplied by British agents, he seemed to attack everywhere at once. A trader in the overhill settlements of the Tennessee country would be found dead and scalped inside his cabin; sometimes he'd been scalped by the same Cherokee he'd been trading with for 10 years. A small party on their journey to settle west of Asheville, the new town that sprung up seemingly overnight in the Carolina colony, would be attacked one day, their horses driven off and livestock slaughtered. A week later, Dragging Canoe and his band would attack as far south as the growing town of Augusta, Georgia.

While the first years of the Revolutionary War involved several bloody engagements between Patriots and Tories in southern states, the frontier Patriot militia from these states, unlike their coastal neighbors, also had to contend with rambunctious Cherokee on the frontier. Thus, in 1776, several raids were sent against the Cherokee from the various coastal cities. First, a youngish, undistinguished man, Colonel Samuel Jack, led a small party of 200 Georgia Militia against the Cherokee towns at the headwaters of the Tugaloo. However, they found the area around old Tugaloo Town almost entirely deserted by the Cherokee. In fact, the several Cherokee families they did find were so welcoming, the Georgia Militia couldn't force itself to destroy their homes, and this small raid resulted only in the burning of several Cherokee barns that had been rebuilt in the old town of Estatoe four miles upriver from Tugaloo.

The South Carolinians on the other hand were quite angry at Dragging Canoe and his continued raids into their upcountry settlements, raids which, of course were supported by the Tories. In order to meet this threat, the South Carolina assembly voted a bounty of seventy five pounds per Cherokee scalp—an unheard of amount in that day—and this resulted in a large number of volunteers for the expedition to make war on the Cherokee. Thus, Colonel Andrew Williamson, the same man who destroyed Tugaloo Town many years previously, went on the march again. He brought with him eleven hundred money-hungry men from the lowlands, and rode into the Cherokee towns twenty miles to the east of the Tugaloo River Valley. There they burned any Cherokee cabin they came across, and attacked anything that moved. Riding past the now abandoned Fort Prince George, these men rode into the old settlement of Seneca which was upriver on the banks of the Keowee. Wyly, who was active in both the South Carolina and the Tennessee militia, was serving with Williamson's raiders. He tells the story of the opening of the Seneca Battle.

"Upon reaching the old Cherokee settlement of Seneca, our scouts noted that the lodges were dilapidated; further the fields had not been farmed recently, so we concluded that the town was abandoned. The lodges on both sides of the river ford were deserted, and some of the roofs had caved in. Thus, we naturally made no preparations for a fight, but continued our marching by twos (two militiamen abreast). This formation is the most effective option for making good time on wilderness trails, but it is a very ineffective way to march into a battle, and that mistake cost us dearly. Many a man was marching or riding with unloaded muskets, and they died in that fashion.

James Wyly's Diary, Winter, 1980

The two lines of men marched in good order into the ford and across the shallow river at Seneca getting wet up to their knees. When perhaps one third of the column had crossed, all hell erupted with the crack of a single musket. As men scrambled under fire to climb the opposite bank, more shots erupted from all sides of the settlement—Dragging Canoe, his warriors, and a few of his Tory allies were well hidden in every lodge, tree, and firepit. The first volley took down almost 20 militiamen, and started a general route of the invading force. Militiamen fell wounded on both sides of the ford as well as in the river; some of the wounded drowned when they fell face down in the water. With their muskets unloaded, other militiamen had no way to return fire; many threw down their weapons and began to run back up the trail. Wyly himself escaped the initial fire, only because he was riding and his horse reared at the initial shot. As he was not yet into the river, he began a prudent retreat back up the trail.

However, Williamson's second in command, Col. Duncan Hammond, had ridden into town near the middle of the line, unlike Williamson who, along with his staff, usually rode towards the rear of his force. Hammond immediately saw the danger and ordered all of his remaining men to stand fast, and to load their muskets. He shouted that they would defend their fallen brothers on the other side of the ford. All knew what would happen to wounded men who were left on the field in the hands of Dragging Canoe and his Cherokee; it was the same fate that these militiamen had planned for every Cherokee they encountered–hasty death and quick scalping. In a flash, Hammond rushed his horse to the front of the soldiers, all of whom were on foot and shouted; *"We can't leave the wounded across the river. If needs be I will ride to their rescue myself!"* With that, he turned and charged his horse into the cold waters of the river ford.

Hammond's bravery thus, had immediate effect. Many of the militiamen who had been retreating stopped dead in their tracks, as did Wyly, and his Tennesseans. These men were the first to fire, since no frontiersman ever traveled the wilderness with an unloaded rifle. Others in the column began to load their muskets. Some fixed their bayonets and followed Hammond into the cold, bloody waters of the river and across the ford. Much to their surprise, they found that despite their initial success with the first volley, the Cherokee themselves were withdrawing. Wyly explained this withdrawal in his papers many years latter.

"Throughout this period of unrest by the savages, powder and lead were as precious as gold to the Cherokee; indeed to everyone in the colonies. As a result of the general shortage, these essentials for waging war were always in extremely short supply among the Cherokee, even with the British agents supplying what they could. Often this worked to the advantage of our militia, as it did during the raid on Seneca. After a second musket volley with the Tennessee militia showing no sign now of retreating, and the rally of the South Carolina men, the Cherokee themselves had to withdraw.

In that engagement, Williamson lost 28 men, with another 13 wounded, as his men made up the front of the column. No Tennessean was lost. Still, our force held the ground and within the hour, the Cherokee Town of Seneca was gone. The dilapidated cabins and lodges went up like lighter-wood under the torches of our militia, and many of our Tennesseans collected Cherokee hair for bounty, on that day, since the more genteel gentlemen from South Carolina were still somewhat squeamish about collecting scalps. That was a squeamishness they would soon loose."

James Wyly's Diary, War Report 1780

Williamson's force, unlike the earlier, smaller raid by the Georgia men, continued into the Blue Ridge, across the first ridge-line and into the lower towns of the Cherokee. The warriors under Dragging Canoe fell back to Neowee Pass near the town of Estatoe, five miles north of old Tugaloo Town. There Dragging Canoe prepared another ambush. Again, the militia fell into the trap, and again Hamilton saved the force—he ordered a direct charge on the enemy front, while he personally led a force over a mound of high rocks to outflank the Cherokee. He shouted: *"Loaded guns advance; empty guns fall down and load,"* as he charged the rocks and began his climb. Again, the Cherokee fired two volleys and fled, leaving several dead and wounded for Williamson's men to scalp.

As Williamson forced his way through the Neowee Pass, he found himself only 20 miles from the valley towns of the Cherokee, and unlike the lower settlements of Keowee or Tugaloo Town, these valley towns were very much occupied by the Cherokee in 1780. Williamson's thousand man army went on a rampage, and the Cherokee fled into the deeper mountains, leaving their cabins, their livestock, and their fields to be destroyed. When the South Carolina Militia did find a few Cherokee, the savagery shown by Williamson's force reached epic proportions. Women and children were not spared, but received even more cruel treatment than did the few warriors captured alive. By this point in their foray, the South Carolina men had indeed lost their squeamishness. In fact, every convention of civilization was ignored by these bounty hunting militiamen from the lower counties of South Carolina, and no atrocity was beyond contemplation. The most horrific tortures were conducted upon Cherokee captives as if they were mere entertainment for the militiamen around their campfires at night. In one case a captured Cherokee woman and two children were tied together at the waist and chopped apart one arm or leg at a time until all were dead. Such is the nature of border warfare for an unimportant war, embedded within a larger Revolution which is itself, embedded within the conflicting colonial and geopolitical claims of empire-building world powers. Cruelty compounds itself as conflicts become both less important historically, and simultaneously, more personal.

Ultimately, Williamson's force ran low on supplies in a couple of months, and retreated having destroyed several of the middle Cherokee villages. They took

75 scalps back to Charles Town for the bounty. Of course this only enraged the Cherokee more, and given their Blood Oath, Williamson's raid ultimately lead to reprisals by the Cherokee.

Thus did Dragging Canoe's War progress, embedded within the larger history of the Revolution. The Cherokee would raid outlying farms, scalp the occupants, and melt into the Blue Mountains, and white militias of Georgia, Virginia, or the Carolinas would take to the field, raid the Cherokee towns in the Blue Ridge while reaching higher and deeper into the scared hills with each passing year. At this point, the Tugaloo River Valley and the small hill that was the focus of our story, was now considered to be open to settlement by whites, though few came, because of the trouble with the Cherokee.

In November of 1780 Dragging Canoe and his band of Cherokee on the Georgia Tennessee border had noticed that many of the frontiersmen were off yet again to the east fighting among themselves. The local militias were fighting their British King and of course, agents from Great Britain had been encouraging revolt among the Cherokee since the Revolution began. As the over-mountain men left for the Battle of King's Mountain in September of 1780, the Cherokee under Dragging Canoe determined that this would be a wonderful time to drive the whites from the Blue Ridge and Great Smoky Mountains once and for all. At that particular moment, all the militias typically used for defense of the white settlements to the west of the Blue Mountains were now engaged far to the east at Kings Mountain. Thus did Dragging Canoe, in a final desperate act to save his people, determine yet again to make war. Once again the warriors of the Cherokee were called together from many villages, and were told to prepare to fight the whites.

When the call for warriors came to the Cherokee village of Hiawassee, a middle-town in the Georgia Country some 60 miles west of the Tugaloo River Valley and just below the higher mountains, many warriors were off beginning the long autumn hunt. Stands-Tall, the son of Runs-To-Water was in the hunting grounds with his son Ridge far to the west. Stands-Tall had inherited his father's size, and was known to be a good hunter, with little love for the white man. He worked hard to instill that hatred of whites in his son. Still not all of the Cherokee hated the whites, as did Dragging Canoe and Stands-Tall. In fact, many were opposed to continued war with the whites. While all Cherokee knew that land was being lost to white settlements, some argued that the Cherokee should give up the old ways, and find new ways to live with the whites—a policy of assimilation. Even the Cherokee in the middle and over-mountain villages were coming increasingly under the influence of white culture—at that point, no Cherokee considered himself equipped for battle without a rifle or musket; war hatchets, or arrows would not do on the modern battlefield of 1780.

Nancy Ward, as one example, was convinced that continued war with the whites was foolish; she was sure that driving the whites back to the east of the Blue Ridge was a dream, and no longer a real possibility. Moreover, this woman knew war intimately—and hated it; for this was the same woman who had chewed lead for her husband, Kingfisher, in the Battle of Taliwa against the Creeks many years before. She knew the blood, the pain and death—the very face of war. More recently, she had separated from her white husband, Bryan Ward, and left his mill and cabin along Ward's Creek in the Tugaloo River Valley, and moved in with her cousins in the Cherokee villages in the higher mountains, eventually settling in a Cherokee village some 60 miles to the west of the Tugaloo, called Echota.

Knowing war herself, she detested fighting; based on her bravery and her first hand experience, she had now become a "Beloved Woman" of the Cherokee, and as such her wise council was heeded on many matters. Throughout the Revolutionary War, she had worked to save lives on both sides. Moreover, she believed whites and Cherokee could live together. Her daughter was now married to an Indian Agent from Virginia named Joseph Martin. Given her marriage to a white, as well as her daughter's, and her status as a "Beloved Woman" of the Cherokee, she was a living example of assimilation.

When Nancy Ward heard of Draggin Canoe's most recent plan to attack the white settlements in the mountains, she went into the Cherokee council house and argued vehemently against it. She marshaled every argument she could think of. She pleaded with Dragging Canoe yet again to avoid war with the whites. She used her age, and her reputation to advantage, but the anger among tribal members was just too great. She left the council, dejected, and sure that her tribe was doomed.

Of course, Dragging Canoe would hear no talk of peace—he'd been waging war against whites all his life, and had witnessed things no man alive should ever have to witness. He had become that most fearsome warrior of any historic period—an enraged man, viciously angry, and yet confident that he was defending his people's very existence by killing his enemy in any way possible. Such are the makings of both a terrorist and a hero, depending of course, on one's point of view.

When Dragging Canoe sent out his call for warriors in 1780, the Cherokee were of different minds about continuing the war with the white settlers. Many days did the Cherokee spend in council during late September and early October of 1780, debating the wisdom of an attack on the white settlements north of the Great Mountains, and as the debate ebbed and flowed, more warriors in the distant hills received the message that the tribe was going to war. This delay proved costly.

Dragging Canoe, like most of the whites then on the North American continent, was certain that the British and Tories would ultimately be victorious, if not in the fall of 1780, then certainly the next year—for the Patriots were on the run everywhere. Thus he believed the British and their Tory allies would destroy the militias from the Tennessee, Georgia, and Carolina mountains. He was astute enough to realize that each time the Patriots fought, they seemed to loose, and he knew of Gates' earlier defeat by Cornwallis on the plain of Camden in the South Carolina Colony. He had every reason to believe that the white settlements on the western side of the Blue Ridge were unprotected, and would not be well protected for the near future, at least until more militia units could be raised. He assumed that these would then be comprised of younger, inexperienced men. As he made these points in the council house, others saw the wisdom of his plan, and agreed; his argument ultimately prevailed and the Cherokee determined to make war on the white settlements of Tennessee once again.

In this thinking, however, Dragging Canoe was entirely wrong. These stubborn "over-mountain men" didn't loose to the Tories at King's Mountain, as Dragging Canoe had assumed. Thus, the militia units from Tennessee were not destroyed as Dragging Canoe hoped. Further, within two months, they were literally headed back over the Blue Ridge into the Tennessee country, before the Cherokee warriors could gather for Dragging Canoe's War.

Nolichucky Jack Fights Again

When John Sevier returned to his home along the Nolichunky River in Tennessee, he found his wife serving tea to a Cherokee woman that he had never met, but whom he knew just the same. By 1780, Nancy Ward was getting on in years, but there was vigor in her voice, and fire in her eyes; Her long brilliant white hair was bundled behind her head and flowing down in the back. Nolichunky Jack knew a Beloved Woman when he saw one, and while he hated all things Cherokee, he also maintained civility when the situation called for it; clearly this woman was his wife's guest.

This unique woman, with little preamble, looked directly into his face, and without rancor or hatred, spoke. *"I am Nancy Ward, of the Cherokee. I have come to tell you that our young warriors have decided to make war on the whites in the Tennessee country, while they believe the men are away fighting the British."*

Seiver realized that he was in an important council, so he reflected a moment on this news, and then asked. *"Why then, do you come to warn us of this attack?"*

That was both a simple and direct question, but the answer for Nancy was anything but simple. In retrospect, we can see the conflict that such a question would have caused this deeply spiritual Cherokee leader. Why indeed would she betray her own people? Is that what she was doing by coming to the militia leader to warn him? How could she explain to this white man, a man who has caused so much bloodshed among her people, that she hoped to save lives by sharing this information; both white and Cherokee lives?

All she was able to say was, *"I believe God meant for the white and the Cherokee to live together in the Blue Mountains."*

For Col. Jack Sevier, that was enough conversation. He now believed that the Cherokee were soon to make war and he wasted no time. He immediately called together the Tennessee militia that had just disbursed to their homes, and he also sent word to Virginia and the Carolinas for assistance. Wyly himself received word of this call, within an hour after returning to his home in Jonesboro, Tennessee, and subsequently spend one harrowing night, November 2, 1780, riding through the outlying settlements around the town gathering the militia for the newest conflict. His written papers reflect his thoughts on that night.

"While Dragging Canoe is a savage of the first magnitude, he is a cunning savage. He understands that hitting the outlying settlements while the militia is away is his only opportunity, and he is wise to plan this type of attack. The Cherokee are the best woodsman in the world; they can attack with brutal efficiency instantly, like a flash of lightning, and disappear just as quickly. I saw that in South Carolina with Williamson's force. These demons kill savagely, and then melt into the night.

I rode with fear in my heart that night. It was not a fear for my own life as I had fought many times. Rather it was fear of what I might find. I knew that at any moment I might ride into a war party on the trail, with fresh scalps hanging from their war hatchets. In each cabin where I stopped I might have found the bloody remains of a family disemboweled by the Cherokee, with the young women missing..."

Diary of Cap. James Wyly, Nov. 25, 1780

Many a man from the King's Mountain battle rode alone the final few miles to their cabins in the Tennessee country, spent an hour or two with their wives, then left for battle again. For some of them it was off to the local tavern where they hoped for nothing more than a few drinks and a few jokes with their friends. Instead they heard of the newest call for the militia. These men returned home a bit less drunk that they would have otherwise, and spent a subdued evening there with their families, before they left again, for a new battle. While it took four days for news to reach the North Carolina settlements, they also received the call. Thus, did Early Cleveland and his family, as well as many other veterans of King's Mountain spend barely a fortnight at home before they were called on yet again, to attack the Cherokee.

In a matter of days, Sevier was leading two hundred and fifty over-mountain men down the Warrior's Path from the Tennessee settlements, Watauga and Jonesborough, to the southwest deep into Cherokee Country. The ancient Warrior's Path is a long, narrow valley trail of breathtaking scenery, that stretches between the Blue Ridge and the higher Allegheny Mountains for more than five hundred miles. It begins north of Winchester, Virginia, covering the entire length of the beautiful Shanendoah Valley, and meandering to the southwest between the higher ridge-lines, all the way into northern Alabama. Sevier used this route into the Overhill Cherokee towns to gain speed and surprise the Cherokee before they would otherwise expect him. In fact, in only a week a contingent of Virginia and Carolina militia, with old Ben Cleveland leading the way—still sitting atop Ferguson's poor horse, arrived to assist, but Sevier had already left.

As Sevier's force approached the French Broad River, his scouts detected signs of a temporary Cherokee camp—perhaps several hundred Indians—just up the trail. Sevier and Wyly, who was by then his second in command, rode to the front of the men and Nolichucky Jack noted several things that suggested an imminent ambush. Not only was the terrain perfect for such an attack, but Sevier thought he saw several Cherokee behind trees just up the steep slope. Old Nolichucky Jack, as fine a frontier commander as any of that period, also knew his enemy. He was aware that Dragging Canoe's usual method of fighting involved luring the whites into a trap and then opening fire; for he'd talked at length with Wyly about the Williamson raid on Seneca and had learned that Dragging Canoe had used that same strategy twice in the previous conflict. In fact, in this respect, Dragging Canoe was merely using the same approach that had originally been used by the famous Cherokee War Chief Oconostota against Montgomery's force way back in 1760.

Sevier determined there and then to reverse the situation—he wanted to lure the Cherokee out of their ambush positions, and into an ambush he intended to set up, and he thought he knew just how to do it. Without pointing out the hidden Cherokee to Wyly, Sevier cooly determined his course of action, and the first step of that plan was uniquely original. Wyly reports on that unexpected event.

"Since Col. Sevier had determined that the Cherokee had established an ambuscade up the slope from our position, he wished to maintain normalcy and chose to refrain from pointing out the savages to me or the scouts. In fact as he sat atop his horse under an oak tree along the trail, he paused a moment, then dismounted, unbuttoned his codpiece and calmly took a piss in a thatch of grass. I'd never been so shocked in my life! I thought this quite indiscrete, as I'd never seen him present himself as anything other than a true gentlemen previously. I'm glad that, in retrospect, our esteemed Col. subsequently chose to share his desire for unsettling our enemy with me. After he relieved himself, the Col. loudly asked I and the scouts to return with him back down the trail. Once there he shared his awareness of the waiting ambush, and we made our plans. It takes a unique man to calmly relieve himself under the guns of his deadly enemy, even while planning his own attack!

James Wyly's Diary, Winter 1780

Sevier would send the scouts back up the trail in command of one small company of men—50 in all—to be "ambushed" by the Cherokee. Once they were attacked, they were told to grab all of their wounded, and then flee back down the trail the way they had come. Meanwhile, Sevier would set up his own ambush on the trail where his army stood. Sevier laid his trap by moving his main company further back down the trail—perhaps an additional 100 yards—to create the "end of the box." As he faced in the direction of the Cherokee ambush, he called on the veteran Jessie Walton to lead a contingent of 75 good riflemen into the trees and up the hill on the right flank. He then ordered Col. John Tipton to lead another 75 men into the trees on the left flank, thus creating the "sides of the box" and establishing his ambush. When the scout contingent was attacked and fell back, they were told to flee all the way down the trail and take cover behind Sevier's men, at "the end of the box." When the Cherokee followed, the two flanks would encircle them and kill every Cherokee warrior they could. The Cherokee would be caught in a deadly crossfire, from three different directions.

It is an interesting, though often unrecognized, fact that the left and right flank in a battle plan change, depending upon which direction a man or an army is facing. Sevier's plan would have worked brilliantly, but Tipton was facing Sevier rather than standing beside him—as did Walton—during this hasty meeting on the trail that day. Thus when Sevier gave his orders to Tipton to take his force to the left flank, Tipton looked to his left–which was Sevier's and Walton's right. In that instant, he made the biggest mistake of his life. Unfortunately for this man, this single blunder is the only aspect of his life that has been preserved by history, and we may only imagine the dubious distinction of being remembered in history solely for one's single biggest mistake.

Being inexperienced and somewhat new to the mountains, Tipton ardently desired to make a good showing of himself; all he really managed to do was become entirely turned around. Instead of taking the left flank, he led his men in behind Walton's force on the right flank, insisting that they take cover high enough up the hill to be invisible to the Cherokee below. Thus, this commander left a glaring avenue of escape for the Cherokee. His men, of course, realized that they were behind Walton's force, and some even questioned him. Still, Tipton insisted he'd heard his orders correctly and that they were on the correct side of the trail!

The first part of Sevier's plan worked. In only a couple of minutes, the scout force was "surprised" by the Cherokee, and fifteen brave men fell to rifle fire and arrows. This force then collected their wounded, and retreated hastily down the path into what they assumed would be a killing zone for the pursuing Cherokee. Just as Sevier expected, Dragging Canoe and his band, upon seeing the whites flee, grabbed their powder horns, shouted their war cries, and charged down the trail in pursuit. Within two minutes, rifles sounded from the trees on the right flank as Walton's force opened up; within a minute Sevier's main force was likewise

Battle Of The Warrior's Path

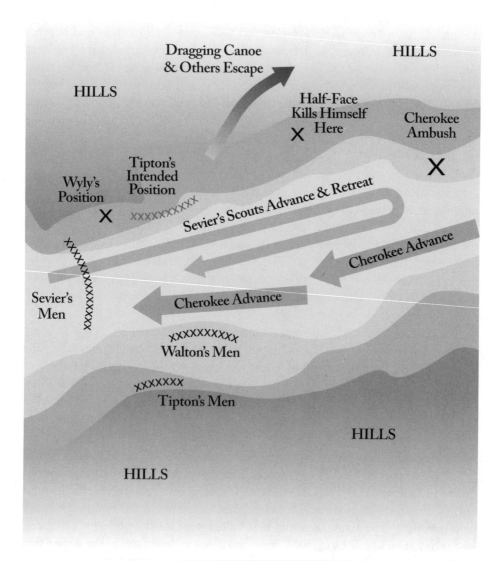

engaged. In the killing zone of the trail, Cherokee warriors began to fall.

When Sevier reloaded his Kentucky rifle after his first volley, he looked to the right flank, and sure enough Walton and his men were giving the savages hell. However, he quickly noted that no fire was coming from the left flank, and he shouted to his subordinate, Wyly, *"Where the hell is Tipton?"*

Wyly, ever eager to assist his commander, immediately made for the left flank where Tipton was supposed to be—thus was the young, yet experienced, Cap. James Wyly, the only white man that ever took the left flank in this battle.

Meanwhile, Tipton was realizing that he had, in fact, led his men the wrong way, and was now all but frozen in indecisiveness. Several of his men looked toward him with disgust, since they had previously realized the stupidity of this inexperienced commander. Moreover they were pissed since they were missing the chance to kill Cherokee. Still, these rugged over-mountain men knew how to join a fight when there was a fight to join, so most of Tipton's men simply refused to stay up the hill. After they saw Walton's men fire their first volley, they ignored their inexperienced commander and headed down the mountain a few paces to join Walton's line well hidden behind the dense trees.

Now the Cherokee under Dragging Canoe were instantly aware that they were trapped between a force on the hill to their left and a force in front of them. Once they recovered from the volley of lead which came screaming in seemingly from several sides, they began to head directly up the hill to their right away from the carnage. At that point, they were certain that there would be a brief reloading pause from the other side of the trail, and unlike the trail, the slope to their right offered some cover. Thus, they headed away from Walton's line.

Only 12 yards into the woods, one large warrior ran directly into James Wyly, body-blocking poor Wyly to the ground; Wyly quickly realized that on the left flank of the battle line alone was no place to be. Still, he was lucky; while his Kentucky rifle was unloaded at that moment, the warrior who literally tripped over him had no lead in his rifle either, so that warrior merely got up and continued running up the hill away from the battle.

However, the Cherokee, while choosing the right direction for escape were wrong in expecting a reloading pause. The brief pause which should have offered the Cherokee a few seconds—perhaps 10 or 15 seconds—to retreat into the woods and find cover, was not to be. Rather, their advance into the wood line to their right coincided precisely with the impromptu advance of Tipton's men—all of whom still had lead in their Kentucky Rifles. These mountain men took positions beside Walton's men and took aim. A wall of lead, fire, and smoke blew from the trees, and 55 Cherokee warriors fell; many hit in the back, and most were dead before they hit the ground. Wyly, now under fire from his comrades along with the fleeing Cherokee, was again realizing that he was definitely in the wrong place. He had the presence of mind to jump behind a log and escape this deadly volley-fire uninjured. He was clearly the luckiest man in the battle that day, having escaped death twice within only 10 seconds.

One of the first to die in this particular fight, was a tall Cherokee with a war hatchet in his belt, and an unloaded musket in his hand. After Stands-Tall had fired his weapon at the men in the woods, he ran into the woods on the opposite side, where he was sure there were no white faces. This assumption was wrong, in that he quickly bumped right into one, but rather than fighting him he ran on a few steps and then ducked behind a low log only 40 feet from Wyly. Here Stands-Tall began to reload his old musket—a task which he never finished. A ball from a Kentucky Rifle, this one was named "Horsefly," found the back side of his skull below the raised end of the log. The shot took off his face but left his topknot of hair—one of Walton's men would collect that trophy later and turn it in for the bounty. Thus, did the only surviving son of Akala and Runs-To-Water die—the very son conceived on their wedding night so long ago in distant, peaceful town of Tugaloo.

In this manner did Stands-Tall join his ancestors in the folklore of the Cherokee. For several warriors had seen him run into the white man, and duck behind the log—loosing his face only moments thereafter. This story, like so many others has long been remembered in the tales of the Cherokee; he died in battle, while loading his gun behind a log on the Warriors Path in Tennessee, many miles from his ancestral home along the Tugaloo River. He died, as had his now famous father, fighting the whites who took his land.

After the horrid second volley from the line of men in the woods, the Cherokee fled in earnest up the opposite hill away from the guns. This gave Sevier's men one final opportunity to take a shot as the forty or so remaining Cherokee escaped, many exposing themselves to fire before scrambling up the hill away from Walton's force. Sevier and several mounted men chose to pursue the Cherokee, but most of his men began to collect scalps.

One man from Walton's company, while running up the hill, tripped on a white man lying behind a log, and tried to shoot him before realizing he was white! He then looked at Wyly, and out popped the obvious question, *"What in hell are you doing over here?"* Without waiting for an answer, the man ran on up the hill to pursue the Cherokee.

After ten minutes of rambling through the woods, Sevier and his adjutant, a Lieutenant Dunham, cornered a lone Cherokee warrior hidden inside a hollow tree. He was highly unusual looking, in that half of his face seemed to be missing, but that was apparently an old wound; for he bled only from an open wound in his upper right thigh. It was apparent that his leg was broken, and he was in great pain. Once spotted, Half-Face realized that he would not escape these white devils, so he pointed his rifle toward the nearest man, but held his fire thinking that maybe they wanted to talk.

Sevier and Dunham assumed that the musket was not loaded, but seeing the intensity in the eyes of this older warrior, and noting his horrid wounds from many years earlier, Sevier said, *"Take care, Dunham. That fellow will soon shoot you!"*

Hearing the commander's voice, Half-Face assumed Sevier had ordered his execution, so he turned his rifle to Sevier and fired. Still, this was to be Nolichucky Jack's lucky day, as it was Wyly's. Just as the savage fired, his horse reared and the lead ball missed Nolichucky Jack by only a few centimeters, taking off a piece of hair by his left ear. Dunham saw the hair fly, and mistakenly thought that his commander had lost the better part of his brains, so he turned his rifle on the savage and prepared to fire. However, much to his surprise, the wounded Cherokee drew his knife from his belt and defiantly looked directly into Dunham's eyes. He then rammed the knife upward into his Half-Face, slicing through his throat, and into his brain. Thus did Half-Face die, bravely, denying the whites the privilege of killing him. For good measure, Dunham fired into the savage's chest.

Half-Face was already gone; he'd already begun his journey to meet Kanati, in the Blue Mountains. This brave old warrior felt nothing when the pistol ball tore into his chest and entered his newly silent heart. Dunham immediately scalped him. The body of the warrior Half-Face, like that of Stands-Tall would lie hairless, only to be savaged by raccoons and bears, eventually to decompose on the ancient Warriors Path, as had so many Cherokee for so many centuries.

Dragging Canoe escaped up the hillside with approximately a fifth of his warriors—some 35 in all—and while their hatred was far from over, the end of the conflict known as Dragging Canoe's War was at hand. Limited raiding would continue for another year, with no major engagements. Further, the men who would settle the Tugaloo saw no further action. In fact, the Virginia militia arrived only after Sevier's force left for this battle, and Early Cleveland saw no action at all during these months at the end of 1780. Thus, for the second time in two months, Cleveland, Walton, and Wyly had finished another battle, and headed home from war.

Grabbin' The Land

After the end of the Revolution, and the few subsequent battles with the Cherokee, Jessie Walton was, as always, feeling the need to move. Moreover, he soon determined that his land speculations in Jonesborough were not progressing as he would like. In fact, because of the horse stealing raids by the Cherokee from the Indian settlements to the west, the "savage threat" was still a problem to new settlers and even to established settlements like Jonesborough. As a result, there was little white migration into the eastern reaches of Tennessee immediately after the Revolution. Thus, Walton's choice lots in the town of Jonesborough—carefully selected by him when he laid out the street plan for the settlement—were sitting idol and unsold rather than making him rich. Within only a few months of returning home, he was considerably dissatisfied with his overall future prospects and, given that he was a drifter by nature, he began to look longingly at the high mountains to the south.

While historical records are silent on the issue, some historians have surmised that Walton may also have been uncomfortable with the way his Tennessee neighbors treated their local Cherokee. Of course, Walton had fought these damn Cherokee all his life, and when it was necessary, he was not above a gruesome killing or scalping when the raid called for it. Still, as a wanderer himself, and something of a quiet, spiritual man, he did have a certain respect for the wandering, spiritual souls of the Cherokee he'd known. He couldn't tolerate pure unreasoned hatred of the Indians and he believed that such hatred would always cause trouble in the Tennessee country.

In contrast, his friend "Nolichucky Jack" Sevier detested anything Cherokee. For this frontiersman, Indians were a scourge on the land and had to be either removed or eliminated. Once when visiting a Cherokee village north of the Smoky Mountains, one of his white colleagues had commented on how healthy the Cherokee children looked as they played their Chungkee ball games. Sevier looked over at the children and was heard to mutter, *"Little nits make lice."* He thus expressed his burning desire to kill even the Cherokee children; his hatred of the Cherokee was pure and unabated. Clearly with this attitude on the part of Sevier, the leader of the entire Tennessee militia, Walton may well have sensed increasing Indian troubles for Jonesborough and all of the other frontier settlements.

Thus in 1783, Jessie Walton headed south with, as he phrased it, *"An eye to removal"* of his family to the lower Blue Ridge. He remembered fondly the land that he had hunted as a boy along the Tugaloo River—the gentle sweep of the lower, more moderate hills of the Southern Blue Ridge, in contrast to the higher peaks to the north. He remembered the small Indian village where he and Early Cleveland had once watched an Indian raid. Thus, this wanderer of the frontier set off to found yet another frontier community in which he would make his home and, perhaps, his fortune. After many days guiding his horse down the trails, Walton crossed into the Georgia country and immediately sought out his friend and former comrade in arms, Elijah Clarke.

Now Col. Clarke, still totally illiterate and quite proud of his "serious wound from the Battle of King's Mountain," demanded that everyone call him Col., even though this was fairly rare. Most militia leaders after the war quickly resumed their former occupations of farmer, lawyer, or judge, and were thereby addressed by either their civilian title or their first name. In spite of this inflated pride, Col. Clarke was nonetheless making a name for himself across the lower Blue Ridge. He had argued in the newly established state legislature of Georgia for many petitions that resulted in settlers moving to the north towards the mountains, rather than merely remaining clustered around the southern river cities of Savannah and Augusta. Thus, he was a major proponent of settling the middle Georgia region, and towns such as Washington, Milledgeville, Greensboro, and Macon were soon founded in central Georgia.

When Walton arrived in Georgia, Clarke was busy in the Georgia legislature, in Savannah, Georgia—the capital of Georgia in those days. Atlanta, the worldly city of southern commerce and the future capital of Georgia would not exist for another 50 years.

Once these two men met, Clarke was able to assist his friend Walton by telling him of the "Bounty Grants" that had just been enacted by the Georgia legislature, under the guidance of the new republic. Like many newly established governments, the new "Articles of Confederation" drawn up as the governing document for all thirteen colonies after the Revolution, was both poorly thought out and doomed from the start. In a desire to escape the harsh realities of absolute and total authority such as the authority of the King of England, the Patriots and their political leaders created a central government that was intentionally and quite explicitly weak. Indeed, they feared any strong power not in the hands of the individual colonies, each of which had, at the end of the Revolution, become a state. In those days, the Patriots considered these states separate governments, very similar to European governments which were separate such as France, England, and Germany. Over these separate governments of the states, the limited central power of the national government under the "Articles of Confederation," lay like a light blanket that was much too thin for the winter cold. That national government was merely for mutual defense and had essentially no powers of any kind. Things such as taxation, minting money, raising militias, or navies, and even the delivery of mail were controlled by the thirteen separate states. There was no president during this period, nor any other strong national leader, and each of the new states had their own coinage, militia, legislature, and post office.

As one might expect, this "plan for chaos" resulted in total paralysis in the new states within a fortnight. As one example, it was easier to get a letter from Savannah to London, half a world away, than it was to get one from Savannah, Georgia to Charlotte, North Carolina, only 120 miles upland, since the letter traveling to Charlotte involved crossing two state boundaries—one into South Carolina, and one into North Carolina—whereas the letter to London could catch any one of hundreds of cross-ocean merchant vessels. In effect, these Articles of Confederation served as nothing more than a disorganized in-term government from 1881 until 1889, when the new Constitution of the United States was enacted. Most Americans today don't really even realize that the Constitution we so venerate, is in reality our "second choice" option for a national government, instituted because our first effort—the Articles of Confederation—failed so abysmally.

With these widely recognized failures of the new national government during those years noted, a few things were accomplished after 1781, particularly when that national government worked in conjunction with the various state governments. After the Revolutionary War victories in the South and Cornwallis' defeat at Yorktown, those in power had to award something to the men who had made this victory possible, and giving away land that ultimately didn't belong to the new government anyway seemed to be one way to do that. Thus, the new government began to encourage states to give away the land of the Cherokee and other Indian tribes who had sided with the British in the recent war, as bounty grants to the veterans. Of course, no one bothered to inform the Cherokee; perhaps the whites merely assumed that they would realize they were defeated and leave.

This innovative land use policy—today's terminology—also held the added advantage of hastening the settlement of the upcountry and mountains of the Blue Ridge in the various southern states. Those states, from Virginia down to Georgia, tended to be settled primarily on the coastal plains, and the new governments in these former colonies wanted to encourage settlement more broadly. These "bounty grants" helped move settlers inland. Finally, these new settlements would soon secure the western borders of these states from hostile influence—either Indian or French. In this fashion, leaders of various companies of militia during the Revolution were granted land, and several of the "bounty grants" happened to be in the Tugaloo River Valley adjacent to the small hill that is the subject of our story. Many family names that today are still prevalent in the Tugaloo Valley, originated from these bounty grants. Names such as Mosely, Cash, Warten, Thompson, Elbert, Cleveland, Walton, Wyly and many others in the Tugaloo Valley result from this influx of settlers, moving onto bounty grants from the state of Georgia in return for service in the late Revolution.

By 1785, Early Cleveland had added even more poundage, and weighed in at 309. Because of his leadership in the Revolution, he collected a bounty grant in 1785, right on the Tugaloo River. It was clear that Cleveland had received a generous portion of good farmland, as well as some of the lower mountains in the Blue Ridge. There was an interesting circular mound just to the west of the river, and several of the old drunk Cherokee who hung around Billy Sharpe's store and tavern, spoke of that particular hill as if it was holy somehow—this hill had once held the Tugaloo Council House of the Cherokee. Cleveland remembered watching an attack on this very Cherokee village in 1755, when he was just a boy, but he knew nothing of Cherokee mysticism, and really didn't place much stock in those tales of Cherokee religion or worship. Further, he really didn't care what that small hill was on his bounty grant, as long as he got a good share of the rich bottomland along the river which he knew had been farmed before, though not recently.

Early was happy to learn that his friend, and long time hunting buddy, Jessie

Walton, had visited Georgia and subsequently petitioned the government for a Bounty Grant. In fact, Walton had gotten the land grant just to the north of Cleveland's own land. By talking early with Col. Clarke, Jessie Walton had done well for himself; he'd gotten a grant of 400 acres of beautiful woodlands and rich farmland along the Tugaloo River, including control of the best spot to ford the river within ten miles. Thus, the town that grew—in just a few short years in that river valley became known as Walton's Ford; it would bear that name for over 100 years. Of course, the area had been called Tugaloo Town for something like 200 years previously by the Cherokee, but most Cherokee had scooted out to the west, and the ones who remained seemed to stay drunk most of the time, so that name was lost for a while.

Ekaia, another veteran of King's Mountain, had indeed come down from his tree-top perch on the eastern end of battlefield. He then quietly disappeared again, and merely headed home. However, as always, he was quite creative in his ability to hide, and had studied the white man much like he studied any other prey. In addition to taking a white name after the destruction of Tugaloo Town in 1760, by 1781 he'd invented a respectable past for himself claiming that he'd come up the river from Savannah in 1773. He was also claiming to have fought on King's Mountain—which was true as far as it goes; However, Prather was now claiming he'd been fighting as a Patriot!

Tom Prather, a man who always knew how to disappear, realized early in life that the best way to hide is in plain sight. He figured that if he claimed to be both a Patriot and a white man, few folks would, or could, ever challenge that. Of course on certain occasions, some folks—even veterans of the battle—would question him about his role at King's Mountain. When necessary, he could most certainly describe the action at both ends of the mountain top, having had by far the best vantage point to watch the entire engagement. In recounting the battle, he'd merely find out where he questioner had fought, and then place himself with a Patriot unit at the other end of the hill.

He'd managed to pull this delusion off so well, that Bryan Ward, often more drunk that sober by this time, once swore to a magistrate near Augusta that he'd known Tom Prather all his life. Ward even swore that old Tom had indeed come from Savannah and fought at King's Mountain. Thus Prather became both a Patriot and veteran of the Revolution, and thereby had a right to a bounty claim all his own! By 1784, posing as a white man and a patriotic veteran, he road down to the county seat of the newly established "Franklin County" in Georgia and calmly claimed a very large section of land north of the river, just 3 miles northwest of old Tugaloo Town. No one ever disputed his claim. In this way, Tom Prather came to own many fields that had originally been cleared by his ancestors—the Cherokee. Throughout history, this man stands alone, as the only Tory veteran of the American Revolution to have claimed a bounty grant as a Patriot.

Thus did the early white citizens begin to converge on the Tugaloo River Valley. After Walton acquired his land grant, he communicated with other Revolutionary War leaders, and many men from King's Mountain ended up coming into the Tugaloo Valley. James Wyly, a neighbor of Walton's in Tennessee, having recently married and had his first child, likewise chose to pick up a bounty grant and move south with Walton. Jessie Bond, Edward Cash, Edward Rice, and several other families would likewise move from Jonesborough to the Tugaloo, and some of these men chose, for safety sake, to move their families together. For it was well known that the Cherokee occupied the many mountain valleys, and no one could ever tell where these Cherokee might be raiding next. When traveling such a distance, there was safety in numbers.

Thus, unlike the great "westward" movement that many today envision as the settlement of this country, much of the lower Blue Ridge, including all of North Georgia, much of northern South Carolina, and north Alabama, was settled by people moving almost directly south rather than west. Such a flight from northern states to southern states would not be seen again until the economic boom two centuries later, marked by the rise of the great southern cities of Charlotte, Savannah, Atlanta, Charleston, Dallas, and Houston in the 1970s, the 1980s, and 1990s.

Heading Back Over the Mountains

The Cherokee were up in arms about the giveaway of some of their ancient land, and thus were a danger to any settler crossing their territory. Walton and Wyly determined early on, that any route directly across the southern mountains would be dangerous indeed. In this they were correct; history records that in the single year after the Revolution ended, some 200 frontiersmen were killed by the Cherokee. Neither man relished the thought of fighting the Cherokee again, particularly with their families tossed into the middle! Thus, it soon became apparent to these men that, in the settlement of the lower Blue Ridge, obtaining land through a bounty grant was the easy part. The hard part was the actual move to the new land along that bloody frontier in Georgia. Walton and the others had to move their families, their household goods, their funds, and their livestock from Jonesborough, Tennessee almost due south, to their new home on the Tugaloo River in Franklin County, Georgia.

Now Early Cleveland faced the same daunting task, but he had an easier route, because he was still settled at that time in Surry County, North Carolina; thus he was still on the eastern side of the formidable Blue Ridge Mountains. Also, the Great Philadelphia Wagon Road went right past his home, and skimmed along the Eastern slope of the mountains all the way to the Tugaloo River. While that road could be quite muddy, at least it stayed on one side of the mountains so

Early and his family didn't have to cross any high mountain passes. Moreover, the Cherokee who were still left to the east of the Blue Ridge were rather docile now, and posed no threat to settlers moving along this road. It was the Cherokee to the west of the mountains that posed the problem from 1781 through the 1830s.

In contrast to Cleveland's proposed travel route, Walton, Wyly, and the other families escaping from eastern Tennessee would have to re-cross the high mountains, using the famed "Wilderness Road" running through the mountains, just south of the new settlement of Boone, North Carolina. As recently as 1900, this Wilderness Road, at best a rough wagon road across the high Blue Ridge, was horrendous. It was described by one traveler in 1899. *"Despite all that has been done to civilize it since Boone traced the course in 1790, this honored historic thoroughfare remains today as it was in the beginning, with all its sloughs and sands, its mud and holes, and jutting ledges of rock and loose boulders, and twists and turns, and general depravity."*

Walton, Wyly, and the others with their families and all of their possessions in tow, proposed to cross this road for the second time going in the wrong direction—almost directly east. Then they would join the Great Philadelphia Wagon Road on the eastern side of the Blue Ridge, and from that point, they would follow along behind Cleveland, heading southwest into Georgia. While Walton, Wyly and the others in Jonesborough were geographically much closer to the Tugaloo River Valley than Cleveland, when their journey began, there was no road that headed due south through the Great Smoky Mountains—through the heart of Cherokee country. Thus, instead of having a shorter distance to travel than Cleveland's family they had, essentially twice the distance, and a major mountain ridge to cross.

It may help to understand this decision on their route, as well as the subsequent history of the Tugaloo River Valley, if we reflect on what the Cherokee threat meant to these settlers. Terror in the modern mind brings mental images of death in aircraft or explosions of mud-brick buildings in some foreign or domestic city-scape. Much has been made of the "terror" associated with life in the modern world and the possibility of death in virtually any action one takes. Still, it behooves us to reflect that our ancestors knew terror; they feared it in the same sense as we do today. Whites on this frontier faced instant death by war hatchet, arrow, or musket, in the hands of hostile savages who attacked indiscriminately all along the entire frontier, seemingly on a whim. A man may be clearing new ground on his farm, or cutting firewood, only to be struck down by an arrow in the back. A woman may be picking beans or churning butter and die with a hatchet in her head, before she could even warn her children. All of this, because of the "Blood Oath" of the damned Cherokee!

Every frontiersman and all of his family, knew of and despised the "Blood Oath" of the Cherokee—an oath that made all whites guilty for any crime committed against the Cherokee by any white. The everyday lives of these people were governed by this knowledge and they surely knew terror. That is why, these frontiersmen lived in small clusters, often behind walls for protection, and their very routes of travel changed as a result of this terrible warfare.

The Cherokee, in turn, knew terror in the sense that their villages could be destroyed at any time; they were all suspect for any Indian on White crime, since all Indians—Cherokee, Creek, Catawba—were viewed as the same. Indians were considered savages and scourges on the land. For that reason, Cherokee life was difficult, and often brutally short—as was the life of Runs-To-Water, not to mention his first wife and daughter. The point is that terror is not a modern phenomenon, nor is chronic, daily fear exclusive to the 21st century. These men and women of the Blue Ridge knew terror, and in that stark reality, they found ways to calmly go about their business tilling the earth, milking their cows, slaughtering hogs, raising their children, teaching them their "letters" using the only book in the house—the Bible; thus did they live their lives, and even enjoy their existence, in spite of their constant terror. Each member of these mountain communities, both white and Cherokee—sought and found great solace in the spiritual gifts of their respective cultures, and only in following these religious dictates of their lives, did they survive the terrors of their world. Perhaps, there is a lesson here for us all. History seems to suggest that terror is the fundamental human condition, and that in the face of terror, only a life dedicated to the spiritual thrives.

To add even more troubles to the travels of the Walton party, these early migrations over the Blue Ridge, unlike the organized wagon trains that eighty years later would cross the great plains of the continent, tended to be rather unorganized affairs. This was the first great western migration, and the settlers didn't understand what they were doing. They really didn't know what to take along and what to leave behind. Thus, they loaded their ox-team wagons with everything they had, only to discard much of the wooden, hand-hewn furniture along the way; for the two ox typically used to pull the family possessions simply could not pull the weight of the entire household up a steep mountain pass. Moreover, the wooden creations could be replaced in their new home, with wood from their new farm. In fact, along the rugged mountain trails, by every ford in the river, and along every sharp rise in elevation, piles of discarded brick-a-brack could be found in those years— merely from settlers discarding what they'd finally decided they didn't need. One settler, moving to Jonesborough in 1782 remarked to his neighbors; *"We left with a couple of tables, a quilting frame, and three stools for our cabin, and tossed 'em within a fortnight. But that's all right, 'cause about 20 mile ago, I just picked up some more stools that another idiot had finally tossed out along the trail, and that's what I got in my cabin now!"*

The only advantage Walton and the others had during this trip was the fact that they had all made the same mistakes before. Thus, before leaving, they sold what wooden objects they could to their neighbors in Jonesborough, since those could be replaced with a bit of carving once they reached their new home. Instead, these experienced frontier settlers loaded only what they had to keep. First, the family Bible, one change of clothes for everyone, and their metal objects such as cooking pots, knives, or ploughs were loaded so they could be used when they reached the Tugaloo Valley. Next, seed corn, meal, cured hams, and garden seeds were carefully loaded in jars, pots, or bags. The rifles, powder, and lead went in last since they might have to get to it quick on the trail. Axes were in plentiful supply, and second only to muskets or rifles, axes would determine their ability to live on the new frontier along the Tugaloo River.

Thus, on the morning of August 1, 1784 did Walton, his wife, four sons, and a daughter begin their trek eastward across the Blue Ridge to migrate south into the lower Blue Ridge. This date allowed them to harvest their crops in Tennessee and do a bit of hunting, but still promised the possibility of reaching the Tugaloo before the cold days of December arrived. Walton road one of his eight horses as did his oldest son. These men carried the two Kentucky rifles owned by the family, and acted as scouts—often riding ahead of the group a mile or so up the trail. Other horses were loaded down with various items. Three milk cows were tied behind the wagon, and five pigs and several sheep were herded along behind by Walton's two slaves. One goat—hogtied—road atop the load in the wagon, since any frontiersman knows that you can't "trail" goats. A couple of cages held an assortment of chickens; most of these would be cooked and eaten along the way. Walton's wife Margaret, was allowed to ride in the wagon and she drove the two oxen, while the rest of the family walked along beside, with a couple of dogs barking at all the action.

Wyly's small family, loaded out in much the same configuration, joined the Waltons within a mile, as did two other families. Thus, this group of four families formed a fairly large group, as they traveled backward along the Wilderness Road to the east over the Blue Ridge.

With the Cherokee still attacking settlers all along the Tennessee and Nolichucky Rivers, these folks didn't run into a single group of settlers heading west—a fact which confirmed for Walton that he'd made the right decision in this move; with no new settlers heading into Tennessee, he was surely not going to be able to sell those choice lots in Jonesborough. In those years right after the Revolution, many folks looking to settle to the west were still unsure that the settlements over the high mountains would survive—by this point, Jessie Walton shared that concern.

The journey would take between eight and ten weeks, and most of that time would be spent re-crossing the trail heading east over the Blue Ridge. In contrast, once the settlers reached the Great Philadelphia Wagon Road, their direction would change from directly east, to southwest, and the journey would involve crossing only a few moderate rivers and no high mountain peaks.

On the second day out from Jonesborough, the migrating settlers got a taste of what their trials would be like. On that day they came to a tributary of the Nolichucky River, which was itself a tributary of the Holsten River further north. Walton thought he'd hit a section of the French Broad River, a meandering stream which wrapped all the way around the eastern end of the Cherokee country, flowing through the Carolinas and into Tennessee, but in this he was mistaken. He'd run into a rain-swollen section of the Nolichucky, and it was "in a fiddle" on this particular day. A massive rainfall only 30 miles to the northwest had swollen the river, from the usual depth at this ford of 3 feet, to almost five feet, and it was running swiftly. One look at the river and Jessie Walton, a normally mild mannered man, spit out his chew and launched into a cussin' fit that would have rivaled any of Early Cleveland's most famous efforts. *"Gol, dangit. When in tarnation hell has any damn fool seen this damn river so goddamn high, a'fore?"*

His wife, Margret was simply appalled at such foul language, and immediately sent the children off to the Wyly's wagon which she hoped was out of earshot. She then closed her eyes and began a loud, slightly offensive prayer for the "damned soul" of her foul mouthed husband. She was one of those women who seemed to know God's will much better than did anyone else, and she was never above "praying for the soul of the sinners." Finally, she considered everyone but herself and whatever local pastor happened to be in the neighborhood, sinners. Walton's two boys, who were used to such ostentatious religiosity on the part of their mother, merely snickered nearby. They were at that stage of male adolescence when each day is an adventure and all occurrences have some humor in them—particularly if the occurrence had the effect of pissing off their parents.

About that time, Wyly road up, looked over the situation, and simply said, *"We better unload 'um and hogtie everything across."*

Walton hated to hear those words, but it was the only course of action available for crossing the 80 feet between the shore lines of that swollen stream.

It took them two days to cross that swollen river. First, the wagons were unhitched, and four oxen along with several men crossed the swiftly moving water. They then hitched the oxen to the ropes on the far side, while the families unloaded each wagon almost totally. Only a few metal objects could be left inside any of the wagons, since everything remaining in the bed of the wagons was likely to get wet. Next, one man, or one boy, was stationed beside each wagon wheel to manually roll it over any large rocks on the river bottom that may have washed into the ford. Next, the wagons were tied to ropes on both sides of the stream. With the oxen on the eastern side pulling, and oxen on the western side giving resistance to the ropes, the wagons were "floated out" into the high river and pulled across.

Of course, these rough wagons didn't "float" in any sense—that was merely the expression used at the time; the term "floated out" could best be translated as "get the damn thing in the river and watch it sink like a stone." The dual rope procedure did effectively prevent the wagons themselves from being pulled downstream by the swift current and subsequently destroyed.

When the wagon was finally pulled up the other side, the chicken cages, barrels of seed, corn meal were tied off to ropes on both sides of the stream and were hoisted across the river without getting wet. Once in a while a barrel of corn meal would get wet and thus be ruined, but the real tragedy was losing a keg of gunpowder to the river. Corn could be grown on the Tugaloo, but gunpowder costs cold hard cash! Thus, getting the powder wet was unforgivable.

Now just for fun, every once in a while, one of Walton's or Wyly's boys manning the ropes on the far side of the river would intentionally leave too much slack, and thereby wet a cage full of chickens. This resulted in nothing more harmful than extremely loud cussin' from Walton, equally loud praying from Walton's overly religious wife, and an incredible additional racket from a flustered cage full of wet, pissed off poultry! Both roosters and settin' hens can really toss up a noise when they get wet, and watching the infernal birds in their cramped cages attempt to "flap 'um dry", flapping their wings in the cages and slapping each other silly, was even more fun! This didn't happen often, but the boys did have a good time with birds belonging to several families, and after his cussin' even Jessie Walton got a good laugh. Once the goods were on the other side of the river, the individual families would carefully reload each wagon.

With the Nolichucky behind them, the families were set to really cover some ground and Walton promised them that they would make great distances now, which they did—at a steady five to seven miles each day. They could reach such astronomical distances only because they traveled for ten to eleven hours daily—leaving just before dawn and traveling steadily until dusk. In the evening, by the time the wagons were unhitched and the horses and oxen rubbed down, the women would have built a fire, and several chickens—wet or dry, made no difference—would be killed, plucked, and cooked. Corn meal would be cooked flat against a rock beside the fire, and dipped in the steaming chicken broth, after the chickens were consumed. On some evenings, one family or another would break out a cured ham, and fry part of the meat, just to add some variety to the meal. After a cup of coffee around the campfire, everyone would go to bed, save one of the older boys, who would guard the camp. Such was the way of frontier travel over the Blue Ridge in the 1780s.

The most difficult days involved climbing the pass over the Blue Ridge itself. When the Wilderness Road ascended sharply up the mountain toward the high peaks, the wagons again had to be pulled by several oxen teams. While there was no threat of getting anything wet, the top-heavy loads of wagons stacked high with household goods and food, meant that they again had to be partially unloaded, for any climb over a 15 to 20 degree grade. Two oxen teams from the other wagons, would be taken up the steep slope some 20 to 50 yards, and ropes attached would allow those oxen to pull the remaining weight along with the ox team still hitched to the front of the wagon. In this manner, every steep slope that the families came to, took a full day just to ascend, since four wagons had to be "climbed up" the hill. In one or two places, the descending trail across the ridge was steep enough to require the same procedure in reverse, and those hills took even more time.

With these difficulties taking up every day on the trail, it is no wonder that Wyly, ever the sly one, wondered many times, *"Couldn't this region use a trail right through Cherokee country?"* Wyly knew that any man who could negotiate safe passage through the mountains on the intricate system of Cherokee trails would be a wealthy man indeed; for certainly he could charge a toll for use of the trail, as was, in fact being done all along the Great Philadelphia Wagon Road in those days. With these difficulties to face, and this thought on his mind, Wyly moved his young family, along with Waltons and several others to the Tugaloo in 1784. In that distant Tugaloo River Valley, beside old Tugaloo Town, would these settlers from Tennessee make their new home.

With many rivers crossed, and several high mountain passes climbed, the families made their way to the eastern side of the Blue Ridge, only to find Early Cleveland waiting for them with an uncreative string of his usual obscenities.

"Well kiss my ass and clean my coffee pot! Look at this sorry lot' o frontiersmen, scurrying back'ards 'cross the mountains. You boys loose your way, or couldn't ya' find the sun to follow to the western country? Apparently you is slow as old women too! I thought you' all's leave on the first, and here it is near the 20th*! Guess that'll teach you, you cain't do nothing without ol' Early Cleveland helpin' ya out! What the hell took you'll so long, anyway?"*

They rested the oxen for two days, while Early and his Misses packed up their household goods, along with all of his boys, his livestock, and his four slaves. From this point on the Clevelands would travel along with the Walton's, the Wyly's and the others.

One other fact should be noted about this migration—the arrival of slaves. Early Cleveland and Jessie Walton would be the first whites to bring black slaves into the Tugaloo River Valley, though slavery had existed in southern Georgia from the 1740s onward. Further, there had been some Cherokee sold into slavery off and on over the prior years, but with the migration in 1784 slavery took hold in the agriculture that was soon to dominate this beautiful river valley and it would take almost 100 years to rid the valley of this horridly "peculiar institution." Thus, within four weeks, around September 25, 1784, this large and soon to be influential group of white settlers—with their black slaves in tow, came into the beautiful Tugaloo River Valley.

The Early Settlers of Walton's Ford

Once in the Tugaloo Valley, these new settlers nestled in within half a mile of the hill on which Runs-To-Water was buried. In the Valley, they found a half breed, Billy Sharpe, running a tavern along with his rotund, loud wife, and a drunk—Bryan Ward—pretending to run a grist mill. There were some farms belonging to various Carmichael's down the river a bit, towards Augusta, and a number of Cherokee, mostly drunk, still living in the area. In a few months they'd met Tom Prather, who seemed to keep to himself, but claimed he'd been in the big fight at King's Mountain. Walton, Wyly, and Cleveland couldn't remember him, but there had been almost a thousand Patriots in that fight, and these men never met most of Clarke's Georgia soldiers. However, given the misinterpreted orders, and the post-battle killing of unarmed prisoners which by now everybody was ashamed of, if a man wanted to keep quiet about his role in that battle, other veterans would ask few questions.

From the perspective of history, it may also help to consider also what these early settlers didn't find in the Tugaloo River Valley of 1784. They didn't find any homes in which to live, no fields to plant, and no real stores in which to purchase goods they might need. They found no blacksmith, no tannery, indeed no manufacturing of any sort, no roads, other than the Philadelphia Wagon Road upon which they had traveled, no postal service, and no other settlers to speak of. It would be true to say that these individuals felt they were at the frontier on the very end of the world, for nothing existed to the west except Cherokee Country and, further to the southwest, Creek Country. To the north were the formidable Blue Ridge Mountains. At that time, these were the northernmost white settlers on the southern slopes of the Blue Ridge, and in that direction one would have to travel all the way to Tennessee to find other white faces.

Early Cleveland's land included several meadows which soon became cleared fields, and some stands of young pine that appeared to be from 15 to twenty years old. These pine stands were, of course, the fields that once produced selu for the Cherokee, but any man of the mountains will tell you it doesn't take pine many years to reclaim a field. Still, Cleveland knew he could clear this ground in short order. He had his four slaves, and he had his sons, Absolom and John. Both of these boys were unsavory characters who took their father's good natured cussin' and overindulgence in drink several steps beyond good natured fun. Still they both provided labor and support for the family in their own fashion.

"Devil John" in particular, the younger of Early Cleveland's sons, helped his father for about 10 years, and then purchased a large piece of land from him along the Tugaloo River adjacent to Toccoa Creek, and began his own plantation. He was later known for abusing his slaves and his wives alike. We shall hear more of this unsavory character later.

Still, like all frontiersmen, these sons of Early could work hard when the times called for it; thus they, their Dad, and the slaves—standing shoulder to shoulder—began to fell trees for a cabin, and to make room for crops next year. Early's other boy, Absolom, was known to be somewhat dim-witted. Still, he was a fairly good shot and unlike his obese father, Absolom was in fairly good shape, so he hunted almost full time to feed the family and the slaves. Deer were still around—in fact they were more plentiful with the absence of the Cherokee. Raccoon were abundant, as were bear, wild turkey, panthers, rabbits, duck, and many other delicacies. This land even supported a few buffalo—though these would soon disappear. Hunting was usually enough to supply the families needs, but when all else failed, as it did sometimes, the family could always kill a hog. Thus, did plantation life begin on what would become the famous Cleveland Plantation. This land is still known by that name today, and some two hundred twenty years later it is still in the hands of the same family, and still nestled along the banks of the Tugaloo River.

Walton was proud of his bounty grant, and looked forward to building a small farm and perhaps a grand plantation. However, he quickly noted that the only road in these parts, the Great Philadelphia Wagon Road, came right through his land, and anyone on that road had to use the ford on the Tugaloo River that Walton now owned. Walton immediately saw an advantage to building his home right by the river, so he could eventually build a bridge over the river–it was only 100 feet wide and three to four feet deep for most of the year—getting a bit deeper during the Spring thaw. Once he completed his bridge, he hoped to collect a toll for crossing the river. He also noted that a number of fields were clear of rocks and tillable, but small pines, hickory and oak trees that seemed to be about 20 years old, were growing in the bottom lands. He, like Cleveland, began to clear land that only 25 years before had fed the Cherokee of Tugaloo Town.

Wyly had two "Bounty Grants." One piece of land was adjacent to Early Cleveland's land, and unfortunately for Wyly, was mostly swampland, many years later this would be known as "Owl Swamp," a marshy area running along south of Toccoa Creek reaching almost to the Tugaloo River. This was the swamp through which Utani, the Longknife had once tracked a huge bear, only to see a young toonali kill it with a stone.

Wyly's other grant was tillable land away to the west of Walton's, approximately 8 miles distant. Bryan Ward's grist mill was located on a trail running beside Wyly's land, and others had gotten various land grants in between this land and the river. Still, Wyly noted one prominent feature on his grant of 500 acres—he now owned both the eastern and western slope of a large mountain that stood alone—away from the other mountains—towering above the plateau below by some 900 feet, with a stark rock face toward the east. During his first week in the Tugaloo area, he made a point to climb that mountain and take in the view. Thus, did Currahee

Mountain, the home of Kanati, the Great Spirit and first man of Cherokee legend, come into possession of James Wyly in 1784. Wyly would clear some land in each of his grants, and build a cabin near the eastern end of Owl Swamp, to be nearer his Tugaloo neighbors. The forest around Currahee Mountain would be left largely uncleared for another 100 years.

In this way did three of the four men from the Battle of King's Mountain come to the Tugaloo. Early Cleveland brought dreams of building a plantation, farming the rich bottom lands. Walton took one look at the ford he owned, and thought to build a toll bridge. Thus, the settlement would be known as Walton's Ford. Wyly, ever the planner, cleared some land and began to farm, but couldn't help looking north towards the Blue Ridge and Cherokee country, still thinking, *"Somebody should build a road through there!"*

Of the four veterans of King's Mountain who would drastically impact this valley and the whole of the lower Blue Ridge, these three, Walton, Cleveland, and Wyly, were now living in the valley. In contrast, Robert Jarrett had not arrived; in fact he would die without ever living in the valley. After fighting in the Revolution, Jarrett didn't have any continuing troubles with the Cherokee. His home in Pendleton Court House, some thirty miles to the southeast of the Tugaloo River, was a bit too far south for the numerous Cherokee raids to impact, so his war years ended with the Revolution in 1781. He spent a few years in Wilkes County Georgia, approximately 60 miles south of the Tugaloo Valley, and then returned to his store and his South Carolina home and did what all soldiers tend to do at that moment—he enjoyed his wife. Within just a few months she began to show, and sure enough, a young boy—Devereaux Jarrett was born in 1785.

Unfortunately, Robert Jarrett died young, passing away from consumption before his son was born. His impact on the Tugaloo River Valley would come through this son, Devereaux Jarrett. Within a few short years, this boy was to build a store into the upper part of the county on the eastern side of the Tugaloo. It seemed destined that as he grew to manhood, he would become a merchant like the father he'd never met. However, through these humble beginnings, Devereaux Jarrett would become the most wealthy planter in the Tugaloo Valley, arriving approximately 18 years after the others; once at the river, he would build an empire.

Bloody Raid at Walton's Ford

In spite of the industriousness of the new settlers, and their continuing efforts to establish a life here at the settlement known then as Waltons' Ford, this beautiful river valley was not destined to know peace as yet. Some say it was the very beauty of the place that attracted so much lustful attention from various groups—Cherokee, Creek, early frontier settlers, or British invaders. Others say the conflux of early transportation crossroads here made this a magnet for invasion and military expeditions. While this question may never be answered fully, we can note that certain areas on the globe, for whatever reason, seem to attract more than their share of wars and conflict—perhaps this would only be expected for an area such as the Tugaloo River Valley, which became the gateway to the entire southern Blue Ridge and most of Georgia and Alabama. This valley, because of the Great Philadelphia Wagon Road, and the terminus of the navigable portion of the Savannah River system was truly, the "Interstate Highway" of its century, and it is no accident that even today, Interstate Highway 85 passes within 10 miles of Tugaloo Town at the junction of South Carolina and Georgia. It, like the Great Philadelphia Wagon Road before it, parallels the eastern slope of the Blue Ridge, just at the base of the mountains.

Just as things seemed to be settling down in the lives of these veterans of King's Mountain however, trouble arrived in the form of a Creek raiding party. The event—what turned out to be the final Indian attack at Walton's Ford, was duly catalogued by Wyly in his diary.

"While the Cherokee threat had mostly been removed from the Tugaloo River Valley, by 1785, our plantations still labored under the threat from the savage—specifically from the Creek in the Georgia flatlands to the Southwest. At times a few cows, sheep, or horses were stolen, as young Indian warriors proved their manhood in the way of the savage for thousands of years—steeling the property of others. We planters saw such thievery for what it was—threats to our very livelihood rather than some harmless right of passage for young Creek warriors. In particular, the Creeks who had migrated to the Southwest some decades before, often saw it as a further test of their manhood to hunt in the ancestral hunting grounds that they had shared, unintentionally, with the Cherokee.

By 1788, these were settled lands, with more whites coming daily from Augusta, Georgia all the way up to the Tugaloo. Still, the Creek would travel to this valley to find the deer and bear that were still plentiful in these lower ridges of the Blue Ridge Mountains. While most of the buffalo had been hunted out of these parts, the deer population had rebounded in a few short years after the Cherokee had moved to the west, and thus, these Creeks felt it only right that they should harvest from this bounty of deer in the area. We, of course, killed as many of these Creeks as we could."

James Wyly's diary, November 1788

On one such hunting party, the seven Creek warriors involved managed to change history. Jessie Walton was growing older—he'd been 16 when he watched a Creek raid on Tugaloo Town in 1755, so by 1789 he was well past his fortieth year, when devastation struck. He and another new settler, Duncan McIntyre, were just closing a deal for Walton to purchase a couple of McIntyre's cows when several rifles sounded from the tree line. All of the first shots, which seemed to be coming from the direction of the trees behind the horse coral to the south, missed, but both frontiersmen knew the danger immediately—Indians. Neither knew at that moment if the danger was from the Cherokee, which they would have suspected, or Creek, a possibility much less likely. Both took action immediately; they fell in unison behind a stack of nearby firewood, and grabbed their rifles.

McIntyre peeked out first, saw the Creek in the trees, and shouted, "*They's come for the horses, Jessie!*" The two men let go the ropes tied to the cows they'd been bartering over and quickly sought their Kentucky rifles. Walton—still using the weapon he'd had a King's Mountain—and McIntyre both returned fire. Next, they did what many in the civilized worlds of London, New York, or Charleston would have considered impossible. They charged the horse coral, and they reloaded their rifles on the run. Each accomplished the task without thinking about it, and it took each man no more than 15 seconds, while on the run the whole time.

Had Major Patrick Ferguson been alive and around to see that performance, he would have been shocked at the dexterity of these men and their use of these amazing weapons. No army in the world in that century had trained their infantry to reload on the run–any military man anywhere on the planet at that time would have said it was all but impossible to do so. Yet frontiersmen did it routinely; for them it often meant the difference between life and death. In fact, had Patrick Ferguson witnessed this, he would have finally understood his own defeat on King's Mountain. These frontiersmen could reload while running, or for that matter, while climbing a tree. By the time McIntyre and Walton crouched behind a split log watering trough near the coral, they'd finished reloading and were looking again for targets.

But these Creek were wise indeed; they had divided their forces for this raid, and what's even more impressive, each of the warriors had stuck to the plan! The initial two shots from the tree line had been the bait in a trap. Walton and McIntyre had hidden exactly where the Creek wanted them. Suddenly four more Creek opened up from behind the cabin to their rear—both McIntyre and Walton had literally run right past these attackers who were hidden by the side of the log structure. As fate would have it, all of Walton's sons and his slaves were working in the distant fields about ½ mile away, and the only one in the cabin was Walton's wife, who had already begun her loud beseeching of God for help—she always seemed to pray when she was most needed doing something else.

The second volley of fire from the Creeks caught Walton and McIntyre by surprise, and both were wounded. McIntyre was hit above the elbow in the upper arm, and he would lose most of the function of that arm for life. Walton's wound was more serious. He was his hit twice in the back, with one piece of hot lead entering his right lung.

Still these tough men managed to get off another volley in the rough direction of the new threat, and they saw these four Creek retreat back into the forest behind the cabin. What neither realized was that the seventh Creek on the raid, a warrior they hadn't even been aware of, had managed to use the 30 second battle to sneak from behind the barn and swipe the cows that McIntyre and Walton had been negotiating over in the first place. This Creek had run for the cattle as soon as Walton and McIntyre had run the other way; those cattle were now on the trail back to the Creek settlements far to the southwest, thus becoming the property of the Creek. While horses were more treasured, steeling cows was also highly valued by the tribe.

When Walton's wife reached her prone, badly wounded husband, she took one look at the scene and immediately fell to her knees and began to pray loudly again while swaying from side to side.

McIntyre, leaning over his wounded neighbor couldn't believe it. He looked over at this useless woman, and in his Scottish brogue, he said, *"Are ye daft woman? Stop your damn wailin' and help me get this man to a doctor."* He didn't know Walton's wife at all, and thus didn't realize she had a history of praying loudly and offensively for almost any reason whatsoever, and thus rendering herself completely useless for any emergency. She never realized the need to distinguish between the time for religious reflection and time for action—thus she was relatively useless for both.

Walton's oldest son had now arrived. He ignored his mother's noise, and said, *"Ain't no doctor here. Early Cleveland's got a slave, though, Anabell, who knows herbs."*

McIntyre looked again at the loud woman, still on her knees wailing and communing as best she could with her God, and decided on the obvious fact that the family had known for years—she really was daft. After finding no decision-making help there, he looked into the face of Walton's 14 year old son, and knew he'd make the determination of what to do. He also realized it would be a good idea for him to see some type—any type—of doctor too, so he said. *"I guess that 'll have to do. Hitch up that wagon, yonder."*

With that, McIntyre and Walton's boys picked up the badly wounded man, and continuing to ignore their mother, laid him in the back of a wagon, hitched up the oxen and proceeded to the Cleveland farm across the river using the ford by the cabin. Early took one look at the wound in his friend's back and said, *"Jessie, Gol' dangit. I recon' you caught a who heap o' damn trouble this time."*

Jessie, seeing the worry in his life-long friends' eyes, merely responded, *"Yea, I guess I did."* Early took another look at the wound and sent out to the fields for Anabell.

While Anabell did know herbs and could create a poultice for a cough or other mild elements, a lung shot was totally out of her league. However, she did what she could, and slowed the bleeding a bit. Still, Walton continued to cough up blood for over a day, and within three days, his wound had festered such that everyone knew he was soon to expire. Thus, in the home of his lifelong friend Early

Cleveland, Jessie Walton slowly died. In his forties, and hardened by a frontier life, he was tough, and his body willed itself to resist. Still, infection and continued loss of blood took its toll. He lingered for a week, then a few more days, which was long enough to dictate a will to his friend Early Cleveland. That document has been preserved in the historic records, as were some additional notes in Wyly's diary. With certain provisions for his wife, Walton left most of his estate to his sons, who themselves were approaching manhood. They would soon sell out to James Wyly and Early Cleveland, for those two never let a good piece of land go by without at least considering the purchase of it. Wyly's diary, among the various historical records, offered the most appropriate epitaph for Walton many years after his death; thus did Wyly memorialize his mentor, his comrade in arms, and has friend.

"Jessie Walton had fought Indians, mostly Cherokee, all his life. He was a hero of King's Mountain, but his real victory was his opening of this valley for others. He moved from Virginia to North Carolina, to Tennessee, and then on to Georgia where he and others settled the Tugaloo River Valley. He made his last move specifically to get away from the threat of Indian attack. It is somehow fitting that this remarkable man, a frontiersman, a veteran of King's Mountain, a contemporary of Daniel Boone, and the founder of Jonesborogh, Tennessee—the first white settlement across the Blue Ridge— would die of wounds from an Indian rifle. Such was the life on the frontier of the lower Blue Ridge along the Tugaloo River in 1789. While he had personally lived in the valley along the Tugaloo for only five years, his descendants remain to this day. Moreover, this remarkable man was the only frontiersman of the eighteenth century to found not one but two of the westernmost settlements on the frontier of the fledgling United States– Jonesborough, Tennessee and Walton's Ford, Georgia. Only Daniel Boone himself, in the next century, would do more to settle the western frontier of our new nation. Finally, in lasting tribute, the small settlement Walton founded along the Tugaloo River will bear his name—Walton's Ford—forever."

Diary of James Wyly, 1822

Wyly's assessment was correct in every particular save one. While the name Walton's Ford, was commonly used for the next 100 years, at least one historical document from the mid 1800s refers to the growing town as Wyly's Ford— obviously dating from the period after Wyly purchased the ford, the bridge, and the home from Walton's descendents. Jessie Walton was buried near his cabin along the Tugaloo River within a ½ mile of the old Tugaloo Town Council House Mound of the Cherokee. He was buried at the base of a small hill, along the south side of Toccoa Creek some 300 feet below a large pile of boulders, which none then noticed. These were the rocks that covered the remains of a great Cherokee leader, Runs-To-Water. Of course, the white settlers of the day did not realize that the older Cherokee grave was even there. All they knew, as they laid this great man to rest, was that the wanderings of Jessie Walton, had finally come to an end. Eventually, both the Walton cabin and Jessie Walton's grave were lost to history; with both near the deep channel of the Tugaloo River, each was buried by the construction of Lake Hartwell, in the mid 1900s. Jessie's wandering had ended; he had finally found his home. His bones rest today beneath Lake Hartwell, and his spirit thus joined the mountains that defined his life.

Early Cleveland's Line

Even with the death of his lifelong friend and hunting companion, Early Cleveland continued to work his land, and build a future for his family. As the number of early settlers began to grow, the first settlers in the Tugaloo Valley prospered. By 1795, Early Cleveland's growing plantation was prosperous. His land holdings grew, and the number of slaves he owned had doubled several times over; he now held some twenty eight slaves, an ownership of human beings that, in those days, represented not moral depravity as it does in our view today, but rather respectability, not to mention a great deal of wealth.

Still, building a plantation in the antebellum south of the late 1700s was not a easy proposition. It often involved several transitions; first from Indian fighter and frontiersman, to small farmer, and then from farmer to plantation manager, then to aristocrat. First these frontiersmen, lately turned into farmers, had to clear land for their own subsistence farming. Early was like most in that he began with some seed corn and a few skinny hogs; he may have had several cattle, perhaps a mule, certainly an ox or two. He clearly had a wife whose dual purpose was to work like a slave, and to produce as many children as she could bear. Early also owned several horses. Slaves were the real advantage, not common for most, though Early, as we have seen did have several to begin with.

Early Cleveland was lucky in that he had managed to confiscate many fields which once belonged to the Cherokee of Tugaloo Town. Pine trees that were from 15 to 20 years old now dominated these fields, and these were relatively easy to "girdle and fell," much easier than the old growth oaks and hardwoods that others found on their property. The "girdlin' was merely skinning the bark off the tree for a distance of about 12 inches, all the way around the trunk at the bottom. This damaged the growth potential and nutrient system of the tree, and would generally kill the tree in fairly short order. Then the tree was simply cut down with a crosscut saw, and the roots pulled out with an ox team. Much fine timber was felled in this manner; in fact, many trees dropped in this fashion became the logs for neighboring cabins, or slave huts as the farm expanded.

Of course for the first decade or so, it was all any frontier farmer could do to plant enough corn and beans to feed himself, his few slaves, his hogs, and what cattle he may have had. It often took ten years or more before these rugged farms returned sufficient crops for selling at the end of the season. When that magic moment came, the farm became a "plantation" and typically the frontier farmer assumed more of a managerial role, doing less of the direct field work himself. Thus, did many a mountain man, along with their scrawny, underfed wives and children, reach a point where they could now build a "real house with real floor"—for wood floors in their original farm cabins were nonexistent. More importantly, at that point, the "farmer" became a "Planter!"

While today's mental image of the "antebellum aristocracy" of the Old South brings thoughts of grand mansions with columns out front, and *"Gone With the Wind"* dresses in the shade of the front porch, these mansions were to come in the second or third generation on the plantation. The first planters were quite content to have a two or four room house, with a wooden floor. In later years, this type of house has come to be known as "Plantation Plains" style, the bottom two rooms were generally a drawing room and a formal dining room which were separated by a hallway—essentially a breezeway with doors opening front and back to catch any breeze offered—and a stairway to the two bedrooms upstairs. The kitchen and the "necessary" (i.e. toilet) were both in separate buildings out back. The kitchen was removed from the house to prevent a fire hazard—a strategy that would continue into the early 1900s—and the necessary was kept outside for obvious reasons. In these plantation plains homes the first generation of plantation owners built their fortunes, with the great antebellum mansions generally coming one or two generations latter.

By 1795, Early Cleveland's plantation had been transformed; by then he and his family lived in a four room, plantation plains house. He was now a substantial owner of slaves, and he'd begun to export his excess down river to Savannah or overland to Charlestown. He was considering his next expansion, and was almost set to begin planting cotton, as did many of the larger established planters down towards Savannah and the newer settlement of Augusta. However, when sharing a tankard of ale in the tavern of Billy Sharpe one evening with his friend James Wyly, another thought emerged.

Wyly, ever the shrewd one, was always searching for ways to expand his holdings, as well as other ways to get ahead. The talk soon turned to the next planting season. *"I'm of a mind to try some cotton this Spring, since the prices were so damn high last year,"* Early said, as he took a swig of his ale.

"Well, Early, you won't go wrong with cotton, if'n this ground 'll grow it, but I'm not sure we got the right fields for it." Wyly responded.

"What 'a ya mean? We got the best goddamn fields of the lot right here on the Tugaloo, with water a plenty and slaves to work it," says Early. *"You damn well better be about plantin' some your self. I knowed you got a plenty of slaves, and you're a wasting them if you don't plant cotton."*

Wyly, ever the thoughtful one, took a sip of ale—unlike almost everyone else he always sipped his ale in Billy Sharp's tavern rather than drinking it down in one or two gulps. He did it simply because he never really acquired a taste for ale, but to others it gave him an air of dignity and an aura of great wisdom. He soon shared his thoughts with his friend.

"I'm thinking that, with everybody else in Georgia doing cotton, some folks might need more corn this year, or more beans or sorghum as fodder for their herds. In fact, I was talking to one of my factors." Factors in those days were brokers who served as "middle men" representing buyers in London or Bristol, whose offices were located in the top floors of warehouses along the Savannah riverfront, where they purchased commodities for their buyers. *"He told me he'd take all the corn and beans I could ship him this fall, and he gave me a good price. He ain't gonna ship oversees to London. Instead he's gonna warehouse it, and then sell it back to other plantations through the winter."* Wyly took another slow sip of his ale, and then looked directly at his friend. *"Sort of makes a man think doesn't it?"*

Early was not immediately trusting of this information. *"Why the hell would any damn fool, whose mama raised him with one eye, one asshole, and half sense, pay for corn he could grow his own damn self on his own land?"*

Wyly laughed at his friend's never-ending string of original curses. *"As I see it, the plantations down the river have been cleared longer than our land, and they already have the inside track on cotton."* He took another sip of his ale—again, demonstrated to others both his class, and his wisdom. *"But they put all their slaves to work the cotton fields, and with all their land in cotton, they can't feed themselves. With our climate, we'd do better ignoring the cotton, which we'd have to ship further to get it to market anyway. We can just do corn, beans, hogs, and buy a few deerskin to sell, and we'll do a damn sight better, than trying to compete with the folks down near Savannah or Charleston on the large cotton plantations."*

"Well, James, you can't drink worth a shit, but you do make damn good sense, on most things," said Early. *"I'm gonna put my brain to work on that."*

Talk between the two then turned to the next court week and Early ended the evening entertaining the entire tavern with one of his stories, peppered with his creative language. While neither realized it, in that conversation lay the long term success of many of the plantations of the Tugaloo River Valley. While growing plantations all over the new states of the south would compete for the best cotton prices for almost a century, history tells us that the few plantations of the Tugaloo would become the "farmers' market" for the other plantations down river all the way to the coast. Thus, was their prosperity assured. Even when the cotton prices in distant London took one of the several nosedives during the next decades, the Cleveland and Wyly plantations, and the soon to emerge Jarrett and Prather plantations would do well, planting mostly corn and beans. For even in tough times, the slaves on every plantation in Georgia and South Carolina, like their masters, needed to eat, and much of their fare—corn, vegetables, hogs, cattle, sheep—was grown and/or butchered right in Walton's Ford, the gateway to the Blue Ridge in the Tugaloo River Valley.

Before Early Cleveland could get his field's planted that year however, an interesting controversy arose concerning, of all things, where exactly his plantation was. By a strange quirk of fate, Early Cleveland's land was mostly on the eastern bank of the Tugaloo River, and in those years, everyone assumed that the entire Tugaloo River Valley was in Franklin County, Georgia. Cleveland had been paying his taxes and voting in Franklin County, just like all of his neighbors. However, with the Revolutionary War only recently ended, the various new states had not really gotten around to determining exactly where the boundary line was between Georgia and South Carolina this far north. Of course, the Savannah River was the boundary coming up from the coast, but in the lower reaches of the mountains, that river split into innumerable smaller streams, and one had some difficulty telling which was the largest; the Tugaloo River was only one of the possibilities.

Thus, when Cleveland first moved into the Tugaloo, he was pretty sure he was living in Franklin County, Georgia. Early Cleveland even ran for office from this area of Franklin County, and served one term in the Georgia legislature during those early years. However, that particular brand of politics wasn't for Early, since most of the other legislators came from civilized towns far toward the coast such as Macon, Augusta, and Savannah. Most were planters with significant education, whereas Early had earned his limited education fighting Cherokee, and taming a frontier—his cussin' wasn't even prized or praised by his peers in the legislature, as it was in the Tugaloo Valley. Thus, Early didn't enjoy serving in the legislature much and, of course, folks in the Tugaloo realized that, and none were surprised when he chose not to run for a second term.

Still, he was a leader to be respected, and destined it seems for a life of public service; he was in short order, named "Magistrate Judge" for the Franklin County district of Georgia. He now weighed over 350 pounds—even with the hard work of building a plantation, it seems Early could somehow manage to gain weight— so folks began to talk of him as "the fat Judge", an appellation which Early himself rather enjoyed.

However, a decade later in 1798 or so, when the state line boundary was finally fixed as the Tugaloo River itself, Cleveland found he'd been living in South Carolina during all of those years, since the bulk of his bounty grant had been on the Eastern Bank of the Tugaloo, rather than the western. Never one to be upset by a minor confusions, or artificial lines on a map, he calmly "transferred" his Judgeship to South Carolina, and without really asking anyone's permission, he went about his business as if nothing had happened. In all of recorded history, Early Cleveland, this fat, loudmouth braggart, who was known to be foolishly brave, scrupulously honest, and to cuss like the worst sailor in history, was the only

South Carolinian to ever serve in the Georgia legislature, without ever living a single day in Georgia.

Meanwhile, Early Cleveland' s sons Absolom and Devil John continued to bully and terrorize the entire Tugaloo River neighborhood. In particular, bear baiting and chicken fights seemed to be preferences of Devil John. During the 1790s, he always seemed to have one or more animals tearing each other apart in his barn on any given Saturday night.

Once, Old Tom Prather—who everyone agreed was the best hunter in the valley—had managed to trap a bear cub up near Panther Creek. Tom had killed the mother, and butchered it before he realized there was a cub just above his head in the tree. He captured the cub, by clubbing it senseless with a hickory branch. He then tossed it in a pile of deerskins in his flatboat along with the meat from the other bear, and brought both to the Jarrett store in Walton's Ford for sale.

Devil John immediately saw potential in the cub, so he paid Tom ten buckskins for the young bear. Within two years, Devil John had turned this bear, now weighing over 425 pounds, into a raging monster. For never did a week go by without Devil John tossing a live rabbit or dog, with legs broken, to the beast who he kept chained in a small cabin behind the barn. He also beat the chained bear mercilessly with a large oak pole; as he phrased it, *"Just to liven it up a bit."* Devil John wasn't raising a pet—he was raising a killer. In this way over the next two years, did he create a horrid machine of death, and many a Saturday night did the men in the valley gather in the barn to watch someone's pack of hunting dogs fight the bear.

These events were usually accompanied by much drinking and betting, and many of the "land transactions" recorded in the Franklin County Deeds of this period had their origin in the bear baiting evenings over in Devil John's barn. Devil John always made sure that he had a few "bucks" (i.e. deerskins) around for trade or to cover his bets, and most importantly, he made sure that the homemade liquor flowed freely during a couple of early cock fights, just to warm up the crowd. Next, he'd let anyone who wanted to, take a whack at the bear's head, just to *"Get his attention."* By the time the bear baiting began, inevitably some drunken farmer would bet on which dog the bear would disembowel first, and more often than not, he would lose a portion of his bottomland to Devil John.

By today's standards these "entertainments" of the frontier are perceived as inconceivably cruel, but that is wrongheaded thinking on our part. In the 1790s, life on the frontier was tough, cruel, and short, and that affected the frontier people in ways we can never understand. Terror, cruelty, and untimely death seemed to rule their very existence. Jessie Walton, as one example, arose one morning to do his farmwork, collect his bridge tolls, and trade for a few cattle, and he ended the day, dying in Early Cleveland's house across the river. Life was clearly unpredictable. Almost anyone struggling on this bloody frontier would need some deep-seated assurance that his fate was not as precarious as, in fact, it was. As cruel as these bear baiting events were, they did drive home the fact of human mastery over the beasts of the wilderness—the human desire to control even one small part of a brutal frontier. Thus these entertainments may have served as something of a psychological release for these people. In fact, many of our species even in civilized societies today, still hunt as a hobby, long after any realistic need for the food obtained from such behavior is past. For some people today, perhaps the same psychological need is met by hunting, as was met in Devil John's barn.

Still, in a broader sense, judging yesterday's characters in the broader sweep of history by today's standards is both insulting to our ancestors, and demeaningly stupid on our part. We can never know or truly understand what impacted life on this bloody frontier, or our ancestor's emotional reactions to the frontier. While we may partially understand the emotional role these entertainments in history played for our ancestors, we can never be empathic with those emotions. Moreover, what do we do today, that will be perceived as stupid in a few short years? How harshly will our progeny judge us for various aspects of our character?

Behold the Spirit: God Comes to the Tugaloo Valley

Such reflections must, of necessity, lead to a quest for the spiritual, and spiritual history is rich in these tantalizingly Blue Mountains. The Cherokee who lived first in the Tugaloo Valley were a mystical people, always seeking "balance" in their lives. Dedicated to their worship of Kanati and their reverence for the sacred fire in the Council House, the spiritual commitment was obvious in their clan structure and the resulting "community" concern for each member of their clan; such thoughts and rituals dominated their lives.

Perhaps this is understandable, given the tough life these marvelous people led. It is one certainty of history that a deep spiritualism makes survival in a harsh world not only possible, but enjoyable. The Cherokee would turn to Kanati, in prayer for every major event—the Green Corn Festival, fall or winter hunts, or raiding parties against the Creeks or the Whites. Their very death songs were prayers to their one God. Each day, the Cherokee began their day in prayers, as they headed as one to the river for the water purification. Each evening, the old men would tell the children the tales of the water beetle of the Cherokee creation story, or where the animals came from, and thus promote the mystic development of the youngest of their tribe. This gave them balance in their world, and ultimately what is man, without a quest for the divine?

However, the spiritual development in the Tugaloo River Valley took a sharp turn for the worse after 1761 when the Cherokee families were driven out. For something like 28 years, few prayers could be heard in these marvelous hills, and between Sharpe's store selling liquor to anyone, any age, anytime, and the bear-baiting, cock-fighting, and general hell raising out by Devil John's cabin, the spiritual development of the community left much to be desired. All of this was soon to change, however, and once again, because of the influence of Early Cleveland.

In spite of his malcontented and disreputable spawn—Devil John—Early Cleveland was to bring much good influence into the Tugaloo River Valley. Within a decade of Early's move into the valley, his two brothers, Larkin and John, took their families from North Carolina and moved into the valley also. Soon Larkin Cleveland began farming and in a few years had established a second Cleveland plantation in the Valley in South Carolina. Brother John, however, went about doing the business of the Lord.

Being a religious man, and unlike his cussin', drinking brother, who was also prone to enjoy the unsavory business of county politics, John was of a deeply spiritual nature. John Cleveland was a man touched by God himself, and by 1789, he had established the Tugaloo Baptist Church. Beginning with only fourteen, his flock soon included some 108 members, and was one of the first churches in the Tugaloo Valley. If the congregation was looked upon with contempt by Devil John, most of the upright citizens in the valley took their religion quite seriously and welcomed this weekly opportunity for both reverence and socializing over a lunch on the grounds. Wyly commented on the typical Sunday morning meeting.

It was an astounding sight–this community worshiping together. Wagons fill the few roads early of a Sunday morning, and by 10:00 AM the rough-hewed log church is filled to capacity by Clevelands, McIntyres, Wards, Jarretts, Waltons, Moselys, Cashs, a few Sharpes, a scattering of Prathers, Wylys and one or two Carmichaels—though this last batch usually sat way in the back; for everyone knew the twisted story of the inbred Carmichael clan. Those few Carmichaels who bathed up enough to go to church were usually somewhat quiet, though they were never otherwise known to be quiet; more importantly, the Tugaloo Baptist Church received even these. The Reverend John Cleveland was known to welcome all; even the darkies of in the community got their dose of Brother John's fiery preachin' late Sunday evening under the trees down by the river.

Diary of James Wyly 1793

The Reverend Cleveland was indeed a man touched by God; He seemed intimate with the Almighty and was known to preach with the loud, certain passion often associated with Baptist Ministers of those years. Many small children spent their early lives terrified by images of hell conjured up by Reverend John. For in those days, it simply wasn't considered to be a really good sermon by either the Reverend or his congregation, unless *"the women were weepin' and the children were wailin' in the old log church down by the river."* Many a Sunday did the spirit move the men and women of this church, and in the harsh existence on the frontier of those days, people needed the solace that a firm, yet kind, religion can bring.

Yes, by all accounts, Reverend John was as profound a spiritual influence as was the very word of the Risen Lord he espoused. While his sermons created discomfort among many—fire and brimstone images were plentiful in his words—all in the valley knew that he was a man who "Walked in the Lord." Never did a beggar go wanting from his door without a piece of bread or a small hunk of bacon. Never did a stranger find him unwilling to travel in the middle of the night, when someone on a distant farm or plantation was dying. Never did Reverend John fail to show tender love for children, for the youth of the community who traveled a "Godly path," or for the many newly wed couples who came to him to "get hitched."

Not only did Reverend John minister to slaves; he was even known to minister to the few remaining Cherokee in the area; *"Drunks the lot of them,"* by the mutual judgment of his congregation. Yet, even these unusual actions were taken as ministering to the savages and were thus seen as doing the Lord's work, even for the little good such efforts would do. As a result of this ministry, Reverend John was one of the few white men—along with Billy Sharpe and Tom Prather—who learned a bit of the native tongue; these few could seemingly travel through Cherokee country further up in the mountains in relative safety.

By 1800 the Cherokee, ever a spiritual people, were largely embracing Christianity, and the Reverend John played a large part in that spiritual awakening. The Indians saw this revered figure as the "White haired man of God," in reference to the shoulder length white mane of hair sported by the Reverend, and indeed, he did preach to the Cherokee whenever the occasion presented itself. However, the eschatology of the converted Cherokee in those years was still a bit rough; in their tongue, Jesus was *"The man on the sticks,"* and they never understood how his death brought them either a personal relationship to the Almighty, or a spiritual life after death.

History records the bravery–not to mention the spiritual certainty–of this remarkable man; for truly he walked with the Lord. Wyly, as usual, played a role in the following events, and every the dutiful recorder, he noted not only the event itself but the very words spoken along the Tugaloo River so long ago, and much of the following account comes from that source.

One hot June evening, while he sat preparing his sermon for the next Sunday, he heard a knock on the door frame of the open cabin door. When Reverend John looked up, he saw a young Cherokee boy, holding his hat in supplication. The boy diverted his eyes, as was proper in his world. While this Cherokee custom drove most whites to distraction, Brother John understood it as a sign of deep respect for an elder. The child spoke, while looking down, in rough broken English. *"My father say you come."*

The Reverend recognized the boy as one of the half-breeds that seemed to hang around Sharpe's tavern, and lived in one of the several dirt floor hovels out in back. Nearly every tavern on the frontier in those days, at least every tavern worthy of the name, either included, or provided access to a whorehouse, and Sharp's was no exception. Brother John, while trying to save all for Jesus, was wise enough to pick his battles; thus he did not ask too many questions, about this collection of shacks, nor did he ever mention the spiritual issue presented in such trade in his sermons. This particular cluster of rough log cabins stood some 200 yards up the hill from the tavern, and was known to house many who could barely identify their own mother, much less their father. Most of these young half-breeds worked in the tavern's stable or in the fields by the river. All were free labor, though there was clearly some African blood, as well as Cherokee and white blood in that intriguing mix. While the community didn't realize it, the Reverend John had been teaching some of these youngsters of dubious ancestry—boys and girls alike—to read the Good Book for some time. Thus, he recognized this Cherokee mixed-blood youngster as one called simply, Moon. *"Are you having a walk this fine evening, Moon, or pray tell me, is something wrong?"*

The boy again diverted his eyes from the older gentlemen in respect, as he'd been dutifully taught by his Cherokee mother, and merely repeated, *"Father say you come."*

Realizing he'd get no more information, the Reverend considered saddling his horse, and then decided to merely walk the half mile to the hovels behind the tavern. As he and Moon approached, the Reverend wondered what might bring the call for his presence. In the absence of a doctor, he was called many times for medical reasons—for which he was no more prepared than any other citizen in the valley. Sometimes he was called in for a birth, but midwives usually handled the routine childbirths. Moreover, most of the plantations around had a slave or two that "knew herbs."

In those days, a bit higher in the mountains, the Cherokee themselves were much more practiced in herbal medicine, and in fact had much better medicines than the whites. History records that the Cherokee used over 700 plants as medicine in those years. Still, the egotistical whites would never dream of sending for a Cherokee in the event of illness—rather a slave or midwife who "knew herbs" would be called, and Brother John called shortly thereafter, if necessary.

On this night, however, the Reverend began to suspect the trouble even before he reached the first hovel. While Moon's ancestry may have been questionable, there was no doubt of some Cherokee blood in him as well as the others that inhabited these hovels, and the Cherokee were still more susceptible to many diseases than were the whites. The Reverend's fears were confirmed before he entered the first shack—his countenance dropped and his heart skipped a beat as he realized the plague had returned.

It is hard for the modern mind to conceive of the meaning of the plagues of history. In an era when nothing was known of germs, much less viruses, plagues were a feared scourge, bringing death unexpectedly to young and old alike. Entire families would be wiped out. Even more tragic, at times only the parents would be taken by the dreaded illness, leaving several young children to be taken in by relatives or merely divided among other families in the community. These diseases could sweep in at any time, and they would be attributed to everything from bad luck to God's will. In some cases, when diseases ran through a community, entire settlements could be wiped out. While this problem is more widely known and documented as a European urban problem in the 1700s and 1800s, the same diseases often savaged victims among rural folk along the American frontier as well. Also, while the Cherokee had built some tolerance over European diseases during the 1700s, there was still increased susceptibility among them as late as the early 1900s.

The Reverend saw an older half-breed whom he recognized, but whose name he did not know stagger from one of the hovels, and collapse on the ground—his face swollen, with large pox clearly visible on his skin. The man died on the ground gasping for ragged breaths, while the Reverend and Moon watched the spectacle in the darkening twilight.

The Reverend said, *"Moon, do you live in one of these cabins?"*

Moon merely pointed to the cabin on the far left, and repeated again, *"Father say come."*

At that moment, the Reverend could have, and perhaps should have walked away; for who could blame him for avoiding such an agonizing death as might befall him? However, such was not the makeup of this man. He knew with a certainty, he would enter the cabin and minister as best he could—some combination of damp towels and prayers most likely—but first he had his duty to the community.

"Moon," he said. *"Go get Miss Sadie Sharpe, Mr. Wyly, and the Fat Judge, and tell them I said come to the tavern at once. Do you know where they all live?"*

Moon merely nodded affirmation, and then pointed once again to the hovel in which his stricken family lay.

The Reverend said, *"I'll tend your paw and your maw, right after I talk with those folks, now run get them; run fast!"*

Good news spreads fast in small communities, but bad news spreads like lightning. In a flash James Wyly, now one of the leading citizens in the valley, came riding in, and on his heals two carriages—one with Ms. Sadie, and one with Judge Early Cleveland; the Judge, in particular, was none too pleased.

"What is Sam Hill's gotten into you John? I was damn near finished the best meal I ever had and I hadn't even finished the damn desert!" Early, because of his nature and disposition, was the only man in the county to show such a foul mouth before the Reverend, and sometimes Brother John rebuked him, but not that night; there

was more important work to be done. At that moment, the Judge saw Ms. Sadie, and while he'd cuss around his brother, just to get his dander up, he didn't want to upset this pillar of the Tugaloo Presbyterian Church! *"Oh, sorry Ms. Sadie. I didn't see you there. I thought maybe that was ol' Tom Prather's carriage."*

The Reverend spoke before Ms. Sadie could reply. *"OK, now Early, just shut your cussin' trap, because we have more important things to consider tonight."*

"We most assuredly do," said Wyly, who'd seen the prone man lying dead in the shadows. *"It's the plague, isn't it Reverend."*

"Yes it is, Brother James," the Reverend answered. *"And I'm afraid it may run the whole town."*

At that, Early cussed for real. *"Oh shit! What in hell do we need this for?"*

Ms. Sadie merely drew a sharp breath, and decided not to get into the Judge's case; for if ever a vulgar word might be permitted it was when the plague hit.

The Reverend continued. *"We'll need to burn these cabins here; I think we can do that without burning the tavern, barn, or anything else. Still, we'll need a place to care for the sick."*

Wyly immediately saw the obvious question, even if the others didn't. *"Who is going to tend them?"* In those days, families tended to their own, even during rough times, but who indeed attended to whores and their progeny when the plague was about?

The question stopped all conversation instantly. In the hushed silence that followed, each of these pillars of the community wished that Walton's Ford had a doctor—none would arrive this night, for none would come into the Tugaloo River Valley until well into the 1850s.

It was then that the greatness of Reverend John Cleveland came forth. When courage is required, when help is necessary, or when fortitude is essential, in those times do true spiritual leaders manifest themselves, as they have done throughout history, in all times, in all cultures. In the twilight dusk, with a corpse at his feet in the darkening shadows, this holy man first looked to his God, whispering a silent prayer for courage. Then he looked within his soul, and there he found the answer he needed. In a quiet, though assured voice, Reverend John Cleveland simply said, *"I will."*

With those simple words, did his name and his courage enter history. For in these times, trifling with horrors such as the plague was no simple matter—many died of various diseases each year, and the Reverend had no more immunity for these than did anyone else. Each of the community leaders thought they'd seen the last great act of a truly spiritual man. For surely the Reverend would die within the week, like almost all of the others. For a moment, there was a hushed silence, as all contemplated this self-less act.

Wyly recovered first, and spoke. *"We'll use the barn behind the tavern. Ms. Sadie, get the women to give as many blankets and towels as they can. Nobody should go within 50 feet of the barn, except to bring the sick. This boy,* (he pointed to Moon) *and any others around here who don't have it yet can bring in the sick and help the Reverend."*

Early then spoke up. *"I'll have some of my boys and the slaves come over and burn these hovels down, as soon as John gets the living out of them. We'll leave the dead in the cabins."* Then he turned to directly face the Reverend, his younger brother that he truly believed would soon perish. He paused for just a moment before he solemnly spoke, *"John, I shall pray."*

For the Fat Judge, that was quite a statement; none present could recall Early Cleveland ever praying in church, or for that matter, ever making such a statement before. He looked at his brother John with newfound respect, as well as love.

The Reverend took the statement for the gift it was. *"Thank you, Early. Now go on and send your boys over."*

Within ten minutes four half-breeds who were still living were collected from the several hovels, and moved into the barn by Reverend John and Moon. Five minutes later, all of those small cabins were burning, several with a corpse or two inside. Meanwhile, Ms. Sadie was riding through the night, up and down the Valley, with the word that the plague had come. She collected blankets and towels, but mostly she merely warned others to stay out of the village for the next month or so. All who got the message avoided the tavern and the town for the rest of the summer.

Perhaps because of this relatively fast action by the community leaders, the plague that year wasn't as deadly as it could have been. Eighteen souls lost their lives in the Tugaloo Valley including the five found dead in the hovels on the first night. Further, an additional eight came down with the symptoms but managed to survive, scared for life, but still happy with their new lease on life. Much to the surprise of everyone, Reverend John Cleveland never came down with the plague.

Nevertheless, the plague that year changed things for the Reverend. After it was all over, his reputation as a man of God knew no bounds. He was invited to speak from the Surrey County settlements in North Carolina all the way down to Savannah, and speak he did—with the same fire and determination that left them weeping in the aisles in his own Tugaloo Baptist Church. He told of his ministry to the heathen community on the frontier, and the genteel folk of Charlestown, Augusta and Savannah would lean forward to hear the stories of this man who preached to whites, to slaves, and to the Cherokee alike. They would marvel at his white mane of shoulder length hair, and cringe when he told of the several deaths he'd attended, corpses mutilated at the hands of savage Indians in the Blue Ridge.

Still, when he spoke of the time when he tended the dying half-breeds during the plague, his courage was manifest, and his determination unbounded. In those moments, the spirit of the Lord would come upon him, his voice would become more stately, and his words like magic. He spoke of those days in a soft whisper of a voice—uncharacteristic for him, but even more powerful by that. Men would shake their heads in wonder, and many of the leading ladies of the distant congregations would cry, tears streaming down their faces; others would simply faint. Truly this man was a man of God; truly he, "Walked with the Lord." Of such leadership are communities formed, and great religions, regardless of beliefs, all rest on the shoulders of men such as these.

The Antics of Devil John

While Reverend John Cleveland was a tremendous influence for good along the Tugaloo, Devil John continued to be an influence for evil in the valley. In almost every frontier community of this period, such trashy, vulgar men were spawned that seemed to reflect the worst aspects of human nature—Devil John Cleveland was such a man. Wyly recorded many examples of this. In the early autumn one year in the 1790s, Devil John's wife, Caty, proposed to join the church that Reverend John had established. Devil John, as one may expect, took exception, and a great spiritual battle arose over this woman's soul. The next Saturday evening in a drunken rage, Devil John absolutely forbade her to join the church, as she planned to do the next morning. Shouting so loud that almost everyone on the several neighboring plantations heard most of his cussin', he "laid her low" verbally, and then struck her across the face, sending her into the wall. Of course, forbidding her to join a church made perfect sense to him, since he himself never attended. Not only was Devil John predisposed to a life of sin, but he was also afraid that too much religion would cut into his profits from his Saturday night activities. His cash reserves depended upon considerable drinking in his barn each weekend, and he wasn't about to let his wife help in any endeavor that might reduce the number of folks willing to lay down a ha'penny to watch the festivities.

Come Sunday morning, Caty snuck out while Devil John slept off the previous evenings frolics. The Reverend John noted the bruise on her face, but was still very pleased when she came in; he didn't even wait until he preached to baptize her, but announced that God's work that morning was to be done at the river! Then shortly after she entered, after only an opening prayer and hymn—he headed down the aisle with both Caty and the whole congregation in tow, leading to the banks of the Tugaloo to do God's work! In record time, Reverend John had her head underwater, baptizing as he always did in the swift cool waters of that beautiful stream. Then and there, unpracticed and with no notes, he preached a two hour sermon singing the praises of the newly saved, and how those who suffered for God's work truly benefited in the next life. After a half-day spiritual experience, which all present agreed was one of his better sermons, Caty returned home, quite content with her new relationship to God.

Now, when he awakened in mid-afternoon, old Devil John must have seen something in her eyes, so he questioned her. *"I supposed you've been baptized?"*

Caty looked frightened, but stood her ground with her husband; at that moment, she had the strength of the Lord in her. *"Yes, I have."* She replied calmly, *"and you can't do nothing about it!"*

Perhaps it was her calmness itself that didn't sit well with Devil John. *"Well, by God, we'll see about that! This minute, you shall have some more of it!"* With that he picked her up and bodily carried her to the river where the baptisms were conducted and there he dunked her under ninety-nine more times, countin' out loud her baptisms. Each time he pulled her head up, as she gasped for breath, he'd shout, *"Is your sorry ass saved yet?"* and then he'd dunk her back under. Some in the village thought he was drowning her, but she continued to scream, and even those who saw this overt cruelty left the two of them alone. In those days no one stepped into such a family dispute. Thus in the entire history of the Tugaloo River Valley, Caty Cleveland was the only woman who was right and truly baptized 100 times in one day.

This, of course, caught the attention of the community, and Devil John was ostracized for an entire week. This rude punishment lasted right on up to the following Saturday night when men who were hungry for diversion from their inconceivable labors began to gather at his barn for the next bear baiting. Caty, meanwhile saw her mistake in marrying this horrible man and left for her parents home in Abbyville, South Carolina the very next day. She never set foot in the Tugaloo Valley again, and one can only hope that she found a better life elsewhere— it would have been difficult to find a worse one!

One interesting escapade of Devil John brought him into direct conflict with his father, Early Cleveland, who was then serving as magistrate for the upstate South Carolina district. Devil John was, once again drunk over at Billy Sharpe's tavern, and had managed to insult Duncan Carmichael, one of the ungainly clan of Carmichaels from down river. This man, well into his cups himself, took umbrage and hit the Devil with a half-full bottle of home made whiskey. Of course, Devil John went down to one knee, with a cut on his cheek, but according to the testimony of Billy and several others present, when he came up was grinnin' *"from ear to ear"* and had his knife in his hand. Billy recalled the fight, and his exact words were taken down in the court records. *"Devil John come up with his knife out and grinnin' from ear to ear. I never seed such devilment in a man a'fore, so's I shouted to Duncan, 'Watch yourself! Devil John got his knife and he's gona cut out your soul if you don't run."*

Carmichael, who was unarmed, saw the wisdom of that suggestion, and managed to get just outside of the door before Devil John caught him. Billy's testimony continued. *"Me and Duncan, and everybody there could smell the stench of whiskey breath and the Devil's smell* (Devil John's unwashed body—he was known to bath twice a year, on Christmas and Easter). *Duncan looked like he was gonna' puke 'cause of the smell. Then the Devil grabbed Duncan's hair, and made to cut his throat. So's I shouted, 'Don't kill him, Devil John. You done scart him enough to pee his pants.' Sure enough there was a puddle under the man, so the Devil just laughed out loud, and cut some hair out of Duncan's scalp. Then he put his knife back in his belt, and beat Carmichael senseless."*

Thus did Duncan Carmichael become the only white man ever scalped by another white man in Walton's Ford.

All during this testimony, the Judge, Early Cleveland, had to endure this scathing rebuke of his son's whiskey'd up antics. Still, old Early Cleveland was scrupulously fair. Weighing in now at 395 pounds, Early sat on the newly reinforced bench, looking down as his worthless progeny; one can only imagine what this father must have felt, looking at his son under those circumstances.

When all the witnesses were heard, Devil John stood up and began to make a "defense" of his own actions. His father, looked only once at his son before he told him to *"shut the hell up."* Early then ordered his own son "Pilloried" for five days in front of the Tugaloo Baptist Church.

This punishment involved essentially having ones hands and head bound between two timbers mounted on poles—what in the northern colonies had come to be know as "the stocks." The water or food the prisoner received during that time, had to come from well meaning members of the community, or family or friends, and while Devil John had a number of drinking buddies, he didn't have many friends. This unfortunate man, however, had never learned that critical distinction; while friends are there for you all the time, drinking buddies tend to disappear when trouble arrives.

Moreover, by being pilloried near the church the Devil's uncle, Reverend John Cleveland, could both preach against the actions of Devil John, and also toss any left over kitchen scrapes on the Devil's shoulders, only to let the ants eat them off his useless nephew's skin. While Early ordered that his family leave Devil John hungry and thirsty during his stay, Early's wife had pity on her misguided son, and each evening she secretly sent a slave to the prisoner with some water and a biscuit or two. After a couple of days, even the Reverend John began to take pity on the younger man. No matter how sinful he was, hungry ants could drive a man insane, so the Reverend stopped tossing his table scrapes on his nephew, and made certain that Devil John had at least a little bread each day.

Thus did Devil John survive this punishment. Still, within a decade, Devil John was to get his back broken in a drunken brawl, and mercifully die, thus ridding the valley of his horrid man. A more useless man has never since lived in the Tugaloo River Valley, though as in many frontier communities, some men have come close.

The Tugaloo Neighborhood in 1805

As more settlers moved in, the Tugaloo neighborhood continued to grow. Another small church began near the river where Walton's home had once stood, and a blacksmith finally arrived in 1795 and set up shop near the ford on the river. Wyly had purchased some land from the heirs of Jessie Walton along with the toll bridge over the river, directly over the ford. For a brief time, some official government documents referred to the area as "Wyly's Ford" but that name never stuck and most government documents, as well as all of the locals, continued to refer to the community as Walton's Ford. Of course, after Wyly purchased his bridge, he charged a slightly increased toll for the crossing which was, as it turned out, merely his first endeavor in making money from travelers.

When the various land grants awarded to Revolutionary War soldiers began to be sold off by their heirs, either Wyly or his friend, Old Early Cleveland, who now weighed just over 400 pounds, were always on hand to buy them up. By 1800, these two became, for a time, the largest landholders in the Valley, and each was very successful at acquiring good land. While remaining best of friends, they were quite dissimilar in every other area. Cleveland, of course, was the fattest man in the Valley, while Wyly was a small man, standing only 5 feet four, and carrying only some 145 pounds. In fact, the few remaining Cherokee in the Valley were all much larger, with the average height of the Cherokee male just over six feet. Moreover, Cleveland was, at this point, quite content to live his remaining years on his plantation, while Wyly, like all frontier wanderers, continued to eye the northwestern horizon, with the age old question on his mind, *"I wonder if I could take a road through there, maybe even all the way to Tennessee?"*

Others did well in the Valley during those years. In spite of the departure of his first wife, Nancy, Bryan Ward had married another Cherokee woman and left five children in the area. While his old grist mill was long since closed, by 1798 his several children still held land on Ward's Creek. Their descendants would live in this valley for two hundred years. Old Tom Prather, who had begun life as Ekaia—the disappearing ghost of the Cherokee—had long since been regarded as a white man by everyone around. Through shrewd trading and hard work, he had managed to not only maintain his farm, but to extend his holdings considerably. His family lived in a small cabin near the river, and he now owned five slaves who had cabins further up the hill behind the house. The Prather farm was a growing concern, with hog lots, cattle, and cash crops of cotton and corn. Old Tom Prather often visited Early Cleveland, who was now approaching seventy years old, and the two would swap stories about this or that Indian raid they'd managed to survive in their youth. Early died having never realized that for years, he was talking with a man who'd been born Cherokee.

After Tom's first wife died—men in this period were often widowed by childbirth or disease, or by merely working their frontier women to death—Tom managed to marry a young, lily-white preacher's daughter named Elizabeth Purkey in 1792. In short order, they'd begun a family together, and with two sets of children from two different wives—not to mention one of the best run plantations in the valley—this family became quite influential.

In fact, Tom Prather's first son, James Wallace Prather, grew up never realizing that he had any Cherokee blood in him at all. When James occasionally asked his Daddy about their family, Tom Prather just said he'd come to the Tugaloo Valley from Abbyville, South Carolina—a place Tom had visited once to buy a rifle. Of such meandering deceptions do family legends come, and today the entire Prather clan—totally ignorant of Tom Prather's Cherokee background as well as his Indian name, trace their ancestry back to James Wallace Prather, whom they say came to the valley from Abbyville, South Carolina just before 1800.

While the original dirt floor cabin used by Tom Prather is long gone, one of the few buildings from 1800 that survives to this day is the original cabin build by James Wallace Prather, just a half mile north of the Tugaloo River. The two room cabin allowed James to begin the expansion of the Prather Clan, a family which would become wealthy, influential settlers later during the antebellum period. Once again, the great southern plantations were not begun in the large mansions known by all today to be the very definition of the antebellum period—rather these massive agri-business concerns were begun in the first two room log cabin or plantation-plains clapboard house that had a "real floor." The Prather cabin is one of the few remaining such plantation houses anywhere on the Tugaloo dating from this period; it is still owned by the Prather family, along with a magnificent antebellum mansion which came some 50 years later. The grave of James Wallace Prather is only 25 feet in back of that cabin, marked with a large memorial placed there by his descendents.

By 1805 everyone in the valley knew that old Tom Prather was something of a loner. He'd disappear hunting for weeks at a time every fall, and sometimes even in the Spring and summer, leaving his son and slaves to run the plantation. None knew that often, during those long weeks of absence, Tom would visit with his relatives living with the Cherokee near Echota, some 70 miles to the west of the Tugaloo. Here he would swap stories with the Cherokee, who still considered Ekaia, to be merely "hiding with the whites." Each could learn the news of the other, and many times white raids against the Cherokee were thwarted because of these secret visits. After a few weeks or so, Old Tom would shoot a deer or bear, skin it, and travel on home to his Tugaloo River plantation, and neither his white wife nor his neighbors were ever the wiser.

A newer settler had arrived by the early 1800s, and the fact that Wyly noted this new comer in his diary indicated the shear personal power of the man.

"By 1805, Devereaux Jarrett, the son of our former comrade in arms Mr. Robert Jarrett, had arrived in Waltons' Ford. He arrived owning some 17 slaves, most highly skilled, which of course made Mr. Jarrett a wealthy man. However, he owned no land and was despairing to acquire some. For he was obviously a substantial man of business—for his slaves had to work somewhere to earn their keep. In fact, he rented them out as smithy's, tanners, wagon drivers, house servants, etc. Some could even count and read, though this was not generally discussed by those in the community."

Diary of James Wyly, Nov. 1807

Indeed most of Devereaux Jarretts slaves were highly skilled; some had even been purchased in London. Many had worked in his stores in the small community of Pendleton Courthouse in South Carolina. Some were butchers while others tended cattle, pigs, or horses. In fact, every one of Jarrett's slaves were skilled in one task or another, thus making them more valuable than the average field hand slave. Even then was Devereaux building his fortune one slave at a time—for when his slaves became skilled, he became more wealthy. Of course he needed land, and was able to purchase some on which to field his livestock from one of the Carmichaels, thus acquiring a parcel of some 20 acres down river from Walton's Ford. He also purchased some of the original track of land given as a bounty grant to Jessie Walton.

Now Devereaux happened to arrive in the Valley during a week when Billy Sharpe was taken ill of the fevers. When Billy subsequently died, Jarrett immediately acquired his old floorless hovel of a tavern on the East bank of the Tugaloo River. Of course, Jarrett wasn't interested in running a crude tavern in the valley; rather, he wanted a dry goods store, a smithy, and a real tavern with a real floor. In short, he wanted to dominate all of the "store bought" trade in the valley. Still, he knew that getting folks into his store—and his store alone—meant getting rid of competitors if he could. Thus, when the opportunity presented itself, he purchased the ramshackle cabin that had been serving as the only tavern in these parts, since the days of the Toothless White Man, with an eye towards closing it down and moving it across the river in a year or two. That is exactly what he did.

Devereaux was also able to purchase some land along Toccoa Creek, where he built a small cabin slightly to the north of the creek. He didn't realize it at the time, but his cabin sat only 200 feet across the creek from where a Cherokee boy—Runs-To-Water—had killed his first bear over 80 years before. In fact, from the porch of the Jarrett cabin, one could look across the creek, up the slope of a small hill, and see a large pile of rocks that was the crept of Runs-To-Water. However, no one would rediscover that grave for almost 200 years. Today an antebellum mansion stands on the spot where that first cabin of Devereaux once stood, and the crept is long since gone, but that is getting ahead of our story. The point for now, is that Devereaux Jarrett, the most influential man in the Tugaloo during his day, had arrived on the scene by 1805, and was running a store and tavern in the area.

Other families who had early beginnings in the valley had flourished also. The Carmichael's who lived down near Ward's creek were beginning their third generation in the valley, still with many questionable family relationships. They'd all sprung from a skinny young Scotsman who had helped kill Runs-To-Water many years ago. While no large land holdings were ever amassed by this family, the staunch Presbyterianism of several of the women of this clan, was one of the most important influences in the Tugaloo Presbyterian Church that had just begun in the valley; second only to the influence of Ms. Sadie Sharpe.

Even before her husband, Billy Sharpe died, Ms. Sadie had become a rock on which that congregation hinged. Ms. Sadie, this onetime whore who was hog-tied and smuggled up river by her husband so many years ago could really belt out a hymn, even at the ripe old age of 65. She'd toss her head back and hit the high soprano notes as well as the youngest maiden in the entire congregation, and with twice the volume. It was said that even the Baptists in the old log church across the river could hear her on the high notes. She and her children, proud Presbyterians all, mustered in the same church she'd attended for almost forty years each Sunday morning. She liked being the loudest vocalist there, if not necessarily the most accomplished. Still, Ms. Sadie thought it important that her grandchildren see her worship each week, and she had the habit of winking at them when she caught them with their eyes open during prayers. She wanted them to know she was always watching.

The life of this remarkable women holds a lesson for us all. It is often the case today that seekers of their ancestors like to idolize their forbearers, often creating aristocracy where none existed, or even claiming some distant ties to European royalty. Of course these connections are often imaginary inventions, claimed many years after the fact. It is a fact that almost nobody who was doing well in the old country came to these shores by choice; why would they? Moreover, certainly no one who was doing well in New York, Philadelphia, or Savannah would come to the rough and bloody frontier along the Tugaloo River in those days. The harsh reality is that as Americans, by and large, we are a nation of migrants; our ancestors were immigrants, wanderers, nomads, second or third sons with no prospects for inheritance, criminals escaping in the only way practical, indentured servants sold into bondage for a specified time, or slaves outright. Most of us do not stem from royalty, or even aristocracy. Rather, we are the rabble and refuse from Europe, Asia, and Africa, and like Ms. Sadie Sharpe or Tom Prather, our ancestors frequently had something to hide.

Still, in fairness to these our ancestors—these wanderers of the night, often hiding from their past—one can point to the likes of Ms. Sadie Sharpe, as a woman who succeeded against all odds. This one-time whore had found herself in a horrid position—hogtied in the bottom of a boat by a half-breed Cherokee savage. However, even in that unlikely situation she not only survived, but thrived, making a wonderful life for herself and her children. Of such women are great nations made, and we should be quite proud to claim the one-time whore from Savannah, the captured African slave, the indentured servant from London, Bristol, or East Anglia, the wandering frontiersman trader, or the "Disappearing Ghost of the Cherokee" as our ancestor. Men and women such as these can teach us to survive the rigors of our world, as they survived and even thrived within the rigors of theirs.

In retrospect, I like the image of the old whore, with her head thrown back and singing so loudly the Baptists across the river were put to shame! Thus did she lead the spiritual quest in that church so many years ago, while winking clandestinely during most every prayer at one grandchild or another. Ms. Sadie was always watchin' and I have no doubt that her soul is watchin' the goings on in the Tugaloo Valley still. I'd be willing to bet that the soul of fat judge is too.

It was a sad day in the valley, when Ol' Judge Cleveland died. He'd become much loved on both sides of the river, and his influence accounted for much of the early migration to the Tugaloo River Valley. He was the third of the King's Mountain Men to expire, with both Robert Jarrett and Jessie Walton having died earlier; the fat Judge passed in the fall of 1806. He probably had a heart attack, but rumor soon spread along the Tugaloo River that he merely "smothered in his own fat," as he slept. Perhaps Wyly summarize this man's life most accurately.

"Judge Early Cleveland will be remembered for his bravery, his leadership, his cussin', his judgeship, and his amazing girth. Among the several of the veterans of King's Mountain, only Early Cleveland, Tom Prather, and I have made the transition from frontiersman to plantation owner, and only Early and I managed to become gentleman. After Early's judgeship was established, and his plantation finally landed in South Carolina, he settled in to quite a life—eating and drinking way too much, and cussin' as always. He offered a witty word and laughter to all, and we shall miss him for that. Moreover, He confronted every danger head on, usually laughing, or telling his stories until the day he died. I'm sure that this valley will never know another man like my friend, Early Cleveland."

James Wyly's diary, 1806

Mr. Wyly's Wanderin Road

The four King's Mountain Men, now reduced to one, were all first and foremost frontiersmen, and frontiersmen are prone to wander. Like old Daniel Boone himself, they never really seemed to settle down anywhere. Once anyone of them got a settlement established, they were up and gone again like "the devil was down a'hind him!" Early Cleveland, recent from Virginia had lodged for a time on the Yadkin River along the Eastern slope of the Blue Ridge in North Carolina before coming to the Tugaloo River Valley. Jessie Walton was no different. He settled in Tennessee, then along the Tugaloo and only his untimely death at the hands of the Creek Raiding party had stopped Walton's wandering ways; no historian doubts that, had he lived another decade or two, he would have soon left the Tugaloo River for the ever greener pastures on the frontier in middle Tennessee. Like many men of their age, these four King's Mountain Men seemed prone to wander, always hovering near the Blue Ridge, as if attracted by some unseen charm of those wonderful, foreboding mountains. They could no more have left those mountains than they could have stopped breathing.

James Wyly, now the only one left, was as prone to wander as the others. Even while clearing his land near the Tugaloo, Wyly was busily eyeing the rich, highlands to the north, and he'd never forgotten the drudgery, boredom, and sheer stupidity of walking toward the northeast in order to travel to the southwest. Still that is what he and Walton had, of necessity, done when they moved from Jonesborough, Tennessee down to the Tugaloo River in Georgia. When Wyly realized that his lifelong friend Early Cleveland was gone, he began yet again to eye the mountains to the north, wondering if a road through those high hills was possible.

Shrewd as ever, Wyly approached his contacts in the new Georgia legislature and began to inquire about the possibility of a road through the mountains from the upper reaches of the Savannah River into Tennessee. He found old Elijah Clarke—the hero of King's Mountain—by Clarke's most recent recollection, still serving in the Georgia legislature, and Clarke was positively euphoric with the idea. In fact, while everyone he approached seemed enthusiastic, all noted that there was still this pesky band of savages—the Cherokee—smack in the middle of the way. Of course, the Tugaloo Town cluster of Cherokee villages had never been seriously resettled by the Cherokee after being destroyed in 1761. However, the Cherokee had not disappeared; they had merely retreated into the Georgia Blue Ridge, further to the north and west. Thus, the nearest Cherokee Towns to the Tugaloo Valley were, in 1813, merely some 25 miles distant up into the mountains, and other Cherokee settlements stretched as far south as the present outskirts of Atlanta—a city which would not begin to be settled for another two decades.

Moreover, land boundaries were always a problem. While the late Revolution against the British had settled the overall independence of the original 13 colonies, the western expanse of those colonies had not been settled, and certainly no borders had been drawn to state specifically where Georgia, Virginia, or North Carolina ended in the west. Some optimistic citizens of the newly independent states drew the map of Georgia to include everything from Savannah on the Atlantic Ocean clear across the North American continent, capturing a large part of what is now Southern California. Other Georgians were at least discrete enough to recognize that Spain had colonial claims to much of the Texas and California country, and discretely ended the state of Georgia on the banks of the Mississippi River— France had ended her claims on that rich land with her sale of Louisiana in 1803. Also, everyone realized that with the whites now moving into the Tennessee by the thousands, new states would have to be formed, but no one seemed sure how to do that, and "right smack in the middle" between the Tennessee settlements, the newer Kentucky settlements, and the upstate Georgia settlements along the Tugaloo River, were the unfortunate Cherokee.

The Cherokee themselves were for the most part acclimating to European culture. Most were now settled on farms, and the yearly hunting parties seemed to get smaller each year. Of course missionaries were moving into Cherokee country, and many were bringing the benefits of literacy and the Bible with them. Some Cherokee were sending their children to mission run schools to learn to read. Others were turning into plantation owners themselves, owning slaves and shipping off their excess produce to other plantations in the south. Clearly, the Cherokee were anything but a pesky group of savages.

By 1810, the new federal government had developed the habit of negotiating with the Cherokee as a sovereign nation. Because of this, the Georgia legislature commissioned a group of men, James Wyly among them, to treaty with the Cherokee and secure the rights to build a road through the Cherokee country. Wyly's diary captured his thoughts.

"I knew that opening the lower mountain valleys would supply the necessary land for the wealth of newcomers from distant Europe. Thus, a road that I'd dreamed of for years would be needed, a road into and across the distant mountains. The proposed road was to follow the ancient Unicoi Trail of the Cherokee, moving west from the Tugaloo River for some 25 miles, and then turning sharply North and subsequently moving through various mountain gaps, and into the high country of North Carolina and eventually into Tennessee. I had hoped that this "Unicoi Turnpike" would bring increased trade with the upstate farms in Georgia, North Carolina, and Tennessee, not to mention opening more of the land for whites from the docks of Philadelphia, Savannah, Charlestown, and other coastal cities; for certainly no land was then to be found along the coast. I knew that all of these newcomers would need land, and tools to work it, and I intended to supply them.

James Wyly's diary, 1819

By 1813, Wyly and his collaborators had secured the treaty and were busily building their road. The Unicoi Turnpike would begin along the Tugaloo River adjacent the lands of Wyly at the settlement known as Walton's Ford. Needless to say, Wyly was ecstatic with the treaty, since he would profit from this road mightily. He even envisioned passenger boat service one day along the Tugaloo River from

Augusta and Savannah to the headwaters of the Tugaloo. With both the Unicoi Turnpike and the Great Philadelphia Wagon Road crossing the Tugaloo at Walton's Ford, and the river bringing passengers, three transportation/migration routes for new settlers would come together at that precise point. This small settlement of Walton's Ford, had therefore become the 'Gateway to the Blue Ridge." With this in mind, in 1815, Wyly began to build a tavern on his land at the beginning of the new Unicoi Turnpike; in fact his establishment was the equivalent of an eighteenth century "hotel, bar, and grill"—soon to be called Traveler's Rest, and it sat right on top of the intersection of these roads!

Construction of that large tavern involved the usual building techniques of the day. First, cutting large logs for the supporting frame. Next, chipping away at massive pine logs, until one had "sided" the logs into large "squared off" support beams. This was done with bladed instruments, since no sawmills were yet operating in the Valley. Today, we can only imagine the drudgery of attacking a 40 foot pine log, some 14 inches in diameter, with a hatchet, until one had chipped away the rounded edges on all sides for the entire length, and thus fashioned a "squared off" timber. This was done thousands of times in order to create the lumber and frame supports of the tavern—timbers which even today bear those markings.

Next, massive piles of river rocks would be selected that were flat sided and thus could be fitted together to build the foundations and chimneys. A chimney would be needed on each end of the building. Next, the wall joists and rafters were cut and matched together on the ground, one of each pair was "notched" to fit within the other. These were then numbered with roman numerals so that they could be rematched once they were hoisted atop the structure—one can still see these roman numerals today some 190 years after they were carved. Of course, while Wyly may have supervised, he also hired contractors who knew how to work in wood, and his slaves did most of the actual labor. It is an irony that often escapes notice that black hands built much of colonial America, from the earliest days onward. The first part of the historic tavern that stands today was built in this time consuming fashion, yet it was finished within 18 months.

Still, Wyly was not content with merely profiting from the Unicoi Turnpike—he wanted real wealth, and he had formulated a way to get it! Specifically, the treaty with the Cherokee allowed for small inns along the line of route, approximately one day's ride from each other. The coaches of the day could travel approximately 15 to 20 miles depending on the quality of the roads and recent rainfall; thus, an inn would be established approximately every 20 miles along the route for the entire distance of the turnpike. Further, the treaty also granted 100 acres of land near each of the inns so that the innkeeper could clear land and eventually grow the vegetables and fruits needed at the inn itself. Wyly intended to own as many of those inns as possible, and ended up owning the first three along the Turnpike!

By 1817, the Unicoi Turnpike was completed, and travelers came to the lower

Blue Ridge in droves. First a family would move in to settle into one of the new land lots opened by the Government, then another, then an entire extended family would migrate—some coming down the Great Philadelphia Wagon Road, others up the overland routes from Charlestown, still others up river from Savannah or Augusta. Wyly's staff would calmly collect their toll—in currency, or deerskins, or whatever commodity the travelers had, and move them along their way, while providing their bed and board for the next three evenings.

While settlers were coming by the score every day to populate the land of the lower Blue Ridge, wagoners hauling freight along Mr. Wyly's Road were even more numerous. The gruff, rude men driving these freight wagons were often unschooled, knowing neither their numbers nor their letters, but they could "recon" with the most savvy business minds on the planet in their day. Using only their eyeballs, and a good dose of experience, these unlettered men would simply "know" how many barrels of corn, how many deer skins, or how much gunpowder they carried, and if some rogue chanced to lift even a penny-weight of their freight, gunplay would quickly erupt. While the wagoners might lose an arm or an eye, they would usually retrieve their freight. One description of these men comes down to us from that distant time, again as the result of Wyly's diary.

"These wagoners were familiarly called "crackers" because of the cracking of their mule whips, I suppose. They are said to be often very rude and insolent to strangers, and people of the towns, whom they meet on the road, particularly if they happen to be genteel persons. These rough wagoners take every opportunity they can to give anyone else, not to mention each other, a thrashing. Even the slaves looked down on these white crackers for their coarseness, not to mention their tendency to remain unwashed for months at a time. There were many who smelled much worse than the droppings of the filthy mules they drove, and one might even understand the disdain slaves felt for these unruly men."

James Wyly's diary; 1822

Clearly, Mr. Wyly's road, while a phenomenal producer of income, was not the safest place to be for the genteel folk of the day. However, Mr. Wyly was not content even with the success of his road and his three inns. First, he bought many lots in Clarkesville, where the wealthy planters from the south Georgia plantations would come during the hot summer months, and from the sale of these he made a tidy sum. Moreover, he was also appointed to the River Commission, that was charged with taxing all land along the navigable Upper Savannah River System, in order to improve navigation all the way past Walton's Ford all the way north to Panther Creek. This project, again, improved Wyly's fortune, and continued well into the early 1800s.

Even with all this progress however, the early decades of the 1800s were almost anti-climatic in the valley. These were the very years in which settlers rushed into the lower mountains on the southern slope of the Blue Ridge, and these were the years, in which the Cherokee "problem"—so labeled by Elijah Clarke, and other Georgia legislators, began to come to crisis. Still, unlike the last 20 years of the previous century, there was no major revolution, and the Indian raids in the east had sharply declined. While the fledgling nation did have a second round of the revolution—the often forgotten War of 1812 with England—that particular war impacted the Tugaloo River Valley not at all. Only a few local men participated, and other than driving up the price of the cattle and hogs raised on the local plantations, no ill effects from that war were felt here in the Blue Ridge. In the lower mountains, small farmers were fighting out a subsistence living in the rocky ground, and a smaller number of plantation owners were growing wealthy. Wyly was feeding the masses as they traveled his road, and collecting funds for each traveler along the Unicoi Turnpike. Meanwhile, all along the Tugaloo, the sons of Ol' Judge Cleveland were sprouting forth children, and grandchildren, and the Prather clan seemed to ever expand. Clearly, all was right with the world, in the eyes of the whites, at least.

In Retrospect...

In retrospect, we can see it now; in hindsight it is clear. All of this early progress towards civilization was accomplished by these King's Mountain Men in combination with the conflux of transportation in Walton's Ford, and all was duly catalogued by Wyly's private writings. Here the men and the opportunities offered by nature's transportation system—the mighty Savannah River system, of which the Tugaloo River was a part—came together. Along with the river, the Great Philadelphia Wagon Road, and the Unicoi Turnpike began the massive influx of settlement, and it all started right here in the Tugaloo River Valley. This bloody frontier was settled by those who moved through the Tugaloo Valley, and that forgotten town of Walton's Ford was truly the "Gateway to the Southern Blue Ridge" in those years.

These men; the King's Mountain Men—Walton, Cleveland, and Wyly, along with Devereaux Jarrett, the son of another King's Mountain veteran, had come to this land when it was yet wild. Here they settled, farmed, raised children, shopped, bartered, lived and died, and in so doing they eventually created a nation from a rough and bloody frontier.

Historical events such as the settlement of these mountains, never truly "begin;" Rather, they often seem to "come together" as in those years along the Tugaloo, and only a blessed few ever realize the import of events as they take place. Our chronicler, James Wyly was such a man of vision and insight. Of course, none of the King's Mountain Men, Wyly included, realized at that time that a new era had begun—an era that would know the joys of white southern antebellum society, the elimination of the Cherokee, or the horrid anguish that was slavery. Rather, these mountain people merely knew that their daily lives were getting easier, as the frontier faded into the sunset of the western lands.

Unlike the first settlers, few travelers along the Great Philadelphia Wagon Road of 1817 knew of the harsh conditions in that Valley just 30 years previously. Fewer still would notice the squat, lower hill, just to the north of the final bend in the road. Wyly's diary, again provides insight.

"These travelers along these frontier roads, by the 1820s arrived at Traveler's Rest in Walton's Ford hungry after a long day's travel, and they rarely looked out at the unnamed hill on which my friend Devereaux Jarrett was finally buried. They neither knew nor cared for our history along this river. Rather, they came weary, and ready for their evening meal; They were a dirty lot, tired, and no doubt irritable; few true Gentlemen among them. None would know the story of our struggles in this valley. Many a boy in the new century, both plantation owner and slave, would hunt squirrel or rabbit along those primitive roads that only 30 years before had been Cherokee trails. Many would walk over the battleground of Tugaloo Town, and hunt among it's ruins, never realizing a fight had taken place there, though by the 1820s the bear had largely moved into the distant mountains, and the buffalo were long extinct in these parts."

James Wyly's diary, 1825

Still, we today cannot fault these travelers from the past for their ignorance of this rich history; for today we are the same. How often do we travel across the Tugaloo River between Georgia and South Carolina—today we call it Lake Hartwell and cross it on Interstate 85—not realizing what took place here? We ride comfortably, breezing along in air conditioned mini-vans, never realizing that a mere 7 miles upriver, a young Cherokee boy once killed a bear, or that he was to die on a low hill, killed in the battle that destroyed his beloved Tugaloo Town and extinguished forever the sacred fire of the Cherokee. Here recorded history began for the frontier of the lower Blue Ridge, and while the route of the road has changed a bit more to the south and east, Interstate 85 still parallels the Great Philadelphia Wagon Road all along the slope of the lower Blue Mountains in South Carolina and upper Georgia. Here the once-famed Unicoi Turnpike began—now it is called Highway 17. Here many generations of many races—Cherokee, white, and black lived and died—their bones and the bones of their children are scattered in unmarked graves from the 1700s and early 1800s.

Most of those older graves lay in small plots on small farmsteads, buried near the cabins that no longer exist—the graves and the cabins both long forgotten. Some of the unmarked graves however, appear as small depressions in the earth in the older churchyards of the mountains, and are thus at least visible. Some lie among more recent gravestones, in areas that were once churchyards or family cemeteries. Even those early gravestones are worn down by time and no longer legible, in the cemeteries that are covered today in vines and grasses along the mountain byways. Most of us drive on by those unmarked forgotten graves, as did our predecessors, never contemplating the mystery of what happened here; we pass by this history never even knowing, never understanding...

Chapter 5:
Nunna Daul Tsuny—The Trail of Great Weeping
1839 – by the European Calendar
In the Indian Territories of Oklahoma

The old Cherokee warrior sat on the rock hearth of the simple cabin, holding his son's body and waiting for his killers to arrive. He'd found his son still breathing only minutes ago when he came into the cabin. Now his son was dead with several rifle shots in his body, having died in his father's arms. With the final breath of the son, all of the vitality left the father. By this point in our story, Ridge had lost everything; his wealth in slaves, his plantation, his wife and most of his family, and his only surviving son. Most of all he'd lost the respect of the Real People, and for any leader of the once mighty Cherokee, that was a loss that none could bear.

Throughout his life, he had tried to lead as best he could; tried to make wise decisions for his family, his clan, and his people, but that had not been enough. Under his father, Stands-Tall, and his uncles Ekaia and Half-Face, he'd studied the warrior way of the Cherokee. In this first year in the Oklahoma territories, he was one of the few true Cherokee warriors left, since he possessed the skills of the traditional Cherokee warrior with the blowgun and the bow and arrow. Not only that, he'd also mastered the learning of the whites; he was one of only a handful of men of his era to ever be equally comfortable in the white or the Cherokee world.

As a Cherokee planter in the early 1800s, he'd built a thriving plantation on the Georgia frontier, and earned the respect of the Cherokee and whites alike. He'd learned his letters and sums early, eventually mastering much of the knowledge of the west. While not classically educated in the way of his contemporaries Jefferson or Madison, he was nevertheless quite educated for the Cherokee. He'd been the Leader of the House of Representatives—the legislative body of the government of the Cherokee Nation, prior to the removal of the Cherokee. Clearly he was a man of substance and respect.

Now, all this had been taken from him. He'd done everything he could for himself and his people, but it had not been enough.

At this low point in Cherokee history, his people were displaced and dying, ousted by gold, and by the sheer beauty of their native Blue Mountains. Plague, the greed of the whites, and the expansion of a growing republic on the eastern coast of the continent had doomed his tribe. Most of his family was long since gone, his wife dead on the Trail of Tears. He'd lost everything that was dear to him.

On other days, at other times in his life, Ridge would have stood and fought as his son's murderers returned; for he was not a man to give up easily. The grandson of the famed Runs-To-Water was neither a coward nor a shirker. In his better days, he would have raised the war hatchet that his son John had, no doubt tried to use against his attackers. A rifle was unloaded leaning in a corner of the cabin, so John had had no real time to prepare for the attack that took his life. Still, there was blood on the war hatchet lying in the floor; thus Ridge knew that his oldest son John had managed to disable at least one, perhaps several of his assailants.

Ridge himself had fought many battles; like every man he had won some and lost some. He was seasoned enough to realize that ultimately, the meaning of one's life lay not in the winning or losing, but in the fighting spirit one showed; for therein lay a man's true character. Like his famous Grandfather, Ridge had many victories; he'd once saved the life of the President of the United States on the battlefield; how many men in history can say that? Even on that distant day in 1839–Ridge's last day of life—songs were written about him by the younger men, at least by the men who still treasured the old ways—the true ways of the Cherokee.

But having watched his son's last breath only moments before, Ridge felt no more spirit for any fight. He could not even find it within himself to stand before his assassins returned. For by now they surely knew he was here and—he was sure—they would be coming for him.

The old warrior simply sat, holding the body of his son; his destiny had demanded too much of him. Without his realizing it, he began to speak to the Great Spirit Kanati of his life—his victories, and his worries; his women, his wars, his children, and ultimately, the meaning of his life. He would greet his assassins like this, seated, with the body of his son before him. Thus, he began his death song as a simple whispered chant, in the tradition of the Cherokee. From the deepest recesses of his mind, he spoke to his God, of his life.

"Great Kanati. Thank you for my life. Thank you for my father Stands-Tall, and my wives and sons and daughters. Thank you for my son John." At this he paused a bit to compose himself, with John's still warm body before him, then he continued. *"Thank you for my victories; victories over the Creek at the Horseshoe, and for my many hunts. I remember each deer and bear I killed, and I thank you for them. I remember each battle I fought, and each victory and I thank you. I thank you for letting me live in the Blue Mountains most of my days. I thank you for the sunrise and sunsets of my life, each has been beautiful. Great Father, I do not understand why so many of the mighty*

Cherokee needed to die. I do not understand why our mountains were taken from us, or why the whites hated us so. So many of the Real People are gone now, and I have failed my duty to my people; I am ashamed. Only yesterday we lived in the beautiful Blue Mountains, and Great Father, I remember many, many happy times…"

The Great Cherokee Council of 1804

They met in the Valley of Nacoochee in the council house atop a ceremonial mound that would stand for over 300 years (the mound is there even today, in the beautiful valley near Helen, Georgia). The council house was squat, and like all others rounded. In the center was the sacred fire of the Cherokee, and arrayed around the fire were the seven spaces for the seven great Cherokee Clans. On this day, early in the Green Corn Month, in the year the Europeans called 1804, the spaces were all filled. Everyone knew that this was an important council; this was the council that was to determine the fate of the Cherokee. Many felt that the Cherokee had been at war with themselves for some time, and all hoped that this internal conflict would end at this meeting as the clans sat in council.

Ridge, in particular was conflicted—not at balance within himself. He'd lived his entire life with one foot firmly in the Cherokee world of his ancestors, and another in the white world—a world accessed through the missionaries that taught he and many other Cherokee to read and do their sums. He wanted to know where his future lay.

No one who was present that day could have stated why they sensed that this particular council would be so influential. Perhaps it was the visitor who was expected to speak; perhaps it merely seemed that the time was right. By the summer of 1804, the Cherokee existed almost as a two separate tribes, with the various Cherokee settlements split between the traditionalists and the assimilationists, or the "White Cherokee." Both older traditionalist leaders and younger, more "assimilated" leaders were present on this day. The older more traditionally oriented Cherokee who had known Cherokee life prior to the dominate influence of the whites were realizing that they might have to yield control to those more in favor of assimilation. These traditionalist Cherokee tended to come from the over-hill towns on the northern boundary of the Cherokee nation; those Cherokee settlements were further from the older white settlements on the coast, and thus were the last to be impacted by the dominating influence of the whites.

Many Cherokee in the over-hill settlements still built traditional Cherokee lodges, worshiped Kanati, told the traditional Cherokee myths of creation, and the warriors hunted in the traditional ways. The tradition of the "Blood Oath" of the Cherokee was still strong among these Cherokee, and that seemed thoroughly uncivilized to the more cultured Cherokee of the lower southern and eastern slopes of the Blue Ridge. Of course, it was widely known that two veterans of the famed

Battle of Taliwa, the fight which drove the Creeks from the Blue Mountains, were to be here, and this gave the traditionalists courage. For surely those revered leaders would side with the traditional ways of the Cherokee.

In contrast, many of the assimilationists or "White Cherokee" were here also. These were the Cherokee who chose assimilation rather than confrontation with the whites, and their influence was clearly growing. These Cherokee were largely settled on farms which were owned by the tribe or by they themselves. They ploughed their fields, bartered their produce, accepted Christianity, and the teachings offered by the many missionaries in the Blue Ridge. These Cherokee did not engage in the traditional "long hunts" for weeks at a time in the fall and winter, since such long hunting trips were regarded as "dangerous" as most of the young warriors found trouble on these long hunts—trouble with Creek, or whites which often turned bloody. The missionaries actively discouraged such winter hunts among the Cherokee.

Many of these Cherokee wore "white" clothes. Because of President Washington's policy of assimilation several years before, many of their wives had acquired spinning wheels, and much high quality cloth was generated in the log cabins of the Cherokee. These women were thus able to make the simple cloth common in white frontier settlements, and some even sold their excess, much as their husbands had once sold deerskins, to the whites. This group wanted to become a part of the larger white civilization. They did not consider themselves "sellouts" to white culture; quite the contrary, they believed that assimilation was the only way they would survive. Ridge, like many present on this day, had one foot in both worlds.

With these groups present, there was some sense that in this historic council, the old would confront the new, and these contrasting visions of the future of the Cherokee would somehow be brought together, and balance would be restored to the tribe. For balance in all things was the single greatest desire of all Cherokee. All hoped that some solution could be found that would result in the Cherokee reclaiming their tribal identity, and not losing any more territory to the whites. With the cumulative wisdom of the assembled leaders from throughout the Cherokee nation, expectations in this great council were high.

In the center sat an old woman, with few teeth left. She was diminished by age, her skin almost translucent, and showing many wrinkles. She was by 1804 almost a living God among the Cherokee. For this was the Beloved Woman who had chewed her husband's shot in the great Battle of Taliwa so many years before. One of the few veterans left of that great battle, so influential in the life of the Cherokee, Nancy Ward had not aged gracefully. She was an outspoken woman, given to strong opinions and heartfelt positions, and such persons—in any culture, at any point in history—do not wear their years well. Still, at 74 she had a head full of long flowing hair which was almost as white as that of the Reverend Cleveland from Walton's Ford who occasionally traveled through these parts. Moreover, Nancy Ward was known for her seasoned wisdom, and while she was often boisterously loud, her council was much revered by the Cherokee Nation. Stories of her bravery had been told for generations by the hearth fires in the Cherokee lodges, and in the log cabins where most Cherokee now lived. By 1804 she was one of the most influential members of the entire Cherokee Tribe. Many a warrior in the council house that morning was raised hearing stories of this great one, and some felt almost a religious zeal when she rose to speak to the nation. The clans waited for her words this day, but in the beginning on this morning she kept to herself, while the other revered leaders still gathered.

Her son, "Oak," who knew his letters as a result of the teachings of the missionaries that were now streaming into the lower Blue Ridge, was sitting several rows behind her. He had received an education of sorts, and like many Cherokee of the day, he had embraced Christianity. He sat waiting with pen and paper, to write down the deliberations and decisions of this council; for all present knew this to be a historic event.

Little Carpenter, perhaps the greatest Peace Chief in the history of the Cherokee, was seated in the clan section for the Blue Clan. As an older man with many victories to his credit, his word was respected. This Cherokee Peace Chief, while trained in the traditional warrior way, and therefore subscribing to the Blood Oath, was nevertheless known to get along well with the whites. He consistently argued for peace and assimilation with the whites. With that stated, like many assimilationists he was unwilling to give up the traditional Cherokee homeland in the Blue Mountains. His council was always revered, and he had already lead the Real People for something like 40 years.

His counterpart, Dragging Canoe soon entered. Dragging Canoe was, at this point, the War Chief of the tribe, and everyone knew his position. Having escaped the ambush by Sevier's men on the Warrior's Trail in 1780, he was still a formidable warrior, and still led the break-away Chickamauga Cherokee who lived on the mountain that would one day overlook Chattanooga, Tennessee. In quiet dignity, and dressed in his traditional Cherokee garb, he walked to the center of the council house. Here he turned and did a slight bow to each of the clans in turn. He paused, as was proper, when he spied Nancy Ward, sitting on the front row in her clan section, and offered a second bow to acknowledge her in particular; he did the same with Little Carpenter.

At that moment, everyone expected Dragging Canoe to speak. However, the meeting this morning was the beginning of the third day of this council, and Dragging Canoe, having spoken previously, decided that he'd hear the words of the others. His own position was well known; no assimilation, but war on all whites west of the Blue Ridge. He completed his greetings and took his seat in the first row of the section of the Paint Clan.

Ridge, of course, was already there. By now, he was a seasoned warrior of some 28 years, and he was recognized as the son of Stands-Tall, and the grandson of Runs-To-Water; still he was not a chief so he arrived early, as did most of the others. Ridge had grown to the great height and girth of his grandfather, standing some six feet three inches, in an age where the average white frontiersman was only five and a half feet. Ridge looked very much like his Grandfather, Runs-To-Water, but he had not yet assumed a leadership position in his clan, and he would not speak on this day. Further, he'd arrived early to take a seat; for only the chiefs, the great warriors, and the Beloved Women came at the last minute and got to make an entrance before the whole tribe.

Had anyone thought about it, most would have realized that on this day, Ridge was deserving of much more respect than he received; for he was one of only a few Cherokee who knew the old ways of the tribe. He was one of the few who could still make and use a blowgun, or hunt with a bow. Of course, he rarely did, preferring the rifle like almost all Cherokee by this period. Nevertheless, the traditional Cherokee skills were much revered by his tribe, and his skills were a point of pride in the new settlement of New Echota in the Georgia Blue Ridge, some 70 miles west of Tugaloo River.

Of course, publicly, Ridge was known to hate the white man. As a youth, he had attended a missionary school for a time—just long enough to learn his letters and his sums, and to sense the disdain which the whites of that era felt for all things Cherokee. After complaining many times to his father, Stands-Tall, of these attitudes of the whites, his father allowed him to stop attending the school, and he could then concentrate on developing his warrior skills.

In his early life, Ridge had often prayed to the Great Spirit to let him have the opportunity to kill white men. All his life he'd heard the stories of his brave Grandfather, Runs-To-Water, who died charging into the guns of the white man in Tugaloo Town, so that his family might escape across the Tugaloo River. He'd heard how his father, Stands-Tall, had died fighting the whites in Dragging Canoe's War on the Great Warrior's Path, only 20 years later. Moreover, he could see how the whites seemed to be endless, ever encroaching on the land of the Cherokee, and cutting the forests in the Blue Mountains to plant ever larger crops of corn, beans, and tobacco. Many whites were living across the Blue Ridge in land that had been promised to the Cherokee forever, and Ridge, like Dragging Canoe, wanted to drive the whites back to settlements along the coast. Certainly Ridge had every reason to hate the white faces.

In spite of this fact, however, Ridge determined to keep his mind clear; for he—like his fathers before him—was spiritual in nature and sought balance in all things. He knew his decision would be made when the time was right for such a decision, but until then, he kept an open mind. He would hold his own council until he had heard this mysterious visitor from the north speak, and that speech was expected today.

It was just at that moment that Ridge detected a white face in the council house! In fact he did something most uncharacteristic for a Cherokee—looking twice in that direction and thus doing a double take—directly at a man seating high up in the last row across from him in the section of the Deer Clan. This man appeared to be white, and whites were not permitted in council, unless invited. Still Ridge realized that many Cherokee by 1804 were dressing in the fashion of the whites, and that included many in this council house. Then Ridge decided that this man was merely a Cherokee who had chosen the affectation of white dress. Only then did Ridge recognized him, noting that his shirt was more fine than many others here. Ridge had told his two sons many times of this man, and this man's reputation was to live within Cherokee folklore for many centuries.

Of course, Ekaia, known in Walton's Ford as Old Tom Prather, knew that he'd been spotted by some upstart young warrior across the way, and he knew of the rumored hatred of Ridge for all white men. Still, this aging "Disappearing Ghost of the Cherokee" was not overly concerned. He had known not only Ridge's father, Stands-Tall, but also his revered Grandfather, Runs-To-Water. Further, as a full blood Cherokee, he had every right to be at this council. In fact, he would not have missed this council of his people. He came, like all of the others, to hear the words of the guest from the north.

The Prather plantation along the Tugaloo was doing very well under the overall management of Tom's son James Wallace Prather. The Prather plantation was now famous for not only fairly large cotton production, but also for a variety of wines. Moreover, in the tradition of many of the Scots-Irish immigrants to the lower Blue Ridge, the Prather family made a very fine sour-mash whiskey which was run off in a still near the two room cabin just a half mile from the upper Tugaloo River. James Wallace had received a fine education, having learned his letters early, and attended university in the state of Virginia—taking his classes in the famed school that claimed Thomas Jefferson and James Madison among it's many alumni—The College of William and Mary.

With the plantation in such skilled hands, Old Tom—Ekaia—found that no one missed him much if he disappeared for a few weeks at a time. Thus, he could hunt for longer periods each year, and thereby visit his Cherokee people more frequently in these days. He looked back from the upper row of the council house, and bowed slightly to Ridge, who immediately returned the bow. Then Ekaia waited for the leaders to speak; like Ridge, he quietly maintained his own council.

Before anyone spoke however, more dignitaries were to arrive, and as if on cue, the ancient, stooped warrior Doublehead entered the council house. Doublehead was the only other veteran of Taliwa to attend, besides Nancy Ward. He was even older than she—having now counted some 84 winters. His hair was long, and his tattoos told of his many battles. While younger Cherokee had long ago abandoned the custom of body tattoos, Doublehead was born in a time when all great warriors wore their victories on their skin, so he continued having his tattoos redone every so often. He was not an outspoken leader, and had not been for decades, but as a veteran of the great Battle of Taliwa, he was revered nonetheless. He turned to greet each Clan as was proper, and his eyes rested for a moment on each section of the seven sided house. He noted that no section was empty, and that many held as many Cherokee as the benches could seat. After a full circle, he took his seat.

Several lesser figures came in the wake of Doublehead, and quickly took their seats, seemingly almost embarrassed that they had entered after the great chief. While the great chiefs and veterans of earlier battles were recognized as the leaders by all present, one irony of this council is how the younger, future leaders were ignored; for this council held an incredible collection of men—Ridge among them. Many others were future leaders of Cherokee and several would be remembered by history as great white leaders, but as yet all were unrecognized as men of great destiny.

George Gist, a Cherokee of the Over-Hill Towns, entered just after Doublehead. He typically went by his adopted white name, as did many Cherokee in the early 1800s. However, history would later know him as Sequoyah, a Cherokee who would do more to educate the masses in his time than anyone else on earth, in any culture. In time this man would invent the written form of the Cherokee language, which was to be the only written native American tongue throughout history.

In the section of the Paint Clan, high up in the benches and dressed in traditional Cherokee fashion, sat a young man who was obviously white. He was, in that year, only 17 years old, but he was very tall for a white man, and while he wore his hair in Indian fashion, he was clearly not Cherokee. Still, everyone present knew his story, and none minded his presence. He had abandoned his white family in Nashville, Tennessee, because of a drunken father when he was only nine, and since that time had been raised as a Cherokee among the Over-Hill Towns, raised as the son of a Cherokee Chief named John Jolly. Indeed this young white man may have been more "Cherokee" than many full blood "White Cherokee" by this time. His Cherokee name was Kalanu, or "The Raven," a name given him by his adopted Cherokee family, but in time the world would know this incredible man as General Sam Houston. Houston would first acquire public acclaim two decades later as the Governor of the State of Tennessee, but later still he would defeat General Santa Anna of Mexico and win Independence for the "Lone Star" nation of Texas. He would then serve as the first President of the Republic of Texas. This man of destiny was too young to be noticed at the Great Cherokee Council of 1804, yet like the others, Houston came to hear the guest from the north.

Another youngish man, just a boy really, but a boy who had acquired his letters, snuck in at the last and took a seat. As unlikely as it seemed at the time, that lanky young man, John Ross—a man who was only one-eighth Cherokee, would one day lead the Cherokee Nation. One can sometimes see hints of a great man of the future in a young boy, as was the case with both Ridge and Sam Houston—both being large and dignified. However that was not the case with John Ross. Overly educated—at least in the eyes of many—and knowing little of the ancient Cherokee ways, who would have believed on the day of this great council, that this gangly adolescent boy would become a great Peace Chief of the Cherokee?

It was then that the expected guest came into the council house, followed, by several warriors. Some in the assembled group gasped in surprise, for this guest was not Cherokee, and important councils such as this were generally only open to tribal members. However, the Cherokee leaders who had expected this arrival were not surprised, and the crowd quickly calmed down to listen to the words of the single most hated man of his generation—Tecumseh.

The Molding of a Man of Vision

While the Cherokee Indians assembled that day in the council house were willing to listen to Tecumseh, he would have been killed on sight in any white settlement on the frontier between Canada and Mexico. Almost every white man, woman, and child on the frontier anywhere in the Americas hated this man with a passion. It was widely known that this warrior from the Ohio territories was stirring up trouble for all of the towns on the frontier from New York all the way down to New Orleans, and many on the frontier in those years ascribed any death at the hands of Indians to Tecumseh. Some thought he represented the devil incarnate, since his dangerous views lead to so much meaningless death. In this age of racial hatred, and publicly sanctioned genocide, Tecumseh was the most hated man alive.

However, history will, at times, take a kinder view of a man than his contemporaries. In retrospect, Tecumseh was a man with a vision, and men of vision are always dangerous. His vision could potentially have reshaped history; for he envisioned a united Indian Confederacy that would war on all of the white men living west of the Blue Mountains. To understand the importance and the evolution of this vision, it is necessary to understand some things of Tecumseh's background.

Tecumseh was born a Shawnee, in 1768 in a small settlement along the Mad River in the Ohio territory many miles to the north of the Blue Ridge. With few substantive mountains as a barrier to white settlement that far north, and more rivers for navigation inward from the colonial cities along the coast, whites had, by the 1760s, settled much further to the west in those northern states than in Virginia, the Carolinas, or Georgia. Thus, the Indians of the Ohio territory engaged in the struggle for land with the ever growing numbers of white settlers even before the Over-Hill Towns of the Cherokee in Tennessee. Fearing the encroaching whites, Tecumseh's mother moved further west, leaving Tecumseh to be raised by his eldest brother in the Ohio country. That brother, a Shawnee warrior himself, trained Tecumseh in the traditional ways of the Shawnee. Thus, from his earliest memories, Tecumseh was learning not only the ancient ways of the Shawnee warrior, but also a fierce hatred for the white settlers encroaching into the frontier. Further, his entire early life had been disrupted from the normal family routines of his tribe by the growing number of whites. In such a hotbed of disruption, hatred is often the natural by-product.

Tecumseh's first military encounter occurred against a white army led by George Rogers Clark into the Ohio Country in 1782. Tecumseh, at 14 years of age and seeing an intense battle for the first time, responded badly; he ran from the battle as other warriors died. Just after the warrior's face next to him exploded from the strike of a musket ball, Tecumseh fled the field, thinking that all the other braves would likewise retreat. With blood and brains from his compatriot covering his face, chest, and upper arms, Tecumseh must have been crazed with fear. Tradition holds that he ran until the blood from that warrior's mortal wounds dried on his own body; only then did he wash the offal from his face, arms and chest.

Thus, did this young warrior run from his first battle, only to be humiliated before his friends and family. Some days later, he found that other warriors had not run, but stood and fought to the death. With no one pointing a finger at him, he nevertheless acknowledged publicly his humiliation, and moreover, he swore before his fellow warriors never to run again. Only rarely in history does any decision by a 14 year old boy hold so much potential for disrupting civilized societies, as that fateful decision by this young Shawnee brave. For in truth, Tecumseh fought the whites from that day forward with a vision and a zeal that singularly held the potential for postponing successful white settlement in the west for many decades, if not stopping it altogether. Further, as he'd decided on that fateful day, he knew he'd seen the worst that battle can offer, he knew death, and thus, he would from that day forth, take it in stride. He never ran from a battle again.

Tecumseh, with his newfound resolve, quickly grew into a brave warrior—some would say a foolishly brave warrior—and he eventually became a Shawnee leader. By 1791, Tecumseh found himself in yet another battle against the encroaching whites. This time, he fought against a group of frontiersmen in the Indiana wilderness, and while all the warriors fought bravely that day, it was noted by all that Tecumseh fought like a man possessed of great medicine. He ran swift and true, always forward, loading his rifle as he ran, and once it discharged, he struck out with the butt end, or with his war hatchet, or his knife. At one point he attacked three whites at once, killing all with his flashing knife before they could reload their weapons. Others watched as Tecumseh took the battle forward, and only then did they follow. On this day he was a fighter that would have been revered by any culture at any point in history; for he was a warrior with something to prove, and no man going into battle was ever more deadly. In that battle, the Shawnee emerged victorious. Tecumseh's actions and courage was noted by all, and commented on by the chiefs after the battle. Thus did Tecumseh become one of the most trusted leaders of his tribe.

From that point on, songs were written about him, and his name was sung proudly around the camps of the Shawnee. Moreover, younger braves were drawn to him because of his unquestioned courage, as well as his emerging oratorical gifts. It was often said of him that his speeches to his people were mesmerizing. Within only ten years, his fame had spread into the white settlements along the frontier. One white leader, William Henry Harrison, who would later became the President of the United States, noted this oratorical ability. Harrison was then Governor of the Indiana Territory, and he spoke of Tecumseh as *"...one of those uncommon geniuses that spring up occasionally to produce revolutions. I've seen young warriors shaking with emotion and brandishing war hatchets, as this Tecumseh speaks to them of their lost land."*

Tecumseh frequently called for violent resistance against further white settlement on any land claimed by Indians, a plea which the Cherokee of the lower Blue Ridge were well prepared to empathize.

In yet another early battle—white frontiersmen against Shawnee—Tecumseh again fought like a man possessed of great power, but this time his tribe lost and the Shawnee warriors were scattered. Tecumseh and many other escaped alive from the Battle of Fallen Timbers in 1794, but many other warriors were killed. After that defeat, many of the Shawnee lost their will to continue the struggle for their land. Thus, did many tribes living in Ohio sign the Treaty of Greenville, in 1795, ceding almost the entire Ohio territory to the whites. Tecumseh, of course, did not sign the treaty. However, the treaty is important, in that it occasioned much thought by Tecumseh and his younger brother Tenekwatowa—latter known as the Prophet. That repugnant treaty, like Tecumseh's fateful decision to never run again, combined to change history in ways the whites could never have foreseen.

Tecumseh Seeks A Vision

In contemplating how the militant Shawnee should respond to this treaty, Tecumseh chose the path of warriors who sought communion with their gods; he fasted alone for several days in a location along the Ohio River, taking only a few sips of water each day. After the first day, when his body was weak from hunger, he chose to challenge himself with a feat of strength, as warriors often did in those times. While the exact spot is unknown today, it is said he climbed a rugged bluff overlooking the river. He could have easily scaled that bluff in normal times, but with his strength depleted by fasting and his spirit sore from the recent battles, the climb was a challenge. Forgoing food for another day, and having only a few sips of water, he determined to sit on that bluff above the river until the Great Spirit decided to speak to him. Many more hours did he sit, through sunlight, dusk, and darkness, and through the same cycle yet again, waiting for his God to speak. On the next morning, even weaker from hunger, with his stomach in cramps, he still sat; he would have continued to sit until his life ceased, such was the depth of his spirit's pain. However, God is benevolent with those who are dedicated. After some seventy nine hours of self-imposed starvation, he had his vision.

It came to him in the spirit of a bald eagle—that great bird, the majestic hunter of the rivers. The Great Spirit found a fern branch very near the warrior from which it too, could look into the depths of the river. As it searched for fish, it spoke to Tecumseh. *"I see a great warrior, and leader of his people searching in the river. Why have you come to my river on this fine day?"*

Having heard a voice as distinctly as if another Shawnee warrior were talking with him, Tecumseh responded without realizing his vision had begun. *"I have come because my heart is in pain. We lose more and more of our land to the whites, and I do not know what to do."*

The eagle, without looking at Tecumseh, spoke again. *"You have fought and lost many times to the whites, Tecumseh. Do you really think the red man can defeat the white?"*

Tecumseh, by then aware that this mighty eagle was a part of the vision he sought, replied. *"Thank you for coming to talk to me, Grandfather. My heart is sick, and I need your thoughts on what to do with my life. As for the whites, I do not know if we can defeat them, but I know we must try."*

The eagle looked sideways at Tecumseh, and then returned his gaze to the flowing waters of the Ohio. *"Why must you try this task, my son? Is there no room for them between the eastern morning and the close of day in the west? Surely there must be some deer for you to kill toward the sunset, while they plant their fields toward the morning sun."*

"Yes, my father. I am sure that you have provided plenty of land to hunt, but they do not seem to know that. They want only to fell the forests and build their cabins. Then they tell us that we cannot hunt in our own lands."

The eagle considered this for a few moments, showing his respect for the words of Tecumseh. Then he continued. *"I hunt the waters where ever and whenever I please, and they do not molest me."*

Tecumseh considered this. *"Great father, the whites hate us. They kill us whenever they have the chance. I too would like to think we can live with all men, but it is not the case. There has been too much war between us already."*

The Eagle, spotting a fish in the river, lifted his great wings, and flew down in a perfect attack angle, coming up with a small fish. Tecumseh followed this miracle of perfection in hunting and killing and marveled at the skill of this eagle. Reclaiming it's perch on the same fern branch, it tossed the fish into the air, caught in it's beak, and swallowed. It then spoke again. *"All creatures need to eat, and all creatures need room to grow, to hunt, and to live. Perhaps, the whites could take land to the East of the mountains, and let the Shawnee people and my other peoples—the Catawba, the Cherokee, and the Creek, have the land to the west."*

Tecumseh contemplated that thought—for it was a thought he'd often heard voiced before. Then he responded, *"In the last war when the white man from here fought the whites from England, the British soldiers promised that if they won, they would restrict the whites to the eastern slope of the mountains. That was not to be. In fact, often our people, drunk with their whiskey, sign treaties to give away our land. It sickens my heart."*

This the Great Spirit considered for a moment. *"How can one of my people sign away land that belongs to the wind and the sky? Who is it that signs these treaties?"*

With that question, Tecumseh's mind seemed to explode into a jumble of simultaneous thoughts! Who indeed, could sign such a treaty? Who had the power to give away everyone's land? In a flash, he knew he'd had his vision. Tears began to stream down his cheeks as he contemplated his racing thoughts; for how could any single Shawnee sign away land belonging to all Shawnee? In fact, how could any Shawnee sign away any land without every Shawnee signing?

Tecumseh felt a surge of strength, certain in the knowledge that he'd found his vision; that he'd found his answers. He wanted to stand immediately and run share his new wisdom with his people, but he first had to finish his communion with his God.

With fresh tears streaming down his face, he looked directly at the eagle, who returned the stare from only twenty feet away. Tecumseh spoke; *"Thank you, Grandfather, thank you for talking with me. I know now what I must tell my people. Thank you!"*

The eagle, cocked it's head sideways, as if realizing that it had perched so near a human. The Great Spirit spoke only once more. *"You are welcome my son. Now I go to catch my fish. You may go talk to your people."* And with that the eagle, once again just an eagle, flew away.

Tecumseh was immediately shown by the Great Spirit that any treaty, in fact all treaties, were invalid because only a limited number of Shawnee signed them; clearly all those Shawnee effected must sign such treaties for them to be valid. Moreover, was not any treaty invalid unless all the Shawnee signed it? His final thought was, why should this be so only for the Shawnee? Do not all Indians living west of the Blue Mountains have some interest in what happened to the land on which they live? Were not all Indians impacted each time another white family moved to the frontier?

This was perhaps the first time such a revolutionary thought had occurred to any Indian leader, that all Indians west of the mountains—regardless of their tribe, all Indians from Canada to the Gulf of Mexico—should have to sign treaties together before any land west of the mountains could be given up to the whites. This single thought—this vision—immediately suggested the possibility of uniting all of the Indians in the west. Of course, it was a short jump from that revolutionary thought to the idea that all Indians should, if necessary, fight the whites together. Tecumseh knew in an instant that his vision could reshape the world, and like any great man, he would dedicate his life to realizing that vision. He thanked the Great Spirit again, watching the eagle fly into the distance down the river, then stood to walk back to his lodge.

By 1804 Tecumseh had shared his vision with his brother, Tenekwatowa. The Great Spirit had shown him that the only way to beat back the white invaders was to do it in unison with other tribes. Thus, did Tecumseh become the first Native American in history to seek a unity of all of the tribes west of the Blue Ridge and Allegheny Mountains. He sought nothing less than a confederacy of all Indian tribes; for the Great Spirit had shown Tecumseh that no single man, or even a single tribe could own the land. Thus, only all tribes together could turn land over to the whites, and therefore treaties with single tribes were invalid. Tecumseh also knew that Indians united together would have a better chance to chase the whites back across the mountains.

Thus, during the next ten years, Tecumseh visited the many tribes west of the Appalachian Mountains, spending time with each tribe in council, and trying to convince them to unite together. In this fashion, did he come to speak to this council of the Cherokee in 1804. Of course, making these arguments in the various tribal councils was easy but creating such a confederacy was not. While the logic of a collaborative effort seems compelling in retrospect, such a confederation would mean that Indian tribes who had made war on each other for generations would have to establish peace among themselves. This, of course, had never been done before.

For example, the Cherokee could easily fight beside the Shawnee, since the lands and hunting grounds of those two tribes had never overlapped, and there were no outstanding "Blood Oath" debts to be settled among these peoples. However, in order for Tecumseh's vision of an Indian Confederacy to become reality, the Cherokee would have to agree not only to war beside the Shawnee, but also to put aside their differences with the "filthy Creek," with whom they had fought forever. That was, clearly, no easy matter. Much blood had been spilled and many warriors lost by both sides in that century long tribal struggle. Such wounds were not likely to heal easily, and building a confederacy among such mortal enemies was going to be difficult at best.

Still, Tecumseh came to the Cherokee Council House in 1804 to make his argument. Thus did Ridge have the opportunity to hear this great visionary of the Shawnee speak in council with the Cherokee. History was to be made in that council, and all present knew it. As soon as Tecumseh entered, and the crowd became silent.

The local chief, Two Drums, who was presiding at this critically important council, stood and offered the scared "smoking pipe" to Tecumseh, and they smoked together. Two Drums then tossed some tobacco on the sacred fire in the council house, as an offering to the Great Spirit. He then indicated his desire that Tecumseh should speak, and the great visionary stood and slowly looked around the council house. He did not know Cherokee Protocol, and thus did not face each Clan separately for any extended period. He did note that a number of women were present, and had this been a Shawnee Council, that would not have been the case. Still, he was here to build the Indian Confederacy he envisioned, not critique the Cherokee for their unusual reliance on women in affairs that were strictly male decisions among the Shawnee. Thus, Tecumseh determined to ignore the women. Nevertheless, without realizing it, he did make eye contact with many. After turning in a full circle, he raised his voice, and his words were duly recorded for history by Oak.

"We have all lost land to the whites. I know that you have spoken of this for the last two days. Know that we Shawnee have also lost land, as have the Creek, the Catawba and many others. The way, the only way, to stop this evil is for the red man to unite in claiming a common and equal right in the land, as it was first, and should be now, for the land was never divided.

We gave them forest-clad mountains and valleys full of game, and in return what did they give our warriors and our women? Rum, trinkets, and a grave.

Brothers—My people wish for peace; the red men all wish for peace; but where the white people are, there is no peace, except it be on the bosom of our mother." Here Tecumseh looked directly down, indicating the Mother Earth.

"Where today are the Pequot? Where today are the Narrangansett, the Mohican, the Pakanoket, the Tuscarora and many other powerful tribes of our people? They have vanished before the avarice and the oppression of the White Man, as snow before a summer sun. Everywhere our people have passed away. We no longer rule the forest.

The game has gone like our hunting grounds. Even our lands are nearly all gone. Yes, my brothers, our campfires are few. Those that still burn we must draw together. We can no longer trust the white man. We gave him our tobacco and our selu, and now there is hardly any land for us to grow these sacred plants. White men have built their castles where the Indian hunting grounds once were, and now they are coming into your Blue Mountains. Soon there will be no place for the Cherokee to hunt the deer and the bear. One day, when my heart was troubled by this, I fasted and considered this problem. My medicine brought me to the Great Spirit who came to me as an eagle, hunting for his food in the waters of the Ohio River, many days-run to the north. As we spoke, he asked me who signed the treaties and by what right did they sign? How could anyone sign away land for everyone to the west of the Blue Mountains?

Thus did the Great Spirit share this vision with me—that we must all decide together whether to keep our lands or to give them away. I invite each of you to join with us in our struggle to fight the whites together. We will need all warriors of every tribe to drive the white devils back across the mountains. Even now, more come to take our land, and when we fight as small tribes, we cannot win. Together, we can stand victorious and live on our land forever.

It may be that, if we fight, we die together. Yes even together we may fall in death, but together we have a chance. The tomahawk of the Shawnee is ready. Will the mighty Cherokee raise the tomahawk? Will the Cherokee join their brothers the Shawnee?"

With that Tecumseh sat back down beside Two Drums. After a few minutes of silence, in which all present considered the words they had heard, it became clear that the great leaders, all of whom had already been heard, were not of a mind to speak. However, one chief of a town far to the east—a small Cherokee town on the banks of the Oconaluftee River in what would one day become the Great Smoky Mountain National Park, rose to speak. His name was Junaluska, and he spoke with the conviction of his many years.

"Brothers. It has been years, many years, since the Cherokee in our country have drawn the tomahawk. Our braves have forgotten how to use the scalping knife. We have learned with sorrow it is better not to war against the white brothers. We know they have come to stay. They are like leaves in the forest, there are so many. We believe we can live in peace with them. We have moved into the high mountains, where our fields will be small. No more do they molest our lands. Our crops grow well, and we live in peace."

Junaluska then sat back down, as all considered his words. Perhaps moving higher into the Blue Mountains was the answer, but that meant abandoning the fields their ancestors had cleared for generations, and all were repelled by that thought.

No one else seemed inclined to speak, and after two minutes while the assembled Cherokee considered the words they had heard, Two Drums cleared his throat loudly, and then stood. He first turned to each Clan, to gather their attention, on what all assumed would be the final morning of this council. For at this point, each of the leaders had been heard, as had their guest, Tecumseh. Two Drums wanted to sum up the deliberations, as he understood them, on the tedious position of the Cherokee.

"My Cherokee brothers, we know that the Great Father Jefferson has bought all of the land from the French beyond the great river; land that stretches all the way into the land of the Shoshone to the west. He has paid the French to leave that land, and the French have agreed to do so. Now much land, far to the west of the Blue Mountains is already settled by whites. Their town Nashville grows daily, and many have moved on to the banks of the great river itself far to the west, while we still live in our Blue

Mountains. We are surrounded on all sides by the whites, and I do not think we can hold on to our land.

The Great Father Jefferson has also told us of a place to which we can go on the other side of the Great River. He thinks we can build our cabins, and plant our fields there, and raise our children. He even suggested that we set up a government like the United States on those lands. Now we have been offered another treaty to pay us for more of our land in the Tennessee country. Whites already live on that land, as we know, and the bear, turkey, and deer are hard to find; the buffalo have been hunted out. Our question is this. If we do not take this new land, can we hold on to these Blue Mountains? Even if our mighty warriors fight against the whites, where will we get our powder and shot? While our warriors are strong, the whites are many, and they have guns and powder. They surround us, and more come every day. Who among us has not rode to a distant valley in these Blue Mountains for a fall hunt, only to find the valley cleared and a white family building a cabin? Can we survive? Should we fight along side the Shawnee? Can we fight alongside the Creek? This we must decide."

In this assessment, Two Drums was essentially correct. President Jefferson had indeed bought the land to the west in the famed Louisiana Purchase in 1803, and when a delegation of Cherokee Chiefs lead by Little Carpenter and Junaluska visited him in the capital at Washington, he did suggest that the tribe consider moving to land to the west. Jefferson negotiated with the Cherokee as if they were an independent nation, and thus from the Cherokee alone, comes the tradition of referring to all of the various tribes of Indians as "Nations." By this date in 1804, white settlements were plentiful on the Northern slope of the Blue Ridge; while less plentiful south of the mountains, there was still sign of development. The town of Clarkesville, Georgia for example, was growing only 25 miles to the South, some 20 miles west of the Tugaloo River. A new University had been formed by the Georgia legislature only 50 miles to the south—a school for the sons of the landed white aristocracy—a seat of knowledge that would eventually become the University of Georgia. Other towns such as Chattanooga, Dalton, Rome, Asheville, Knoxville, and Sevierville, were springing up in Cherokee Country, and others were sure to follow throughout north Georgia, Tennessee, and Alabama. By this date, every Cherokee in Northern Georgia was sure that their way of life was in jeopardy; for they stood to lose the sacred Blue Mountains forever, and after Tecumseh's words they all understood that many other tribes were feeling the pressure of the whites.

When Two Drums sat, the Cherokee gathered in that council house all realized that all of the mighty chiefs had been heard, and again everyone sensed that the council was drawing to a close. Ridge and the others waited a full two minutes carefully considering the words they had heard, and for a time none seemed inclined to speak again. However, after this respectful pause, the Beloved Woman of the Cherokee, Nancy Ward, rose to speak a final time. She broke with

Protocol and began to speak before facing each clan; speaking instead as she slowly turned to face each clan of the Cherokee. Her speech was more powerful by that breech of Protocol. *"I have thought many times about the whites and the Cherokee; I have thought about what they know and about what we know. I have had a white husband, and I have had a Cherokee warrior for my husband (here her voice rose a bit),* **and I can say that Cherokee is better!"**

Many in the crowd smiled at that joke; some laughed outright. For this Beloved Woman of the Cherokee had provided exactly what was needed at that moment–a moment of laughter! She then turned serious, and continued.

"Still, the whites will continue to come, and some of their ways are better than some of our ways. Do not we all use their rifles and powder and shot? Do not we all wear cloth from the spinning wheels they provided? Do not our children learn to read and count from their missionaries? I think the Cherokee must become strong again, but the way to become strong is to learn the ways of the whites, and to become like them. The Cherokee should farm our land, and raise our cattle, our corn, our squash and beans, and sell these to the whites. We can earn many buckskins, and even trade our food from our fields to the whites for powder and shot for our rifles." Here Nancy, paused and took a deep breath, thus theatrically demonstrating her age; for in this council age was a definite plus, and such theatrics helped make her next point.

"I am now an old woman, and I have known many things. I have known war, and I have known peace. I have chewed shot for my husband's rifle, and I have killed many Creek to defend our Blue Mountains (With this reference to her role in the Battle of Taliwa, the assembled Cherokee were reminded that they were listening to a person who, for them, was a living legend). *This I say to the Cherokee. In war one can live a lifetime in only a day, and in peace the days can turn into years overnight. I have known war and I have known peace and I can tell you now that peace is better than war* (Here she paused again, and when she continued, her voice was softer; Ridge and the others leaned forward to hear what was said).

As these old bones get older they speak to me more each day. Who among us has seen more than sixty winters without his bones talking loudly? (Again the crowd chuckled). *These old bones often tell me that I will not be able to rise on many more mornings, and after a time, it is probably best that old bones not rise at all. I will not see the mist in the Tugaloo Valley again, or hear the rivers in these Blue Mountains for many more winters. Still, I would like to get up tomorrow and have peace with my neighbors. I would like to learn the ways of the whites that are better than ours. I want peace so I can plant my selu patch, and my grandchildren and my great-grandchildren can bring cool water from the river for my dinner. I want to watch these Cherokee children play in the village, and learn the ways of life in these Blue Mountains. I want them to know peace.*

I do not want to hear again the sounds of battle. I do not want our brave young warriors to die needlessly in a Blood Oath against the whites. The older I become, the more I long for peace."

With that, the old woman—seemingly the very heart, soul, and spirit of the Cherokee Nation—sat back down. All present were respectfully quiet for several minutes while they carefully considered her words. Many suspected that this would be her last great council, and all knew they had witnessed history as she spoke; for she was a Beloved Woman of the Cherokee. In fact, it was her last great Cherokee council; she died peacefully in her sleep within three months. Still she is both remembered and revered by Cherokee and whites alike. Today her burial mound is still visited by well wishers, and is visible just off Highway 411 in Eastern Tennessee.

When it was obvious that none of the others desired to speak, Dragging Canoe determined that he would share, once again, his thoughts. His thoughts were quite different from those of Nancy Ward, and he needed to sense the direction of the assembled group. One final time, Dragging Canoe stood to speak. First he looked into each area of the clans, turning slowly to connect with the eyes and hearts of his people. He looked directly at the guest, Tecumseh, and bowed his head respectfully to that great visionary from the north. Then he solemnly spoke.

Once again, because of the half-breed son of Nancy Ward, these words from that great council of the Cherokee, have been preserved for all time.

"I hope that the Great Spirit Kanati hears my words this day. I want him to consider my words, and I want all Cherokee to hear them. I thank the great chief Tecumseh for sharing his vision with us. His medicine is strong, and he sees the balance of this world through the eyes of the Great Spirit. I too have sought that spirit. Often have I prayed for the Cherokee in the cool streams and in the tall hills in our Blue Mountains. I have prayed on Currahee Mountain many miles to the east, and I know that the great Peace Chief Runs-To-Water prayed on that sacred mountain many times. I have prayed beside the gentle Oconaluftee River with Little Carpenter and with the great chief Junaluska, who is with us today. I have climbed alone, the high mountain where the wind blows (today this is called Clingman's Dome, and is located in the Great Smoky Mountains National Park), *and there I prayed to the Great Spirit. Many times when I prayed in the heart of our Blue Mountains, I felt the Great Spirit with me, telling me that these are our mountains for all time. Many times did my father and his father pray in these mountains, ever since Kanati let the animals escape, and since we drove the filthy Creek away. Doublehead, and Nancy Ward, two who are with us today, said their prayers that day and fought in that battle so many winters ago, that we Cherokee might have these Blue Mountains for all time. We honor them, and we thank them for their courage on that day; for we have enjoyed these mountains for many years since that battle.*

Now the white man comes to take these mountains from us; they come like wolves, in numbers that we cannot count. They come to take my land again. Often have I fought for my land, the land where Cherokee have prayed for so many years. I know that I will fight again for my land, and perhaps my sons, who have all become brave Cherokee warriors will fight the whites (Dragging Canoe had already lost one son in a fight with the whites, and this reference reminded the Cherokee of that sacrifice). *I do not know if we will win, because our brother Two Drums is right that the whites seem to have no end. They cut trees and kill the deer and bear in our forest, and when one begins to farm five more whites will soon show up to farm close to him."*

At this point, as he continued speaking, Dragging Canoe began to repeat himself. Without realizing it, his words were almost exactly what they had been many years earlier in a similar council—for he had made these arguments scores of times in various Cherokee councils, not to mention hundreds of times when speaking to a few young warriors while hunting around the campfires of the Cherokee.

"Once we had hoped that the white men would not be willing to travel beyond the mountains. Now that hope is gone. They have passed the mountains and have settled upon Cherokee land. Finally the whole country which the Cherokee and their fathers have so long occupied will be demanded. The land where we have prayed for generations is no longer ours, and the remnant of the Ani-Yvwiya, the Real People, once so great and formidable will be compelled to run once again to the west to seek refuge in some distant wilderness. There they will be permitted to stay only a short while before they must move west again. When there is nowhere else to retreat, the few miserable Cherokee will fight and there they will die; and the Real People will cease to exist. Should we not fight here? Should we not fight now? Should we not fight, rather than submit to further loss of our country? Learning the ways of the whites, while they steal our land with treaties may be all right for men who are too old to hunt or fight. As for me, I have my young warriors about me; I have my sons with me. We will have our lands, the lands where I and my fathers have prayed for generations, or we will die fighting to keep our land. This I say to the Cherokee, I will fight to keep my lands even if I fight beside the Shoshone, the Shawnee, or even beside the filthy Creek, I will fight forever to keep my land, or I will die. I have spoken. I want you all to hear my words."

Thus, did it become clear that no consensus had been reached; this all important council of the Cherokee broke up without any decision whatsoever, and history judges harshly the leaders of any people who cannot make a decision on which direction to pursue. Perhaps all of the Cherokee should have agreed with Dragging Canoe and fought to the death to hold their sacred Blue Mountains. Perhaps, each warrior present should have followed the visionary leader Tecumseh and chosen to fight as one great tribe of warriors against all the whites all across the frontier. In retrospect, either decision would seem to have been better for the tribe overall than no decision at all. Still, this great council of 1804 was to break up with various Cherokee leaders leading their small bands in various directions—a reality that would haunt the Cherokee, and most Native American tribes, for the next two hundred years. For one of the few certainties of history is that indecision quite often breeds disaster.

Ridge Chooses Sides

It seems inexplicable to the historian, but one ironic result of the Great Cherokee Council of 1804 is the determination of Ridge, the young grandson of Runs-To-Water, to learn the ways of the whites. It was known by all Cherokee leaders that Ridge entered that council hating all white faces, and for a very good reason—those faces had stolen his land and the lives of the men in his family for generations. Still, Ridge had kept an open mind about the best solution to the white problem, and thus he'd entered the council with an open mind. He wanted to hear the words of the leaders of his tribe and their guest, Tecumseh, and clearly something said in that council, at a minimum convinced him that the future lay in assimilation rather than overt war.

Now no one doubts that, at the end of the Great Council, Ridge still hated the white invasion of the Blue Mountains. Still, he'd seen enough of white civilization to know that it was wise to be able to read and count—for otherwise, how could one know the fair value of one's buckskins when selling them downriver? Moreover, Ridge had determined that his own survival, and that of his family was tied to their understanding of white culture. If he needed to learn to farm more and hunt less, that would just have to be acceptable. He did not leave this council hating the whites any less, nor did he ever foresee a day of total reconciliation between the races. Still, he did believe, like Nancy Ward and most of those in favor of assimilation, that his immediate future lay with the assimilationist Cherokee—the "White Cherokee." Therefore, as he left this Great Council, he had decided to learn the ways of the whites.

After the great chiefs and the northern guest had departed the council house, as Ridge was standing to leave, a man appeared by his side, seemingly with little effort, like a ghost. The man wore fine white clothes, but he moved effortlessly and with great dignity, like a Cherokee. He said but a few words to Ridge, but those words coupled with the thoughts that had been shared in the council over the last three days, would change the way Ridge related to the whites. *"My family has done well, in learning the ways of the whites, and building a farm in our Blue Mountains. My children grow in peace. This is better than dying in a meaningless battle that we cannot win. Besides, it is no dishonor to learn the ways of one's enemies."*

With those words, whispered to the grandson of the great leader Runs-To-Water, Ekaia—Old Tom Prather—left the council house, seemingly as mysteriously as he'd entered. Tom had decided that he'd owed those words and thoughts to the grandson of the leader of his people from Tugaloo Town so many years ago. Ekaia hoped that Ridge would reach the same conclusion; for Ekaia was sure that if Ridge maintained his hatred for whites that this grandson of Runs-To-Water, like his father and his grandfather, would fall before the guns of the whites. Ekaia knew that Ridge thought deeply before making a decision, and if Ridge was smart, he'd see the wisdom in assimilation.

Only by happenstance did Oak, standing a few feet away, hear those few whispered words from Ekaia. He later jotted them down, not in his catalogue of the great speeches from this council, but in his personal diary, which like the catalogue has survived to this day. This is the only written hint or record preserved by history as to why Ridge would later become a "White Cherokee."

Thus, did Ridge begin his journey towards assimilation—not because he valued whites or hated them less, but rather to learn the ways of his enemy. He was greatly conflicted about these thoughts, but he knew that learning how the bear fed, or where the deer slept was the first step in good hunting. Of course, bear and deer were gifts from Kanati and not enemies, but the same principal applied—if one wanted to survive in these Blue Mountains, one had better learn the ways of the other inhabitants of these mountains, including the whites.

In 1805, as Ridge still considered his thoughts on the whites, he saw something that impacted his heart deeply. In that summer, with the warmer weather, the plague of smallpox, again returned to the settlement where he resided in the Nacoochee Valley, and many died. Ridge lost his youngest son—he had three sons at that point—to the disease. The Cherokee, while having suffered this disease many times, did not understand what to do to curtail the problem so many just went about their business, and continued interactions while those infected spread the disease even more rapidly in the Cherokee settlements than in the white communities in the Blue Ridge.

It was then that, for the first time, Ridge saw something good in the character of a white man, and it turned his world upside down. For just as the disease was reaching its peak early in the Green Corn Month (June to the Americans) an old white man with a long mane of silvery white hair rode into New Echota, looked over the village as if he owned it, and much to the surprise of everyone, he then began to speak in the language of the Cherokee.

The Reverend Cleveland had fought the plague many times, including once in Walton's Ford, and several times in the newer town of Clarkesville. Immediately upon hearing of it in the Cherokee village far to the west, he'd saddled his horse, and left Walton's Ford for the journey to fight his old nemesis. With no preamble whatsoever, he merely looked around the village from atop his steed, and began his mission. While the words were spoken in flawless Cherokee—a shock to many in the village that any white man knew their language—an even bigger surprise was the caring nature of the message. *"I have come to tell you that the Great Spirit does not want your children to die in their lodges. He does not want to see your women barren or to see your village die, but you must fear the Lord, our Great Spirit, and you must do as I and the Lord command you, if you wish to live."*

With that, this man of God dismounted, and sought out the council house, walking boldly into it even before the Cherokee village leaders could enter. Clearly, this old man, this imposing, commanding figure had something to say to the council, so the Cherokee, most of whom had never heard their tongue spoken by a white man before, gathered to hear his words.

Ridge had heard many times of this man with the white hair and the commanding voice, and had even seen him from time to time in other Cherokee villages. He knew that this man spoke of Christianity—the man of the sticks, Jesus, who was a God for the whites and even some Cherokee. Still, Ridge wanted to learn anything that might save his other sons.

Within two hours, the Reverend Cleveland had convinced the tribal leaders to do as he commanded. He first identified one lodge as a "pest house" and, only a few minutes later all of the Cherokee were taking their sick relatives there to be tended by the Reverend. At first, some of the women were skeptical, thinking that the Reverend meant to collect all of the sick in one location and then murder them. Still, some stood by and watched the caring way the Reverend would wet a rag and mop the heads of the sick; clearly he meant no harm. The Reverend would also run the healthy Cherokee away as soon as they brought in the ill, and many did not understand why the Reverend could stay with the sick and not the other family members. Some insisted that the mother stay with a sick child, but when these women subsequently died, the Cherokee began to understand that the Reverend and his God somehow controlled this disease, and they became even more inclined to follow his instructions.

Within two months, the disease had subsided, and the town was still intact, though somewhat diminished—in that episode, 25% of those in the village had died, but all the Cherokee realized that it would have been much worse had the Reverend not arrived and taken charge. Many more converted to Christianity which was one goal of the Reverend—he preached every night around the campfire before the pest house, without letting his growing congregation get too close. Ridge went many times to hear of this Jesus, this man of the sticks, thinking that this would be a good time to learn as much as he could about the whites. In time, he began to understand the courage of this man Jesus, and while he was not terribly clear why the man of the sticks should be of importance to him, this tall white Reverend with the white hair clearly had saved many of his people. Further, he showed great courage in going into the pest house, when all inside were dying.

In this fashion, by striving to keep the Cherokee village of the Nacoochee Valley from succumbing entirely to the plague, did the Reverend Cleveland facilitate the eventual demise of the Cherokee in Georgia. He certainly did not mean to have that effect. However, his actions—his undeniable courage and leadership—helped to convert Ridge to the position of assimilation; thus did a future leader of the

Cherokee determine his course, and that leader would eventually impact the entire Cherokee Tribe.

Of course, the arguments in favor of assimilation would grow in the years to come, but the real reason Ridge turned to assimilation was the influence and personal strength of the Reverend Cleveland. In this fashion did Reverend Cleveland impact history yet again. The Reverend, having never realized the leadership role that Ridge would assume among the Cherokee, merely returned to his flock in the Tugaloo Baptist Church in Walton's Ford, and waited for the next call of God.

In his lodge, a few weeks after the Reverend left New Echota, Ridge determined to discuss his mixed feelings about the whites with his wife, after his children slept. His wife, like many Cherokee women, was wise in many things, and Ridge felt glad to have a confidant with whom he could share his thoughts. He said, *"I have seen a white man do good for our people, and he knew things about the smallpox that we did not. He saved our village, and may have saved ourselves and our other children. We must study the ways of the whites. I believe that we must learn to farm and to build our holdings beyond this lodge and this selu patch. I think that tomorrow, I will go and find some land to the west along a creek that has not been cleared and begin a new selu patch that will be all our own."*

Corn Blossom, his wife, knew that this would mean leaving their comfortable lodge, and beginning a new farm. While she did not mind the work—in fact their oldest two children could help with that—she was concerned with this new direction in their lives, and wanted to know what lead to this statement. She said, *"Have our fields here produced no selu, or no squash?"* In point of fact, their fields, under her careful eye, were among the best in the neighborhood, and they both knew it. Still she spoke; *"Are we to starve this winter from lack of food?"*

Ridge, looked at her and smiled, as any husband would when he knows his wife is being somewhat sassy, not to mention intentionally obtuse. *"Our fields are fine, and you do a good job with our children here. Still, here we do not own the land, and cannot work others on it. That would not be fair to the Cherokee. However, if we clear land next winter, we can buy a black slave to work it with us. We can set up a farm, and learn the ways of the whites who have many slaves. However, we will never abandon the ways of the Cherokee; we are Cherokee and our children will be raised Cherokee."*

Once Ridge and Corn Blossom determined their course, each began to consider all of the things that whites did successfully, and masterful students they were in that regard. Within a year, Ridge had cleared a small patch of land along two rivers in what would one day become the city of Rome, Georgia. He'd also purchased a black slave—a strong buck—from a trader in Clarkesville, and began to work that slave on the small selu and beans patch on the new farm.

Moreover, he visited in secret, the growing plantation of the Prathers many miles to the east near Walton's Ford. For one entire Spring in 1806, he left his family on the new farm, and hired himself out for labor to his distant cousin—Ekaia—on the Prather Plantation. Of course, none of the other Prathers ever realized that Old Tom had spent any inordinate amount of time with this Cherokee laborer. Still, clandestine lessons in farming and management of plantation farm books were undertaken in one of the slave cabins that was provided exclusively for the use of the young Cherokee. If Tom's wife and children thought it unusual that an entire cabin was provided for only one free Cherokee laborer, they didn't mention it. After all, their father was known to be secretive and somewhat peculiar, and the strong young Cherokee was a good worker. In fact, after the planting season of five weeks ended, the laborer seemingly disappeared one evening. Old Tom merely moved another slave family into the cabin and never mentioned the laborer again to his family. In an interesting happenstance of history, the chimney of that same slave cabin still stands to this day, on the Prather Plantation, in Toccoa, Georgia; it has served in history as the hearth to both Cherokee and black slaves.

However, in spite of learning the many ways of the whites, Ridge also kept his pledge to Corn Blossom to raise their remaining children Cherokee. Two sons and one daughter survived the plague, and were immediately sent to the nearby missionaries to learn their letters, and counting, much as Ridge had done. Ridge knew that the missionaries were attempting to destroy everything Cherokee, so while adopting Christianity and many ways of the whites, Ridge and Corn Blossom made certain that their children knew the Cherokee ways. The children were taught the ancient Cherokee skills—the toonalies were taught to use a blowgun, to make a dugout canoe, and to set fish traps. The daughter was taught to weave baskets, and to plant and harvest selu in the old ways. They were taught the sense of balance sought by all beings, their sense of the forest, and even the Cherokee myths of creation.

Almost every evening, while sitting in their new cabin dining with the family and their slave Ceasar, Ridge would tell one of the old Cherokee myths. One evening, his daughter, a delightful child of four named Two Winds, was speaking of the missionary school, and said, "*Today we learned how God made the world in seven days.*" Her mother, Corn Blossom, beamed with pride, since her daughter was excelling in the letters and other teachings of the whites, but Ridge, having finished his dinner saw this as a chance to speak of the legends of the Cherokee.

"*I am sure that the white man's world was created as you say, but these Blue Mountains were created for the Cherokee. I will tell you how the Cherokee world was made. In the beginning all was water, and the animals lived above in Galunlati. It was very crowded there with so many animals, and they wanted more room. The water beetle offered to leave the place above and find land below the water. It went below the water and brought up soft mud which became the earth. Then many birds were sent down to find a dry place to have their nests, but the Great Buzzard flew too low. Now this was a large buzzard, much bigger than what we see today, and he flew too close to the soft mud, while it was still soft. His wings began to strike the ground and make valleys, and where they rose, they brought up the mountains. That is how Cherokee country, these Blue Mountains, were created, and we have lived here since that time before time."*

In this fashion did the myths of the Cherokee get passed down from one generation to the next—as they had for centuries. Ridge also told his children many other legends of the Cherokee. He spoke of Nancy Ward, the Beloved Woman of the Cherokee, and the children sat enthralled, hearing of her chewing the shot for her husband, and then taking up his rifle to continue the fight. Ridge spoke to his children of their great Grandfather, the mighty Chief Runs-To-Water. He told of Runs-To-Water killing a bear when he was seven, and later of how he led the war party into the village of Taliwa. Most importantly, he told them the legends he'd heard of how Runs-To-Water had died, charging into the British guns above Tugaloo Town, while his wife and children escaped across the river to safety.

Thus, in this small enclave, in this one cabin many miles to the west of the Tugaloo River, did the stories continue into the fourth generation distant from Tugaloo Town. This is the essence of these spiritually rich Cherokee legends. Such legends helped the Real People survive; for as long as the legends exist—spoken of in a reverent whisper around the family hearth at night, the Cherokee will always be Cherokee.

Back in Walton's Ford

When the Reverend Cleveland returned to Walton's Ford, after the plague left the Cherokee, he found things much as he'd left them two months previously. His congregation was still meeting each Sunday for prayers together. James Wyly and Devereaux Jarrett were still purchasing land at every opportunity. Ms. Sadie Sharpe was as outspoken as ever, and one could hear her singing for miles along the river whenever she jumped into a hymn she particularly liked. Other settlers were still arriving on the Great Philadelphia Wagon Road, and many soon got work on the local plantations, or purchased some farmland themselves, if any could be found for sale.

Devereaux Jarrett, a man who would become a leader in the area several years later, had moved his store from the South Carolina side of the river to a location on the Georgia side, and purchased a tavern from James Wyly. That house, growing more famous as Traveler's Rest, would play host to congressmen, vice-presidents, governors and other political leaders.

Just downriver, the Carmichael clan was producing ever more children, so that no one, including the Carmichaels themselves, could keep one generation straight from the next. This would be a recurring problem in that clan of misfits.

On the Prather plantation, James Prather was doing an excellent job in managing the growing business interests, and if the older man—Tom Prather—got more eccentric with each passing year, the family was at the very least, in good hands. All in all, Walton's Ford was growing into the type of civilized settlement that would soon pass that ill-determined line and become an "upcountry city," and the Reverend Cleveland was then sure that he would have even more work to do saving souls and walking the path of God.

In those years, as the new century began, his untimely death came as quite a shock. On one unexpectedly cool evening in the fall, when everyone in the new settlement was headed to a wedding, the powerful spiritual leader of Walton's Ford suddenly fell dead at his own pulpit as he prepared for the service. The planned wedding was obviously canceled, as this frontier town prepared to mourn one of its leading citizens. However, even in death this great man was to give something of meaning to his world—perhaps this gift has become his greatest legacy.

Tradition holds that the author of the now famous poem is unknown, but that is not the case. Anyone today in the Tugaloo River Valley can tell you just how the traditional lines—lines that have meant so much to so many worldwide—originated. It was several years after the last visit of the dreaded plague to Walton's Ford, on the day of burial for the Reverend John Cleveland, when the poem was first read publicly. It was a moving day, a powerfully spiritual day, as this small Blue Ridge community gathered to mourn their Reverend, this spiritual giant.

At the funeral, the Tugaloo Baptist Church in which the Reverend Cleveland preached was overflowing—everyone in North Georgia seemed to come–many traveling all night to pay their final respects to this great man. Even old Elijah Clarke, the hero of King's Mountain, came—having ridden his horse hard all night; for Elijah knew a good political opportunity when he saw one, and many voters would be in that church for that service. James Wyly was there, and Tom Prather; Devereaux Jarrett, the store keeper of Walton's Ford was in attendance with his growing family. Ms. Sadie Sharpe drug in her entire clan, Presbyterians the lot, but there that sat on this fateful day in the Tugaloo Baptist Church. The descendants of Early Cleveland–many children and grandchildren—were there, as were many slaves from the Cleveland and the Prather Plantations. All knew that the Reverend Cleveland had ministered to everyone, and all were there to mourn his passing.

The crowd filled the little church and many had to be content standing outside in front of the open double doors where they could at least hear the service. His body, hidden in the inevitable pine box coffin that awaits us all, lay on the rough table in front of the congregation, as his newly ordained son Richard Cleveland, stood to speak.

Richard had often served in his father's absence, while his father ministered to the growing number of distant churches or to the Cherokee. In the same strong senatorial voice known well to this valley, did the son, thus carry on the work of the father. *"It was often said of my father, that he walked with the Lord."* Richard said, as he looked out at the crowd before him. He continued. *"I believe that he did walk with the Lord, and as I see so many of you whom he helped in this life, I think you believe it too. Often did my father and I walk along the Tugaloo, leaving our footprints in the sandy bank, and as I think of his walk through life, I realized that my father, our minister must have often walked there with our Lord Jesus, as he raised his evening prayers.*

They must have walked along beside that river quite often, leaving footprints as they went. In many ways, the lessons he taught are his footprints; you and I are his footprints, and those footprints will last long after this day, the day in which he joins our Lord Jesus for his final walk.

My father was a strong, dedicated man, but there were times when he was not beaming with certainty, and while we saw those times in our cabin, I'm not sure many of you did. One time, when he'd lost a member of the congregation, he was so sad that he wept, sitting alone at the table in the cabin. I happened to come home early that day from the field, and found him there crying, just as he was kneeling to pray.

I asked him, 'Father, what is it? Can I pray with you? Will that help?' My father looked up, surprised to see me there, and with tears on his face, he smiled, and told me that I could certainly pray with him for the departed spirit who was so important to the church, and to him. Then he said something I'll never forget. He said, 'Son, I walk with the Lord, and when I cannot walk any longer, our Lord Jesus carries me.'

My life changed at that moment, when I heard him say that. This powerful man, my father, weeping before my eyes, knew that when he could not walk any further, the Lord would carry him. From that moment on, I knew that the Lord carries us all, through everything we have to face, and now, you know it too.

When times are impossible, our Lord is there. If our children die from the plague in their cribs, or our wives are cut down by Creek arrows, our Lord will be there. When our fields burn with a lightening strike before the harvest, or our cattle and sheep are carried away by a flood, God is still with us.

When our children are born dead, having never taken a breath, God is with us then too, even as he is greeting them in heaven. He is in the mists of these mountains, over the river in the morning, and he hears our crying. He tests us as he has tested our fathers before us, yet he loves us and would never leave us. We can never escape from our God, and when we can walk no further, when we can bear no more, He will carry us."

The young Reverend Richard Cleveland then read a rough version of the poem still known today the world over. The traditional poem, known simply as *"Footprints"* has become familiar over the ages, and while many versions currently exist, the poem's author is never specified. Still, the original poem evolved from that very requiem for the Reverend John Cleveland, in the Tugaloo Baptist Church, as any citizen in the valley will tell you to this day. While somewhat edged in pathos by today's standards, that poem of yesteryear does sum up the life of the Reverend John, not to mention the many other ministers and missionaries who brought God into the Blue Ridge.

In all cultural traditions and in all periods of history, the harsh demands of life simply require a spiritual dimension, and the tougher life becomes, the more the human condition craves God. To reject that lesson from all cultures throughout history is to arrogantly ignore the fundamental human condition, and that is an error in judgment made today, only by fools. The Reverend John Cleveland understood that fact, and lived his life serving God. This man brought his God into the Tugaloo River Valley, and he could have performed no greater service for the people of that area.

His church, the Tugaloo Baptist Church, still stands today on the original site by the Tugaloo River. It was to become the "Mother of Churches" for all of north Georgia and northern Alabama; for many congregations were formed there for distant churches in various valleys of the lower mountains. Services are still held in that building along the Tugaloo every Sunday. Surely the footprints of the Reverend John Cleveland echo still in this valley of the Blue Ridge, and the poem in it's original form, is still a fitting requiem for this great man.

> *"One night, I had a dream,*
> *that I was walking by the river with the Lord.*
> *As we walked, we talked.*
> *We shared many things, throughout my life,*
> *and as we passed hardship after hardship,*
> *we left our footprints in the sand.*
> *We continued the walk throughout my whole life,*
> *and in looking back, I noticed that*
> *at times there were two sets of footprints.*
> *At other times there was only one.*
> *Then I noticed that, when there was only one set of footprints*
> *I always seemed to be having a difficult time in my life.*
> *So I asked God, why he'd left me alone.*
> *'Lord, why, in the difficult times in my life,*
> *Did you not continue to walk with me?*
> *Did you not know that I needed you the most at those times?'*
> *God then smiled at me, as he continued walking.*
> *Then he said, "My precious, precious child.*
> *I am a God of love and compassion,*
> *and I am always here for you.*

I would never abandon you.
At those times, when you had the most difficulty,
At those very times when you see
only one set of footprints in the sand,
It was then that I carried you."

The Reverend John Cleveland, pastor of the Tugaloo Baptist Church, truly walked with the Lord. In understanding the Blue Ridge and the harsh trials faced by everyone in that region in the distant past, we must seek to understand the depth of their spiritual quest as well as their spiritual certainty. For both the Cherokee, and many of the white settlers who followed, living in these mountains was first and foremost a spiritual existence, and as we today enjoy these hills, these sharp rocky crags, the higher peaks, and lower valleys, we can still hear the call of the spirits. It is this very mysticism that brings us today—by the scores of thousands— to seek out the beautiful Blue Mountains; for the spirit is here in these mystic hills. It is just there, as we listen quietly in the morning mist just before the first rays of sunshine hit the top of the distant peaks, the haunting sounds of the mountains seem to speak to us of the spirits worshiped here. One can almost hear the distant prayer of Reverend John Cleveland, baptizing his flock down by the river, or the reverent chant of the ancient Cherokee, standing in the shallows of the water just over the next rise. This is the meaning of these mountains; it is their richness. For just as the Reverend John Cleveland did in his time, these haunting mountains can tell us of a time when God walked and talked with us all, if only we are wise enough to listen.

The Cherokee Fight The Creek Again

While the War of 1812 did not drastically impact the lower Blue Ridge, that war did impact the Cherokee in several subtle ways, and in particular, it impacted Ridge. The Cherokee, by choosing to fight beside the Americans essentially conceded that the whites would forever be living to the west of the mountains. Thus, this war, as much as anything else, assured the ultimate victory of the assimilation policy of the Cherokee, among the Indians themselves. They could not, at that time, realize that the whites had outgrown the policy of assimilation first proposed under Washington's Presidency two decades before; the whites would soon betray this policy as they had previous commitments, and would demand the total removal of the Cherokee. Still, that demand was unanticipated in the first decades of the nineteenth century. Thus, when the call to arms came, many Cherokee—warriors who wanted to fight the filthy Creek as their fathers and grandfathers had done for generations—assembled to fight beside the Americans against the British and their Creek allies.

In the decade since the Great Council of the Cherokee in 1804, Ridge had acquired substantial holdings in land and quite a few black slaves. His first slave, Ceasar, served as his overseer, and managed the fields, organizing the work crews among the 15 other slaves that Ridge had purchased. Ridge's growing farm, not yet quite large enough to be termed a true plantation, did produce substantial cotton, and many vegetables for sale in the growing upcountry towns in Georgia, so by 1812 Ridge was a rich man among the Cherokee. In terms of his education, he had little formal schooling, but he could read and cipher, and with his clandestine lessons from Old Tom Prather, he had become quite the businessman.

He'd even built a two room cabin from which he oversaw his holdings, and his growing family. His oldest daughter, Two Winds, was growing more lovely every day, and Ridge was sure to lose her to some young warrior within the year.

Moreover, Ridge had tempered his hatred for the whites, and in addition to Reverend Cleveland, Ridge had found many others whom he respected—thus he had many whites to emulate. When interacting with the white world, he often dressed as a white, and modeled himself on any of the great Southern plantation owners. Thus, was life moving along well for Ridge and his family.

Then came the War of 1812. When an upstart white cavalryman named Andy Jackson, a Tennessee man, sought a leader among the Cherokee that could be trusted, it was natural that he pick a plantation owner, and a Cherokee who desired assimilation. Moreover, as Jackson considered which Cherokee he would utilize to manage his scouting force, he wanted a man whom the Cherokee themselves respected.

Now most of the traditionalist Cherokee had contempt for the "White Cherokee," but among the "White Cherokee" Ridge was clearly different. This man was also a "warrior" in the traditional sense, and knew more of the traditional Cherokee values than did many of the Christianized, assimilated Cherokee of that period. Moreover, Ridge came from a revered family among the Cherokee people, many of whom still spoke the legends of Runs-To-Water's final charge, or of the death of Stands-Tall. Thus, Ridge had the admiration of both the traditionalists and the assimilationists among his tribe. Like his grandfather he was a fighter, and a natural leader among his people; he was clearly the leader Jackson wanted. Jackson interviewed him only once, but finding him to be physically large, as many natural leaders are in many cultures, and knowing of his reputation, Jackson appointed Ridge a "Major" on the spot—thus did Ridge acquire the name by which history would know him for all time—Major Ridge.

When his militia was finally called out in 1812 they chose to meet in Nashville, Tennessee. As the militia gathered, Jackson's scouting force of 500 Cherokee also assembled, with Major Ridge at the head of the scouting force. Jackson and his army marched south to confront the Creek, and their British sponsors. The British held a base of operations in New Orleans, and a Creek army had been moving freely along the coast, and the lower hills, attacking settlements on the frontier in upstate Georgia, Tennessee, and in the Alabama Territory. Several skirmishes were undertaken over the next months, without conclusive results. However, in March of 1814, hearing that a band of Creek warriors were encamped along the Tallapoosa River, Jackson started in that direction, with his small army in trail, and his Cherokee scouting force eager to close with their age old enemies. Soon the battle would be joined—a battle which would end the dominance of the Creek in the Southeast forever, tie the Cherokee to the newly formed United States, and subsequently produce a president.

At the Horseshoe

Today, the stately pines and hardwoods stand sentinel to the peaceful fields near the river. As one walks along near the unusual horseshoe shaped bend in the Tallapoosa River in east-central Alabama, one is aware of the gentle breeze and the unusual quiet of the place. The mixed pine and hardwoods seemingly creep down to the distant shoreline. Here the river cuts back on itself, to form a peninsula of land—a natural fortification—jutting some 2500 feet towards the southwest. This unusual bend in the meandering Tallapoosa enclosed just over 100 wooded and open acres; at the northeastern end of the bend, the river is separated by only 1200 feet of gently sloping ground from itself. Pointing down the center of the horseshoe shaped landmass is a finger of higher ground, with gentle slopes to the river on all sides. For the set-piece defensive battles of the early nineteenth century, God could not have produced a more defensible fortification than these rolling hills at Horseshoe Bend.

An isolated island stands in the river on the western side of the horseshoe. Because of this island, the river flows more rapidly on the western most branch around this island, almost as if it had a mind of it's own; as if the river were seeking to change it's course and enclose even more land in this atypical landlocked configuration. Today, the quiet woodland sounds speak of tranquility, but in March of 1814, in this splendidly peaceful woodland setting, there was no peace; here over a thousand men would die.

On March 26, 1814, a number of Creek Indians who had been fighting with the British were encamped here. The Creek, like the Cherokee before them, had heard Tecumseh speak of his vision to unite the Indians. These Creek had chosen to fight with the British in the hope that, with a British victory, the British King would force all whites to withdraw from west of the mountains. Based on this desperate hope, the Creek had fought and lost several battles in the War of 1812, and by March of 1814, they were desperately trying to cling to any hope they could find. About 1000 warriors and perhaps 400 women and children had made their home in the village then nestled on the horseshoe shaped peninsula. The village was not old—having grown into a substantial village only during the previous six months, as many Creek sought refuge from the various battles towards the end of that forgotten war.

Camping only six miles north of the village, was a battle tested army of men committed to it's destruction. General Andrew Jackson arrived with his American forces on March 26, 1814. Supporting Jackson were 3000 lightly armed, highly aggressive men; this makeshift army traveled with what each man could carry on his back, but they also had two small cannons which could provide light artillery support.

Jackson, who would later become President of the United States, was then living in Nashville, Tennessee and was serving as a Major General of the Tennessee Militia. His core force was comprised of 2,400 fighters—some were "regular" infantry from the U. S. Army's 39th Regiment. Others were Tennessee militiamen from the frontier who had fought Indians all their lives, and included among that number was a young upstart who would become famous in only a few years as the essence of the frontiersman—a man who preferred to be called David, but history would forever remember as "Davy" Crockett.

These whites were all battle tested veterans. Also, some 500 Cherokee warriors, never ones to miss a fight with the Creek, were waiting for the chance to kill their ancient enemy. Major Ridge had his Cherokee force scouting each flank, as Jackson's army moved on the long march through upper Alabama. Strangely enough, there were even some 100 disgruntled Creek warriors fighting with Jackson's makeshift army, who would, in the coming battle, be fighting against their own tribe.

On the night of March 26, the Cherokee huddled by their campfires. While they traveled with the American army, the Cherokee were considered "scouts" rather than regular troops, and always fought as a separate unit under command of their own leaders. However the bigotry of Jackson—not to mention virtually every other white leader of the day—demanded that several white officers be appointed to "lead" the scouts. Nevertheless, Jackson was savvy in his dealing with "savages" and had, thus placed only a few white commanders in charge of his Indian allies. In spite of his own prejudice, he chose to vest the true authority in the Indian leaders themselves, such as Major Ridge. Of course in his mind, this made the Cherokee allies somewhat less reliable than army regulars or the Tennessee militia, but Jackson had a special mission in mind for the Cherokee—a mission to which they would be well suited. He intended to use them, not in the main assault, but as a reserve blocking force in order to prevent the Creek from escaping across the river. Jackson had already told Major Ridge of this plan.

That evening, as the Cherokee spoke among themselves of the battle plan, every warrior realized that they would get little opportunity to kill Creek, if they were used only to prevent escape across the river. This upset the Cherokee terribly—Cherokee who had marched across the entire state of Georgia and Tennessee for something like 16 months for the sole reason of killing their historic enemies. Still, Ridge managed to silence the rumblings in fairly short order by having his men bed down early in preparation for the fight the next morning. Thus, all of the Cherokee, unlike their white allies, slept a sound sleep the night before the battle.

Early on the morning of March 27, Jackson changed the battle plan. Realizing how narrow the horseshoe bend in the river really was, and how wide an area the river retreat was, he added the Tennessee militia to the Cherokee blocking force. Thus, the Cherokee and some Tennessee militia crossed the river downstream from the town to approach it from behind. Here they would prevent escape of the enemy. At 10:30 in the morning, Jackson and his forces arrived at the top of the horseshoe landmass ready to attack, and only then did they note the hastily constructed defensive works. The Creek had fortified the northeastern end of the land bridge with a rough construction that would prove to be a problem for Jackson's command. The barricade was some 1200 feet long, reaching from one shore of the river to the other, and effectively closing off the entire landmass inside the horseshoe of the river.

Creek Chief, Menawa, a veteran of many battles, was leading the Creek. He had participated in battles between white forces before, and he therefore knew the advantages of defensive works when a smaller force was attacked by a larger force. In the nineteenth century—as in most other historical periods—the attackers were virtually assured of losing more men than the defenders, and even a small defending force, if provided with appropriate defensive works, could often hold off a much larger attacking force. This rough barricade had been constructed at Menawa's orders, specifically in order to give the smaller defending force a fighting chance.

Jackson contemplated his situation, but he could see no options other than a frontal assault. He ordered his regulars to form a line facing the barricade. In the west and slightly to their rear, the remaining Tennessee Militia formed a second parallel line, and would reinforce the regular army units. Well forward and slightly to the right of both lines, on a rise about 250 yards from the breastwork, Jackson had placed his two light artillery pieces. The General had seen enough breastworks to realize the skill with which the Creek had built their barricade. In his journal on that morning, he wrote of his surprise at finding such defenses on the field.

"It is impossible to conceive a situation more eligible for defense than the one they had chosen and the skill which they manifested in their breastwork was really astonishing. It extended across the point in a concave fashion, such that a force approaching would be exposed to a double fire from either end of their defensive works, while they lay entirely safe behind it. It would have been impossible to have raked it with cannon to any advantage even if we had had possession of one end of the line."

In Jackson's mind, these Indians may have been savages, but they knew how to fight. Within minutes, Jackson had informed his commanders of his decision to attack, and he ordered fire on the barricade at 10:45 in the morning, in the hope that his cannon could unearth the Creek forces. Thus, as quickly as the regular army artillerymen could reload, cannon shot from his twin six pounders tore into the barricade, killing or maiming a few unfortunate Creek warriors.

Still, the Creek had built wisely. While such a cannon-pounding would have reduced any brick fortification of that period to rubble, the Creek—using the only materials at hand—had made their barricade out of the soft sand and mud of the surrounding land, along with stout hardwoods from the forest. In many cases, the non-explosive shot from Jackson's cannon merely embedded themselves into the barricade and sprayed river mud over everything in sight. At other times however, the shot would hit an oak beam, splintering it into thousands of deadly projectile splinters. These would pierce any flesh behind that section of the wall, and some Creek warriors died from pounds of wood embedded in their eyes, their cheeks, their faces, or their bodies. However, regardless of this pounding, the soft earthen barricade would not go down. The sustained bombardment lasted for 30 minutes before Jackson called a halt to inspect the works. Using his spy-glass, he inspected the earthen wall carefully. Finding it very little effected he ordered the cannonade to resume. Sixty minutes, then ninety minutes passed, with only sporadic pauses for Jackson to inspect the wall. Even after nearly two hours the fortification remained generally in tact, and strong enough to prevent the attackers from marching through it. Jackson had no choice—his men would have to storm the wall. Jackson determined to send his men into the hell that surely awaited behind the barricade, and he, once again considered his options and plans for attack.

The Cherokee, meanwhile, waited across the river to the southwest, hearing the bombardment, and yet realizing that if the plan worked, they would be left out of the thick of the battle. This many warriors found intolerable, and there seemed to be more grumbling with each cannon shot.

"*The General cannot expect us to remain unengaged, once the battle is joined,*" said a gangly warrior who was dressed in "white" clothes. This youngish man had grown since the Great Cherokee Council of 1804, and was now a substantial landholder with eight slaves of his own. Like Ridge, he'd been selected by Jackson because of his white education and his leanings towards assimilation. John Ross had now become a leader among his people, and while he was not yet a Chief, his council was respected. Jackson had noted this, and when he'd awarded Ridge the temporary rank of "Major", he'd likewise awarded Ross the rank of "Captain."

Major Ridge—who'd chosen to dress in the traditional Cherokee garb for this battle—responded. "*Our warriors cry out for battle. Why would the General not use them?*"

Ross replied. "*I'm sure that the General has plans that we are unaware of.*"

Major Ridge merely grunted, thinking that Captain Ross might be right; Jackson might have plans that he, for one reason or another, had decided not to

The Battle Of Horseshoe Bend

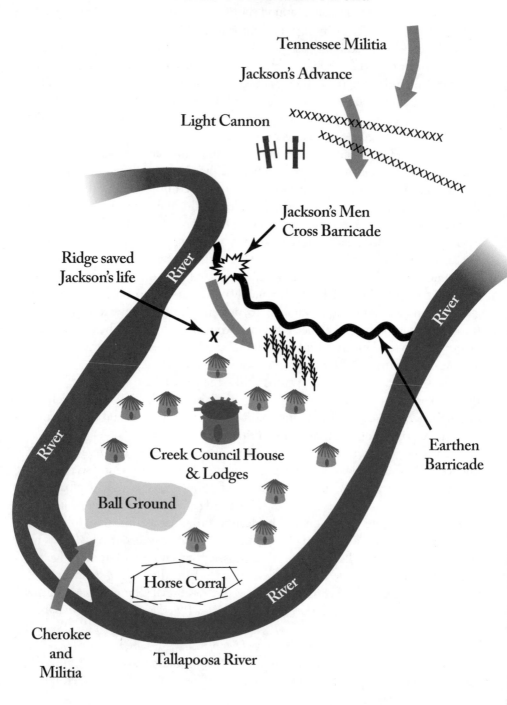

Tennessee Militia

Jackson's Advance

Light Cannon

Jackson's Men
Cross Barricade

Ridge saved
Jackson's life

River

River

River

Earthen
Barricade

Creek Council House
& Lodges

Ball Ground

Horse Corral

Cherokee
and
Militia

Tallapoosa River

disclose to the Cherokee. Still, it would be terribly poor leadership indeed to not inform one's commanders on the field of the general plan of battle. Upon reflection however, Ridge realized that in the crazy world of war, such stupidities were entirely possible, because the whites distrusted the Cherokee so completely. Meanwhile, like all the other Cherokee, Ridge continued to look across the river for any Creek foolish enough to show his head. At that moment, some 600 rifles were loaded, primed, and aimed across that small river, and in the hands of these Cherokee warriors and Tennessee militiamen, each would have been deadly accurate, had a target presented itself. None did.

At just the moment that Jackson ordered a resumption of the barrage on the barricade at the east end of the battlefield, a lone Cherokee warrior, lustful for the blood of his enemy, decided he could take no more. Indeed it seemed to happen without any forethought, and certainly without orders. One foolishly brave–and very young—Cherokee warrior left his post behind a large oak tree, handed his rifle to his companion, and moved slowly into the strong current of the western section of the river. As the water crept up his torso, he began to swim across. This brave man—no one that day even recorded his name, and it has been lost to history—was positioned slightly behind the western island, and was thus, fairly sure that he could not be seen from the Creek village itself.

When Ross saw this stupidly brave act, he was beside himself with anger—for this young warrior had come from his own company. *"Identify that man,"* he said to his adjunct, *"and I'll have him shot for deserting his post."* Not sure that such a punishment was sufficient, and becoming more angry with each breath, Ross continued. *"Find out who he is, and I'll flog him and then I'll shoot him myself!"*

Major Ridge, on the other hand was much more seasoned in battle, and like all good commanders, he knew a good idea when he saw one. Within a minute he and forty other Cherokee warriors were moving behind the island, which for some unknown reason, the Creek had left entirely unfortified. With no order given these men—strong swimmers all—left their rifles along the shore. With only their knives and war hatchets, they waded in, swam, and reached the island within five minutes. They immediately crawled to the other side, to look more closely at the Creek village. However, the first warrior across, was not yet finished with his brave exploit. Now feeling both confident and cocky, as only a young warrior can, he quickly swam across the next small section of the river in full view of the Creek village, and found to his surprise that no one in the village had noticed his exploit.

Of course, he now found himself within the village, with no weapons other than his knife and more importantly, no real thought as to what he would do once he got there. Thus, he determined to do what young warriors did best, demonstrate their bravado by stealing something from his enemy. He crawled to one of the Creek canoes along the riverbank, untied it and pushed it into the stream. He paddled furiously, under the watchful gaze of 500 other Cherokee, none of whom could believe the Creek had been so foolish as to leave their rear unguarded. The young warrior paddled not to the Island, but to the far shore and the waiting Cherokee.

When others saw him nearing the shore, the larger band of Cherokee, Ridge and fifteen others, swam the last section of the river and brought back sixteen other canoes. These were quickly loaded with rifles, shot, and powder which could then be ferried across the river dry. In spite of all of this activity, and the unavoidable, though minimal, noise of this haphazard river crossing, the Creek appeared to be none the wiser.

Unbelievable as it may seem, within ten minutes most of the Cherokee and a mixed force of Tennessee militia had swum the river with their powder and rifles dry in the canoes, all without firing a shot. The Creek warriors were 300 yards away at the barricade and looking the other way. We, today can only speculate on how this could have happened. Of course, the Creek warriors were hunkered down and under attack behind the barricade to the northeast. Further, they were under bombardment, and nothing commands one's attention like being on the receiving end of a two hour artillery barrage. Still, how could the Cherokee manage to cross the river without some of the Creek women or children, in the village just above the riverbank, noticing and raising the alarm? On such unexplainable circumstances does the tide of history sometimes turn.

When all was ready, Major Ridge shouted, "*Charge,*" and as one the Cherokee ran into the Creek village from the rear.

Bloody death was the order of the day; no compassion was expected, and none was shown by these Cherokee warriors as they attacked lodge after lodge. A Cherokee would enter a lodge, to find a woman huddled with two, three, or four children. In some lodges an old woman, or even an older man, long past his warrior years, were present. The Cherokee warrior would not waste his powder and shot on any among such a group. Instead he would draw his war hatchet and would kill the mother first, since mothers can be quite aggressive when forced to watch their children die. Thus, most of the Creek women died with their skull cleaved in two from horrid wounds which could only be made by a war hatchet; such terribly bloody wounds have not been seen on any battlefield on earth in the last 100 years. Any old men present would die next, and only then would the warrior put away the bloody hatchet and draw his knife along the neck of each of the children. Thus did the Creek families die in their lodges, terrified by the specter of a Cherokee warrior, fully painted according to his clan and his own particular medicine, some tattooed in the traditional way across their faces, arms, chests and thighs. The poor Creek died, often staring at each other unable to speak or even breath through their sliced throats, as life ebbed away with their blood leaving lifeless eyes staring a pitiful few feet across the earthen floor into other lifeless eyes. Many of the children used their last strength to crawl toward their mother's now lifeless corpse, so the dead were often found in huddled masses of two, three, or four bodies. Only a few of the Cherokee bothered to take prisoners. They looted what they could, and then burned the lodges as soon as they'd killed all of those inside.

Jackson's forces had advanced and were set up for a general charge, but were still blocked by the barricade. Nevertheless, when Jackson saw smoke rising from the village and heard rifle fire, he realized instantly what had happened, and knew it was time to force the battle at the barricade. At just that moment, he noted a number of Creek running to face the threat from the rear, so he decided to waste no further time. He would assault the barricade directly. It was almost 12:30, when Jackson ordered a roll of the drums to signal the beginning of the charge, and a mass of men, red and white together, clad in the skins of animals or merely in breech cloth, ran into the guns of the Creek behind the earthen wall.

What followed was one of the most extreme examples of battle hell ever seen on the North American continent. While the slaughter in the village had been closer to murder than to war, the men at the barricade witnessed the worst face of bloody, nineteenth century hand-to-hand warfare; ferocious fighting, characterized by a deadly knife fights; a hitting, biting, stabbing, bleeding, terror—all the while each warrior shouting at the top of his lungs, and fighting with wild abandon. One shot with an old musket or Kentucky Long Rifle, and then these men would plunge into the fray with nothing but a knife, maybe a single shot pistol, and if one was lucky, a quick reaction time.

The whites thought they were fighting the Indians from hell; for the Creek looked formidable that day, painted in war paint, smeared in blood, covered in mud from their barricade, many with burning splinters sticking out of the flesh of their face from the explosions of the hardwood supports of the wall, and every Creek warrior fought like there was no tomorrow. The younger Creek in particular fought with wild abandon; for they were convinced there would be no tomorrow should they lose, so they fought like demons. Jackson later reported that the fight was one of the bloodiest he'd ever seen, this metal to metal, blood to blood horror. He stated later: "*The action was muzzle to muzzle through the holes in the barricade and many of the enemy's musket balls were welded to the bayonets of our muskets.*"

Once the breastworks were overtaken at the northwestern end, hand-to-hand fighting ensued on the other side of the barricade towards the village. The cannon now shifted their focus, like some ancient, deadly predator, to the eastern end of the barricade, but the gentle river breezes spread the smoke to cover the entire bloody battlefield. In the acid smoke and the splintered wood from the cannonade fighters on both sides could see only a few dozen feet, and none knew how the battle was going overall. When a white militiamen fell, the Creek warrior would often stab him several more times to assure his death, and only then turn a look for another enemy for his knife or his war hatchet. All thought of loading muskets now gone, since the fighting was so intense. When a white man stuck his knife into the eye socket, or the breast, or the rib-cage of some damn Creek, he'd pull it out and immediately cut the man's throat for good measure, only then looking for another target, as his enemies' body fell to the ground at his feet. Man to man they fought, bled, and died—most without ever realizing what was happening only thirty feet away.

Slowly, the superior numbers of Jackson's fighters overwhelmed the Creek warriors, and even more slowly did the Cherokee warriors fighting through the entire village and their American army allies come together toward the northwestern end of the barricade. The Cherokee had subdued most of the village and fought on through the town to approach the barricade portion of the battle from the southwest. Once the forces under Jackson joined together, the Creek were forced to the northeast and backed into an ever shrinking position between the back side of the barricade and the river. For a time, the poor dwindling Creek force faced Jackson's men to the northwest, the Cherokee from the southwest, cannon fire from the north, all the while hemmed in with the river to the east. The Cherokee and Tennessee militia could smell victory, but the fighting continued man to man, and the smoke was still thick. Suddenly the cannon were silenced, since the artillerymen could not tell where the enemy was in the smoke. Still, the muskets flashed frequently enough to continually renew the smoky haze that covered the bloody ground.

Then History Changed

Then history changed once again. At one point, General Jackson himself stood exposed on the Southwestern side of the barricade, having mistakenly assumed that the battle line would move toward the village and not back toward the barricade's east end. Major Ridge approached him, realizing the danger to the General even before Jackson's aides. At that very moment, a Creek warrior plunged from the smoky death only fifty feet away and letting out a bloodcurdling war cry, he charged with his war hatchet directed at Jackson. He ran screaming like one of Satan's henchmen, with blood streaming from wounds in his face and upper arms, and burning embers buried deep in his cheeks. He seemed, at that moment, to be a minion of hell, looming large, dominating the landscape; he covered the distance to Jackson in seconds, with his mighty arms raised and his war hatchet ready to cleave Jackson in two with one blow. No one who saw that charge would ever forget it, as Jackson stood paralyzed by this specter of death, as well as the surprise at the terrible fear he felt. He watched his own death approach without moving and—to his credit—without flinching at all.

The Creek was now within eight feet of Jackson, but just as the bloody demon warrior raised his hatchet even higher for more strength, another demon from hell—dressed in the battle dress of the Cherokee—side-tackled the Creek, taking him many feet from Jackson. The general and his several aids stood transfixed as they watched Major Ridge, disengage from the Creek while drawing his knife in his left hand and his own war hatchet in his right. These two warriors—bloody enemies for generations—slowly circled each other for only a moment, before the death fight began.

While any one of a number of Tennessee militiamen could have shot the Creek dead at that moment, none thought to do so; all knew this was a fight between two warriors whose ancestors had fought for centuries—one a young strong Creek, covered in the blood of his people, with wood embedded in his right cheek; the other a wise, decisive Cherokee leader, respected for his traditional warrior skills as well as his white education. Thus, was this singular battle joined; two men faced each other and one was, most certainly, going to die.

Ridge's white education didn't count for much at that moment however, for after only a few seconds, the Creek saw the opening he was looking for, and instantly tossing his war hatchet from his right to his left hand he spun around and swung a might blow towards the head of Ridge from the left. Jackson and his aides were dumbfounded at this maneuver; how did one change hands with a weapon so fast in battle? It was so fast so as to be nearly invisible!

Ridge, much the wiser and more seasoned warrior, had assumed that this Creek would fight equally well with both hands; any warrior could. In fact, Ridge had created that momentary opening in his battle stance intentionally, to draw the Creek off balance, and once the Creek's momentum committed him to the left-handed swing, Ridge quickly did a forward summer-salt that would make a modern gymnast proud, moving into the blow toward the Creek's left. As the Creek spun, Ridge rapidly flipped over his own weight without touching the ground, still inside of the Creek's hatchet, the hatchet missing him by only three inches and connecting only with air. Ridge stopped in a fraction of a second, as his feet again connected with the ground, and began his own attack to the Creek's weak side, even before the Creek could recover his balance. During his roll he'd dropped his hatchet, and in a flash he tossed his knife to his right hand, and pivoted back to the exposed left side of the Creek. He then plunged that knife deep into the exposed lower rib-cage of the Creek warrior, behind his left arm—the knife sinking for nine inches up to the bone handle. Ridge used his mighty left arm to block the anticipated return swing from the Creek, but even then he did not let go of the knife embedded deep into the body of his enemy. Rather, Ridge twisted that powerful knife in the man's side. The entire engagement from the tackle of the Creek to his death took no more than eight seconds. At the end, they stood paralyzed together for a few brief moments, their faces only inches apart and their eyes locked on each other as the Creek died. In the last moment of his life, the Creek warrior looked at Ridge and nodded his respect for a great warrior, a superior fighter, and a better man. His life then ended.

Jackson, his aides, and almost 20 of the Tennessee Militia stood transfixed for those seconds, watching an Indian knife fight, and by the time they realized what had happened, Ridge was extracting his knife as the Creek fell dead at his feet. He wiped the knife on his breechcloth, and over 25 whites stood in awe at this Cherokee warrior. While any one of these frontiersman—Jackson included—could fight with a knife, every man knew he would never be the equal of either this Creek or this Cherokee. They felt that they had watched a miracle, and in a way they would never have understood, they had. For this was to be one of the last great Indian to Indian battles east of the Mississippi. The days of Indian on Indian warfare in this region were coming to a close.

Within a few short years, Ridge would be a leader known and respected by the entire Cherokee tribe, and of course, Andrew Jackson would be President of the United States, a position which he would use to expel every single Cherokee from their traditional homeland in the Blue Mountains, without exception and without remorse. Even Major Ridge and his family would be sent west to starve and eventually perish. Only a decade later would Ridge regret having saved Jackson's life at the Battle of Horseshoe Bend. In an understatement, typical of great Cherokee leaders, Ridge would state, *"Had I known what Jackson would do to my people, I would have let that Creek kill him that day at the Horseshoe."* Still, this event is historic; Major Ridge is the only man in history who has saved the life of a future president in battle.

Meanwhile on that fateful day in March of 1814, the most vicious fighting continued amid the smoke toward the eastern end of the barricade. Slowly the Creek were reduced in number, until only a few continued to fight. What followed has often been described as a slaughter. The American Army regulars and the Tennessee militia, along with the Cherokee killed any Creek warrior they could find. For example, when some creek hid in a stand of pines along the higher ridge, the Cherokee set fire to the timber. When the Creeks emerged, they were shot down immediately. The bloodshed continued until dark, with many victory cries from the Cherokee. The next morning, as the village was searched, some 16 Creek warriors were found hidden under the banks of the river; they too were killed immediately, even though some were clearly unarmed; for such was the way of the Creek versus Cherokee conflict over the generations.

By the end of the battle, 548 Creek warriors were dead, and most were mutilated. Some 250 to 300 more were shot in the river and drowned—these floated downstream, and were never accurately counted. Further, the Creek women and children who died could not be counted, since many bodies had been burned in the lodges. Suffice it to say that this Creek village was wiped out entirely. In contrast, only 49 Tennessee militia men died at Horseshoe Bend. However, another 154 were wounded, and many of those would die later as a result of festering wounds.

The count of Cherokee was neither noted by history, nor by the men on the field that day; for the Cherokee mourned their own, and by midday on March 28, the bodies of the Cherokee were burned along with the dead Creek.

Among the Tennessee Militia was 27 year-old officer named Sam Houston. Having been raised with the Cherokee, Houston was more Cherokee than not. He could have fought just as easily with the Cherokee warriors under Major Ridge in this famous battle. However, he'd been living with a white family in the new town of Nashville when the call had come, so he had fought with Jackson's militia forces at the barricade. His bravery was noted by Jackson, and Houston was to become Jackson's protégé. Years later, after Houston achieved fame in his own right as the Governor of Tennessee, he described the results of the battle: *"The sun was going down, and it set on the ruin of the Creek nation. Where, but a few hours before a thousand brave warriors had scowled on death and their assailants, there was nothing to be seen now but volumes of dense smoke, rising heavily over the corpses of painted warriors, and the burning ruins of their fortifications."*

With this victory, the power of the Creek nation ended forever. A few discredited Creek chiefs were found who had not fought with the British, and with these, a peace treaty was signed. As a result of fighting to preserve their land and their way of life, the Creeks in defeat lost both. They were forced to give the United States over 23 million acres of land—much of what is today western Georgia and almost all of Alabama. Moreover, this victory brought Andrew Jackson national acclaim. As a result, only fourteen years later—in 1828—he would be elected the seventh President of the United States. In an ironic twist of fate, His presidency would spell disaster for the Cherokee, and that is when Major Ridge would openly state his sorrow for having saved Jackson's life at the Battle of Horseshoe Bend.

One other man that would be noted by history fought with the Cherokee that day at Horseshoe Bend. George Gist was never a great fighter, but like all men of the frontier, he could shoot a rifle, and like most of the Cherokee, he fought with Major Ridge and the Cherokee who overtook the village from across the river. Gist would leave the field that day convinced that the Cherokee should be able to communicate with the written word; for he had seen how Jackson wrote down his plans for his other commanders, and how the Cherokee had no such tools, even though many Cherokee like Major Ridge and John Ross, did read the writing of the whites. Throughout the war, Gist had noted that he and the other Cherokees were unable to write letters home, read military orders, or record events as they occurred. He had noted many times, as he did that day at Horseshoe Bend, that the whites could communicate completely, with few misunderstandings with the written word, and he'd watched as the Cherokee commanders—Major Ridge and Captain Ross—had been left out when the main assault had been planned. He felt that the Cherokee would always be inferior unless they too developed their own version of the written word. While he had been toying with the need for literacy among his people for some time, this battle left him committed to the idea.

The Cherokee Renaissance

Between the end of the war in 1814 and 1835, the history of the lower Blue Ridge can best be described as the Cherokee Renaissance, though the seeds for the renaissance had been planted years before. George Washington, in one of the first acts of his presidency in 1789, had instituted a "civilization policy" through which native Americans, including the Cherokee in the southwest were provided looms, and encouraged to have their children learn to read in the missionary schools that were being established throughout the frontier. While many Native Americans resented this change from the old ways, most recognized that some change would come, and some, the assimilationists, gladly greeted these changes. Over time, this policy lead to the assimilation of many Indians in various tribes, but no tribe was to establish itself as well as the Cherokee. By 1814, the Cherokee were unique among native American tribes. They were allies of the United States in the recent war, and within only a few years would establish their own elected government, modeled after the United States. They would soon devise a written language, a tribal Constitution, and a solid agrarian economy that rivaled the economic output of many smaller European countries in those years. Indeed, within that time-span a new Nation—a Cherokee Nation—was created, and no other native tribe ever achieved so many steps toward developing something akin to Western civilization. It was during those years, that the Cherokee began to be referred to as the Cherokee Nation, and that terminology was eventually applied to tribes that accomplished much less in their move towards western civilization.

One leader of that Renaissance was George Gist. This man, unique in human history, invented a syllabary, which would educate scores of thousands, in less than 18 months. Gist, better known to history as Sequoyah, had been born in 1776, when his father, Nathaniel Gist, a Virginia fur trader had married Wut-the, a Cherokee maiden. The name "Sequoyah" means "Pig's Foot" in Cherokee; it was assumed for years that Sequoyah bore this name because his left hand had been partially paralyzed by some accident early in life. Others have speculated that Sequoyah might have had a subtle birth defect—some type of disability resulting from some childhood trauma. History never noted the cause of this infirmity, but like many among the disabled who are destined to greatness, this disability seems to have provided the spark in the young boy that allowed him to envision—to dream—to see things as they might be. That visionary ability subsequently allowed him to accomplish great things for his people.

With the continuing encroachment of the whites into Cherokee territory, Sequoyah had fled Tennessee in the early 1800s, settling eventually in northwestern Georgia, where he learned to work with silver. In 1809, when a local white man purchased some of his work, he requested that Sequoyah sign the work on the bottom as was the custom of silversmiths in Savannah and the other coastal cities. At that point, Sequoyah did not know how to write, so he visited another local white, one Charles Hicks, who was a successful farmer in the area.

Hicks was sitting on the front porch of his cabin, when Sequoyah walked into his yard. Several chickens scattered around the "swept yard" of the cabin as Sequoyah walked past. Swept yards—yards with only dirt showing—characterized almost every home in the nineteenth and early twentieth centuries in the western lands. Lawn grass was neither cultivated nor desired when snakes were in abundance and "lawn mowers" were still in the distant future. Thus, everyone "swept" their grassless dirt yards periodically in order to remove leaves and protect the chickens and children from snakes.

Sequoyah saw Hicks on the porch and smiled. Looking Hicks in the eye, he said, *"Charles, I could use your help this evening."* Sequoyah was a mixed blood and he knew of the ancient Cherokee tradition looking elsewhere when one spoke—of never looking others in the eye. Still, Sequoyah was also aware that whites considered it essential to look at someone directly so he adopted the "white" conversational tactic for this evening.

Charles, who knew Sequoyah as George, replied. *"I'd be happy to help, George. What's on yer mind."*

"Kinda ashamed to tell ya," George replied, *"But I don't have much schoolin' and a customer asked me to sign a silver platter I made for his wife's birthday. Could you help me out, and show me how to write my name?"*

Charles scratched his head, and said, *"Well, I guess I can show you on a piece of paper but can't you just make your mark?"* It was traditional on the frontier that, in the absence of literacy, men could "make their mark" and that would suffice as a personal signature. Some men made a large X, while others made various marks that were specific to them.

George replied, *"I could I guess, but I'd just like to sign it like they do in Savvanee and the other big towns."*

Charles then said. *"OK, I ain't got no paper, but we can write your name in the yard."*

And that is what they did. A Cherokee, son and grandson of a proud people, a spiritual people, had to ask a poor white farmer how to write his name in the dirt of the front yard. Moreover, he had to adopt the speech patterns, the language, and the cultural communication cues in order to learn his own name. Of course, the written name, "George Gist" was also a "white" name. History records that, at that specific moment, Sequoyah's attitude crystallized; At that moment, he made a life changing decision that his people needed a written language of their own. That decision was only to be reinforced by the many battles Sequoyah saw during the War of 1812, when he saw his leader, Major Ridge, relegated to an un-important battle responsibility and eliminated from receiving any written orders.

After the war, Sequoyah began in earnest to create a writing system for the Cherokee language. Initially, Sequoyah tried pictographs—symbols which were small drawings of the concepts or words that they represented. However, he soon discovered that the number of symbols in the Cherokee language would be in the thousands, and that seemed an impossible task. Next, he began to create symbols for each syllable the Cherokees used. This was the essential step in creating the syllabary.

Whereas the English language of today is "phonetic" in that various letters represent discrete sounds, the syllabary of Sequoyah was based on some phonetic symbols and some symbols that represented entire syllables of words rather than discrete letter sounds. Thus, using a sound based system for various syllables in Cherokee, after over twelve years of struggle, Sequoyah created the "Talking Leaves" of the Cherokee. The syllabary devised by Sequoyah originally contained 115 characters, but seeing some of those as unnecessary, he reduced this number to 83 by 1818. Later, three additional sounds were added bringing the number up to 86 distinctive shapes which, today, make up the Cherokee written language.

Sequoyah's first pupil was his own daughter. Tradition holds that his little girl, Eyoki, learned this syllabary with ease. Once he could communicate with her, he demonstrated the use of his syllabary to his cousin, George Lowrey. For the first demonstration of the written language, Sequoyah sent Eyoki outside, literally making her leave the cabin. He then ask Lowrey to answer a question. Next, Sequoyah wrote the answer down using the 86 symbols, and had Eyoki return and read the answer to Lowrey. Lowrey, who was completely astonished by this, encouraged Sequoyah to demonstrate the syllabary in public. When he did a similar demonstration several days later for three local chiefs, he was immediately accused of witchcraft. Several chiefs fled the scene in horror, but one or two others asked for another demonstration, and within a few weeks, Sequoyah was teaching his syllabary to their children.

Word spread quickly of Sequoyah's invention throughout the valleys and ridges of the Blue Ridge. Everywhere the Cherokee lived, the new syllabary was studied. It was quickly discovered that anyone who could speak Cherokee could learn the syllabary within two weeks! Thus, did Sequoyah's years-long struggle result in a dramatic increase in literacy within what had been a population that was almost totally illiterate. By the flickering light of the fire in the cabin fireplace, in the early evening, after the chores were done, the Cherokee—almost as one mighty family—sat together to learn to read. This scene was repeated in scores of villages, hundreds of cabins across the Blue Ridge. Within months, thousands upon thousands of Cherokee began to study the syllabary, and within only weeks they were not only reading, but teaching their children, their parents, their village to read. Within only a year, the entire tribe was reading and writing in their own language! At a time when most frontiersmen in towns like Walton's Ford, Clarkesville, or Nashville could not read, the "savage" Cherokee could do so with ease. There is no known parallel for this dramatic increase in literacy anywhere in human history, at any time, anywhere on the globe.

Not all Cherokee were pleased with this development. In fact, Sequoyah was about to learn the penalties which are frequently exacted from men of vision. After heated discussion in the council house of New Echota, Major Ridge was sent in 1820 to arrest Sequoyah for the development of the syllabary.

Major Ridge was, by that time, leading the "Lighthorse Patrol" which served as a tribal police force for the Cherokee. After the War of 1812, Ridge's leadership skills had lead him into politics within the new government of the tribe. With his "white" education, and his status as a respected plantation owner, when the government needed a leader for the newly established police force, it turned to Major Ridge.

The patrol was ordered to find Sequoyah and punish him for trying to create the syllabary. At that point, the leaders of the tribe felt that this written language was the work of the devil. The Patrol was told to find him, and force him to stop. The tribe had ordered Ridge to remove the "tops of his fingers" in order to make Sequoyah desist from writing his syllabary—a punishment which was never carried out.

Within months the tribal leadership reversed itself, and recognized the value of the syllabary. In 1821, 12 years after the original idea, the Cherokee Nation adopted Sequoyah's alphabet as their own. Later, in 1824, a gold metal was struck by the tribal leadership in Sequoyah's honor. The Cherokee were wise indeed to honor this accomplishment. In a few short years Sequoyah had achieved a means of communication that had taken other civilizations thousands of years to accomplish. While most whites missed this miracle of literacy entirely, some—mostly missionaries in the Cherokee country—noted this staggering accomplishment. For in this work, lay the seed for printing the Holy Book in Cherokee—thus could the various missionaries spread the gospel more readily throughout the Cherokee people.

That is how our chronicler, James Wyly, learned of this remarkable feat of education. Ever interested in forces that impacted the Blue Ridge, Wyly inquired of several missionaries then traveling in upstate Georgia about this growing use of the Cherokee written language, and hearing the same remarkable story—that virtually all of the Cherokee could now read their own language, he became convinced of the importance of it, as shown in his diary.

"The most remarkable man who has ever lived on Georgia soil was neither a politician, nor a soldier, nor an ecclesiastic, nor a scholar, but merely a Cherokee Indian of mixed blood. This man invented a written language and single-handedly taught his people to read. Thousands upon thousands were reading the Good Book in their

own language within only a few months. No other human in history can lay claim to so great an educational accomplishment as this. And strange to say, by his action, this Indian—Sequoyah—acquired permanent fame, neither expecting nor seeking it."

Diary of James Wyly, December 1826

The Cherokee Renaissance continued at a remarkable pace, and the accomplishments of this tribe far surpassed the accomplishments of every other tribe on the continent. First of all, the entire Cheorkee people, now much more literate than the population of the large, growing nation just to their east, supported the new national government of the Cherokee Nation. John Ross was soon elected President of the Cherokee Nation, and Major Ridge was elected as the Speaker of the House—the governing legislative body which met at the Cherokee capital of New Echota, Georgia. Moreover, a newspaper had begun for the Cherokee— the *Cherokee Phoenix*—which was printed in both English and Cherokee, using Sequoyah's 86 character syllabary.

In one of the first acts of the new government, the ancient "Blood Oath" was outlawed; many assimilationist Cherokee saw this as their final barrier to the ultimate civilization of the tribe, and were thrilled when that legislation passed, Major Ridge among them. Clearly the Cherokee had made great strides and should have been granted the respect of other peoples who move toward civilized government with such single-minded determination. No other Native American tribe in the Northern Hemisphere could boast anything remotely resembling this impressive set of accomplishments. This newly emerging nation could have provided a second democratic nation on the continent, and a worthy companion for the fledgling United States, but history was to take a different turn.

Along the Tugaloo River

During this period along the Tugaloo River, things seemed to move along peaceably into the new century. Ms. Sadie Sharp was still singing loud as you please in her church, and Devil John Cleveland, the worthless progeny of the Fat Judge, had finally expired. The Carmichaels, down on Ward's Creek seemed to breed like rabbits—so fast that you couldn't tell one generation from the next; indeed they had trouble keeping up with that themselves. The Prathers were doing quite well, though Old Tom seemed to get crazier every year. Most of the folks in Walton's Ford, along the Tugaloo River just seemed to accept that Old Tom was losing his mind—not that he ever said anything, just that he seemed to look at all the newly arriving settlers with something akin to distrust in his eye. He was gone more on his huntin' trips too. Folks began to suspect that he ran a whiskey still in the mountains someplace, and stayed drunk for days on end.

Of course, Tom did nothing to discourage that notion, but it was a total falsehood. In his extended absences, which his family still referred to as his hunting trips, he was merely living with his Cherokee relatives in the Tennessee foothills many miles to the northwest of the Tugaloo River Valley.

Yes, all in all the little settlement of Walton's Ford seemed to move from day to day, with the easy grace of an autumn leaf floating along the slowly moving Tugaloo River. The only big news in those years, was the moving of Jarrett's Store.

Devereaux Jarrett had done well, as a merchant during his younger years, on the South Carolina side of the river. By 1805, he'd moved his store from the South Carolina side, to the western bank, making him a citizen of Georgia. Early tax records indicate that he first paid taxes in Georgia on some 17 slaves, but during his first years on the west side of the river, he owned no land. Still, he'd done well for himself with those early slave purchases, since history records that slaves skilled in tanning deer hides, or blacksmithing, or carpentry were much more highly prized than mere field hands. There were times when Jarrett and James Prather traveled to Richmond, Virginia, Charleston, South Carolina—once even to London—to purchase skilled slaves. Buying and or developing talents and skills in one's slaves was farsighted, as the value of the slave increased dramatically once a skill was acquired, and Jarrett understood this better than his contemporaries. He was clearly building a long-term fortune for his young family.

In 1815 he showed just how savvy he could be when he purchased the building that was to become known as "Traveler's Rest." He paid James Wyly the princely sum of $8000, and at the time, no one could understand why a smart man like Devereaux could be taken in by Wyly. Why would anyone pay that price for a few acres and a big house? Of course everyone knew old man Wyly was cunning as a fox, since folks had finally figured out that he all but owned the Unicoi Turnpike outright! Still, time proved the whole community wrong and Devereaux Jarrett right; Traveler's Rest was to soon make him rich. For like Wyly, Jarrett knew potential when he saw it, and like Wyly, he realized that the influx of white settlers was only going to increase. He knew that when everyone is passing by, it paid to have a hotel along a busy highway, just where the newly established stage run needed to stop for the night. Thus did the land that had belonged first to the Cherokee in the days of Runs-To-Water, subsequently to Jessie Walton, then to Wyly, become the famed home of Devereaux Jarrett. It would remain in the Jarrett family for over 175 years.

However, even in those relatively peaceful years, tensions with the Cherokee ran high. In spite of the increased literacy brought about by Sequoyah's Talking Leaves, and the other accomplishments of the Cherokee Renaissance, the Cherokee were still viewed as "savages" in their own land.

James Wyly's road—the Unicoi Turnpike—became a thoroughfare opening the lower Blue Ridge and the southern slopes of the Great Smoky Mountains to settlement; for a period, the inconsequential Walton's Ford became the Gateway to the West! Thousands upon thousands of whites, mostly displaced Scotsmen and Scots-Irish, came along with their families, their Presbyterianism, their meager hopes for land of their own, and their love for sour-mash whiskey. If these families had nothing else, they had a Bible, a black-bottom kettle for making whiskey, and determination to own land, and these rugged folks with the funny Scottish names and funnier Scottish/Irish accents, were more than willing to die fighting for any one of those valued possessions.

Landing first in Philadelphia, or Charlestown, or Savannah, they headed inland quickly; for they soon saw that the good land in the coastal plains areas was taken. Still these peasants would die rather than forfeit their quest for the commodity that had driven them half-way around the world, for they longed for land of their own. When they found no land available in the flat-lands, they moved into the lower slopes of the mountains, where they claimed a patch of land—it may be land tilted at a 35° angle, but it was their land and it was tillable. When their teenage sons married some young 14 year old girl from the local church congregation, that family would settle in just up-slope of the first frontier family. By 1820 it was not uncommon to find three or four generations of frontier families living just up-slope from each other in most of the "hollers" (i.e. valleys) of the lower Blue Ridge. Land that was considered unfit for the plough by earlier settlers was cleared and tilled by the next generation, continuing on up the hill. In some cases land rising as much as forty-five degrees was cleared and ploughed. It was rumored that these folks grew their mules with two legs on one side shorter than the two on the other, so the mule could plough furrows across a steep terrain and stand straight up while doing it!

The Cherokee, meanwhile, watched this increased migration with great fear; they knew they were losing their lands, and while most Cherokee, by 1825, were "assimilationists" in outlook, even those White Cherokee feared the encroaching white tide. The Cherokee, in adapting to the dominate culture of the white man, had taken an impressive number of actions to protect themselves and to live within the growing influence of the white culture.

Still, the historical facts are repugnant, indisputable, and undeniable. In spite of the impressive, unique accomplishments of the Cherokee Renaissance, members of this tribe were subsequently treated like cattle by their white neighbors. Those neighbors would soon ignore not only Cherokee law, but the Supreme Court of the United States as well, when they began to strip the Cherokee of their land in earnest. The whites would round up the Cherokee like livestock, stealing their lands, homes, and possessions. The Cherokee would be herded into stockades where they would die by the thousands. Only the concentration camps of the Boer War in the early 1900s in Africa, or Hitler's tyranny in World War II can compare to what was done to the Cherokee. Today, we can hardly grasp such an event on American soil, but the reasons for this butchery of a race of people are clear, in the stark relief of historical hindsight.

Between 1790 and 1830 the white population of Georgia increased six-fold and that group of Scots-Irish immigrants simply swamped and overwhelmed the Cherokee. This northern and western migration—much of it passing directly through Walton's Ford, and the Tugaloo River Valley along the Unicoi Turnpike—directly threatened Cherokee lands, increasingly resulting in Cherokee attacks on whites. These new Georgians continued to take land, whenever possible. By 1825, the few Creek remaining to the south had been completely removed from the state, and the new frontiersmen turned their attention to the Cherokee.

It is a historic fact that the state of Georgia had an overly-simplistic claim on all of the land owned by the Cherokee that dated to the American Revolution, a claim that would not stand up to serious scrutiny. During the Revolution, in order to raise both funds and militia for the war effort, the state of Georgia was promised the land of all Indians who waged war against the new nation. This claim had lead to the original land grants to white veterans in the Tugaloo River Valley, and for several decades that land had been enough to satisfy the hunger of the white settlers. However, the frontier was ever moving west and northward into the Blue Ridge and Great Smoky Mountains; as the whites in Georgia demanded more land, the Georgia legislature demanded that the federal government live up to it's promise and clear the state of the savages to make the promised land available to settlers.

In 1802, Georgia became the last of the original colonies to cede its western lands—land that would become Alabama—to the federal government. At that point, everyone in Georgia expected that Indian land would be forfeited, since those Cherokee had fought against Patriots in the Revolution. However, this never took place, because the new government was busy with it's own problems and the Cherokee on the frontier did not seem that critical, so the Cherokee continued to occupy at least some of their ancestral homelands.

Still, new immigrants to Georgia continued to encroach on Cherokee lands, and in 1828 Georgia passed a law pronouncing all laws of the Cherokee Nation to be null and void after June 1, 1830. Thus, the constitution of a sovereign nation, the Cherokee Nation, was disclaimed, as were the elected government officials and all statutes passed by that government. This is the only time in history that America, a democratic nation ever acted to disestablish another freely elected government anywhere in the world.

This action was intended to force the federal government to live up to it's promise to remove the Cherokee. Further, a series of "land lotteries" were held by the government in Georgia in the 1820s and 1830s, essentially giving away land, small farms, or even family cabins that were still occupied by the Cherokee families who built them. There were many instances in North Georgia in which a white family would show up at the family cabin of a Cherokee family at dusk with the local sheriff in tow, inform the Cherokee that their cabin no longer belonged to them, and give them a generous 10 minutes to pack what possessions they could and vacate. Clearly, the Cherokee were violently angry—gunfire often erupted and some were killed on both sides. The matter would have to be addressed, in some fashion. However, two other events in the late autumn 1828 settled the fate of the Cherokee in their native homeland.

In that most beautiful of all seasons, when the radiance of the autumn color of the Blue Ridge tantalizes all with the promise of winter, two simple events doomed the Cherokee. First, Andrew Jackson—a frontiersman who hated Indians passionately, was elected President of the United States. Second, an illiterate frontiersman named Benjamin Parks tripped in a creek while hunting deer.

Gold!

He had traveled up from the lower valley near Clarkesville, Georgia, and was hunting deer near the Chattahoochee River, just off of a little stream called Duke's Creek. Even back then no one could quite recall who "Duke" was or how that particular creek got its name. Old One Eye Benny, as he was called by everyone, liked to hunt alone, since he didn't have to divide up his buckskins with anyone that way. Benjamin Parks had earned the name "One Eye" years before because he had a way of squinting when he talked to anyone, appearing to keep his left eye shut most of the time. Some of the mountain folk said it was because he spent so much time *"sightin' deer down the barrel"* of his rifle–others said *"He's jest born that-a-way!"* He called his Kentucky rifle "Deerhide" for obvious reasons; no hunter brought in more buckskins than One Eye Benny.

One Eye had been out for four days, and had collected 3 buckskins already; he planned on bartering the buckskins for powder and shot, and maybe a drop of homemade whiskey at the local tavern in Clarkesville—for there was always some sour-mash whiskey to be had in Clarkesville. The best was usually cooked up by a family named McKintyre in their barn, but several other families were just as skilled. Clarkesville usually had some of the best whiskey to be had in all of North Georgia and it made the lonely nights on the trails of the lower mountains a bit more tolerable. Old One Eye was contemplating having some this very weekend, once he got back into town.

It was late afternoon, with only an hour or so before evening, and One Eye was walking quietly on the river rocks that lined the creek bed, moving ever so slowly through the shallow water. Years of practice and the patience of Job, had taught him how to move so slowly through the water that he made neither a noise nor an extra ripple in the rushing stream. Just as he slowly rounded a bend in the creek, he saw the buck he'd been tracking along the opposite side of the creek some 40 yards distant. A 40 yard shot was child's play for his Kentucky Long Rifle—Deerhide was already primed and loaded. He slowly raised the rifle to his shoulder.

Just then, the deer, for some reason, looked the other way towards a noise in the darkening forest, giving One Eye Benny a perfect opportunity for a killing lung shot. He quietly cocked the hammer, with the rush of the cool mountain stream over the rocks covering the sound. He lived up to his name, squinting down the long barrel, as he took aim, and fired. The buck was dead before he fell to the ground, knocked a few feet by the blast.

As the large deer fell on the opposite bank, One Eye noted that this deer had a rack that sported eight points—hunters then and now estimated deer weight and size by the number of tips on the deer's antlers. This buck would yield a fine buckskin, and he'd been hunting long enough to know that he'd eat well on this deer's meat that night. Still, as he recovered from the recoil of the shot, he shifted his weight and stumbled a bit. Then, as he lowered Deerhide from his shoulder, he looked down to make certain of his footing in the cool river, and noted a shiny rock. Ignoring the deer for a moment, he thought, "*I'll take that home to my daughter Mandy,*" so he reached down to pick it up.

On such unimportant moments as this does the history of a people sometimes change—in some cases history changes for the worse. The Cherokee were to lose their land in the Georgia Blue Ridge, with that simple gesture. One Eye Benny's life was to change in that instant also, no less than that of the Cherokee. For by the time One Eye stood up, both of his eyes were wide open. He realized that he was holding a nugget of gold the size of his own thumb! His heart missed a beat and his breath caught in his chest, as he took a closer look at his find. He'd seen gold coin before, three or four times in his life, mostly in rough taverns down in Savannee when he traveled downriver to sell his skins for a better price. Once or twice some had showed up in Clarkesville. He'd once hunted as far north as Rutherfordton in the Carolina hills, and there'd been gold mining in those parts for a decade or so. He'd seen gold before so he knew that gold was firm but malleable. He next put the small nugget between two of his few remaining back teeth. Like many in the frontier, all of his front teeth were long gone, but he had a few good ones left in the back so he put that metal in his mouth and he bit down hard. It hurt like hell, and probably cost him one of his few remaining molars; for in only a moment he'd managed to inflame the infection that had taken three of his teeth in just the last several weeks. Still he was happy as a "bug in the sourmash." He was laughin' like a drunk man and, in reality he was feelin' no pain at all. By then he knew he was holding gold—the metal had given just a bit under his bite, just like it was supposed to.

With all thought of the deer now gone, One Eye Benny quickly put the inch long nugget into his pocket, and began to turn over other river stones where he stood. In that moment, when he looked for his second nugget in the little stream flowing into the Chattahoochee River, the Georgia Gold Rush—the first major gold rush in the United States—began.

Within an hour, Benny managed to find four sizable nuggets of gold, and by then the sun was setting. He determined to take what skins he had, and move overnight back towards Clarkesville, where he intended to stake a claim on this land along the creek, or to buy it from whoever owned it. He never even skinned the dead deer across the creek that night.

Two days later, once he claimed some land, his friends asked him why he wanted land so far from town when there was still plenty of land to be had much closer. One Eye Benny didn't tell them anything, so, of course, his friends and neighbors really began to talk among themselves. He'd been savvy enough to show his gold to only four folks—the local doctor who had the only scale in Clarkesville at that time—and could thus help him weigh his gold—his wife, and his younger brother. He'd also had to tell the local sheriff. He'd staked his claim with the sheriff in Clarkesville, by drawing a rough map of the area around Duke's Creek. Beginning at a sharp bend in the creek, he told how many hours he had walked from the bend of the Creek down to where it flowed into the Chattahoochee. He'd been smart enough not to try to sell the gold or spend it, and with the information held that closely by old One Eye, it took almost an hour before every single soul in Clarkesville—all 689 adult citizens—knew of the new gold strike in the Georgia Blue Ridge. As it turned out, the sheriff mentioned the gold to his wife, and One Eye's younger brother just had to tell his cousin; word spread initially in about 5 minutes.

Six hours later everyone in Walton's Ford on the Tugaloo River twenty-miles away knew of the gold strike, since Timmy Carmichael was headed back to Walton's Ford anyway, having purchased a new mule that morning in Clarkesville at the behest of his father. A flat bottom riverboat, loaded with some 1400 deerskins was just leaving the dock at Walton's Ford, when Timmy shouted the news to his cousin Seth. Now Seth, who was helping to "raft" the flat-bottom boat downriver to Augusta, Georgia, spread the news to folks on the docks in Augusta the very next night. At that point, both the deerskins and news of the gold was transferred to a steam powered riverboat, which quickly moved from the Augusta docks on down toward Savannah. Thus, folks down river in that seaport knew of the gold strike within four days of the filing of the claim.

The local Savannah paper, in the total absence of facts, printed the many rumors that had spread around the docks about the Gold Strike on Duke's Creek off the Chattahoochee River the following day. Thus, in just over a week, almost everyone in Charleston, South Carolina, New Bern, North Carolina, Norfolk, Virginia, Philadelphia, Pennsylvania, not to mention most of the port cities in the Caribbean, knew of the gold strike in the Georgia mountains. Those were the towns that traded most heavily with Savannah, Georgia, and as soon as word spread—given the oft lamented lure of the rich yellow metal—many persons in each of those cities began packing their bags, to head to the goldfields, where everyone was certain you could merely *"bend down and pick up gold!"* Some were on the trail within 48 hours of hearing the news, heading toward the new gold strike in Georgia—the paper from Savannah said you could pick the gold up in almost any mountain creek! They knew that thousands of folks were heading to the same destination because the papers from Savannah said so!

Of course, upon arriving in the North Georgia mountains, many of these would be prospectors, quite simply got lost. It seemed that no one was quite sure where the correct stream was, and some ended up panning worthless creeks well into the lower hills of South Carolina some 75 miles from the gold rich mountains of Georgia. Most, however, did manage to find the Chattahoochee River. Still, even with all the excitement and directional confusion, and a steady stream of whites pouring into the Cherokee region, no one cared about finding the "right" stream. Within three weeks placer gold was found in many other tributaries in and around Duke's Creek.

Now placer gold is most often comprised of pen-head size, light flakes that have broken off the main gold vein and been carried downstream by the river currents over thousands of years. Thus, placer gold could be had with only a cooking pan, a streambed, and a steady determination. Of course, finding placer gold in a streambed generally meant that every single prospector wanted to follow the stream up to find the "gold mountain" which hosted the rich veins from which the placer gold had come.

Within the year the easy placer gold was taken, and the miners began looking deeper into the earth. By 1829, with a steady stream of 29'ers still arriving, gold claims on creeks that had actually produced some gold were becoming increasingly difficult to find. A few still discovered a few flakes of placer gold; of course others didn't.

Some of the 29'ers, after arriving in the gold fields and looking over the situation, were quick to realize that their fortune lay not in the stream beds but in the towns that quickly grew in the gold county. Towns seemed to spring up almost overnight in the winter of 1829 and early 1830—Auraria, Dahlonega, White Path, Gainesville, Jackson Camp, Tiger, Clayton, all sprung up around the streams that held the gold. Some of these towns are gone now, but others survive as small mountain communities today. In 1829, however, these towns represented not only the goldfields with the roughest, meanest, most ornery citizens to be found in the entire USA, but also the frontier of that period. Like the boom towns of the far west in the later part of the 1800s, these Georgia Gold Rush towns sprung up overnight, moving from a few ramshackle tents housing rough, uncouth men, to substantial houses of trade within just a couple of weeks. James Wyly, ever the keen observer, noted the dramatic growth of these gold rush towns.

"I was amazed at the rapidity of the growth of these inhospitable places. After only

*a few months of a tent city, real towns seemed to spring forth from the very Earth!
In a few short weeks, where nothing had been previously, stores could be found where
a miner might buy his kit—shovel, pan, and perhaps a little coffee and a few beans.
Saloons, brothels, and the ever present assayer's shack rounded out the early settlement.
A few houses were put up by shopkeepers, but most tended to live in the back or on the
second floor of the shops. Of course whiskey and women were the main commodities for
sale, since these were the commodities that the ungentlemanly rogues from the gold filled
creeks really wanted. Any visitor would note that these commodities were immediately
available on any corner of any of the towns. Finding a church anywhere near the gold
fields, however was quite a bit more difficult, as no true man of the cloth would have
dared proselytize in so horrid a place.*

*The only saving grace I find in these rough settlements is the increased trade brought
to the Unicoi Turnpike, as my tolls have increased mightily."*

Diary of James Wyly, June 1831

Five Men Spend an Evening Together

It was in this rough early gold-rush period when Major Ridge determined to
get a sense of what was happening. As a leader in the new Cherokee Nation, he felt
it to be his duty to understand what was happening in the gold fields; for he and
many others quickly realized that this development threatened their new nation,
even more than the whites who merely wanted to steal Cherokee land for farming.
Thus, on March 18, 1830, five men spent an evening together, sitting on a slope
just above one of the original gold claims on Dukes Creek. That evening, three
uncouth and uneducated white men would share their limited thoughts on the
gold rush and the threat of the Cherokee, and two old Cherokee warriors would
glean an education.

The three white men sat near a camp only 15 feet from the rushing mountain
water; the two Cherokee warriors were 20 feet up the steep slope, flat on the
ground. The white men were talking about their early claim on the gold lots.
Chester Carmichael, a member of that ill defined Carmichael clan of the Tugaloo,
sat with his back against a large pine tree, warming his hands toward the fire,
against the coolness of the evening. Chester was a fat man, who nevertheless could
work a ten hour day pannin' the creek, and then tell stories until all hours of the
night. He could eat a horse and drink most men under the table, but he put that
aside when he was in the gold fields at his diggin's. On that particular evening, he
spoke up first; *"Recon' we'll need to do some diggin' soon; we panned nearly all the
placer we'll ever git from this damned sand. Ain't but so much sand down there, and
I recon we's re-panin behind ourselves."* Chester had hit on a sore point for many
miners. No miner wanted to re-pan the same sand, since he'd already found any
possible placer flakes from that pan full of creek-bottom sand the first time, if he'd

done it right.

Old One Eye Benny sat beside him. *"Jest make damn sure that you keep to your side of the line on this creek. I'd hate to have to bust you a new eye with Deerhide!"* Benny laughed at his own joke, and Chester smiled with him.

Able Ward smiled too, as he puffed his clay pipe filled with sweet tobacee from Carolina. He said, *"Don't you rile him, One Eye. Chester has two eyes and he's a better shot than you."* At that crack the three friends all laughed together.

It was not uncommon for the gold claim lots of the day to stretch only a hundred feet along any particular stream, since so many 29er's had crowded into the area so quickly. While all these men worked their claims during the day— sun up to sun down—many retired to the nearby tent camp during the evening; towns such as Auraria and Dahlonega sprang up seemingly overnight. There they bought women for 15 minutes at a stretch, or whiskey for a penny a glass—paid for, of course, by placer gold held on account. Some purchased both on Saturday evenings when they'd panned enough out that week. Others, like these three, knew each other well enough to just camp next to their adjacent claims along Duke's Creek. In fact, Chester had heard about the gold strike from his cousin Timmy Carmichael on the day after the find. That is how he'd managed to stake a claim to a hundred foot lot right next to One Eye Benny's original claim. Able Ward, on the other hand, had purchased his claim from another man who'd rushed to the gold field early, staked a claim along Duke's Creek, but given up and sold his claim within two months.

These men were comfortable with each other, and that meant that they were comfortable in their bawdry—sometimes gross comedy—as well as their long silences together. While none got rich in the gold fields—including old One Eye who'd first discovered the gold, each would sell his gold lot claim well within a year or so and make more cash than he'd ever had before. Still on this night, they sat in silence for a while, contemplating what the next day's pannin' might bring, and thinking of the weekend of women and whiskey they were likely to enjoy. One Eye and Able tended to settle in to the life of the gold fields for months at a time, but Chester Carmichael usually traveled on weekends, back to Ward's Creek near Walton's Ford along the Tugaloo. There he could spend an evening with his wife, and his old pappy was known to make the best sour-mash along the Tugaloo. He figured he could save his placer gold and still enjoy the coming Saturday evening at home where he paid for neither whiskey nor the company of a good woman.

There they sat, three friends and colleagues enjoying the silence of the Georgia Blue Ridge in the evening by the campfire; they were certain that they were quite alone.

Less that 20 feet away from the three white men sat a ghost who was either a white man or a red man, depending upon whatever mood struck him. Ekaia, the ghost of the Cherokee, was now well over 80. He still spent a limited number of months each year as "Old Tom Prather," the slightly crazy patriarch of the Prather Plantation along the Tugaloo River. When he was with his white family, he was now barely tolerated, and certainly not really consulted on matters of importance to the family or the plantation. His white wife was long since dead, and while his oldest son, James Wallace Prather, still showed him grudging respect, James was now clearly the leader of the growing Prather clan, having married well and produced grown sons himself. Old Tom was considered something of a senile old creature by most of the growing white population along the Tugaloo, and thus Ekaia felt little remorse slipping into his Cherokee life more and more as the years went by. Of course, that perception by the whites of Old Tom Prather's craziness served as a disguise that was both more believable and more effective than any other disguise imaginable. More often than not, Ekaia spent his time "hunting" for long periods—and most of that he spent with the Cherokee. In spirit, he had all but abandoned his white family–the Prathers of Walton's Ford—since with the Cherokee he was respected as a great warrior and hunter—he'd become an honored elder in the Cherokee settlements to the west.

His forest skills had not deserted him—indeed he was more adept in the woods now than he'd been as a younger man. One would never have seen him nestled behind and slightly above the three white men just down the slope from him. Thus, once Major Ridge determined to visit the gold fields to see for himself what was happening, it was quite natural for him to consult with Ekaia—the legendary tracker of the Cherokee and his longtime mentor and friend. Together, they decided to look over what the white men were doing to the mountain streams that nourished the Cherokee. When these two phantoms of the forest—each a veteran Cherokee warrior—had smelled the smoke of the distant campfire, they'd slowly slithered near to hear what could be heard from these white men. They listened for a few hours that evening, and the white men below never realized they were there.

Of course, both Ekaia and Ridge were quite comfortable in "white cloths" and had sported them for years when dealing with whites in the white world. When in their white garb, each was considered an aristocrat by others in white society. Each now held title to more land than any of the three white men just down the slope would ever dream of. Each of these Cherokee could read, cipher, do accounts for a large plantation, and each held ownership of scores of black slaves. Still, in their hearts they were Cherokee.

Either of these Cherokee could have donned their "white man's clothes" and approached any of these three men just down the slope some afternoon, and then merely inquired about the gold fields, but who knows if that tactic would result in the truth? Ridge and Ekaia had decided it was better to see for themselves what was happening in the early days of the Georgia Gold Rush, and listen in a bit. They sat in silence so profound that not even animals in the forest detected their presence until they approached within one or two feet of the perfectly still warriors. The Cherokee listened to see what they could learn.

Just down the slope, Chester stretched his arms, and grabbed at the lice that infested his armpit—the Carmichaels were never known for cleanliness. He scratched without thinking about it. *"Ready for bed I recon. Don't know how long I can stand sleeping here on this pile of damn river rocks, pannin' for nothing!"*

Able piped up at that point. *"Find you a nugget the size of your pee-wee, and you'll hush up about the sleeping arrangements out here."*

Each of them laughed at that, and not to be outdone, Chester replied, *"Yea, but if we find one that big, it'll take a buckboard to get it into Dahlonega!"* Chester thus showed the usual modesty of the Carmichael clan. In his mind, his manhood was never in question, and a gold nugget as large as his manhood would definitely involve a serious transportation challenge! He laughed loudly at his own joke.

One Eye took a more thoughtful approach. *"Don't bitch so much about sleeping out here. Question is, are we sleepin' in the right spot? I think this section's about played out. We'll need to move up the creek and find a spot that ain't claimed yet to see any more yeller in this damn stream."*

Chester replied. *"I don't know about that. Some feller in Dahlonega the other day was talking up this "water cannon" idea. Said to stake your claim, pan out the creek, then wash the hillside away through a slew that does the pannin' for ya."*

The water cannons were the next step in mining after all the placer gold had been "struck." The water cannons fired a steady stream of high pressure water at the mountainside, flushing the resulting mud–and possibly some gold—down pannin' troughs and into the creeks of the Blue Ridge. From the 1830s through the 1840s, many a mountainside was washed into the creeks throughout the mountains, leaving horrible scars on the land the Cherokee considered sacred. In contrast, the whites realized—even if the Cherokee didn't—that the placer was the easy stuff to find, and after it was gone, you had to get serious with the mountains that hid your gold.

This water-cannon idea quieted the three down a bit, but only for a moment. *"You really gonna try a cannon? Don't you think they's creekside that-a-way that ain't been claimed, just waitin' to be panned?"* Able asked, as he waved his arms vaguely toward the higher mountains to the north and west.

One Eye said, *"I'll bet there's nothin left to claim up further, at least not 'till you hit Cherokee country."* At this, he spit into the fire, and reconsidered. *"Hell, we's probably in Cherokee country now!"*

Able took another drag off his clay pipe, enjoying the cool feel of the smoke in his throat. He said, *"What damn difference does that make? Most of 'um are so drunk you can take their cabins, their women, or their land for the price of a bottle."*

At that comment, the two warriors up the slope merely looked deeply into each other's eyes with sadness. Each knew that there was some truth in that cruel statement; for each had witnessed that truth many times; such was the present condition of the once mighty Cherokee.

One Eye continued the thought. *"Yea, I don't think the Cherokee are long for this earth, what with old Andy Jackson getting those damned Washington dandies shaped up pretty soon."*

Able continued the thought. *"You're ignorant most times, but you sure are right about that. Old Hickory hates Indians more'n most, and he'll kick 'um all out right proper soon enough—he'll kick 'um out or kill um."*

Only a very few times in anyone's life does one's future become crystal clear, but that statement was such a moment for these Cherokee warriors; that statement sounded like the death songs after a great battle to both of the Cherokee on the slope of the hill above Duke's Creek that night. Once again, for a long, sad moment, Ekaia looked into the eyes of his old friend on the dark mountain slope beside him. Then seeing the pain, despair, and embarrassment, on his friend's face, he diverted his eyes. Neither had said a word, but both knew they'd heard prophetic words from this ignorant, smelly white man. The Cherokee were doomed in the lower Blue Ridge, doomed by the curse of the gold in the creeks and river bottoms. More personally, as Ridge reflected on it, his heart ached for saving Jackson's life so many years before at Horseshoe Bend. At that moment, he wished for the wisdom of his father, Stands-Tall, or his grandfather Runs-To-Water. This night, he would pray to ask their help and guidance.

Only a few moments later, the whites let the fire die down and bedded down for the evening. Chester stood and walked a few feet towards Ekaia to pee, and the stream of yellow urine reached to within three feet of the totally immobile Cherokee warrior sitting behind the next rhododendron bush. Chester, content to relieve himself in what he thought was a private spot well away from the campfire, never saw this famed ghost of the Cherokee. He returned to the fire and bedded down under his bear skin blanket, like his friends. In an hour, Ridge and Ekaia crawled off, having never spoken a word to each other, but having glimpsed their fate as surely as if they had glimpsed their own death.

The Politics of Theft

Able Ward had been right that night in the early months of 1830 in the Georgia Gold Fields along Duke's Creek. Andy Jackson hated Indians, and once he became President, he moved as soon as he could to *"Kick 'um out or kill 'um."* In some ways, this new President appeared to be different from those who came before. Whereas all of the previous Presidents had been aristocratic planters from the original colonies—indeed a majority of the Presidents to date had been from only one state—Virginia, this rough frontiersman was the first man from a western state. Jackson was the first "Man of the people" type politician to move into the

White House. While he, like the previous presidents was a landed aristocrat, he played on his background in the Tennessee country, and his Indian fighting skills. He was the first presidential candidate in history to present himself as a "common man," and thus he began a trend in presidential politics which would continue, off and on, for at least two hundred years. Of course, this image was a myth in some respects—Jackson was quite wealthy, holding title to a major plantation near Nashville, Tennessee. Still, this "common man" myth won Jackson the Presidency in 1828.

In one respect however, this Jackson frontiersman persona was accurate; unlike the previous Presidents, Jackson did not have as fine an educational background as had some of his predecessors. He was not widely lettered like Adams or Jefferson, and his thoughts had neither the depth nor the wisdom of Madison, Monroe, or Washington. Rather he was born of the frontier west, and he was raised fighting the savages on the frontier. He liked his whiskey from a sourmash still, rather than some fancy bottle from London or Paris, just like the rowdy Westerners who elected him. Thus, the common frontiersman could relate to Jackson's background, and would be willing to overlook the fact that he had done well with his plantation. These rowdy men of the growing American frontier sensed that Jackson was one of them. This affiliation was in evidence during Jackson's first inauguration; Washington society was scandalized when home-made whiskey rather than a nice foreign wine was served at the Inaugural Ball in the White House, and for the first and only time in history, various frontiersmen actually swung from the chandeliers in the main hallway of the White House! Clearly, someone different was in the Presidency now!

After the drunken brawl which celebrated Jackson's inauguration, this President soon got down to business. In late 1830, under the urging of the Jackson administration, the Congress of the United States began debate of the "Indian Removal Act" one of the most blatantly bigoted pieces of legislation ever debated in Congress. While many on the frontier favored the enforced removal of all Indians east of the Mississippi River, others saw this legislation for what it really was—a license to steel land and gold.

The Georgia delegation, to a man, favored passage of the act. Georgia harbored many more Cherokee than any other state—a fact little recognized in today's world—and the Georgia citizenry wanted the land and the gold fields. Many Georgians believed that the United States Congress should have kicked out the Cherokee back in 1780s like they had promised after the Revolutionary War.

However, many other Americans were against the act, most notably a new Tennessee Congressman named David Crockett. Crockett was already quite popular in Washington society. In an era when "Indian fighters" were worshiped in the national press, Crockett was a living legend. As a protege of Andy Jackson, Crockett was clearly the favored son of the sitting President, and that commanded attention then, as it does today. Moreover, beginning with Jackson, such frontiersmen routinely became Presidents between 1820 and 1850. It would not have been unlikely for a man with a national reputation such as Crockett's to have eventually succeeded to that office, given Jackson's backing.

However, Crockett surprised everyone in Washington—most importantly Jackson himself—when he decided to fight against the Indian Removal Act. As much as it shocked everyone, Crockett was willing to risk his own future to try and defend the Cherokee! During this lively debate in Congress, Crockett's love of the Cherokee was apparent as he fought this legislation at every turn. At one point, he shouted to his fellow Congressmen in the halls of the House of Representatives itself to *"Leave the Cherokee the hell alone!"*

As his debate tactics were derided by his colleagues, Crockett held firm, knowing that this travesty of legislation would mark a low point in history for the United States. He was heard to comment, *"I would sooner be honestly damned than hypocritically immortalized."* As the debate in Congress raged on, he fought the removal of the Cherokee with every ounce of his being, convinced that this moral outrage would be a black mark on the history of the new, experimental democracy. In the end his efforts were to no avail. Jackson's mandate was too strong, and this immoral and cruel legislation was passed through Congress and signed into law.

With his future in politics destroyed when he crossed political swords with Andrew Jackson in the White House, Crockett chose not to run again for Congress; for Jackson was also a Tennessee man and his friends in that state could easily sabotage Crockett's re-election. By supporting the Cherokee and fighting against this law, this one-time Indian fighter stands before the alter of history as a man who voted his conscience, and he paid a dear price for that single vote. He could not accept the forced removal of his beloved Cherokee and for that view, he was to leave national politics forever. However, as a man possessing honor, courage, and a conscience, he soon found other historically worthy endeavors. As he left national politics, he shouted a final time to his congressional colleagues; *"You can all go to hell! I'll be going to Texas!"*

And that is just what he did! History records that only six years later, Crockett was immortalized while fighting for Texas independence; He died covered in glory with the other Texas heroes in the Battle of the Alamo.

Even after losing Crockett as an advocate, the Cherokee attempted to fight their removal legally by challenging the federal law and various state law courts. John Ross, the elected Principal Chief of the Cherokee Nation brought suit against the United States in a case that quickly moved all the way to the U.S. Supreme Court. In 1832 that court ruled in favor of the Cherokee in Worcester v. Georgia. This decision meant that the state of Georgia could not issue land lotteries to give away Cherokee farms, cabins, or territory because the Cherokee were an independent nation, and could not be removed from their land without a treaty approved by Congress. Specifically, Chief Justice John Marshall ruled that the Cherokee Nation was sovereign, making most of the removal laws in all of the related states completely invalid. Thus, in 1832 the executive—President Jackson—and the judicial branch of government—Marshall and the Supreme Court—were at loggerheads over the removal of the Cherokee.

President Jackson solved his thorny constitutional problem by merely ignoring it. One evening in the oval office itself when consulting with his cronies and kicking back with some fine Tennessee sour-mash whiskey, Jackson was heard to render his final thought on the matter; *"Marshall has granted his ruling; now let him enforce it!"* Of course, enforcement of the law was, by constitutional mandate, the job of the President, and it was Jackson's duty to enforce the court's decision. Nevertheless, with the legislation already passed, and the wheels of motion for the removal already turning, Jackson did nothing to enforce the ruling of the highest court in the land, and the Cherokee removal went forward, in total disregard and abandonment of the Constitution.

Who would ever believe that such a miscarriage of justice was possible? Certainly most Cherokee ignored the ruling, knowing that it could not stand. Still, by 1835 the Cherokee were divided and despondent. Most supported Principal Chief John Ross, who fought the encroachment of whites. However, a vocal minority—perhaps 500 or 1000 Cherokee in the Georgia Blue Ridge—followed Major Ridge who advocated for removal.

One may well ask how had Ridge come to this unlikely position? How had the traditional Cherokee warrior who had once hated all white faces, come to believe that the Cherokee should give up their homeland? How had the man whose father and grand-father had died before the guns of the whites, decided to yield his plantation without remorse? Clearly, for Major Ridge, this would have caused great psychological conflict; in fact this decision would have been particularly painful on many levels. First, he knew he stood to lose all of this land holdings (which were substantial) not to mention his 64 slaves, if he removed himself to the Oklahoma territories as the government demanded. Perhaps more importantly, however, he would have needed to believe that he was leading his people in the right direction. One may only guess how many hours he agonized over this decision, in tortured self-examination and debate. He clearly debated this again and again with his peers in the Cherokee government.

Unfortunately, today we can only surmise his thoughts. While he was a lettered man, he was not a writer. We have no public papers or letters from Major Ridge; we have no diaries revealing his innermost thoughts, nor even any reflections on his inner debates from his contemporaries. In the absence of firm evidence, we can make only one conjecture; we can state that he was a man who was at home in two different worlds—that of the assimilated Cherokee, owner of a plantation, successful businessman—and that world of the traditional Cherokee warrior. We may also note that, typically, persons at home in two such diverse worlds, tend to be completely comfortable in neither.

Ridge was aware that, over the last few decades, many Cherokee had chosen to move to the lands west of "the Big River"—the Mississippi. Nor were the Cherokee the only tribe to be moved; the remaining Creek, the few Catawba left, and many others were likewise to be moved into the new Indian Territory. Still, there were many more Cherokee that would be transplanted, and today, we mistakenly think of this bleak period as impacting only the Cherokee. At some point, Major Ridge decided—and apparently truly believed—that such a move held the only hope for Cherokee survival. He remembered the words of Dragging Canoe many years before in the council house, and he never forgot that night along Duke's Creek, when he'd heard the words of an ignorant white man spell out the fate of the Cherokee so clearly. Thus, it is reasonable to assume that he advocated removal for one simple reason—he saw it as the only way his people could survive.

In this fashion did Major Ridge, while serving as the Speaker of the House in the Cherokee government, begin negotiating a treaty with the federal government for removal of the Cherokee tribe. This group, soon to be known as the "Treaty Party" included Ridge, his son John, and several other Cherokee Chiefs. Acting in defiance of the Principal Chief John Ross, they signed the *Treaty of New Echota* in 1835. Despite the majority opposition to this treaty among the Cherokee, the traditional homelands of the tribe in Georgia and Tennessee were sold to the United States Government for $5 million dollars. By treaty, the Cherokee agreed to move beyond the Mississippi River to the Oklahoma territory. In that document lay the death of the Cherokee Nation.

That treaty, even though it was supported by only a small minority of the Cherokee, gave Jackson the legal document he needed to remove the tribe to the distant west. The quick ratification of the treaty by a single vote in the United States Senate sealed the fate of the Cherokee. The treaty required the Cherokee to move within two years. General Winfield Scott and an army of 7000 men rounded up the Cherokee in 1838; by the fall the last of the Cherokee were ordered from their cabins, into concentration camps, to prepare to be force marched to the West. Thus began one of the darkest days in American history.

History records that none of the promises within the Treaty of New Echota were kept. Even the provisions required for such a journey across a third of a continent were not provided to the Cherokee. It is enough to note here that on this trek, many of the brave, though vanquished Cherokee froze to death or starved; they died by the thousands.

The "Trail Where They Cried"
1838 – by the European Calendar.

She was a beauty, and was universally loved by all. Like a distant ancestor whom she would never know, she was named Akala, and she was lovely, in the way that only the pure blood Cherokee of that period could be lovely. She had an olive skin, the color of which complimented the rough lightly tan homespun cloth dresses worn by most Cherokee girl-children of that period. She had a large rounded face, that seemed to suggest a peaceful countenance. Her hair was rich and full, falling far past her shoulders. She sported a pug nose that was sassy but subtly so, and she had large slightly rounded, highly expressive eyes. Her eyes were shadows of mystery, tantalizingly dark and yet naively nonjudgmental. Still, all the elders of the tribe had the sense that when this child looked toward them, a wiser, much older person was conducting an in-depth examination of their personality. Her easy demeanor matched her beauty; for she was a young Cherokee angel of sweet disposition, ever willing to help others in a way that was characteristic only of much older children or adults. She was the youngest daughter of Major Ridge, and Ridge had chosen to name her after the first wife of his famous grandfather, Runs-To-Water. Of course, Akala had heard the legends of her ancestors—Runs-To-Water and Stands-Tall, all her life—though the mention of the first wife of Runs-To-Water was not shared by legend, so this child did not know the origin of her own name. Ridge had never shared that with her, for some reason known only to himself.

This amazing young girl was only nine when she survived hell. With her father, her mother, and two brothers, one younger and one older, she made the overland trek which, in the Cherokee tongue, was called *Nunna daul Tsuny.* In translation this term roughly meant the "Trail Where They Cried," but history would record this shameful episode as the Trail of Tears.

Like the Bataan Death March, the Rape of Nanking, the slow, steady westward migration of American slavery, the Cultural Revolution of China, or the Holocaust, the Trail of Tears would, in perpetuity, teach all mankind of our common tendency towards unimaginable cruelty. Images of Cherokee women and children, walking without moccasins through snow as they starved to death—having been promised provisions that never arrived—can only tear at our heart today. She lived those long days—never realizing in her child's mind, that her life could be or ever would be more than this dismal daily travel amid so much despair and hopelessness.

Akala and her family were in the first overland group, traveling the longer route to the Indian territories in present day Oklahoma early during this trek. Today, in the modern mind, the Trail of Tears is thought of as unified journey in which all the Cherokee, Creek and others traveled westward one large group—that is not the case. There were sixteen different groups to make that trek—many taking different routes, and some groups fared better than others. The group in which the family of Major Ridge traveled, was one of the more deadly of the various treks that together make up the Trail of Tears.

Major Ridge, by 1838, was known to be a respected leader who truly felt that the future of the Cherokee lay to the west. He determined in that year that he and his family would move from their beloved plantation. He realized that he would lose all of his work, in clearing the land, and extending his fields on his Georgia plantation, but he did determine to sell his slaves prior to his departure. Thus, would he have some funds in reserve for beginning his new home in the west beyond the great river. Ridge knew that this was terribly unfair—losing many of his holdings to several white families with no compensation at all, but he realized that with the reserve funds he would be better off than many Cherokee.

Initially, to effect the round-up in an orderly fashion, General Scott had thirty one forts constructed to house the Cherokee, thirteen in Georgia, five in North Carolina, eight in Tennessee, and five in Alabama. All of these forts were near Cherokee towns, but they served only as temporary housing for the Cherokee. While the forts offered some comforts—such as close proximity to their home, those comforts were not to last. Within the month, the Cherokee were transferred from the removal forts to eleven larger internment camps that were more centrally located—most were located over the Blue Mountains in the southeastern part of Tennessee. The Cherokee were rounded up from the valleys and hillsides of the Southern Blue Ridge, just as they were rounded up in the Tennessee Country, the hills of the Carolina's and Virginia. Men, women, and children were herded into makeshift forts, most of which were little more than cattle pens.

While many today associate the Trail of Tears with the beautiful eastern slopes of the Blue Ridge in the Carolinas, most of the Cherokee who made that famous journey came from the state of Georgia. While Tennessee, Virginia, and North Carolina each contributed between 1000 and 2000 Cherokee to this debacle, over 8000 were rounded up in the cattle pens of North Georgia, more Cherokee on the Trail of Tears came from their homes in Georgia, than from all of the other states combined. By late July of 1838, with the exception the fugitives hiding in the mountains, and some distant scattered families that had been overlooked, virtually all the Cherokees, some 16,000 to 18,000 individuals of all ages, were in the internment camps.

While sixteen different groups totaling over 16,000 Cherokee began the journey, only about 9,000 would arrive. This was to become the most deadly, and the most shameful, traveling genocide in the Western Hemisphere. While most walked the entire trek, some of the groups made part of the journey by boat under equally horrible conditions; all knew hunger.

Private John G. Burdett, one of General Scott's men serving in North Georgia, could read and write, making him somewhat unique for the lower ranks of the army in which he served, and his papers have survived. Of course, almost every Cherokee on the trek could read and write, but none had the materials to do so, and we have no Cherokee written accounts that date from the actual trek itself. Burdett's papers are critical for history since they can be trusted as accurate. While most officers on that march had some education and some wrote accounts of the trek, their writings may have been colored by their career goals, whereas the written words of a lowly private like Burdett may be taken to heart. *"I seed the Cherokee arrested, dragged from their homes, and driven at bayonet point into the stockades. In the chill of a dampin' rain come an October morning I saw them loaded like cattle or sheep into six hundred and forty-five wagons and started toward the west. Most broke down, given no real trail to the west, so then the Cherokee walked. On the morning of November the 17th a terrific sleet and snow storm come up with freezing temperatures. From that day until we reached the end of the fateful journey on March the 26th, 1839, the suffering of the Cherokees was an awful sight to see. The trail of the exiles was a trail of death. They had to sleep in the few wagons that didn't break down, or sleep on the wet ground without a fire. I have seen as many as twenty-two of 'um to die in one night; mostly of pneumonia, or ill treatment. Some simply died in the cold."*

Clearly for this barely literate soldier, this trek was a moral outrage. Despite the promises of food and shelter, human losses among the first groups on the journey were so high that Chief John Ross made an urgent appeal to General Scott, requesting that the general let his people lead the tribe west, rather than be escorted by the army. General Scott agreed, and Ross then organized the Cherokee into smaller groups and let them move separately through the wilderness along the way so they could forage for a bit of food. In spite of leaving in the fall, with the prospect of winter coming, the parties under Ross fared better than did the earlier groups. The last Cherokee arrived in Oklahoma during the brutal winter of 1839, cold and starving. Still under Ross' leadership, most of the later groups arrived alive.

While one death may be tragic, death in the hundreds, the thousands, or the millions, seems to become merely a statistic in the human mind. Neither the soldier's writings from the period, nor the horrid numbers of deaths from this tragic journey tell the true horror, so perhaps we should let the Cherokee people themselves tell the tale. There is a Cherokee account, written long after the fact. This horrible experience was remembered many years later, by that same Akala—that beautiful nine year old girl-child of Major Ridge. Some sixty nine years later, her mind was still sharp and her memories were still vivid, they seemed alive in the eyes of the old woman. In the oft' under-stated way of the ever modest Cherokee, Akala told her tale to her great-granddaughter, who in the 1907 wrote it down. That granddaughter was my grandmother—and thus was this personal story of that tragedy preserved for history—one of the few written accounts by a

Cherokee on the Trail of Tears. Sitting by a log fire in a cabin on the distant plains of Oklahoma, one evening in the early Spring of 1907, Akala was in her seventy-eighth year, as she told the tale for the final time. She would die in June of that year, before the Green Corn Festival.

"One day was much like the others. I was a little girl, who liked to run and play, and as long as I had dried fish, or deer, corn or beans to eat I was happy. My mother carried a small basket of dried corn on her head for the entire journey, and that saved our family—for the fish or dried deer meat quickly ran out, but we had dried corn to eat when others had nothing. I still have the basket.

I did not know at first that so many were dying. We followed creeks and rivers when we could and we children played in the water, until we had to run to catch up to our mothers. Near the creeks and rivers we could get water, and sometimes our old warriors could shoot a deer or a bear.

I remember we woke up each day, and had to eat whatever was left from the night before, since we were not allowed by the soldiers to make cooking fires. Morning cooking fires would slow us down, since there were so many of us that we had to walk many miles just to gather wood for the fires. We were allowed to cook only every other day, and then only in the evening when we finished walking, and then only if we had gathered wood along the way.

Every morning, we began to walk before the sun rose in the sky. We ate our first meal of the day walking. Usually, we had a few bites of dried meat to eat—sometimes dried fish or some dried beans; sometimes just the corn. We drank water from the creeks and rivers. What we had was what we brought; the soldiers never gave us anything to eat. Each night we slept below the stars, using several blankets that my older brother carried in a bundle on his back.

Each morning, my father, Major Ridge, would mount his pony, and with his oldest son, John, he would move to the head of the line, with the soldiers; For a Chief did not walk, and warriors such as my father and my brother had to be ever prepared to ride off to defend the tribe.

We had almost 30 soldiers riding beside us on the rough trail—their job was to keep us moving. Some said that the soldiers had wagons full of food, but I never saw those—if there were wagons of food, they were many miles behind where I walked. The soldiers had taken most of our rifles so that we could not escape.

By this time, most of our warriors did not know the ways of the bow or the blowgun any longer and they could not hunt at all without rifles. However, my father kept his rifle, as did some of the other older chiefs that the soldiers trusted; sometimes they brought down a deer to eat.

I remember one day, many days into the journey, an old woman decided to walk away. The path we followed went down to the river, but this woman walking in the group in front of me, turned and walked into a valley heading to the North. Now I was walking with a group of other children, and we called to her, "Mother, we walk this way, not to the North," but she just turned, waved goodbye, smiled, and resumed her walk. One young toonali ran to get his mother to come and help guide the old woman back to the path—we thought she was just confused. But the mother, merely said, "Let the old woman walk away if she wants. Maybe she will find food.

I never saw that old woman again. It was said she died in the forest. We were always passing many beside the path who were just too tired to walk anymore. Some were dead already, but others would die soon. All merely died where they fell.

We walked on, day after day, and after a time, the children no longer played together as we had at first. By the time we passed near the town of Nashville, I knew everyone was hungry; I was hungry. One of the women wanted to make a winter camp on the high bluff along the river, and send the men out on their traditional winter hunt, but the soldiers would not allow that—they said we had to keep moving, since we had not moved west earlier when we had been told to.

I remember then when the flower first appeared along the trail that fall. Along that river in the Tennessee country, a type of flower grew, that I will always remember—it is called the Cherokee Rose. The rose is white, and in our legends that color represents the tears of the Cherokee Mothers—the mothers cried because they gave no milk to their young children; their breasts had no milk to give because they walked all day with nothing to eat themselves. Many watched their children die in their arms, and had to abandon the dead bodies along the trail with no burial and no death songs. The flower has a gold center that represents the gold that the whites stole from the Cherokee lands in the Blue Mountains. That gold killed our People. The flower has seven leaves on each stem, and these represent the seven Cherokee clans that made the terrible journey. The mothers of the Cherokee grieved so much for their children that the chiefs—lead by my father—prayed for a sign to lift the mother's spirits.

I do not know if he prayed to Jesus or to the Great Spirit Kanati, but it helped. That day God gave the Cherokee mothers new strength to care for their children; that same day, God made the first Cherokee Rose. From that day to this, a beautiful new white and gold flower grew wherever a mother's tear fell to the ground, or wherever a Cherokee child died."

After exhaustive research I discovered that my ancestor, Major Ridge—my family's patriarch—and his family traveled in the second overland group, not the first, though he may have believed he was among the first. The records indicate that his group included some 2800 Cherokee. In that early group, 1931 Cherokee made it into Oklahoma; over eight hundred died, including one young son of Ridge, and his wife of many years. Ridge reached the new lands in Oklahoma with only his remaining children, including his small daughter Akala.

Historians have mused many times over the failed policies that lead to the Trail of Tears which devastated the Cherokee. This marvelous group of First Americans, despite their accomplishments, were nevertheless treated just like all other Native Americans. Clearly the will of the whites was, as was once stated, to *"drive 'um off or kill 'um."* In a historical sense, the Cherokee are probably the most tragic instance of a failed, morally bankrupt policy. All the things that Americans proudly proclaim as hallmarks of civilization were accomplished; in short, the Cherokee did everything they were asked. While they had become mostly Christian, were certainly more literate that the white population of the United States, developed a representative government, and passed moral legislation to govern themselves, the final reality is that they were Indian. In the end, being Indian is what killed them.

Perhaps the legend of the Cherokee Rose, the legend of the tears of Cherokee mothers, tells the tale best. The legend of the Cherokee Rose still persists among the Cherokee in Oklahoma, pretty much as it is reported here. Moreover, the famed Cherokee Rose itself still flourishes along the general route of the Trail of Tears; even today it is considered sacred by the Cherokee both in the Blue Mountains and far to the west in Oklahoma. In an ironic twist of fate, it later became the state flower of Georgia—the state where the Cherokee were most hated.

Death in the Cabin
The Oklahoma Territories, 1839

And that is how Ridge, one of the most distinguished leaders of his people came to be holding his son's body, sitting near his hearth in a cabin in the Oklahoma territories in 1839. He was to die far from the beautiful Blue Mountains he loved; far from the home of his father and his grandfather. Such was the fate of this remarkable man.

While it is fitting that leaders of nations pay for their mistakes, none in history ever paid more dearly than Major Ridge. He lost everything, family, his plantation, his livelihood, and most importantly, the respect of his people, the Cherokee. Thus did his lonely, desperate life end, seemingly, without balance.

Perhaps those that killed my great, great, great, great grandfather were merely seeking to establish balance among the Cherokee in those distant lands. In early 1839, only a few months after the deadly journey, with the devastation of the horrid Trail of Tears being ignored by the white press of the day, the Cherokee were quietly counting their dead. As the number mounted into the thousands, the Cherokee became angry, and the younger men wanted revenge; they began to curse the leaders who had reduced the tribe to such a state. With a total lack of wisdom and restraint, a mind-set that sometimes characterizes decisions of younger men, the younger warriors sought blood.

Within several months of arriving in the new territories, several leaders of the "Treaty Party" were killed by the Cherokee themselves, including Major Ridge, his son John, and several other tribal leaders. These leaders had made a horrible decision—trusting the white government and signing the *Treaty of New Echota* in 1835. They had lead many of their own people to their death. They therefore had to pay the ultimate price—the ancient Blood Oath of the Cherokee demanded it.

In contrast, John Ross, who had fought against that immoral treaty in every way possible, became a man much respected. He lost a wife on the Trail of Tears, but he survived and continued to lead his people in the west for a time. This group of displaced impoverished Indians, in time, became the Western Band of the Cherokee.

However, not all Cherokee were driven away; some had remained in the mountains. Sixty Cherokee families—Cherokee who owned land which they had purchased from whites in the rugged mountains of North Carolina—were allowed to stay, as those land claims were recognized by the courts in that state. It was the only time in history prior to the twentieth Century, in which courts sided with the Cherokee in a land claim. However, in that case the decision did not favor the Cherokee in particular; rather, that decision was rendered by the North Carolina courts in order to uphold the rights of the white settlers to sell land to whomever they chose—not to defend Cherokee land rights.

After the devastation of the long march to Oklahoma, several Cherokee leaders took a look at the dismal conditions in Oklahoma and determined that every promise made to the Cherokee had been broken. No tools were available to help the Cherokee till their soil, no seed corn was provided, the hunting in that distant plain was poor, and the few streams in the area held nothing like the abundance of fish which could be found in the rich waters of the Blue Mountains. Thus some Cherokee quietly left their new homes, and began the same trip in reverse, coming back to their ancestral home lands, to encamp with those who had managed to escape the round up. All told, some 1000 Cherokee remained in the Blue Mountains by 1839, or returned to them over the next year or so. That small group of Cherokee became the ancestors of the Eastern Band of the Cherokee.

Still, Major Ridge would never know any of this. He believed that all or most of his people had made the trek to the new lands; he died believing that the Cherokee would never hold claim to any of their sacred Blue Mountains again. Moreover, he knew that many Cherokee had perished. As he sat in his cabin that night, holding his son's warm body, having come upon the scene of the killing within only moments of the deed, he would certainly have thought himself a failure.

One may only imagine what might have gone through his mind—this complex man—at once a great traditional Cherokee warrior, and in contrast a successful "assimilated" Cherokee planter, owner of a plantation and numerous slaves. What could he have possibly felt, but defeat, given that his last leadership decisions in this life had turned out so poorly for his people. With no witness ever owning up to this crime, we have no way of knowing if Ridge sang the death songs for his son, or for himself. Tradition holds that he did not fight against the several attackers when they returned later that evening to the cabin. Rather, he simply sat, holding his son's body across his lap, waiting for the war hatchet to fall on his neck, or the knife to enter his chest.

Some warriors are destined to die in battle, as did Runs-To-Water, Utani-The-Longknife, The Kingfisher, Half-Face, or Stands-Tall. Others, like Doublehead simply die peacefully as old men. Unfortunate warriors die when they realized they have failed in their task—such was the fate of Major Ridge. Ridge had done his best to lead his people, and had made horrible decisions in that process; by all accounts he failed in his leadership. Still, by not fighting his attackers, he knowingly paid the ultimate price for those mistakes; he could pay no higher a price.

With that in mind, it is possible, in fact quite believable, to suggest that when the knife came, Ridge may have been content. Perhaps by not fighting, he was acknowledging his mistakes, and thus seeking his final balance in this life. If he had not succeeded for his people, he was at least dying for them, and thereby achieving the balance that he—and they—needed. For the ancient Blood Oath of the Cherokee, while recently outlawed, still governed the hearts of many in the tribe, and Ridge, by virtue of his training as a warrior, had been raised to respect it's deadly provision. As required by that oath, he would have gladly paid with his life for such a mistake. Therein lies a lesson of true leadership.

History does not record any grave for Major Ridge. It is not known if anyone sang death songs or where, exactly he died; for the cabin that once stood on those distant Oklahoma plains has been lost to history. Our family tradition tells us that within a hour of the final murder that evening, Akala, his nine year old daughter, came back to the cabin from the creek where she was playing with the other Cherokee children. She saw the bloody devastation, saw the bodies of her brother and father, no doubt horribly mutilated, and taking in the scene of terror in an instant, she fled screaming from the cabin.

In the traditional manner of the Cherokee, John Ross, took her into his cabin, as his daughter. Once he calmed her, on that terrible night, he went quickly to the cabin of Ridge, with only his own son to assist him. There he removed some of the family property from the cabin—a few deerskins, several blankets, a bloody war hatchet, a couple of rifles, and an old corn basket. Without calling for any help from the other neighbors—least the murderous act stir up more hatred among tribal members—he burned the cabin with the two bodies inside.

No mention was ever made of these murders by John Ross, or the young girl, Akala. While some may have assumed that Ridge and his son John simply disappeared, others were certain they had been killed. Still, with all of the challenges of the establishment of the tribe in Oklahoma—and the struggle of this group for recognition as the Western Band of the Cherokee—the murders were simply never brought up. Thus, by his death, did Ridge did ultimately establish balance for his people.

Perhaps that is our lesson from Major Ridge. On some occasions, even in abject failure, victory of a sort, can yet be grasped. A calm dignity—which was always so characteristic of Major Ridge as it was of all of the Real People–goes a long way to establishing balance in the world. Our world today could well benefit from that lesson.

As a descendent, I can only hope that the spirits of Ridge, and his son John, found their way to peace, even from the desolate plains of Oklahoma, when the Great Spirit Kanati called them up. This is my prayer for my forefathers—that peace—that balance—was their destiny. I like to think that Ridge joined his father, Stands-Tall, and his famous grandfather Runs-To-Water in the great beyond. There they will tell each other of their victories and their defeats—for such is the very definition of a warrior, as indeed it is of every man. They will laugh, and joke, and hunt together in the traditional way of the Cherokee, seeking deer and bear. They will purify themselves in the river each dawn, and say prayers to their Great Spirit. The will eat selu each evening, and drink from crystal clear streams that remind them of the Tugaloo River, in a breathtakingly beautiful terrain that looks exactly like the Blue Mountains, that they so loved.

Epilogue

Thus did it end. In one sense, the story ended when my ancestor, Major Ridge died while holding his son's body on that three legged stool in a rough, dirt-floor cabin in Oklahoma in 1839. His hopes and dreams for his family and his people had died previously, and his sense of failure must have been unbearable. The Cherokee were never to know this wonderful land in North Georgia again, and to this date, no sacred fire burns on the ceremonial mound in Tugaloo Town, Estatoe, Seneca, Keowee, or on any of the other council house mounds in the lower Blue Mountains. Cherokee mounds stand in the Nachooee Valley near Helen Georgia, and in Franklin—a city in the distant Blue Ridge of North Carolina—none has ever known the sacred fire of the Cherokee again. Near Tugaloo Town, only a small historic marker by Highway 123 reminds visitors that any Cherokee ever inhabited these beautiful Blue Mountains, and in Georgia—the state that once held the largest population of Cherokee—none now exist.

My family spent the next seven generations on the distant plains of Oklahoma. The Cherokee women of Oklahoma strive desperately to hold their families together, while too many of the men drink themselves to death; I pursued that path to failure for many years, and in that way did I fail myself and my ancestors. It was a futile search for meaning, in the bottom of the bottle, and I found nothing there. The warrior's life had ceased to exist for me.

However, for the Tugaloo River Valley in the lower Blue Mountains this story was only beginning. The King's Mountain Men—Devy's people—had tamed a rough frontier, and the 29'ers of the Georgia gold rush had eliminated the threat posed by the Cherokee from that area once and for all. White settlers, with Scottish or Irish accents mostly, came down the Great Philadelphia Wagon Road from the growing cities of the coast. Some came overland from the port at Charlestown, or up the river from Savannah. The frontier of the lower Blue Ridge, was frontier no more. The early families did well over the next fifty years; the Jarretts, Prathers, Clevelands, Carmichaels, Wards, and Waltons, flourished around Walton's Ford, and many of their descendants are there today. There is much more to tell of these marvelous mountain peoples of the Tugaloo River Valley and of the unnamed hill on it's western escarpment.

In some sense, then, the next decades in the story of the Tugaloo River Valley, and the unnamed hill are Devy's story and not mine. While he lived, he and I left no stone unturned in researching our common ancestry. It was the only meaning two old, failed men had managed to find in the later years of their lives, and we clung to each other, and to this research as if our lives depended on it; in some ways, I suppose they did.

We spent many hours in the libraries of the great southern universities such as Clemson University where John C. Calhoun's plantation once stood—only 20 miles from the Tugaloo River Valley. At a slightly greater distance, the University of Georgia stands proudly, where all of the Jarrett, and many of the Prather men in subsequent generations would be educated. We read for many hours, seeking what we could find of those common people who were our families and our ancestors.

Moreover, we investigated in a hands on way. If the hundreds of hours in dusty book rooms of the universities were dull, Devy and I both came alive when we could dig into our ancestor's past; often we literally dug into the ground of this valley, the ground of their very lives! We trekked through swamps, fields, and woodlands all along the Tugaloo seeking hints of our people. We searched graveyards with no markers—the simple wooden markers having long since rotted. We walked for miles and then picked up the spade or trawl to help researchers from those universities dig up the past. Using old maps still in the hands of Devy's family, we discovered the actual site of Estatoe—the home village of Runs-To-Water. With technology today, archeologists can accomplish amazing things with only a few shards of pottery, or a few bones—fish, foul, or human. Estatoe is still and active archeological site, and will share it's secrets for many years to come. Each new insight brings home to me how my ancestors thrived; this is the very village where my ancestors lived in these wonderful mountains. The local historical society has undertaken a project called the "Tugaloo Corridor" to develop a historical preserve including the village of Estatoe which will serve as a guided study area on Cherokee history in the Blue Ridge. However, the village of Tugaloo Town itself is now covered by Lake Hartwell, and no more can be gained from excavations there.

Devy and I spoke many times before he died of what we were gaining by these efforts. A sense of the raw courage, fortitude, and diligence of these people—Cherokee and white—continues to inspire me. These people knew a world that was at once more gentle and more cruel than ours—more gentle in that things happened more slowly, and movement was more restricted; thus one had some minutes or hours to contemplate things. However, their world was also more cruel, in that death was ever present, moments away by arrow, bullet, or plague, and the tools with which one fought such capricious demise were limited to one's own skills with a weapon, and one's prayers to God.

More than this indeterminate stress however, we studied the passionate quest for survival demonstrated by our people in the Tugaloo River Valley. We gleaned a sense of their spiritual quest, and we each came to believe that they found more than peaceful acceptance in their beliefs in the Gods. These mountain people found their very meaning for their own existence in their quest for the Divine, and Devy and I—each of whom had long ago given up on any hope for the spiritual nature of humanity—found ourselves refreshed by these studies. The Reverend Cleveland, late of the Tugaloo Baptist Church, might look down from Heaven's lofty heights and find some humor in that; Overall I think he would be pleased with this results of his work, some hundred and eighty years after his death.

Even before the Reverend Cleveland walked the trails in this valley, my ancestors—the Cherokee—heard the voice of the Great Spirit in every wind in these Blue Mountains. As Devy and I uncovered some description of a Cherokee ritual, or a Cherokee myth, we would walk to the banks of the Tugaloo River in the early morning, and repeat the ritual purifications or tell the myths to each other. We wanted to sense what those distant Cherokee had sensed; many times did we "purify" ourselves in the cold waters of the Tugaloo, and those solemn occasions became our quest for religious guidance. We both felt that in those actions, we somehow touched our ancestors. Both Devy and I began to look at the mountain sunsets in a deeper way, as we came to understand the depth of the beliefs held by these wonderful people. We sensed their sense of peace and in some ill-defined way, we came to know their soul.

In memory of Devy, I will continue to write until I finish this tale—the story of the wonderful, rugged people–both his and mine; the mountaineers of the Tugaloo Valley. This is a story of America's bloody frontier writ large over the Blue Ridge of Georgia, Tennessee, and the Carolinas. The antebellum south was established with produce from the plantations here in the southern Blue Ridge. Black slaves lived and died here in uncounted thousands, and we can tell the story of only a few. On the Prather plantation, chimneys still stand in which black slave mothers cooked food for their families in those desperate times, as the march of history continued. Within only 25 years of the death of Ridge, our nation tore itself apart in the great Civil War, and Jarrett men—Devy's ancestors—faced a determined foe from the North across those horridly bloody battle lines. There was even a contingent of Cherokee out of Oklahoma fighting with the Confederacy.

Railroads were built here, sour-mask whiskey—the nectar of Scotland and Ireland, was distilled and sold here, and the first woman to vote anywhere in America was a grand-daughter of Devereaux Jarrett. Only eighty years after the Civil War, men again came to this valley to practice war; The famous "Band of Brothers" first trained within sight of the hill on which Devereaux Jarrett and Runs-To-Water are buried. They marched within a mile of here thousands of times, never knowing the battles of this valley.

Yes, much more must be told of this hill and this river, and if God allows me the strength, I will continue to write. It is my purpose in this life, and I owe that to my friend, Devy, and to myself, also to my ancestors—and to his.

Several months ago, Devy and I began a dig ourselves; it was a personal exploration that we felt we should do alone. Without asking permission or guidance from the authorities we dug into a slight depression on the lower slope of the unnamed hill, below the Jarrett graves at the summit. Amid a scattering of rocks, at a depth of four feet and two inches, we unearthed the skeleton of a Cherokee brave who stood an amazing six feet, three inches tall.

When Devy and I had first climbed the hill to the grave of Devereaux Jarrett and noticed the depression slightly down the slope, we both suspected that the depression was more than a natural feature of the ground. When coupled with my family's stories of the death of Runs-To-Water and the location of the legendary hill—slightly south of Toccoa Creek, in my families oral traditions—both Devy and I believed we had detected his grave.

After we found human remains, I said a prayer in the Cherokee tongue; then we called for help. Working later with both an archeologist and a forensics expert from the University of Georgia, we reverently exhumed and examined the body. It was determined that several severe wounds had been inflicted to this warrior, each of which could have been mortal. The remnants of a war hatchet, a few scattered bear claws and a metal knife fashioned in Savannah, coupled with my families oral history of how Half-Face had interred our ancestor, proved to be the evidence we needed. This settled the matter; we had unearthed the solitary grave my ancestor, Runs-To-Water, Peace Chief of the Cherokee.

Thus did I stand by the grave of my great, great, great, great, great, great grandfather. The generations run as follows: Runs-To-Water, Stands-Tall, Major Ridge, and Akala, are discussed in the narrative above. In Oklahoma, Akala married and had a son named James Panther, who had a daughter Charlotte, who in turn had a daughter, Ianna. Ianna was the grand-daughter who wrote down Akala's memories of the Trail of Tears as a young girl doing a school project in 1907; She was also my grandmother.

By the 1900s my family had assumed the last name "Waters" based on the legends of our famous (famous at least among the Cherokee) ancestor Runs-To-Water. Ianna had a daughter named Annabelle, who I must admit, didn't pay much attention to the family oral histories during the 1930s and 1940s. When I arrived later in her life, my mother neglected to tell me these tails, so my grandmother— believing these stories were sacred—began to tell me of these traditions and legends of the Cherokee. Grammy Ianna raised me in many ways, and to her I am indebted for these many family legends which have, by and large, proven to be incredibly accurate.

I still have her cherished basket. As a child, I remember when my grandmother would tell the stories of the Trail of Tears. She often cried for her ancestors, as she showed us in the family the remnants of the basket. While we knew she revered those tattered woven strands of cane, that old basket didn't mean much to us then. I did not at that time realize the depth of her feeling toward this strange family heirloom. Today, I understand. Now I own the basket, woven almost two hundred years ago, of cane from the banks of some nameless creek in North Georgia. This basket traveled on the Trail of Tears holding the dried corn that sustained life for my family. While tattered, and in rough shape, it is one of my most prized possessions. It is quite incredible to contemplate but I actually own the basket that Akala, daughter of Ridge, great grand-daughter of Runs-To-Water, helped to carry on the Trail of Tears.

After some study of my ancestor's bones and his grave goods, the earthly remains of Runs-To-Water were re-interred upon the hill only last year. Mr. Chas Thomas Ward, a distant Cherokee descendent of Nancy Ward, and something of a local historian in the Tugaloo River area was present, as were Devy and myself. Mr. Ward offered a prayer in Cherokee for my ancestor, there on the slope of the hill, where Half-Face had once prayed. I was emotionally overcome, at that moment, and I could offer nothing but silent tears and quiet reverence. Thus was balance restored for the spirit of my ancestor. I have come to love this distant grand-father that I now know so well. Having never known him in life, I still miss him terribly.

Ms. Elizabeth Hagen—a distant descendant of Devereaux Jarrett—also made the trek up the hill for that ceremony. This vibrant woman is a very young ninety years, and is a through inspiration to all who know her. She and her colleague, cousin, and friend Ms. Edna Prather have devoted themselves to keeping the family oral traditions alive for the Jarretts, Devy and myself included. That is a gift beyond measure, and I thank both of these remarkable women for that. Devy and I saw in these women, the very strengths personified in the lives we sought to understand; the spirit of the Blue Mountains lives in their soul. In particular, I hereby offer a special thanks to Ms. Elizabeth Hagen for her gracious permission for the re-interment of my ancestor in land that is now a family cemetery for her ancestors.

While the spirits of Stands-Tall, Ridge and many others all along the path of the Trail of Tears remain unencumbered by graves or markers, I think Runs-To-Water will like his final resting place undisturbed for now. He has, again, taught his descendents meaningful lessons, as a Peace Chief of the Cherokee should. He has taught me many things. Now, he is with me—he is a part of me. He is, in my better moments, who I am, and I am much richer for that. For this I offer my prayer of thanks to the sky, to Kanati; to God, and to the Great Spirit that Runs-To-Water knew so well in these Blue Mountains; I thank my grandfather, and wish him well.

Once again he rests where he chose—in the mountains, near the sight of his first victory over a bear some 280 years ago. I occasionally see him in the mountain valley, late in the evening, when a gentle wind sweeps the hills clean, moving the autumn leaves only slightly; for in the way of the Cherokee, he is never loud or boisterous; his spirit passes quietly, as a warrior should, in determined dignity. Now and forever, he soars over these beautiful hills, and once again his spirit roams free in the Blue Mountains he so cherished.